Dear Read

Harlequin Regency Romance is proud to present
two lively, full-length tales of love, tears and
laughter by two of our most popular authors,
Gail Whitiker and Stephanie Laurens,
in *Regency Romps*. In August we will be
bringing you two more in *Regency Diamonds*.
Brenda Hiatt's *Azalea* and Paula Marshall's
The Cyprian's Sister are stories you'll treasure
forever.

Happy reading!

The Editor

REGENCY ROMPS

BY

GAIL WHITIKER
STEPHANIE LAURENS

Harlequin Books

TORONTO • NEW YORK • LONDON
AMSTERDAM • PARIS • SYDNEY • HAMBURG
STOCKHOLM • ATHENS • TOKYO • MILAN
MADRID • WARSAW • BUDAPEST • AUCKLAND

REGENCY ROMPS

Copyright © 1994 by Harlequin Enterprises B.V.

ISBN 0-373-31213-X

The publisher acknowledges the copyright holders of the individual works as follows:

A PROMISE TO RETURN
Copyright © 1994 by Gail Whitiker

FOUR IN HAND
Copyright © 1993 by Stephanie Laurens

Printed in U.S.A.

CONTENTS

About the Author

Born in England, Gail Whitiker needed no
encouragement to try her hand at Regency
romance. Now, with three books behind her,
Gail has penned her first sequel. When
Nicholas Longworth first showed up in
Letters to a Lady as a secondary character,
Gail immediately knew he was hero material.
Now he has his own book—*A Promise to Return*.

Gail now lives in Caledon, Ontario.

A PROMISE TO RETURN
Gail Whitiker

To Sydney Gardave,
with affection and gratitude for
her trust, support and friendship

CHAPTER ONE

"YOU WANTED TO SEE ME, my lord?"

The war minister looked up at the gentleman standing calmly in front of his desk and gruffly cleared his throat. "Yes, Longworth, I did. Sorry to call you in on such a dismal day."

Nicholas Grey, Viscount Longworth, smiled briefly. "That's quite all right, sir. I assumed it was important."

Lord Osborne sighed. "Yes, I'm afraid it is. Damned important, in fact." The war minister laced his fingers on the desk in front of him and took a deep breath. "We have reason to believe that Jean Leclerc is preparing to flee France, and that he is intending to come to England."

Longworth's expression never changed. "Are you certain?"

"All indications seem to point to it."

"I see." Nicholas glanced down at the crudely drawn sketch laying on top of the war minister's desk. "Is that him?"

Lord Osborne sighed. "I believe so, though no one seems to know exactly who he is or what he looks like. I swear the man has the ability to change form. Every time I think we have him, he slips through our fingers like a tom-cat through an alley gate. All we know for certain is that wherever he goes, he leaves behind a trail of dead British agents."

"And now he's planning on coming to England."

"So Baker informed us just before he..."

Osborne didn't finish, and Longworth nodded. "Yes, I was sorry to hear about Baker. He was a good man."

"They were all good men, damn it!" The war minister leaned forward in his chair, his broad shoulders sagging under the weight of his guilt. "The war is almost over, yet here I am, still trying to track down their killer—a man who has caused me as much grief as Bonaparte himself." He stared down at the crumpled, yellowed piece of paper in disgust. "God knows, I can't risk Leclerc's coming to England." Osborne raised heavy eyes to Longworth's face. "That's why I asked to see you, Nicholas. Under any other circumstances, I wouldn't even suggest it, but there is simply too much at stake not to."

"Too much at stake," Nicholas repeated softly. "That was the excuse you used for not allowing me to go to France to rescue Lavinia Duplesse, remember?"

"Yes, I do. Unfortunately, this is an entirely different matter. The circumstances make it far more dangerous."

"Are you asking me to go, sir, or ordering me to?" Nicholas enquired with an engaging smile.

Osborne ruefully shook his head. "I'm certainly not ordering you to go, Nicholas. I don't even feel I have the right to ask you, after everything you have already done for England. God knows, you have gone above and beyond the call of duty several times over."

"And yet, you're afraid that if I do not go, there is a good chance that this murderer will be allowed to run free."

"Yes, but on the other hand, if you do go to France, there's an equally good possibility that you'll be shot."

A flicker of amusement appeared in Longworth's clear blue eyes. "I hardly think so, sir. As you said yourself, the war is almost over. No one is going to be looking for me any more. The memory of my last mission will have long since been forgotten."

Osborne raised one grizzled grey eyebrow. "I'm not so sure about that, Longworth. French Intelligence is hardly likely to forget the man who helped Edward Kingsley to escape. Need I remind you that it was Kingsley's information that played such a large part in undermining Soult's counteroffensive in the Pyrenees? Besides, just because the war is in its last days doesn't mean Leclerc will be ready to concede as well. He's a vicious man, Nicholas. You've seen how he works. He's a cold-blooded killer with no morals and no conscience.''

''All right then. If you're hesitant about sending me, who else are you considering?''

Lord Osborne cleared his throat. ''I have a number of qualified agents.''

Longworth regarded the files on top of the desk. ''Are those the candidates?''

''They are.''

''May I?''

At the war minister's nod, Longworth fanned the folders out on the desk's surface. He glanced briefly at each of the names. He had no need to look at the information within. ''You're wasting your time, my lord,'' he said quietly. ''None of these men is capable of carrying off the mission, and you know it.''

Osborne grunted. ''Perhaps not, but if you refuse, one of them is going to have to try.'' He swept the folders back into a neat pile. ''The only other men I would consider sending are unavailable to me.''

''I take it you mean Edward Kingsley and the Earl of Marwood.''

Lord Osborne nodded. ''Kingsley doesn't even bear discussing. His face is too well known. He'd be shot the moment he set foot in France. And with Marwood away on his wedding trip, that leaves only—''

''Myself.''

Osborne breathed a long-suffering sigh. ''Yes, I'm afraid so.''

Nicholas stared at the painting of a horse on the wall behind Osborne's desk. It was an exceptionally fine Stubbs, not unlike the one in his own library. "When do you want me to go?" he asked quietly.

Osborne didn't know whether to look guilty or relieved. "Are you sure about this?"

"Quite sure. In fact, when you think about it, it's only fitting that I do go."

Lord Osborne sighed. "Yes, you certainly have ample cause for wanting to find Leclerc. Given that he was responsible for François Duplesse's death, I can understand your wanting revenge for his widow's sake—"

Longworth shook his head. "This has nothing to do with revenge, my lord. You and I both know that Leclerc, for all his French name, is rumoured to be part English, and that when the war ends he may try to take his place in London Society. We also know that he will continue to be what he has been for the duration of the war—a murderer." Nicholas's firm mouth tightened. "Or have you forgotten the contents of the missive intercepted before Baker was killed?"

"I've not forgotten," Osborne snapped. "Why in blazes do you think I fear so much his returning to England now? He made his plans for dispatching certain British agents—whether it was during the war or after—very clear."

"Then is it not worth the risk to send me?" Nicholas replied softly. "You said yourself only three men are capable of doing this job, and of those three, I am the only one available to go."

"Yes, I know that, but there are . . . extenuating circumstances."

"What? You mean because I am one of the men Leclerc has sworn to kill?"

Longworth could tell by the anguish on the minister's face that he had stumbled upon the true reason for the man's misgivings.

"That missive was supposed to be confidential, damn it!" Osborne growled.

"Yes. So was François Duplesse's affiliation with the British government, but someone obviously found out about that," Nicholas pointed out drily. "It seems to me that if Leclerc knows I'm in France, he'll come looking for me. It may be the only way to draw him out, my lord." He indicated the files on Osborne's desk. "He won't trouble himself for any of those men. You know that as well as I do."

Osborne sat back in his chair and studied the reserved face of the man in front of him. "And what happens if you fail, Longworth?"

One dark eyebrow lifted in amusement. "Do you really think I'm going to make it that easy for him?"

"No. If I thought that, I wouldn't have bothered bringing you in. But if you do fail, what am I supposed to tell your fiancée and your family?"

"There will be no need to tell them anything, my lord, because I don't intend to fail."

"But if you do?" Osborne repeated, needing to stress the danger of this mission one last time.

There was a slight pause, before Longworth's mouth eased into a smile. "If I do fail, you can at least be comforted by the knowledge that you won't have to send another man in to find Leclerc. If I do not make it out of France alive, it will be because I'll have taken Jean Leclerc with me!"

LAVINIA DUPLESSE GLANCED at the outrageously low neckline of the tissue-thin gown the modiste held up for her inspection, and arched one eyebrow. "Gracious!"

Beside her, her seventeen-year-old stepdaughter, Martine, smiled in understanding. "*Oui*, it is a trifle... revealing, is it not?"

"Yes, it certainly is. Madame Fouché, can you show me something a little more...discreet, perhaps?" Lavinia asked tactfully. "This is for my betrothal dinner, after all."

"But zis is 'ow zey are wearing zem in Paris, my lady," the sharp-eyed Frenchwoman replied, clearly startled by her customer's request. "And given zat you are ze widow, zer is no need for...'ow do you say *la modestie?*"

Lavinia carefully hid her amusement behind a courteous smile. "It may be how they are wearing them in Paris, *madame,* but I doubt I should receive a very warm welcome from hostesses here in London wearing such a gown. I own, I am more respectably covered when I am in my night-dress."

The modiste sniffed as emphatically as she dared and clapped her hands. "Josette, bring me ze bolts of blue, yellow and rose-coloured silk. Quickly now. And more fashion plates. *Not* ze Parisian ones," she added pointedly.

Lavinia smiled. "Thank you, *madame.* Under any other circumstances, I myself would be inclined towards the Parisian styles, having spent as much time as I have in France. But as I will be marrying a rather...traditional Englishman, I think it better that I maintain a proper British sense of decorum."

Slightly mollified, the modiste nodded her understanding of the situation. "But of course, my lady. And it is an indication of your own refinement zat you would consider ze sensibilities of others before your own beauty." She sighed dramatically. "Such a pity. And such a waste. *Tiens,* we shall try again."

Shortly, Josette reappeared carrying the requested bolts of silk, along with a set of considerably more conservative, though equally stylish, fashion plates. "Now, I am sure one of zese styles will be more suitable to a lady planning her second marriage," Madame said optimistically.

Lavinia leisurely thumbed through the plates before stopping at one in particular, her eyes brightening. "Yes, this one, I think, *madame.*"

Madame studied the plate and duly nodded her approval. "*Oui*, very flattering, my lady."

Lavinia held out the plate for her stepdaughter's inspection. "I think it will garner a more cordial reception from Nicholas's mother than the other, don't you, Martine? The Dowager Lady Longworth is such a stickler for propriety."

At the thought of the frightfully upper-crust matron who was to become Lavinia's mother-in-law, Martine nodded. "I am sure she will be much 'appier with this gown, *maman.*"

"Good. Now, as for ze colour and ze material?" The modiste pulled forward the fabrics. "Any of zese will look lovely with my lady's wonderful complexion and dark hair."

Lavinia regarded the dainty, pastel shades with a degree of ambivalence, before sliding a thoughtful look towards Martine. "Which colour do you like, Martine?"

Martine's fingers went automatically to the bolt of silk the colour of wild roses. "This one."

Smiling, Lavinia nodded. "Yes, I thought that might be your choice. Madame Fouché, we will have the design we discussed for Miss Duplesse in the rose-coloured silk."

Martine beamed her pleasure. "*Merci, maman,* you are very good to me."

"Nonsense, it is only what you deserve. Now, as for myself..." Lavinia glanced over the collection of pretty pastel fabrics again and shook her head. "No, none of these. Something brighter, I think. Something more...dramatic."

Something befitting a five-and-twenty-year-old widow who is just out of black gloves and ready to start her life again, Lavinia felt like saying.

The modiste deliberated for a moment, and then slowly, a smile began to appear. "But of course, I 'ave it! Josette, *le satin.*" She turned back to her client. "I believe zis will be more to your liking, Lady Duplesse."

And it was. Lavinia caught her breath as the shop assistant returned with a bolt of heavy, lustrous satin the colour of polished sapphires.

"Oh, *c'est magnifique!*" Martine breathed.

The modiste nodded. "And with your colouring, my lady, it will be perfect. See 'ow it looks."

Lavinia carried the length of material towards the glass and held it up to her face. There was certainly no doubt that the colour suited her. The rich, jewelled blue seemed to enhance the radiance of her complexion and deepen the natural blush in her cheeks. Was this how Nicholas saw her? Lavinia wondered, silently studying her reflection.

"My lady?"

"Hmm?" Belatedly, Lavinia realized that the modiste was trying to get her attention. "Oh, excuse me, *madame,* I was . . . lost in thought."

She turned, and in doing so, found Martine's gaze on her. "It is lovely, is it not, Martine?"

"It is, and you will be the most beautiful lady in London when you wear it," Martine replied proudly. "But then, you would always be that."

Lavinia felt a warm rush of love for the girl who had become more like a true daughter than a stepdaughter to her. Martine Duplesse was as opposite from François as it was possible for two people to be, and at times it was difficult to credit that they had indeed been father and daughter.

At seventeen, Martine was a slender wisp of a girl who had somehow managed to come through the years of the war untainted by the fear and hate that had so permeated France. Sequestered behind the walls of the Château Duplesse, she had remained apart from what was going on outside, until finally, the ugliness of war had reached into their own lives and jerked them from their complacency.

When her husband had been killed, Lavinia had known that neither she nor Martine would be safe any more. Lord Osborne, head of British Intelligence, had sent word to

Lavinia to leave Paris immediately. There had been no time
to do anything but grab a few of their most precious be-
longings and flee to the safety of the country.

Lavinia had eventually managed to secure passage to
England for Martine with some close friends who were returning to London, promising the girl that she would follow as soon as she could. But as the days turned into weeks,
and the weeks into months, Lavinia truly began to wonder
whether that would ever come to pass. Her life had become
a series of carefully orchestrated moves in a constant attempt to stay ahead of the French. She had gone into hiding, travelling from one small village to another, living as
frugally as she could and taking care to avoid the watchful
eyes of the French spy network.

Lavinia did not know who had murdered her husband.
She only knew that François had been secretly working for
the English government, and that someone had stumbled
upon the truth of his identity.

Thankfully, however, all of that was behind her now. The
months of running and hiding and scraping out an existence as best she could were over. She was back in London,
happily reunited with her stepdaughter and comfortably
settled in a lovely house in a modest part of town. What's
more, she was engaged to marry the man she had been in
love with from the very first day of meeting him all those
years ago. She had her whole life in front of her.

"Yes, *madame,* this will be perfect." Lavinia carried the
length of fabric back to the table and set it next to the design she had chosen. "Now, both gowns must be ready by
next Wednesday. Do you foresee any problems?"

The modiste shook her head. "Not in ze least, my lady.
In fact, you may expect both gowns by ze beginning of ze
week. You 'ave my word."

The selection of their gowns for the betrothal dinner
completed, Lavinia and Martine rose and made their way
back to their carriage. Lavinia breathed a sigh of relief.

"Well, that is one more thing taken care of. Are you pleased with your gown, Martine?"

"Oh, yes, *maman*, it will be beautiful," Martine exclaimed with pleasure. "Everything is perfect, *non?*"

Lavinia tenderly studied the elfin face beside her. She had not expected to be welcomed by François's daughter so easily. Before they'd married, François had told Lavinia of the closeness that had existed between his daughter and her mother, and had warned her that Martine had taken her mother's death very hard.

Moving into the role left vacant by such a woman, Lavinia had felt her own inadequacy most painfully, and had prepared herself for the worst. What she had found, however, was a young girl starved for love and eager to accept the warmth Lavinia was so willing to give. She had been touched when Martine had begun calling her *maman*, and had found the warm bond of friendship that had sprung up between them a heartwarming change from François's quiet, brooding ways. As far as Lavinia was concerned, Martine's love was the only good thing to emerge from the disastrous marriage Lavinia's drunken father had arranged for her.

"You are a brave girl, Martine, and I am very proud of you. François would be proud, too." Lavinia hesitated a moment. "Are you sure you will be happy living with Nicholas and me after we are married? I know how much you loved your father."

Martine's expression clouded. "Yes, I did. But I think that perhaps Papa was not always... an easy man, and that there was much sadness in your marriage. But when I see how happy you are now, I cannot help but be glad. And as long as your Lord Longworth does not mind living with me," the girl said in her softly accented voice, "I shall be 'appy. I do not know where else I might go."

Lavinia reached across and patted the girl's hand. "There was never any question of you going anywhere else, Martine. You are my daughter now. I just wanted to know that you would be happy living in Nicholas's house. Although," she added with a smile, "if you meet a handsome young gentleman at court this Season you may find yourself setting up your own establishment before the end of the year. I was not much older than you when I married François."

"Yes, but yours was an arranged marriage," Martine said with surprising insight. "I would like to find a gentleman with whom I fall in love and marry because I want to be with him, rather than because I have to be."

Lavinia nodded, her thoughts returning pleasantly to the man she was about to marry. Yes, she wanted to be with Nicholas. How many times during her unhappy marriage to François had she thought about Nicholas, dreamt about him. Her lips curved in a secretive smile. Her wicked, loving dreams—that's what she had called them. And oh, the hours she had spent indulging in them. At times they were all that had kept her going.

"You are very much in love with Lord Longworth, are you not, *maman?*"

Lavinia blushed in spite of herself. "Yes, very much, Martine. He is a wonderful man. I know you will think so, too, once you come to know him better."

Martine considered that for a moment and then shook her head. "I already know all I need to know about him. I see how happy he makes you. That is all that matters, *non?*"

IN AN ELEGANT TOWN HOUSE in Mayfair later that same evening, the Dowager Viscountess Longworth studied her only son across the length of the elaborately set dining-room table and frowned her displeasure.

"What do you mean, you are going away again, Nicholas?" she enquired sharply. "How can you even consider leaving London at a time like this? Need I remind you that you are betrothed?"

"Mother, I—"

"You cannot simply take it into your head to up and leave just because the fancy strikes you. You have responsibilities, Nicholas. Obligations. You must start acting the part of a soon-to-be-married man."

Nicholas took a sip of his wine and waited for his mother to finish. At sixty-two, Lady Longworth was a regal-looking woman—and as imperious as ever. Her silver hair was neatly arranged under her dowager cap, and while her eyes might not be as bright a blue as they'd once been, they still burned with the fervour that had so characterized her younger life.

"Nicholas, are you listening to me?"

Nicholas brought his own deep blue eyes in line with hers. "Yes, Mother, every word."

"Then why did not you answer me?"

"Because I was not aware you had asked a question for which an answer was expected."

The viscountess bristled. "I will not have you being impertinent, Nicholas. I am your mother, after all."

Nicholas sighed. "Yes, I am very well aware of that. Now, what was it you asked?"

"Humph, I do not know that I should bother repeating it if you cannot have the decency to listen to me the first time."

Nicholas quickly bit back the retort that sprang to his lips and glanced instead at his mother's long-suffering butler, signalling for a refill. "Needless to say, I should like to hear it, if for no other reason than to assuage my curiosity. Ah, thank you, Mortimer."

Lady Longworth glanced sharply at her son's glass. "You're drinking more than you used to."

"On the contrary, I am drinking less."

She studied his face intently. "You're not looking well. Are you eating?"

"I have a competent cook, and dine out at my club at least three nights a week."

"Humph. You probably do not get enough sleep." She slanted him an accusatory glance. "No doubt you are out with *that* woman all hours of the night. I might have known that you would—" Abruptly recalling the presence of the butler, Lady Longworth waved her hand dismissively. "Leave us, Mortimer."

The butler bowed and thankfully made his escape.

Longworth swirled the wine around in his glass. He'd been wondering how long it would take his mother to get to her favourite subject—namely, the unsuitability of Lavinia to be his wife.

Nicholas knew that his mother had never approved of his relationship with Lavinia, calling her "that immoral Frenchwoman," even though he had taken pains to point out that she was every bit as English as they.

"I am not out with Lavinia until all hours, Mother," Nicholas said patiently. "She is but recently returned to Society after her period of mourning and is well aware of the edicts governing a widow's behaviour."

"Humph." Lady Longworth's thin hand fidgeted on the table. "More so than you, it would seem."

"I beg your pardon?"

"You didn't waste any time before asking her to marry you."

"No, because I didn't need any time," Nicholas replied simply. "I love Lavinia. I always have. And she loves me."

"Yes, even while she was married to that Frenchman!" His mother shook her head. "I've never heard of such behaviour. In my day, a woman stayed married to the same man her whole life."

For the first time that evening, Nicholas was actually tempted to laugh. "For heaven's sake, Mother, Lavinia didn't have any choice in the matter. Her husband was killed. No doubt she would have remained married to him if he hadn't been."

His mother raked him over with her piercing gaze. "Yes, and all that time lusting after you."

"Lusting!" Nicholas hastily put down his glass. "Lavinia is not the type of woman to go *lusting* after any man. She has always conducted herself with the utmost propriety, and even you cannot deny that she has an excellent standing within the ton. There is not a hostess in London who would turn her away. Even Countess Lieven holds her in high regard, and she is not a lady easily pleased."

"Humph," Lady Longworth said again. "And I suppose you would have wasted your life waiting for her even if her husband had not died so conveniently."

Longworth ran his finger along the stem of the wineglass, a nerve jumping in his cheek. "I have been in love with Lavinia since first meeting her, that much I admit. But it was hardly my fault that I met her on the day she was being married to another man!"

"A lot of time has passed since then, Nicholas," his mother pointed out.

"Yes. And in all that time, I have not met anyone to compare with her."

"Fiddlesticks! You haven't even tried," Lady Longworth replied mumpishly. "You've spent more time at your sports, and in the company of Lord Marwood and his friends, than you have in the company of ladies. You could have had your pick of any number of suitable, well-connected young misses, Nicholas. Instead, you chose to waste your time pining over a married woman. A married woman!" she repeated, her voice rising in agitation. "How do you think that made me feel?"

"I shouldn't have thought it would have made you feel one way or another." Longworth's voice was deceptively quiet. "My name has never been linked with Lavinia's, nor have I ever given you the least cause for embarrassment as a result of my involvement with her. I have always observed propriety. I should have thought you would have been relieved that I was not given to the foolish, head-strong impulses of many of my friends."

"I understand that, Nicholas, but—"

"Instead, you tell me to start acting like a soon-to-be married man and to be mindful of my obligations." Nicholas rose and stood staring down at her almost sadly. "Well, let me tell you, Mother, I am very well aware of my responsibilities. I am not ashamed of anything I have ever done in my life, nor do I intend to start making any changes now. I love Lavinia Duplesse, and I intend to marry her. And I will not hear another word spoken against her, by you or anyone else!"

His mother's cheeks flushed painfully. "Nicholas, you don't understand—"

"On the contrary, Mother, I understand perfectly. I understand that you have taken it into your head not to accept Lavinia, and that you've not even had the decency to invite her here. Very well, that is your choice. But like it or not, Lavinia is going to be the next viscountess and nothing you can say will change that. And as for my going away now, I have given my word to someone and I intend to keep it. Yes, I realize that I am soon to be married, and while I do not expect you to understand my reasons for going, you might at least try to show some confidence in my ability to make an intelligent decision. Good evening, Mother."

With that, Nicholas turned on his heel and marched from the room. The door closed with a firm click behind him.

In the silence following his departure, Lady Longworth stared into the flickering candlelight, her eyes filling with tears as she recalled the anger in her son's voice.

Oh, Nicholas. How could you think I had no confidence in you? She was more proud of her only son than she had ever been of anyone in her life. She had watched him grow from a round-cheeked baby into a man to be proud of. She had followed his progress through Oxford with shining eyes, proud of the fact that, unlike so many of her friends' sons,

Nicholas had never been sent down. She had watched him graduate from university, and then go on to the military. The Horse Guards, no less, Lady Longworth thought, her heart swelling with pride.

And then she had watched him fall in love.

Lady Longworth bit her lip and lifted her eyes upwards, trying to hold back the tears that trembled on her lashes. Oh, yes, she had known the day it had happened. Nicholas had gone to the Honourable Lavinia Ridgley's wedding to the much older and already widowed François Duplesse and had come home afterwards with the strangest glow in his eyes.

Like any mother, she had hoped that the romantic mood of the wedding had rubbed off on him, or that he had perhaps met someone there. But when, in the days following the wedding, Nicholas had not called upon any of the eligible young ladies he had seen, nor mentioned anyone's name, Lady Longworth had begun to realize why. Her son had fallen in love with the very woman whose marriage he had gone to celebrate. And he had remained true to her ever since.

Lady Longworth pulled her shawl more closely around her thin shoulders as Mortimer made his way silently back into the room.

"Will that be all, my lady?"

Lady Longworth nodded wearily. "Yes, thank you, Mortimer. I think I shall retire for the night."

She turned towards the door, her mind going back to her conversation with Nicholas. It was true enough, what he had said. He had never once disgraced himself, or her. Whatever amorous liaisons he may have enjoyed were conducted with dignity and the utmost discretion. Never once had the ugly taint of scandal touched his head.

And now that Lavinia Duplesse was widowed, he was free to marry the only woman he had ever loved, taking him that last, irrevocable step away from Lady Longworth and out of her life. And instead of congratulating him, all she had been able to do was berate and badger him. Was it any wonder he had turned away from her in anger? If only she had the chance to take back what she had said, the viscountess thought sadly, one tear making its way slowly down her lined cheek.

CHAPTER TWO

WEARING THE MAGNIFICENT sapphire gown, Lavinia slowly descended the stairs, very conscious of Nicholas's gaze upon her. She saw the warm glow of admiration in his eyes and felt a tingle of excitement as he reached out his hand and enfolded her fingers in his own.

The gown was indeed a credit to the dressmaker's skill. Shimmering with a life of its own, the richly coloured satin accentuated the whiteness of Lavinia's skin. Her neck and smooth, creamy shoulders were bare, the moderately shallow *décolletage* of the gown just displaying the soft fullness of the tops of her breasts.

Her maid, Hélène, had done an artful job of arranging her long, luxuriant tresses in an elaborate coiffure, winding a ribbon of sapphire velvet, studded with diamonds, throughout. Around her throat, Lavinia wore Nicholas's engagement present to her, a stunning circle of brilliant white diamonds set with sapphires. Matching earrings dangled from her earlobes, while completing the set, a beautiful diamond-and-sapphire engagement ring twinkled on her finger.

Nicholas had not asked his mother for the Longworth diamonds. Even though they were rightfully his, he had known that she would have balked at giving them to him because of Lavinia. Instead, he had gone to Rundel and Bridge and commissioned a new set of jewellery for his future wife. Better that Lavinia never see the Longworth diamonds at all than be forced to wear them unhappily.

But now, as he gazed up at her, Nicholas could not have been more pleased.

"You look magnificent. Everything about you is breathtaking."

Lavinia coloured prettily, but did not look away. "I am so glad you approve."

"Did you choose the dress to go with the jewels, or the other way round?"

Lavinia's laugh was light and charming. "I admit, it was not my original intention, but once I saw the material, I realized it would make a stunning backdrop for them."

Nicholas joined in her laughter, marvelling that he was actually to marry this incredible creature. "No, it is you who provide the backdrop, my love," he whispered, lightly touching the stones. "These are mere decorations."

Nicholas bent his head, brushing his mouth gently across hers. The scent of her cologne mingling with the provocative fragrance of her own body intoxicated him. He dropped his mouth lower to kiss the pulse point in her throat, feeling the icy coldness of the diamonds against the heat of her skin—a heady combination.

"Nicholas!"

His name was a throaty whisper on her lips as she clung to him. She had waited so very long to be with him. Through all the long nights of her marriage to François, Lavinia had dreamt of him, longed for him. When François had made love to her, she had seen Nicholas's face, imagined it was Nicholas's body merging with her own. And now soon, so very soon, there would be no more need for pretending....

"Maman?" a voice said tentatively.

At the sound of her stepdaughter's voice, Lavinia felt the colour deepen in her cheeks and abruptly brought her errant thoughts back to the present. She stepped out of her fiancé's arms and turned to see Martine standing uncertainly on the top step, her cheeks flushed the same delicate pink as her gown. "I am sorry, I did not mean to disturb you—"

"It's all right, Martine, you did not disturb us. Come and say hello to Nicholas," Lavinia said softly.

Nicholas watched the young girl descend the staircase, marvelling, as always, that this charming *ingénue* could be François Duplesse's daughter. She must have taken after her mother, Nicholas decided. There was no physical resemblance to her father at all, and there were certainly no shared personality traits. While Nicholas had had the utmost respect for the Frenchman's abilities, he had never warmed to François as a friend.

"Good evening, Martine," Nicholas greeted her. "You look lovely tonight. Indeed, it will be an honour to be seen escorting the two most beautiful ladies here."

Martine smiled, the awkwardness of the moment gone. "*Merci,* Nicholas. Does *maman* not look beautiful?"

Nicholas turned back to his fiancée and slowly lifted her hand to his lips. "Indeed she does, Martine. Indeed she does."

Lavinia lifted her free hand to stroke his cheek, her eyes glowing. "Have you been to see your mother, Nicholas? Is she coming?"

"Actually, no." Nicholas cleared his throat awkwardly. "She has not been feeling too well of late. She...didn't think she would be quite up to it tonight."

Lavinia watched Nicholas's eyes and listened to his words, well aware that they were not telling the same story. She managed a game smile. "I am so sorry to hear that she has not been well. Perhaps next time."

Nicholas nodded. "Yes. Perhaps."

Lavinia turned as her butler arrived. "Is everything ready, Habinger?"

"Yes, Lady Duplesse."

"Good. I should think our guests will begin arriving shortly."

The words had barely left her lips before there was a knock on the door. Quickly squeezing her hand for luck, Longworth took his place next to her as Habinger went to open it.

Lavinia's face lit with pleasure as she recognized the first of their guests. "Edward! Laura! How wonderful to see you both."

Edward Kingsley stepped forward and kissed her warmly on the cheek. "Lavinia, my dear, you look absolutely radiant. And Nicholas." He turned to enclose his good friend's outstretched hand in a firm grip. "I vow you're looking quite the April gentleman. Or very nearly."

"Thank you, Edward. I must say, I never thought to see it happen," Nicholas admitted, recalling Lavinia's dangerous rescue from France. "And Miss Beaufort, what a pleasure to see you again."

Laura Beaufort was looking enchanting in a gown of soft peach sarcenet. She had always been a pretty girl, but since the announcement of her own betrothal to Edward Kingsley, she had blossomed.

"Lord Longworth," Laura replied warmly, before reaching forward to press her cheek against Lavinia's. "Lavinia, you look absolutely wonderful tonight!"

"Thank you, Laura. I am so glad the two of you could come. May I present my stepdaughter, Martine."

Martine curtsied gracefully. "I am very pleased to meet you."

"But what a lovely gown, Miss Duplesse," Laura complimented her. "And such a pretty colour."

"It was a gift from *maman*," Martine told her. "The colour reminded me of the roses that grew wild in the fields around the château."

Laura's eyes warmed sympathetically. "Do you miss your home, Martine?"

"Sometimes," the girl admitted. "But I am very 'appy to be 'ere with *maman*," she said, her English slipping just a little. "This is my home now."

Nicholas turned back to Edward. "When are the newlyweds due back from Italy?"

Edward chuckled. "Who can say? I wasn't able to get a sensible word out of Charlotte once Devon arrived back in England." He leaned forward and lowered his voice in amusement. "Love seems to make babbling fools of us all. But I'll say one thing, it certainly agrees with you, my friend."

Nicholas nodded, his chest swelling with pride as he glanced at Lavinia, now chatting with Laura. "I can hardly credit how happy I am, Edward. I never thought it would happen." His eyes darkened slightly at the thought of what lay ahead. "But we must talk, my friend. There has been a development in France."

Edward nodded briefly. "Yes, so I understand." He purposely kept a smile on his face for the benefit of the ladies and the other guests who were arriving. "At the club, later tonight?"

Nicholas nodded, and then rejoined Lavinia as Laura and Edward moved on into the reception room.

The next few hours flew by as Lavinia and Nicholas mingled with their guests, accepting the good wishes of close friends and distant acquaintances. It was a large group that had gathered to celebrate the engagement, although some of the guests had come more out of curiosity than from a desire to congratulate the couple.

It was well known that Lavinia's first husband, the Comte du Duplesse, had wasted no time in removing his young bride from England. Immediately after their marriage, he had ensconced her in his sprawling old château in the French countryside.

Lavinia had not returned to her native England once during her four years of marriage. And now that she was back, there were many who were anxious to see how, or if, she had changed.

Unfortunately, those who had come expecting to see a woman ill at ease in London Society were destined to be disappointed. Lavinia was as gracious, as elegant and as charming as anyone could have wished. She took time to speak to everyone in that uniquely soft, throaty voice of hers. And there was no doubting her devotion to her late husband's seventeen-year-old daughter.

In fact, it was the stepdaughter to whom some of the more marriage-minded mamas took exception. With that perfect skin and those huge, soulful eyes there was no denying that Martine Duplesse was a diamond. And with a sweetness of nature not unlike that of her youthful stepmother, she quickly won a place in many hearts, including those of a few of the young men present.

But it was Nicholas and Lavinia themselves who drew the bulk of the comments and stares that night. That they were totally in love was so obvious that it actually brought a tear to the eyes of a few hardened tabbies. The newly engaged pair had but to glance across the room at each other, their eyes locking in silent communication, to show how deeply committed they were.

At midnight, Edward called for everyone's attention.

"Ladies and gentlemen, a moment if you please." He waited for the chatter to die down before continuing. "Now, we all know why we are here. My good friend Nicholas has finally had the good sense to propose to one of the loveliest ladies in London, and Lavinia, poor creature, was foolish enough to accept. No, seriously now," Edward amended, laughing as the expected jeers and protests greeted his remark, "we are here to celebrate the forthcoming marriage of these two splendid people, and to that end, I would ask all of you to raise your glasses and join me in a toast to them. May they know only happiness and joy in their lives together." Edward raised his glass and smiled at them both. "To Nicholas and Lavinia."

"Nicholas and Lavinia!" the crowd echoed.

In the centre of the room, Nicholas waited until silence resumed before raising his own glass to the woman standing beside him. "To you, my darling Lavinia," he said in a strong, clear voice. "for making me the happiest man alive, and for bringing joy into my life after so many years of loneliness. I can never thank you enough. I can only say that I love you, and that I will always love you."

Lavinia blinked rapidly and raised her own glass. "And I love you, Nicholas. So very, very much."

And then, to everyone's delight, Nicholas leaned forward and placed a long, lingering kiss on Lavinia's lips. Ignoring the cheers and laughter that resulted, he pulled her lovingly into his arms. And when he reluctantly drew back, it was to see the shimmer of tears in her eyes.

"Oh, Nicholas," she whispered tremulously.

"To Lavinia," Nicholas said, his eyes holding hers as he raised his glass.

"To Lavinia!" shouted the now equally emotional crowd.

Amidst a great deal of eye wiping and throat clearing, the festivities carried on. Finally, at half past one, the last of the guests departed, leaving only Edward and Laura standing in the quiet of the hall with their hosts.

Nicholas sighed his satisfaction. "Well, I would say that was an unmitigated success." He put his arm around Lavinia's waist and gave it a gentle squeeze. "Everyone here tonight was captivated by you, my darling."

Lavinia laughed. "Impossible creature," she whispered fondly. "It was you they were charmed by."

Across from her, Laura couldn't help but smile. "Do you know, I actually saw Lady Harrington wipe a tear from her eye when you made that toast to Lavinia, Nicholas. I don't think I have ever seen her so moved."

Nicholas shrugged. "I only spoke the truth."

"Ah, but that's the thing," Edward said, grinning. "The members of the ton aren't used to hearing the truth, especially when it comes to sentiments of the heart."

"I think what the English are not used to is two people who are truly in love," Martine said suddenly.

Lavinia turned to look at her stepdaughter in surprise. "What do you mean, Martine?"

"Well, you and Nicholas are so obviously devoted to each other, and you are not ashamed to show it. It happens seldom, *n'est-ce pas?* Are not most aristocratic marriages made for convenience?"

"Yes, a lot of them are," Nicholas granted, "but I am happy to say that I know of at least two marriages besides ours that are not. What say you, Kingsley?"

Edward drew a similarly blushing Laura into his embrace. "I am the first to agree, and I know I speak for my sister as well."

Lavinia stepped forward to put an arm around Martine's shoulders. "Off you go to bed, Martine. It has been a big night for you."

Martine guiltily stifled a yawn. *"Oui,* I am tired," she admitted. *"Bonsoir."*

"Good night, Martine," Nicholas said fondly.

The others said their good-nights and watched the girl climb the stairs. When she had gone, Laura said, "Lavinia, your stepdaughter is charming."

"Yes, I daresay she will be in great demand," Edward put in, adding with a smile, "I saw Lord Hardy's son desperately trying to get her attention earlier."

"Yes, but I think she preferred the company of young Tomkins," Nicholas said. "Although she did spend a fair bit of time talking to Sir Wilber's boy."

Lavinia sighed. "The problem with Martine is that all of this is so new to her. François kept her very sheltered, and I truly don't think she realizes how attractive she is. I had to reprimand her earlier for allowing Lord Fox to take her out onto the terrace—alone."

"I'm sure you needn't worry, Lavinia," Laura reassured her. "She will quickly come to learn what is and is not acceptable behaviour."

"I do hope so," Lavinia murmured. "She is so very trusting of people right now. I should hate to see her get hurt."

"She won't," Nicholas asserted. "Not if I have anything to say about it."

"I say, Nicholas, what happens with regard to Martine?" Edward enquired. "Does she legally become your stepdaughter?"

Nicholas glanced at Lavinia, his expression questioning. "I'd really never thought about that. Does she?"

"I suppose so. She is legally *my* stepdaughter." Lavinia's lips quirked. "And do not a wife's possessions become her husband's once they marry?"

"What a splendid arrangement," Edward quipped. "A wife and a fully grown daughter into the bargain."

"A fully grown one, until we have one of our own," Nicholas corrected him.

"Nicholas!"

Nicholas turned, and was amused to see the colour in Lavinia's face. "Now, darling, don't scold," he said gently. "Children are a natural result of being in love. Isn't that right, Edward?"

"As I recall."

"In fact," Nicholas continued, "given the relative closeness of our weddings, I think it will be interesting to see which couple publishes a birth announcement first."

"Don't forget Charlotte," Edward reminded him. "She and Marwood have a bit of a head start on the rest of us."

"Edward, really!" Laura said, colouring hotly. "This is hardly suitable conversation for mixed company. I shall tell your sister when she returns that you were discussing her so indelicately.''

"Do that, my sweet," Edward said wickedly, "and I guarantee that if Charlotte is not already in the family way, she will dutifully cast me off for having accused her of being so!"

To the sound of laughter and good-natured teasing, Laura and Edward left, finally leaving Nicholas and Lavinia alone. Returning to the elegant drawing-room, Nicholas pulled Lavinia into his arms and tilted her face up to his.

Their lips came together in a kiss of mutual need and longing. He felt the softness of her body melt against the hard length of his as his hands curved into the small of her back. He heard her breath catch as his lips moved round to nuzzle the tender skin beneath her earlobe.

"God, you're beautiful!" he murmured, following the line of her neck and bare shoulder. He felt her shiver as his lips reverently brushed the top of her breasts.

Lavinia moaned low in her throat. "Nicholas, you must...stop."

"I don't want to stop." His mouth came back to hers, catching her lips still parted on a sigh. Her breath was sweet and warm, and he groaned, feeling his desire intensify. "I want you so much."

"And I want you, but I hardly think this is the time or the place," Lavinia replied unsteadily. Her eyes twinkled. "Martine has never been a deep sleeper."

The warning in her voice cut through Nicholas's passion, and he reluctantly set her away from him, knowing that the longer he held her, the harder it would be to leave. "My sweet Lavinia," he said with a chuckle, "am I ever to see you lose your self-control altogether and throw yourself impetuously into my arms?"

"Oh, indeed, my lord. And before too much longer, I shouldn't wonder. Especially if you carry on like that," she scolded.

"Yes, well, I can only hope." Nicholas gazed down into her beautiful, trusting face, and his expression suddenly grew serious. He had to tell her that he was going away. It was only fair that she be prepared for his leaving within the next two days.

"Yes, Nicholas?" Lavinia said gently.

He heard the concern in her voice and took a deep breath. "Lavinia, there's . . . something I have to tell—"

He broke off as the door to the salon unexpectedly opened to reveal Habinger standing in the doorway.

"Oh, forgive me, my lady," the flustered butler said. "It was just that, well, it was so quiet in here, I thought everyone had . . . left."

The butler's arrival shattered the mood of intimacy and caused Nicholas to abruptly change his mind. No, he wouldn't tell her tonight. He couldn't spoil what had been such a special evening for both of them. Let Lavinia have her dreams tonight. There would be time enough for worry tomorrow.

"That's quite all right, Habinger, I was just leaving."

Lavinia touched Nicholas's sleeve with her hand. "Nicholas? I thought you were about to tell me—"

"What I was going to say can wait, my darling," Nicholas assured her. "Right now, I think I'd best leave or the servants will be up all night." He drew her into his arms and pressed a tender kiss against her temple. "Sleep well."

"Shall I see you tomorrow?"

Nicholas nodded. "Yes. I'll come by in the morning." He tried to meet her eyes, but couldn't. He knew he would have no choice but to tell her then.

NICHOLAS LEFT LAVINIA'S house that night, understanding for the first time the kind of anguish his good friend Lord Marwood had experienced the night he had taken leave of the woman he loved before sailing for France to undertake a dangerous mission—the very mission that had brought

Lavinia safely home to England. Now Nicholas knew what it was like to face the prospect of never seeing one's beloved again.

Directing his driver to take him to White's, Nicholas climbed into the carriage. A short while later, he found himself in the comfortably masculine ambience of the gentlemen's club's darkly panelled interior. Edward was waiting for him at a quiet table in the back corner, where they could talk without fear of being overheard.

"I've ordered brandy for both of us," Edward said as Nicholas sat down. "I thought you might be able to use one."

"Yes, I've a feeling I will." Nicholas gave him a lopsided grin. "And probably a few more before I see Lavinia again tomorrow."

"You haven't told her then?"

He shook his head. "I was going to tell her tonight, but I changed my mind. I didn't want to spoil such a pleasant evening."

"So tell me, how did this all come about?" Edward enquired. He glanced around carefully and then leaned closer. "Osborne told me he wasn't willing to risk either of us going back to France to find Leclerc."

"That's what he told me, too, but when I saw the names of the chaps he was contemplating sending, I told him it would be like sending lambs to the slaughter."

"That bad?" Edward grimaced. "So how did you convince him?"

"By telling him that the only way Leclerc was likely to come out of hiding was by sending to France someone he wanted badly enough that he'd risk showing himself. I also told Osborne that if Leclerc wasn't stopped *before* he got to England, it would be a damned sight more difficult to stop him after."

They broke off momentarily as the waiter arrived with their brandy. Setting the tray with a bottle and two glasses on the small table beside Edward, the man moved off, leaving Nicholas to continue, "Osborne isn't positive that the drawing Baker sent is of Leclerc, and with us not being able to positively identify the man, the chances of nabbing him once he's in England are limited indeed. That's why I stressed the importance of flushing him out in his own territory."

While Nicholas was speaking, Edward poured out two glasses of cognac and handed one to his friend. "That's all well and good, but what if you meet the same fate as all the others? Leclerc is no novice at this game. He's damn good. The fact that no one has been able to get to him proves that."

"Yes, but it's his cockiness I'm counting on to trip him up," Nicholas admitted. "Given his rather formidable list of successes in the past, I doubt he will view the arrival of yet another English agent, even one of my reputation, as a particularly imposing threat. And knowing how close he is to leaving France, I am hoping he may grow a little careless."

"Well, I have to say I don't envy you having to tell Lavinia you're going back to France. I remember how she looked when Marwood brought her back. She was scared to death."

"Yes, I know," Nicholas said ruefully. "She's already admitted to me that she never expected to get out of France alive." He breathed a heavy sigh. "And now I have to tell her that I'm going back in."

"Do you think telling her that you're trying to find the man who was responsible for her husband's death will help?"

"Not in the least. In fact, I don't intend to tell Lavinia why I'm going."

"You're not?"

Nicholas shook his head. "Lavinia has obviously heard of Jean Leclerc, and she may or may not suspect that he is the one behind her husband's death. If I tell her that I am going to France to try to find Leclerc, she'll worry herself sick."

"Then how do you intend to broach the subject?" Edward asked.

"I don't know. I'm almost tempted to say I'm just going up to the north of England for a few days. Or down to the coast. Lord knows, it really doesn't make much difference."

Edward drew a deep breath and gazed into the depths of the amber liquid in his glass. "I for one shall be heartily glad when this damned war is over."

"Yes, so shall I, my friend. But the problem with men like Leclerc is that it's never really over," Nicholas said grimly. "For them, the killing goes on. That's why I have to stop him before he gets to England. We can't afford to have Leclerc slip into London Society and then start doing away with whomsoever he pleases." He glanced at Edward sharply. "I'm afraid none of us would be able to rest safely in our beds if that were to happen."

"LORD LONGWORTH, my lady."

"Thank you, Habinger." Lavinia rose and went to greet her fiancé at the door. "Good morning, my lord. I had not thought to see you here quite so early."

"Good morning." Nicholas drew her into his arms and kissed her long and tenderly. "You are looking exceptionally lovely this morning."

"I should be." Lavinia flashed a grin at him. "I am expecting a handsome gentleman caller. Dear me, I do hope he doesn't arrive while you're here."

Nicholas's lips curved in a devilish smile. "Saucy wench, tease me, will you?" He playfully tapped her behind as she went to sit down.

"Nicholas! Behave!"

"I will, but only for the moment. Is Martine up?"

Lavinia shook her head fondly. "Not yet. I fear last night quite tired her out. She hasn't grown accustomed to these late nights yet." She gazed at Nicholas through eyes made perceptive by love. "You look weary, though. Did you not go directly home after you left here?"

"Not immediately, no." Nicholas knew he could not lie to her. "I met Edward at the club and we chatted for a while."

Lavinia frowned, detecting a change in Nicholas she wasn't quite able to identify. "Is everything all right, Nicholas?"

He slowly sat down on the settee beside her. "Lavinia, there's something we have to discuss. Or rather, something I have to tell you."

"Yes, I gathered as much last night." Lavinia's smile faded. "Is this serious?"

"Yes."

"I knew it. What's wrong, Nicholas?"

"Well, there's nothing . . . wrong, exactly."

"Then what is it . . . exactly?"

"I'm . . . going back to France."

"*What?*"

He heard the horror and disbelief in her voice and forced himself to go on. "There is a matter that needs taking care of, and I . . . told Lord Osborne I would go."

Lavinia stared at him in shock. "But how can you even think of returning to France after what happened when you went to rescue Edward? The French will still be looking for you, Nicholas. You can't possibly go back there now!"

"Lavinia, no one is looking to be looking for me," Nicholas said, trying his best to reassure her. "The war is almost over. Bonaparte's intelligence network is all but dispersed."

"Then why are you going at all?" Lavinia enquired sharply. "Did Lord Osborne ask you to?"

"No, not exactly," Nicholas replied. "But the mission is...delicate enough to require the services of a more...seasoned agent."

"A more seasoned agent." Lavinia rose to her feet, the rapid rise and fall of her chest evidence that she was more than a little agitated. "Nicholas, I know it is not my place to tell you what you should and should not do, but in this instance, I beg you to reconsider. We are to be married in less than a month. What if—" she closed her eyes and turned her back towards him "—what if something were to...happen to you?"

Nicholas rose and went to stand behind her. "Nothing is going to happen, my love. I shall go, I shall take care of this business and then I shall return. Simple."

"If it is so simple, why are you not willing to let one of Osborne's other men go?" Lavinia rounded on him. "Why does this mission require the services of a *seasoned agent?*"

Nicholas tried to affect an air of nonchalance. "Lavinia, you're making far too much of this."

"Am I? I don't think so." Lavinia stared into his eyes, searching for the truth. "You're not telling me everything, Nicholas. I know you better than that. Why are you going to France? Why is this mission so important?"

Nicholas managed a convincing smile. "Every mission is important, Lavinia. No one knows that better than you. You were intimately involved from the moment you married François."

"Then tell me what this is about."

He shook his head sadly. "I cannot."

"Can't or won't?" Lavinia held her breath. There was so much he wasn't telling her and she was horribly afraid. Afraid that she was going to lose him just when their life together was about to begin.

"Nicholas, *please* let someone else go. Please do not put me through this torture. I cannot bear the thought of losing you."

Nicholas sighed and pulled her into the circle of his arms, willing her to draw strength and confidence from his embrace. "I can't, Lavinia. If it were less important, I would gladly step aside and let another man take my place. But the consequences of this mission not being successfully carried out are too dangerous to contemplate. I know I can do what has to be done."

Lavinia stepped back out of his arms, afraid that she would burst into tears if she stayed there. The ache in her heart made her want to get down on her knees and beg him not to go. What would she do if he didn't come back? How could she face the rest of her life if Nicholas were killed?

Watching her, Nicholas felt her withdrawal like a physical pain. "Lavinia, please do not distance yourself from me," he pleaded. "I need you now more than ever. I need your strength."

"I have no strength, Nicholas," she told him sadly. "Not for this. I cannot help but remember what it was like when Lord Marwood came to take me out of France. It was so dangerous...." Her words trailed off as memories too painful to remember crept in to choke her.

Suddenly, she looked up at him. "My God, that's it, isn't it? You are going in order to find someone."

Inwardly, Nicholas flinched. The workings of Lavinia's agile mind constantly surprised him. "I am going to look for someone, yes."

"And when you find him?" Her eyes cleared for a moment. "Is this another rescue mission?"

He knew that she was grasping at straws, and he was almost tempted to lie and let her believe it. But he knew he couldn't. It wouldn't be fair. "No, I am not going to...rescue anyone, my love."

A tense silence developed between them. "Then you are going to kill someone," Lavinia said in a flat, dead voice. Dear God, he was putting himself in such danger. "Nicholas, please, I *beg* you to reconsider."

It was only because Nicholas knew Lavinia's own life was in danger that he didn't change his mind and back out of the mission then and there. Her name was on Leclerc's list, too. If he did not go, and the man who was sent to kill Leclerc failed, the danger to everyone would be that much greater. Better to chance his own life than to put the lives of others at risk. Especially Lavinia's.

"I cannot. There is ... too much at stake," he said, inadvertently quoting Osborne's words.

Lavinia walked slowly towards the window, focusing her attention on anything she could to distract her mind from the fact that he was leaving. He saw the fear in her eyes when she turned to face him, as well as the weary resignation. "Nicholas, *please.*"

"I will come back, Lavinia," Nicholas told her urgently. "I promise I will return, and then we'll be married, just as we had planned. Nothing will stop me from having you now, beloved. Nothing!"

CHAPTER THREE

TWO DAYS LATER, Nicholas made his way along a darkened country road, heading towards the small village of Rosières just southeast of Amien. Through contacts, he had learned that a man matching Leclerc's description had recently been seen at Le Cheval Blanc, a small country inn near Rosières. That, at least, had been good news. It meant that Leclerc's business in France was not yet concluded.

Arriving at the inn just before eight o'clock in the evening, Nicholas left his horse with the young boy at the stable. Then, pulling his hood up over his head, he made his way towards the bustling *auberge*. Nicholas knew the dangers inherent with his being in France, even though he had assured Osborne there were none. For that reason, he had dressed in the clothes of a simple cleric, a disguise he had used on more than one occasion, and with considerable success. He pulled out his missal and tucked it under his arm.

The sounds of revelry and laughter hit him as soon he opened the heavy wooden door. Nicholas glanced around the crowded room, noting the faces of the people gathered about the tables. He took care not to stare at any one person too long. He had no wish to arouse curiosity, nor to draw attention to himself. Adopting the humble manner of a priest, he approached the innkeeper. *"Monsieur?"*

The innkeeper, a large, heavy-set man with dark, beady eyes, and a bulbous nose dominating his meaty features, turned and barked, *"Oui?"* Then, seeing the clerical garb, he added more politely, in rapid French, "Excuse me, Father. What can I get for you?"

Nicholas smiled benevolently. "Only a room for the night, my son," he replied, in equally fluent French.

Fortunately, the innkeeper had one room left. It was small and noisy, being located at the top of the stairs. But it was not as bad as some, and as he had no intention of sleeping, Nicholas gratefully took it. If Leclerc was still in the area, he would likely return to the inn for the night. If not, there was always the possibility that Nicholas might overhear something of use from one of the revellers.

Once in the room, Nicholas took off his serviceable brown cloak and laid it on the bed, revealing the cleric's tunic beneath. He then crossed to the window and looked out onto the courtyard below, silently blessing his good fortune. From his window, he had a clear view of the yard.

He carefully pulled the curtain aside an inch or so, and stood watching the people coming and going—until an unexpected knock on his bedroom door caused him to drop the curtain and step away from the window. He tensed, his hand dropping automatically to the butt of his pistol. *"Oui?"*

It was only a serving girl with the simple dinner he had requested. Nicholas let out a breath. He was getting jumpy. Still, the crusty bread and thick slices of cheese felt good in his stomach. He had not stopped for food anywhere along the road, and it had been a long time since breakfast. He tucked one piece of bread into the pocket of his gown for the long night ahead. Then he took up his watch by the window again.

An hour passed. Two. The sounds from the ale-room downstairs grew louder as the locals imbibed more heavily. Nicholas purposely kept the room in darkness, ensuring that he would not be seen from the road. He tensed briefly when a large, burly man suddenly staggered drunkenly out through the front doors of the inn and collapsed in a heap on the ground. But it was obviously nothing. Moments later, a number of his friends came out, picked him up and dragged him back inside.

Close to midnight, Nicholas heard the sound of footsteps in the hall outside his doorway. Leaving the window for a moment, he tiptoed across the room and put his ear to the door. The sound of feminine laughter, as well as a few unmistakable French phrases spoken in a rough masculine voice set his mind at rest. Obviously, the ladies of the evening were beginning to retire. Another high-pitched laugh and the sound of a door slamming next to his own room confirmed it.

Well, at least there was pleasure for some, Nicholas reflected drily, trying to ignore the sounds coming through the thin walls of the room next door. He returned to his place by the window. And not a moment too soon. A closed carriage drawn by a matched pair of greys had pulled into the courtyard.

Nicholas carefully drew back into the shadows. As he watched, the coachman sprang down from the box, and after glancing around the deserted yard, made directly for the inn. Moments later he returned with the innkeeper. He then rapped sharply on the door of the carriage.

Nicholas held his breath as the door opened and a man stepped down. Could this be Leclerc?

It was difficult to tell. The man's curly brimmed beaver hat was pulled down low over his eyes, while the turned-up collar of the multicaped greatcoat made it almost impossible to see his features. But there was no mistaking the furtiveness of his movements, alerting Nicholas to the presence of danger.

The three men spoke in low, urgent whispers. An argument seemed to be ensuing between the innkeeper and the coachman. The innkeeper kept shaking his head and pointing to the road, while the coachman stamped his foot and pointed at the inn. Nicholas tried to get a better look at the face of the passenger, but he stubbornly kept his head down.

"Come along, *mon ami,* let's have a look at your face,"
Nicholas whispered softly. "Look up, damn it!"

Strangely enough, as if hearing his appeal, Fate chose that
moment to intervene. The couple in the next room suddenly brought their lovemaking to a dramatic conclusion.
Nicholas heard the high keening sound of the woman's voice
raised in pleasure, and then a resounding crash—clearly of
the bed collapsing—as the man grunted and reached his own
shuddering pinnacle.

The three men in the yard glanced upwards, the sound
having drawn their attention. Nicholas saw the man he suspected of being Leclerc reach instinctively under his cape.
For a split second he looked up, his eyes scanning the windows on the second floor.

It was all the time Nicholas needed. There was no mistaking that face. It was the same as the one in the picture on
Osborne's desk. He had found Jean Leclerc!

Nicholas watched as the innkeeper put his hand on Leclerc's arm and murmured something unintelligible. Leclerc's hand slowly slid out from under his cape and then he
chuckled, obviously recognizing what had happened. After
glancing around, the three men resumed their conversation.

Nicholas moved closer to the window again, straining to
hear what they were saying. The voices were low, as though
the men were fearful of being overheard. Only one word
came clearly to his ears before Leclerc climbed back into the
landau and the carriage set off—*Calais!*

So it was true, Nicholas admitted grimly. Leclerc was
planning to make for the coast. No doubt a ship waited even
now to convey him across the Channel. He would be in
England by morning. There was absolutely no time to waste.
Nicholas had to stop Leclerc before he reached the coast!

He reached for his cloak. Reversing it this time so that the
black side was turned out, he gathered up his few belong-

ings and left the room. Every minute counted now. He had to cut off Leclerc's escape before it was too late.

Avoiding the busy front entrance of the inn, Nicholas located the back stairs and silently made his way down. He sprinted across the yard to the darkened stables. The horses nickered nervously at his approach. He crept stealthily between the stalls, looking for his mount. Suddenly, he froze, detecting a movement against some bales of hay at the back. He reached for his pistol and drew back into a stall. "Show yourself!" he growled, forgetting for a moment to speak in French.

Nicholas heard a startled gasp. "Do not shoot, *monsieur*, do not shoot!" a young and very frightened voice whispered back in French.

The sinister presence turned out to be nothing more than the young lad who had stabled his horse, and Nicholas quickly put his pistol away. He stepped out of the stall, a dark, shadowy figure in his long, flowing black cape. "Do not be afraid, my child. It is only I," he said, this time in perfect French.

"Mon père?" The young boy's eyes widened until they almost filled his face. "What are you doing out here so late?"

Nicholas held his finger to his lips. "Silence, my son. Where is my horse?"

The boy swallowed and, in answer to the question, ran down to the second stall. He quickly untied the chestnut and brought him out.

"Thank you." Nicholas sprang into the saddle with far more agility than a travelling cleric would ever have possessed, and tossed the lad a coin. "God go with you, my son." Then, wheeling the chestnut's head around, Nicholas set off in pursuit of the carriage. He wished, not for the first time, that he had his own fiery stallion under him, and prayed that he hadn't heard the name of Leclerc's intended destination wrong.

THE CARRIAGE HAD a good head start, but Nicholas was able to catch up quickly. Unaware that he was being pursued, the coachman did not set a breakneck speed. Nicholas followed the road until he heard the rumble of carriage wheels on the road ahead. Rounding a bend, he spotted the vehicle about a quarter of a mile ahead. At that point, he guided his horse into the woods, knowing that the trees would give him the necessary cover.

Nicholas quickly closed the distance, his mind racing as fast as the horse's hooves. There was one man inside the carriage, and the coachman on the box. Nicholas had hoped to get Leclerc alone without shedding any other blood, but faced with the prospect that both men would be armed, Nicholas knew the possibility of that was slim. He didn't want to waste a shot. He would bide his time, waiting for the man who had cold-bloodedly murdered his fiancé's husband.

Nicholas took stock of the countryside as, still hidden behind the line of trees, he drew level with the coach. They were approaching a long, deserted stretch of road. There were no houses in the area, although Nicholas saw what looked to be the dark outline of a barn and some scattered farm buildings set well back from the road. Fortunately, at this time of night, the occupants—likely hard-working farmers—would all be sound asleep. With any luck, the sound of gunfire would not waken them.

Nicholas's thoughts turned suddenly to Lavinia, and he knew a heart-wrenching moment of guilt. *Dear God, please let her forgive me if I do not return this night. I love you, my darling.* Then, putting aside all other considerations, Nicholas pulled out his pistol, took aim and fired.

The sound tore through the night like an explosion. As the coachman grabbed his shoulder and slumped forward, the horses whinnied in fear, their ears flat against their heads, their eyes rolling. Nicholas glimpsed the startled face of a man at the window and heard a voice shouting, "*Les chevaux!* Stop them!"

Yanking valiantly on the reins, the coachman managed to draw the panicked team to a halt before slipping from his seat unconscious, a dark stain spreading around the torn fabric at his shoulder. Nicholas stayed under cover of the trees, watching. There was no sound now but the nervous stamping of the horses. He saw no more faces at the window. Most likely Leclerc was on the floor, or sitting far enough back not to be hit by a stray bullet.

"Leclerc!" Nicholas shouted, his voice carrying clearly in the still night air. "Show yourself!"

There was no sound or movement from within the carriage.

"Leclerc! Come out and throw down your weapons."

"Who are you?" said a voice in heavily accented French.

"That is no concern of yours."

"On the contrary, it is of great concern. Why should I show myself to someone who would kill me?"

"How do you know that is my intention?" Nicholas replied.

"Because you are no highwayman," replied a second voice.

Nicholas raised an eyebrow in astonishment. *English?* His eyes narrowed. He had not expected Leclerc to have a travelling companion. And certainly not an English one.

"Come forward, Leclerc," he ordered. "You *and* your friend. I would have you both face me."

"Are you such a coward that you cannot also show yourself?" the Frenchman taunted. "Or do you intend to stay shut away in the woods like a cowering beast?"

Nicholas felt a hard knot of anger form within his breast. "Do you think me such a fool that I would set myself up as a target? Come out, gentlemen, and throw down your weapons." He waited a moment longer. "You gain nothing by remaining within, for I have the advantage. Your coachman will be taking you no further tonight. Come out, I say!"

Slowly the door opened. The two men stepped down. Nicholas immediately recognized the shorter one as the man he had seen at the inn. But when he glanced at the other man, he was astonished to see that the man's face was bandaged to the point of being unrecognizable. His arm also looked to be caught up in some kind of a sling.

"Come along, gentlemen, let's have your weapons. Slowly now," Nicholas cautioned them. "Don't try anything foolish."

He kept his pistol raised as they both reached under their coats. When he saw the two pistols hit the ground, he gently pressed his heels into the chestnut's sides. Emerging from cover for the first time, he approached them slowly, watching their faces. "So, we meet at last, *monsieur*," Nicholas said softly to Leclerc.

The Frenchman's eyes narrowed. "You know me?"

"I should. Your reputation precedes you."

Leclerc bowed mockingly. "I am flattered."

"You needn't be," Nicholas drawled. "It is not a reputation to be proud of."

He saw a momentary flash of anger in the man's dark eyes. "You should be careful, *monsieur*. I have many friends in France."

"Perhaps, but they do not concern me." Nicholas glanced at the other man. "Who is your wounded companion, Leclerc?"

"He is of no concern to you."

"On the contrary, anyone connected with you is of interest to me. And the fact that he is English makes him even more so." Nicholas addressed the man directly. "Who are you, sir, and where did you sustain your injuries?"

The man started to speak, but Leclerc quickly held up his hand, silencing him. "I told you, *monsieur*, that is no concern of yours."

Nicholas sighed and cocked his pistol. The sound echoed in the darkness. "Who is he?"

Leclerc swallowed. *"Monsieur,* I—"

Suddenly, a second gunshot ripped through the night air, shattering the silence. Nicholas watched in disbelief as the Englishman behind Leclerc grabbed at the front of his coat and then crumpled lifeless to the ground.

Nicholas blanched. "What in blazes...?" He spun in the direction from which the shot had come, his pistol raised. Suddenly, out of the corner of his eye, he saw Leclerc pull a small, deadly looking pistol from his breast pocket and aim it directly at his chest.

Displaying the lightning-fast reflexes that had saved his life on more than one occasion, Nicholas whipped back round and flexed his finger on the trigger. There was the sound of a shot, and Leclerc staggered back against the carriage, grasping his chest. His own pistol discharged uselessly into the air.

Nicholas's face darkened. "It is over, Leclerc. There will be no more murders."

The dying man's eyes were glazed with fear, but he shook his head and laughed horribly. *"Non, mon ami,* it is...not over. You are...wrong." He laughed again, then slid to the road, uttering on his dying gasp, *"Je ne suis pas...Leclerc!"*

Nicholas stared at him in horror. Not Leclerc! Then who the hell—

A split second before the bullet hit, Nicholas heard the sound of a pistol cocking and instinctively dropped. But he wasn't fast enough. A fiery bolt tore into his flesh, knocking him out of the saddle. He hit the ground at the edge of the road, blood pouring from the wound in his side. Then he heard a very English, very cultured voice in the darkness above him.

"So, Longworth, you thought to prevent my leaving France, did you? Well, I'm afraid you thought wrong."

Nicholas gasped and closed his eyes as a fresh stab of pain hit him, causing his stomach to lurch violently. He felt the sweat trickling down his temple. He was going to be sick.

"Nothing to say, Nicholas?" the voice taunted him.

Nicholas fought to hold on to consciousness. Straining his eyes, he could just make out the figure of a tall man mounted upon a horse. He could not discern the man's features, but he could see a thin plume of smoke rising from the pistol in his hand.

"Who—who . . . ?" Nicholas tried, but couldn't get the words out. He was becoming dizzy, growing steadily weaker from loss of blood. His body was on fire.

"Who am I? Is that what you're trying to say, old man?" The smooth English voice was mocking him. "But who do you think I am? I am the one you came to kill. I am Jean Leclerc."

Nicholas struggled to focus his eyes, aware of the chaotic jumble of thoughts spinning around in his brain.

They had the wrong man! The picture was of the wrong man!

"Yes, I've surprised you, haven't I, Nicholas? I must admit, I hadn't expected to. I thought for certain you would have seen through my little ruse."

"Ruse?" Nicholas wheezed out through pain-clenched teeth.

"Yes. The drawing I allowed Baker to have. Clever of me, don't you think? To have him send back a picture of the wrong man. Of course, he didn't suspect until it was too late," the man said smugly. "They never do. But I thought you might have. I know all about your reputation, you see. I could not believe you managed to sneak Kingsley out of France—and right under my nose, as it turns out. I suppose I should applaud your intelligence for that. But—" the man sighed dramatically "—I really had expected a more worthy opponent in a face-to-face confrontation."

"This was . . . hardly a . . . face-to-face . . . confrontation."

He heard the man chuckle. "Perhaps not. But at least it is not I who am lying in the ditch dying. Tell me, Nicholas, is it more noble to die a hero or to live a coward? I wonder. I know which I should prefer."

Nicholas licked his lips. Even the act of speaking was causing him excruciating pain. "So, it was all . . . a lie," he wheezed. "It was not . . . Leclerc."

"On the contrary, it was most definitely Leclerc," the stranger informed him calmly. "Or at least, the man I allowed people to think was Leclerc. He did everything I told him to. As did Ferris." He saw a momentary glimmer in Nicholas's eyes. "Yes, you know that name, don't you. And so you should. He was your leak, of course. I'm surprised old Osborne didn't stumble onto that one earlier. I was afraid he might have. Yes, both Ferris and Leclerc were very willing to go along with my plans . . . for the right price. They enabled me to operate undercover and completely above suspicion. I even let them believe that they were going to England. Pity you came along so soon."

Nicholas was finding it difficult to form words. His mouth didn't seem to want to work any more. "What do you . . . mean, pity?"

"I mean, dear boy, that if you hadn't stumbled along, I would have taken care of these two with no one any the wiser. No one would have discovered that Leclerc was not exactly who the British Intelligence thought he was—as illustrated by the picture I allowed to fall into Baker's hands—and I could have returned to London in complete safety. Even Ferris's duplicity would have gone undiscovered. He would have been hailed as a hero for being the one to kill the notorious French spy Jean Leclerc—sadly, just as Leclerc was killing him. You see, I couldn't risk either of them saying anything about me once they got to England. Just as I can't risk your going back to England now." His lips drew back in a malevolent sneer. "As we both know, I have some . . . unfinished business to take care of."

Nicholas took one look at the man's shadowy face and then lay back. "Traitor!"

The word was little more than a gasp, and Nicholas dimly heard the sound of the man's scornful laughter. "Such an unpleasant word, Nicholas, but yes, I suppose to you I would be. Still, I am sorry that we did not have the chance to meet on a more equal footing. I was looking forward to baiting you in Society, seeing if you could catch me out before I killed you. Now I fear it will be that much easier to dispatch the others—your own dear Lavinia included. Well, I think it is time I left. I hate watching a man in his death throes. Such an uncivilized sight, all that wretched blood. I'd much rather remember you as you were. Besides, I have a ship waiting to take me on a moonlit ride to the gently rolling English countryside. And by this time tomorrow night, I shall be safely in London. *Adieu*, Nicholas."

Nicholas heard the man's mocking laughter, and then the sound of the pistol being cocked. Drawing on every last ounce of strength he possessed, he twisted his body to the left at the precise moment the gun fired, hoping it would be enough.

It wasn't.

Nicholas felt a searing pain in his head and then the sound of laughter growing faint in the distance. It was the last thing he was to remember before everything went mercifully, painlessly, black.

SOMETHING WAS WRONG!

Lavinia stared at the cards in her hands and tried not to cry out as the symbols suddenly became blurred. She couldn't explain the feeling of fear that had just come over her. She only knew she was frightened. She began to shiver uncontrollably.

Beside her, Lady Torbarry crowed in delight. "My hand again! I vow, I have never won so easily before, Lavinia. Wherever is your mind this evening?" The older woman turned towards her in surprise. "Lavinia? Are you all right, dear?"

Lavinia tried to smile, but found the effort more than she could manage. "I am sorry, Harriet. I'm afraid my mind is really... not on my cards." Her voice was wavering. "How much does that make it now?"

"Well, let me see." Lady Torbarry checked her calculations. "That brings the total to... fifty-six pounds you owe me."

Lavinia nodded, and rose rather unsteadily from the card table. "I shall have it sent round tomorrow. If you will excuse me..."

Before the woman had a chance to say anything else, Lavinia quit the card room and made her way back into the lavishly appointed gold salon. Her eyes scanned the room. She located Edward Kingsley across the floor and made for his side at once. "Edward, may I speak with you?"

Edward turned and gazed down into Lavinia's white face, the pleasant words of greeting he had been about to utter dying on his lips. Her breathing was shallow, and he could see the faint mist of perspiration on her forehead. "Lavinia, what's wrong?" he asked urgently.

"I... don't know." Lavinia closed her eyes. "Something has... happened."

Her breathing was becoming more erratic by the minute, and Edward recognized panic setting in. Excusing them both, he took Lavinia's arm and led her outside onto the balcony.

"Lavinia, listen to me," Edward said firmly. "You're breathing too fast. You are going to pass out. Start taking deep, easy breaths."

Hearing the calming influence of his voice, Lavinia closed her eyes. She concentrated on her breathing, gradually bringing it back under control. The light-headedness passed.

"There, that's better," Edward said. "Now, what's happened to upset you so?"

Lavinia raised her troubled eyes to his. "I don't know. I was sitting playing cards with Lady Torbarry when this horrible feeling came over me."

Edward glanced at her sharply. "What kind of feeling?"

"I don't know. I can't explain it," she whispered. "Edward, I think something has happened . . . to Nicholas."

"Nicholas!" Edward stared at her in alarm. "What on earth are you talking about?"

Lavinia shook her head. "I know it doesn't make any sense, Edward, but I can't help what I feel, and I feel inside that something has gone very wrong. Nicholas has been hurt."

There was no doubting the depth of her fear, nor the strength of her conviction, and Edward thought for a moment. "Look, I think I had better take you home, Lavinia," he said finally. "And I'm going to have Laura stay with you."

"What are you going to do?"

"I'll see if I can get in touch with Osborne. Perhaps he's heard something."

Lavinia nodded in relief. "Thank you, Edward." She drew a shaky breath. "What if Nicholas has been . . ." She couldn't bring herself to say the words.

"He hasn't!" Edward said forcefully. "Now, come along. I'll have Laura fetch your cape. Shall I make your excuses?"

Lavinia nodded again. "I should be . . . grateful if you would."

An hour later, Lavinia and Laura sat together in the drawing-room of Lavinia's house, waiting for Edward to return. The nagging fear persisted, and no matter what she tried to do, Lavinia could not shake it. They had not woken Martine.

"But how do you know that something has happened, Lavinia?" Laura asked quietly. "Nicholas is hundreds of miles away."

Lavinia shook her head, her eyes staring into space. "I do not know, but I am certain that it has. I can feel it."

Laura bit her lip. "Do you know, it's strange, but Charlotte once told me that she and Edward had a...special bond. She told me that...she would know in her heart if something ever happened to him."

Lavinia nodded. "I never believed such things possible, and I pray to God that I am mistaken, but I just felt—" She broke off, her eyes turning to the door. "Edward!" She rose immediately. "Well?"

Edward came in and shook his head regretfully. "I'm sorry, Lavinia, but there's been no word. I told Osborne that you were...concerned, but there's really nothing we can do. The only thing we know for sure is that Nicholas was heading for Rosières, but that was days ago. There's been nothing from him since."

Nothing from him since. The words rang in Lavinia's head like a death knell.

"We have to find him, Edward," she whispered, her lips white. "He's been hurt, I know it. He's been hurt and he needs our help." She glanced up at Edward with pleading eyes. "Please, tell Lord Osborne he must send help immediately!"

Edward glanced at Laura in concern. "Osborne has already dispatched someone. If Nicholas is in trouble, we'll find him."

Lavinia closed her eyes and leaned against Laura's shoulder. She would not cry. Not yet. Not while Nicholas needed her to be strong.

Don't leave me, Nicholas Lavinia cried silently. *You promised you would return. You have to come back!*

FROM SOMEWHERE FAR OFF in the distance, Nicholas heard a voice. It seemed to be the voice of an angel. Gentle and soft, it called to him, drawing him up out of his dark, dreamless sleep and forcing the gathering grey mists around him to part.

A heavy rain was falling. He felt the sting of drops against his face. He seemed to be lying in a ditch. He tried to move, but couldn't. His body felt stiff, numb. He couldn't feel his fingers. And there was a pain in his chest. Or was it in his leg?

Suddenly, a hand pressed gently against his forehead—a small, soft hand. And he heard a voice speaking to him. He struggled to open his eyes.

Was this what an angel looked like? Nicholas wondered, glancing up into a child's face surrounded by a halo of white-blond hair.

Her lips were moving, but he couldn't understand what she was saying. He was so hot. And so dreadfully thirsty.

"Pardon?" He formed the word, but nothing came out. His throat was parched. Did he still have a voice? The angel started to move away.

No, don't leave me, he cried silently.

Surprisingly, she stayed. He saw that she was speaking again, or at least, that her lips were moving. Then Nicholas saw a movement at her side. A man. Nicholas sensed him moving around, and felt hands prodding his side. Agonizing pain shot through his body, stabbing his flesh like red-hot irons. Sweat broke out on his brow, and he felt the taste of blood in his mouth as he clamped down hard, stifling a scream. Again he felt the angel's comforting hands on his brow, but even that could do nothing to lessen his suffering.

Sometime later, he felt strong hands under his armpits. He felt the stiffness of wood being slid under his back, and then felt himself being lifted, the movement jarring his side. His mind screamed against the pain before he mercifully blacked out.

CHAPTER FOUR

"HE'S BEEN SHOT."

The words were spoken in a weary voice filled with bitter resignation. "I knew this would happen." Lord Osborne threw down the morning paper and glanced at Edward Kingsley in despair. "I should never have let Longworth go."

Edward studiously ignored the paper. "It isn't your fault, my lord. You couldn't have stopped him."

"Of course I could have stopped him. I *am* his commanding officer, damn it! I didn't allow him to go to France to rescue Lavinia Duplesse, and I shouldn't have allowed him to go after Leclerc, either." Osborne glanced at the paper in frustration. "Now I have to tell his fiancée that he's been shot, and that we have no idea where he is. Still, I suppose I should be thankful that he managed to get Leclerc."

"Yes. *And* the leak in the department."

"Ferris!" Osborne's nostrils quivered in anger. "Never suspected him of being a double agent. Didn't think he had the stomach for it."

"Obviously he did. The fact that he and Leclerc were heading for the coast together proves they were collaborators."

"Well, they aren't any more." Osborne sat down at his desk and sighed heavily. "Both men dead by the hand of an unidentified assailant."

"Except that you and I know who that unidentified assailant was."

Osborne nodded. "All too well. I just wish I could bring myself to feel more pleased about this whole damn mess. All I can think about is that it was probably at the expense of Nicholas's life!"

The morning newspaper had been filled with the sensational story that suspected-French-spy Jean Leclerc and an Englishman travelling with him had been killed four nights ago, during what looked to have been a midnight robbery along the road to Calais. It seemed that the gendarmes had been advised of the accident by an anonymous letter. Upon arriving at the scene, they had found the bodies of Jean Leclerc, a man later identified as Andrew Ferris and a coachman. A paragraph at the end of the article briefly mentioned that a curate was also said to have been killed, but despite thorough investigation of the surrounding area, his body had not been found.

If nothing else, that small, seemingly inconsequential piece of news had given both Osborne and Kingsley the only glimmer of hope in an otherwise tragic report. They knew that Nicholas had been masquerading as a cleric. But it still left them no closer to knowing where he was now.

"How did the English papers get hold of the story, anyway?" Edward asked.

Osborne sighed. "We're not sure. I assume the same person who tipped off the French authorities must have slipped someone at *The Times* a note."

"What do you make of that?" Edward asked.

Osborne shrugged. "It could be that our informer was nothing more than an innocent passer-by travelling to the coast en route for England when he happened upon the accident."

"Then why is he so reluctant to make himself known?"

"Probably fears for his safety. The war isn't over yet."

Edward thought about that for a moment, but shook his head. "Something isn't making sense here, my lord. If the person who reported the accident knew that the priest was still alive, why didn't he stop to help the poor fellow? Conversely, if the priest was already dead, why was his body never found? Obviously, Nicholas was able to crawl off and find shelter, which means he could still be alive."

Osborne shook his head grimly. "I would like very much to think so, Kingsley, but according to the report, there was a great deal of blood on the grass at the edge of the wood, along with a bullet lodged in the mud. And Leclerc's pistol had been fired."

"Then where is Nicholas?" Edward asked. "A dead man doesn't just get up and walk away."

"No, he doesn't. Which is why I've dispatched Gordon to try to find him. I intend to do everything in my power to get Longworth back." Osborne stared sightlessly at the paper. "I refuse to believe he is dead until we have absolute proof of it."

HE WAS SURROUNDED by pain!

Nicholas stared into the shadowy darkness and clenched his fists against the terrible spasms that racked his body and made him gag. He began to shiver uncontrollably, even as the sweat poured off his body.

"Not...Leclerc," he gasped, eyes bright with fever as he tossed restlessly from side to side. "Not...Leclerc." Then, louder, "Lavinia...promise me...promise—"

The words broke off as the agonizing pain caught him, doubling him over. He felt gentle hands on his shoulders, forcing him back. His side was on fire. His whole body was on fire! He tasted the saltiness of sweat on his lips. "Water!" he gasped. "Water..."

Suddenly, the angel was there again. He felt the softness of her hand on his fevered brow as she pressed a water-soaked cloth to his lips. The cool liquid bathed the inside of his mouth and trickled down his throat.

"Lavinia!" he gasped, reaching for her blindly. His mind struggled to break through the suffocating haze. "I told you... I'd come back. I promised you—"

As the pain slashed through his side again like a red-hot knife, Nicholas groaned and fell back, his head rolling to the side as he slipped again into merciful unconsciousness.

LAVINIA SAT ON THE sofa in a delicate sprigged-muslin morning gown and tried to contain her anguish. The morning paper lay open on the sofa to one side of her. Edward sat patiently on the other.

"And you say the... cleric the paper mentions was actually... Nicholas," Lavinia intoned, her eyes fixed sightlessly on the window.

Edward nodded. "I am sorry to say that it was, Lavinia. Nicholas has used the cleric's outfit before, with great success. Osborne and I are convinced he was wearing it the night he was shot."

Lavinia closed her eyes, as if to keep the painful words at bay. *The night he was shot!*

"So it was... Jean Leclerc who Nicholas went to find," she said. "The man who... killed my husband."

"Yes."

"But why did Lord Osborne let him go?" Lavinia whispered fiercely. "If he knew the dangers, why didn't he send someone else? You told me yourself that neither you nor Nicholas could go to France to rescue me because your faces were too well known. Why did Lord Osborne suddenly change his mind and let Nicholas go now?"

"He didn't. Or at least, not willingly," Edward admitted. "It was Nicholas who insisted upon going. Nicholas felt the only way of drawing Leclerc out was to send someone he would make an effort to..."

"Kill," Lavinia finished, when Edward did not.

"Lavinia, you must understand, Nicholas went because he knew the dangers—"

She made a strangled sound of disbelief. "A lot of good it did him!"

"No, my dear, not the dangers in his going, the dangers in his *not* going," Edward corrected her gently. "The dangers in allowing Leclerc to come to England."

Lavinia raised her troubled eyes to his. "What dangers, Edward? The war is nearly over. Napoleon is banished. What dangers could possibly arise from a French agent being in London now?"

"Leclerc did not intend *his* war to end quite that easily, Lavinia." Edward chose his words with care. "We intercepted a letter the man sent to his superiors. In it, he detailed plans for returning to London after the war to...deal with certain people."

"What do you mean, deal with them?"

"To...silence them."

Lavinia paled. "Oh, my God, to kill them?"

"Yes."

"But why?"

"Because the man was a cold-blooded murderer."

Lavinia blanched, marvelling that anyone could be so evil. "Who was he intending to...deal with?" she asked tremulously.

"Certain people whom he'd encountered during the course of the war," Edward said evasively. "Enemies to the French cause. Naturally, when Nicholas learned of his intentions, he was determined to prevent Leclerc's coming to England, well aware that in an unsuspecting Society, a murderer like that would wreak havoc."

Lavinia was silent for a moment. "What of the people on this list, Edward? Was Nicholas one of them?"

Edward steeled himself to give the only answer he could. "Yes."

Lavinia's hands began to tremble. "And you say Nicholas knew that?"

"He did."

"Who else?"

"Myself, Lord Osborne, Lord Winchester, to name but a few."

"Dear God!"

"Perhaps now you can better understand why Nicholas felt the urgency of going to France—to deal with Leclerc on his own ground."

Lavinia struggled to come to terms with this new, highly disturbing information. Of course she could understand why Nicholas had felt so compelled to go to France. The lives of too many people had been at risk.

"But where is he now, Edward?" she asked, gazing up at him intently. "The cleric was supposedly shot, and yet his body was never found. Do you think it possible that Nicholas is still alive?"

"I do. Pardon me for speaking plainly, Lavinia, but Nicholas is not the type to give up. If he wasn't killed outright by Leclerc's bullet—which, judging from the report, he was not—he will be doing everything he can to get back to England."

"Then I must go to France," Lavinia said with quiet yet unshakable resolve. "He must be found. Until we hear otherwise, we must believe that Nicholas is alive."

"And we do, but there is certainly no question of your going to look for him," Edward said flatly. "It is far too dangerous."

"But don't you see, Edward? I must." Lavinia turned to gaze at him with pain-clouded eyes. "I can't just sit here waiting for news. I have to be there. Remember that night when I said that Nicholas was in danger?"

"Yes."

"Well, I was right. That was the night he was shot. I felt his pain, Edward. I knew he was suffering. And if I felt that, surely I would be able to feel if he was near me, and to find him. Dear God, Edward, I have to try!"

He could see that she was very close to breaking down, and he took her by the shoulders and shook her gently. "Now listen to me, Lavinia. I know you're worried about Nicholas. We all are. But your running off to France isn't going to help. Lord Osborne has already dispatched a man—a good man by the name of James Gordon. He will scour the area where Nicholas was last seen, and if he's alive, Gordon will bring him back. You have to trust me!"

"I do trust you," Lavinia said, still dreadfully near tears, "but I can't just sit here and do nothing, Edward. I can't! I feel as though I am going mad as it is."

"But you're not just sitting here doing nothing, my dear. You have Martine, and you cannot leave her alone," Edward said gently, knowing it was the only argument he could use that would mean anything to her. "She is still getting over the death of her father and your own dangerous flight from France. The girl needs some stability in her life, Lavinia. She needs you. Only think what would happen to her if you were to go to France and meet with an accident."

Lavinia stopped dead, her eyes widening. In her fear for Nicholas, she had momentarily forgotten about Martine, and was now overcome with a tremendous feeling of guilt at having done so. How could she have been so selfish? Martine had come to love and depend on her. She was the only family the girl now had. If something were to happen to her in France, how would Martine cope? Who could she turn to for comfort?

Yes, Edward was right, Lavinia conceded reluctantly. She would have to stay in England and wait for news. She had to be strong. Not just for her own sake, but for Martine's. She would have to wait until she heard the news that Nicholas was safe. But dear God, if only the waiting didn't hurt so much!

NICHOLAS SLOWLY OPENED his eyes, squinting slightly against the slivers of sunlight shining down through the barn boards above. The sound of birds chirping caused him to turn his head, as did the sound of a young girl humming somewhere below him.

Was it morning already? He must have fallen asleep. It had been dark the last time he remembered looking out. And he didn't feel as tired as he had. Even the excruciating throbbing in his side seemed to have eased a bit. But his head still felt sore and his mouth was dry as dust.

He went to sit up, but subsided with a moan. There was a stiffness around his middle. His exploring fingers located the presence of a wide bandage. "What the...?"

"Ah, *mon père,* you are awake at last!"

The soft French voice spoke gently in Nicholas's ear, and he turned in its direction. "You!"

It was the angel's face again. Pink and white, with a cap of white-blond curls and a smile to make a man want to confess his worst sins.

"I 'ave brought you some of *maman's* broth," she said softly. "It will 'elp to make you strong."

Nicholas again tried to raise himself to a sitting position, and winced at the pain the movement caused him. "Damn!" He sank down weakly once more, before offering an apologetic, "Excuse me."

"It is of no concern. Here, perhaps you would like some water first?"

"Yes, very much." Nicholas glanced at his tiny nurse. She looked to be about eleven. "Who are you?"

The girl's smile was pure sunshine. "I am called Sophie. My brother and I found you lying injured in the road by my father's field."

Nicholas glanced at his surroundings with a total lack of comprehension. "Where am I? How did I... get here?"

"You are in my father's barn, and you are 'ere because my brother Antoine brought you in the cart. It was Antoine who took the bullet from your side and bandaged your head."

"Bullet?" Nicholas had a vague recollection of being shot, but his memory of the events leading up to it were hazy. "How long have I been here?" he asked quietly.

"A long time. Nine days, I think."

"Nine days!" he repeated incredulously.

Sophie nodded and lifted the cup to his lips. "Unfortunately, for most of them, you were unconscious with *la fièvre.*. Now, drink slowly, *mon père.*"

Nicholas lifted his head and swallowed the water with some difficulty. Nine days. And most of the time delirious with fever. He shook his head in frustration. He didn't know how he had come to be here, or even where here was. In fact, he could remember nothing at all. Not even his own name.

"Do you want some soup?"

Nicholas nodded, and hesitantly opened his mouth as Sophie tipped a spoonful of the savoury broth into it. He swallowed tentatively, then looked at her and opened his mouth again.

Sophie smiled at him with pleasure. "It is good, *mon père*—you are eating again."

Nicholas glanced at her sharply. "Why do you call me *mon père*... Father?"

Sophie glanced at him curiously. "Because you wear the robes. And because you carry the missal. But you are English, *non?*"

Nicholas returned his attention to the soup. Strange. He knew that he was English, but he was also reasonably certain that he was not a man of the cloth. But if that was the case, what was he doing in robes? And why did he feel like his being here was somehow endangering the lives of his young nurse and her family?

"Sophie, I don't seem to be able to... think very clearly right now, but I think it probably best that I...leave as soon as possible," Nicholas said. "I feel my being here is a... danger to you and your family."

Sophie nodded a touch sadly. "*Oui*, I know. It is fortunate that my father did not find you. 'E is very suspicious of strangers. 'E probably would not 'ave allowed us to help you, even though you wore the robes. But Antoine is 'oping to be a doctor one day, and 'e said that a doctor does not turn away from the sick, no matter who they are." Sophie looked proud. "Antoine is very smart."

"I am sure he is."

"I am glad that you did not die, *mon père*."

Nicholas smiled in spite of his injuries. "You saved my life, Sophie, and I shall never forget you or your brother. In fact, I should very much like to thank him if I could."

"It is not necessary." Sophie glanced towards the door carefully, and then lowered her voice even further. "There 'as been . . . a man looking for you. An English, like you."

Nicholas gazed at her intently. "How do you know that?"

"Antoine 'as 'eard the villagers speak of it." Sophie leaned closer. "I believe this English is looking for you."

"For me?" Nicholas felt a swift rush of hope. "Is this man still in the area?"

"I do not know, but I can ask." Sophie watched the handsome Englishman, relieved that he had finally started to improve. "Would you like me to do that?"

Nicholas stared into the girl's face. He knew he didn't belong here. But where did he belong? He had to find out. And the man who was looking for him—did he know? He must. Why else would an Englishman be in the area? "Yes, Sophie, I would."

"*Bon*." Sophie rose and wrapped her shawl more closely about her shoulders. "I will ask Antoine to find out." She glanced at him almost sadly. "If the man is 'ere to take you away, you will want to go with 'im, yes?"

Nicholas nodded. "Yes, I think I probably should."

"*D'accord*." Sophie smiled bravely. "But until then, you must stay 'ere and rest. You are better than you were, but the wounds were very bad, *mon père*, and you lost much blood.

Still, at least you are better off than the other men we found," she said with a noticeable shudder.

Nicholas glanced up at her in surprise. There were other men? Who were they? And where were they now?

Nicholas knew he needed to ask those questions, but even as his mind framed the words, he felt himself drifting back to sleep. He was still so tired. His eyes were so heavy. "Yes, I . . . think perhaps I will . . . sleep, Sophie," Nicholas murmured.

Sophie watched him until he was asleep. Her eyes softened as she reached out to stroke his glistening black hair.

"Sleep well, *mon père,*" she said gently. "I will miss you." Then, taking one long, last look at him, Sophie left the barn to look for her brother in the far field.

WHAT HAPPENED OVER the next few days was little more than a blur in Longworth's mind. Gordon, the Englishman Sophie had told him about, said he had been sent by a Lord Osborne in London, and that he had been scouring the countryside. This news had come back to Nicholas via Sophie's brother, Antoine, just as it was through Antoine that arrangements were made for Nicholas to meet the Englishman after dark.

Nicholas bid a fond farewell to Sophie, knowing that she had saved his life. He kissed her cheek tenderly upon leaving, wishing he had something to give her. She had risked a great deal for him, she and her brother both.

"You are a very brave girl, Sophie," he said softly.

Sophie bravely held back her tears. "Goodbye, Monsieur Longworth." She had heard the other Englishman call him that name. "I 'ope you 'ave a safe journey back to England."

After thanking Antoine for all he had done, Longworth and the Englishman took their leave. James Gordon informed Nicholas that Lord Osborne had been searching high and low for him and that he would be mightily pleased to discover that he was still alive.

Nicholas smiled, but said nothing. It seemed decidedly ungrateful to say that he had no recollection whatsoever of the man who had obviously gone to so much trouble to find him.

THE TWO MEN MADE relatively good time. They travelled on horseback by night, preferring to seek cover in the heavy woods by day. Longworth was forced by the extent of his injuries to rest periodically, but he tried to keep each stop brief, aware that Gordon was anxious to be gone.

"'Tis dangerous country we be in, sir,'' Gordon said as they crouched together, eating sparingly of the food Sophie had managed to steal from her mother's kitchen. "The place is alive with Frenchies, all hunting for you.''

"For me?'' Nicholas shook his head in confusion. "But why? What have I done?''

Gordon gazed at him incredulously. "What have you done? Pardon me for saying so, sir, but you've bloody well done the impossible. Nobody thought Jean Leclerc could be brought down, and you did it single-handedly. Mind, Lord Osborne did say that if anyone was going to do it, you'd be the one. Damn proud he is, sir, damn proud. And I don't mind telling you, I'm honoured to be the man to bring you back. Just hope one of us lives to tell the tale!''

Three nights later, exhausted after a number of near encounters with roving French patrols, Gordon and Longworth crept down to a yacht moored at Le Havre and, under the cover of darkness, slipped out into the choppy waters of the English Channel.

Nicholas, wearied by the travelling and still very much troubled by his injuries, spent most of his time in his cabin resting. The thought of going back to a country of which he had no recollection—as well as to people who would be expecting him to remember them—was daunting, to say the least.

But if he was English, what had he been doing in France? Gordon hadn't told him much, other than that he had brought this man Leclerc down. But who was Leclerc? And what nature of business had caused Nicholas himself to take two near-fatal bullets and be left at the side of the road to die?

He closed his eyes as the ship rolled with the waves. Going to England was like venturing into a new world—a world filled with faces he should know, but would not. How was he to explain that?

"LORD LONGWORTH, my lord."

The two gentlemen in the room slowly rose as Nicholas entered. He felt their eyes on him, studying him. He, in turn, glanced keenly from one to the other. The gentleman standing behind the desk was considerably older. Nicholas surmised that this must be the Lord Osborne Gordon had spoken of. He bowed slightly. "Lord Osborne, I presume."

He saw the man swallow. "Welcome home, Longworth." The man's voice was husky with emotion. "And may I commend you on a job well done. All England is proud of you."

Nicholas smiled vaguely. "Thank you, sir." He turned to address the other fellow, who looked to be more his own age, saying quietly, "Your servant, sir."

Edward's eyes never left Nicholas's face. "Nicholas, do you not know me? I am Edward. Edward Kingsley."

Nicholas stared at the man's face, willing something, anything, to come back to him. But there was nothing— nothing but an empty, gaping hole where his past had been. "I wish I could say that I did, Mr. . . . Kingsley, but the truth is—" Nicholas glanced at the older man apologetically "—I remember nothing."

As he stood and gazed at the two hopeful faces in front of him, Nicholas felt a sense of utter desolation. Nothing had changed. He did not recognize either of them. He gazed about this room with a complete lack of recognition. During the trip across the channel, he had harboured hopes that seeing familiar places and the people with whom he had shared his life might jog his memory in some fashion. But he realized now that such was not to be the case.

He cleared his throat awkwardly. "I feel I should...know you both, but I'm afraid..." His words drifted into silence.

Osborne swore and briefly turned away, the muscles in his jaw working. Edward's face filled with compassion. "Won't you...sit down, Lord Longworth?"

Nicholas started abruptly. "*Lord* Longworth?"

"You are Nicholas Grey, Viscount Longworth," Edward told him.

"Really? I didn't know." Nicholas smiled, almost as if in a daze. "Your man Gordon usually addressed me as 'sir'."

"Have you no memory of your life here at all?" Edward asked.

Nicholas cast his eyes about the room that he should have known, and regretfully shook his head. "None. It is as though I am seeing everything...for the first time."

Osborne had managed to get his emotions under control. He came around from behind his desk and sat down in the chair next to Nicholas.

"Can you tell us what happened, Nicholas? The night you were shot? Do you remember anything about it? Anything at all?"

Nicholas narrowed his eyes in concentration. He had gone over it in his mind time and again, helped along by what little information Sophie, her brother and James Gordon had been able to provide. "I remember almost nothing, my lord. I am told that there was...a carriage. And...a man. A Frenchman."

"Leclerc," Osborne supplied helpfully.

"Leclerc." Nicholas repeated the name experimentally. "Perhaps. But there was another man, too, I think. An...Englishman." ·

"Ferris," Edward added tersely. "He was travelling with Leclerc."

Nicholas glanced up hopefully. "Perhaps it would be possible to question them. They could tell us—"

"They are dead, Nicholas," Osborne informed him quietly. "You were forced to shoot them both. That is how you were wounded. Leclerc—or Ferris—shot you."

Nicholas stared at his commanding officer in astonishment. "I shot two men?"

"That was why you volunteered to go to France," Edward told him. "To get Leclerc."

"But what of the other Englishman?" Nicholas persisted, feeling instinctively that something was missing.

"You shot him, too," Osborne said, assuming Nicholas meant Ferris again. "He was the leak in the department. He was responsible for François Duplesse being murdered."

Nicholas looked confused. "François Duplesse?"

"Yes, Lavinia's—oh, my God," Edward muttered, glancing quickly at Osborne.

Nicholas saw the expression on the faces of both men and knew that something was horribly wrong. "What is it? Do I know this...François Duplesse?"

Osborne placed a hand gently on Nicholas's shoulder. "Not so much François as you do his widow, Lavinia."

"Do you remember Lavinia, Nicholas?" Edward asked, watching for some sign, however minute, of recognition.

"Lavinia." Nicholas said the name and then repeated it, but his expression remained blank. "I remember nothing." He lifted his eyes to Edward's face. "Should I know this lady?"

Edward sighed, more heartsick than he could ever remember having felt in his life. "Yes, my friend, you know this lady. She is the woman you are engaged to marry."

CHAPTER FIVE

LAVINIA STOOD BY the window, anxiously watching for the carriage. She knew that they were coming. Edward had stopped by the house last night and told her. He had also told her, as gently as possible, that her fiancé had absolutely no memory of his previous life in London—or of her. When they met again, it would be for Nicholas like the very first time.

Lavinia had hid her grief remarkably well. She had waited until Edward had gone before breaking down and shedding heart-wrenching tears in the privacy of her room. She had railed against God for taking away Nicholas's memory, and then, in the same breath, had thanked Him for sparing his life.

After all, where there was life, there was hope, Lavinia told herself firmly. As long as Nicholas was alive, there was a chance that his memory would return. Dear God, it had to return!

The sound of a carriage in the street below drew Lavinia's attention back to the window. She watched the curricle pull up and then caught her breath as two gentlemen got out.

Nicholas!

As if hearing her silent cry, he glanced up towards the window and looked at her. Her heart turned over at the sight of his beloved face, the same moment as her hand went to her mouth to stifle the sob. He had not recognized her.

"Lord Longworth and Mr. Kingsley," Habinger announced solemnly a few minutes later.

Lavinia was unaware that she was still holding her breath. Her eyes went immediately to Nicholas, taking in the dreadful pallor of his skin. His face was more drawn than she had ever seen it, no doubt as a result of his injuries. He moved stiffly, as though the wound in his side still pained him. But it was the look in his eyes that troubled her the most.

There was nothing there—no flicker of recognition, no warm glow of love. No spark at seeing her again—the woman he had professed to love.

"Nicholas!" she murmured huskily.

Nicholas advanced uncertainly into the tastefully decorated room, thankful for Edward's presence at his side.

"Nicholas, this is Lavinia, Lady Duplesse," Edward said softly. "Now, I am going to leave the two of you alone for a few minutes, all right? I'll be just outside if you need me."

"Thank you, Edward," Lavinia said.

Nicholas nodded. As the door closed behind Edward, he turned back towards the beautiful woman in front of him, seeing the hope in her eyes, and he felt sorrow so deep it made him want to run from the room.

"I am so very, very sorry," he whispered, his throat husky with emotion. "I know that I should . . . know you, but—"

Lavinia caught her breath and felt the swift rush of tears to her eyes. She had promised herself that she would not cry again, but seeing him now, like this, it was so very hard not to.

"No, Nicholas, you have no need to apologize. It is . . . not your fault. But please, if you would just . . . hold me for a moment."

Nicholas slowly opened his arms and Lavinia walked into them. He felt the warmth and the softness of her body as she pressed against him, and his arms closed automatically around her. She smelled of violets, sweet and undeniably feminine. Dear God, he had been about to marry this beautiful creature?

Lavinia allowed herself a few moments of pure bliss in the circle of Nicholas's arms. She knew he did not remember her, but right now, that didn't matter. All that mattered was that he was alive. He was safe, and they were together again. At the moment, that was all she had.

Forcing herself to smile, Lavinia reluctantly stepped out of his arms, hastily wiping away a tear that managed to escape and trickle down her cheek.

"Please, do not cry for me, Lavinia," Nicholas said suddenly.

Lavinia thought she had her emotions under control, but the softness in his voice proved to be her undoing. She abruptly turned away, unable to halt the flow of tears, while Nicholas stood helplessly by, his hands clenched uselessly at his side. He wanted to comfort her, but he didn't know how. It seemed that his presence was only upsetting her more. "Perhaps I should leave?"

"No!" Lavinia spun around, her cheeks streaked with tears. Then, more softly, she added, "No, Nicholas, please . . . do not leave. Forgive me, I did not mean to cry." She took a deep breath and managed a shaky laugh. "I promised myself I would not, but when I heard your voice . . . when you held me . . ." She cleared her throat and gestured towards a chair. "Won't you . . . sit down?"

"Thank you."

Nicholas sat down slowly, his eyes never leaving her face. She was an incredibly beautiful woman. Even in grief, her loveliness was undiminished. The pale lavender gown did little to hide the womanly curves beneath. Her dark, glistening hair was drawn up into an elegant chignon, her complexion was smooth, her lips reminiscent of a dusky rose.

Yes, she was beautiful, but there was also an underlying strength that Nicholas felt as surely as though it lay open and exposed to him. This was an admirable woman—a woman who had known pain and suffering and who had come through it. An admirable woman, his Lavinia.

His Lavinia. Unbidden, his eyes went to the ring on her left hand.

"Yes, my lord, we are... betrothed," Lavinia said, noting his regard. "Or rather, we were," she said uncertainly.

"I must have been considered a very fortunate man," Nicholas said quietly. "Though given the circumstances, I can understand your wishing to... withdraw your promise."

Lavinia swallowed, trying not to show how deeply his innocent words had hurt her. "Nicholas, I know that...much has happened to you. But you must understand that...my feelings...have not changed in any way. You are still the man I fell in love with, and the man with whom I am in love still."

Nicholas watched the play of emotions across her face. "Edward told me very briefly what happened in our pasts. It would appear that...I have always loved you."

Lavinia smiled. "Yes. We have been through a great deal, you and I."

"But what of us now?" Nicholas asked, knowing that he had to ask, and as soon as possible. "You see that I have no memory of what went before. I know that Edward hoped my seeing you might trigger something in my memory. Indeed, I had hoped it myself, for I confess I have never felt so lost in my life. But now that I have seen you, and realize that I have absolutely no recollection of...what has passed between us, would you not choose to be free? To start your life again? Surely you would not have yourself shackled to someone who is but a ghost from the past. You are young and beautiful. You must have admirers by the score."

Lavinia shook her head. "I care not if I have, Nicholas. You are the only man I have ever loved, and your accident has not changed that. In fact, I have no desire to change anything at the moment."

Impulsively, she crossed to his chair. Lowering herself to the carpet at his feet, she took one of his hands and held it tightly between her own. "I will ask nothing of you, Nicholas, and expect nothing in return. But perhaps, in some way, I can help you."

"Help me? How?"

"By leading you through the steps of your life as it was," Lavinia said quietly. "Perhaps by meeting people and seeing things that were once part of your life, your memory will return."

Nicholas closed his eyes. "I wish with all my heart that it might happen, Lavinia, but I cannot know for sure if it will. The doctor Lord Osborne arranged for me to see told me that my memory may never come back." He opened his eyes and looked down into her face. "Will it not be terribly difficult for you? I cannot lie and tell you that...things are...as they were between us."

"I realize that you no longer...love me, Nicholas," Lavinia forced herself to say. "How can you, when you have no recollection of who I am? But because of what I once was to you, and because of what you still are to me, I would try." She gave a shaky laugh. "God knows, I have little enough to lose by trying, and everything to gain."

Nicholas gazed down at her intently. Then he smiled. "I think I must have been an intelligent man to have chosen such an admirable woman to be my wife." He paused and then came to a decision. "All right, Lavinia, if it is truly what you wish. I see no reason to end our betrothal right now, and I would be heartily grateful for your help."

Lavinia saw his gaze drop to her mouth, and felt a familiar flutter in her stomach. "Was there something else you wanted to say, Nicholas?" she asked tentatively.

"Not say, exactly," he murmured. Slowly, as if unsure of her reaction, Nicholas leaned forward. Would he remember how she felt, perhaps? He lifted one hand and ran his thumb along the edge of her cheek, along her jaw. He could see the flickering pulse in the tender hollow at the base of her throat.

Slowly raising her to her knees, Nicholas pulled her closer. He saw her eyes close, and she swayed towards him almost unconsciously, her beautiful lips slightly parted...

"Hello, I hope I'm not—oh, pardon me!" Edward broke off abruptly, pausing with his head around the door. "It would appear that I am indeed interrupting."

Lavinia hastily opened her eyes as Nicholas drew back awkwardly. She noticed that she wasn't the only one blushing.

"No, it's...quite all right, Edward." Lavinia was the first to regain her composure. She rose gracefully to her feet. "Come in."

"I say," Edward said, glancing from one to the other hopefully. "Things are looking very good between the two of you. Have you remembered something, Nicholas?"

Nicholas shook his head, more confused and upset than he could ever remember having felt in his life. He had wanted to kiss Lavinia Duplesse very much just now, but he wasn't sure why. Apart from the fact that she was an extremely beautiful woman, she meant nothing to him.

"No, I fear not. Lavinia and I were just...discussing our engagement."

Edward's face creased in a smile. "Rather nice way of discussing it, that," he said, winking at Nicholas. "Well, what have the two of you decided?"

"That there is no need to break off our betrothal just yet," Lavinia informed him quietly. She turned to smile at her fiancé. "Nicholas has agreed to allow me to help him go about his daily routine. Perhaps by doing so, we will be able to jog something in his memory."

"Well, I am very glad to hear that." There was no denying the relief in Edward's voice. "The doctor did say that the memory lapse might not be permanent. Perhaps all it will take is some trifling detail, some inconsequential act, to bring it back again."

"I sincerely hope so," Nicholas said. He glanced at Lavinia, and at length, he smiled. "It would seem that I have a very good reason for wanting it to return."

Lavinia blushed, immeasurably pleased that he would say so. But as she bid him goodbye a little while later, one thing became very clear in her mind. From this moment on, she intended to work very hard at helping Nicholas remember. He was everything in the world to her, and if it took the rest of her life, she would make his memory return.

Either that, or she would make him fall in love with her again!

SO BEGAN NICHOLAS'S gentle reintroduction to the life he had led before the mission to France robbed him of his memory. The knowledge that he had been the one to kill the notorious French spy, Jean Leclerc, spread quickly, and his reception was that of a returning hero. Unfortunately, the fact that Nicholas had no recollection of his former life, nor of what he had done in France, quickly put a damper on his reunion with the people that he met.

"No one seems to know what to say to him," Lavinia complained to Laura Beaufort two days later, as they sat together in the front parlour of Lavinia's house. "Nicholas and I went driving this afternoon, and though people were happy enough to smile and nod at him, very few approached us, even though he is perfectly charming to everyone."

Laura sighed. "Poor man. I cannot imagine what it must be like to return to a place I have lived all my life and not know a soul. How dreadfully lonely it must be for him."

Lavinia nodded. She knew the strain Nicholas was under. It was as though he was isolated from everything, from everyone. He held on to both Lavinia and Edward now as though they were his lifelines.

"Have you reintroduced him to Martine yet?"

"I haven't even told him about her. I'm trying not to thrust too much upon him at once. Coming back to London and finding out that he was engaged to be married was one thing, but telling him that he is about to become a stepfather as well..." Lavinia laughed and shook her head. "I could not bring myself to do it. Besides, Nicholas has been spending a good deal of time with Lord Osborne, and on the two occasions he has been here, Martine was out with a friend. But I have invited Nicholas to call round tomorrow afternoon. Martine will meet him then."

"Is she aware of what happened?" Laura enquired softly.

"Yes. I thought it only fair that she know before Nicholas arrived. She did not say very much the whole time Nicholas was gone, but I knew she was worried. And I am very pleased at how well she took the news of his memory loss."

"What of his mother?" Laura asked now. "Has she been to see him?"

Lavinia bit her lip. "We are going to see her this evening, in fact. I received a note from her, asking us to call."

Laura raised an eyebrow in surprise. "Both of you?"

"Yes. Surprising, is it not?"

"Promising, more like." Laura was well aware that Lady Longworth did not hold Lavinia in the greatest of affection. "Perhaps she is mellowing towards you."

Lavinia could only hope that it was true. But in the carriage on the way to Lady Longworth's later that evening, she truly began to wonder. After all, if Lady Longworth knew that her son had been injured as a result of an altercation with the man who had killed her first husband, was she not likely to hold Lavinia in even greater contempt? It seemed a logical assumption. For that reason, Lavinia could only hope that the true identity of Jean Leclerc was never made known to her.

Lavinia felt the growing tension in Nicholas's body. "Nicholas, what's wrong?"

He shook his head. "Nothing. Other than that it seems incredible that I should have no memory of my own mother." He turned and glanced at her thoughtfully. "What is she like?"

"Your mother? Well, she is...a most dignified lady," Lavinia said, anxious to present the woman in a positive light. "And quite a handsome woman...for her age."

"No, no, I meant her character," Nicholas said. "Were we close?"

Oh dear, Lavinia groaned inwardly. How honest should she be?

"I cannot say that you were...close, precisely. You did not see...a great deal of each other," she answered tactfully.

Nicholas nodded thoughtfully. "I see. And what about you?"

"Me?"

"Yes. Did you like my mother?" he asked innocently. "Was she happy that we were to be married?"

Lavinia bit her lip. This was getting decidedly difficult.

"No, Nicholas, your mother and I were not exactly close," she said finally, deciding that honesty—without too much explanation—was probably the best policy. "But then, we have not spent a great deal of time together. I was just recently out of mourning for my husband, you see, and not given to socializing much."

"But surely she was pleased that we were to be married?" he persisted.

"I cannot say that your mother ever told me to my face that she was not."

"Ah. Then I imagine she will be happy to hear that we have decided not to break off our betrothal," Nicholas said with some satisfaction.

"Yes, I daresay she will have something to say about that," Lavinia murmured.

They were greeted at the door by Lady Longworth's butler and then shown into the drawing-room, where a warm
fire burned in the grate. Nicholas walked around the pe-
rimeter of the spacious room, touching objects, studying the
furniture and the decorations. "Was I here recently?" he
enquired.

Lavinia nodded. "Shortly before you left. You and your
mother had dinner together."

"How strange that I have no recollection of it whatsoever." Nicholas's attention was momentarily arrested by the
large painting over the fireplace. "Was that my father?"

"It was," a voice answered from the doorway. "Two
years before he died."

They both turned as the Dowager Lady Longworth
walked into the room. Lavinia curtsied out of respect, but
she had a feeling the woman never even saw her. Lady
Longworth went straight to her son and stared up into his
face. "Is it true, what I have been hearing?" she asked quietly. "You have no recollection of the past?"

Nicholas shook his head. "It is true." He gazed down into
the face of the woman who had given him birth, and felt a
blinding return of despair. "I do not even remember you."

Lady Longworth closed her eyes, an inarticulate sound
escaping her lips as grief welled up in her. *"I am your
mother."*

Nicholas swallowed, and gently brushed her cheek with
his lips, paying her the homage he knew was due. "Yes, I
know. Forgive me."

He straightened, and the two regarded each other in silence. Lady Longworth shook her head. "It is not for you
to ask forgiveness, Nicholas. This is not your fault. Nor had
I the right to criticize you, since I now understand why you
went." She glanced briefly at Lavinia, her blue eyes chilly,
but uncertain. "Did he remember you?"

"No. Mr. Kingsley told him who I was."

Lavinia expected to see a look of satisfaction appear on the old woman's face. Instead, all she saw was a great sadness. "Then am I to assume that your engagement is no longer in place?"

"No, Mother," Nicholas said. "For the moment, we saw no need to end it. The doctors said that the memory loss may be temporary, and that by continuously seeing things that were part of my life, I may suddenly remember something. Lavinia has kindly offered to stay and help me work through this."

Lady Longworth looked at Lavinia with grudging respect. "It is...good of you, Lady Duplesse. It cannot be easy."

Lavinia shook her head in surprise, recognizing that the woman was making an effort. "It is not, Lady Longworth. But I continue to hope."

"Come, let us sit down. Nicholas, why don't you sit here by the fire. I will have Mortimer build it up a bit. The evening is chilly."

"It is quite all right for me...Mother. I do not seem to feel the cold much."

His mother hesitated uncertainly. "Well, if you are sure."

The three of them sat down, Lady Longworth in her usual chair by the fire, Lavinia and Nicholas together on the sofa.

"So, Nicholas, you have earned yourself a hero's welcome." Lady Longworth nodded. "I am proud of you. Though I wish to God you had never gone to France. Was it so important, your finding this man—what was his name—Leclerc?"

Nicholas smiled. "I am told that it was, though I cannot honestly recall my reasons for having gone. Perhaps if I could, I would feel more settled in my own mind. Lord Osborne told me that what I did was of great importance, and that many lives were saved."

Lady Longworth watched him sadly. "But at such great cost, Nicholas. At such great cost."

Nicholas smiled, and strove for a measure of lightness in his voice. "It is not so bad, Mother. I have an opportunity to begin again. Every day is a great adventure. And every day I wake hoping this might be the day it all comes back to me."

Lady Longworth was not so easily mollified. "And you remember nothing of me? Of your father? Your life here?"

Nicholas's smile faded. "No." He paused. "Sometimes I think I am just beginning to grasp something, only to have it...disappear seconds later."

A heavy silence fell, broken only by the crackling of the logs in the fireplace.

"I understand you have a daughter, Lady Duplesse," Lady Longworth said unexpectedly, rousing herself. "How is she adjusting to life in London?"

"Very well, thank you, my lady," Lavinia answered. "It is all a bit strange to her, of course, but I am very pleased with the progress she is making."

"You have a daughter?"

Lavinia turned towards Nicholas, a fresh stab of pain twisting in her heart at the look of surprise in his eyes. "A stepdaughter, actually. Martine is François's child."

"Martine." Nicholas repeated the name, as he always did when a new name was mentioned. "How old is...Martine?"

"She is seventeen."

"Seventeen!" Nicholas continued to look dazed. "Why have you not told me about her?"

Lavinia blushed uncomfortably. "I thought it...better to wait, Nicholas. You had enough to come to terms with. But you will be meeting her tomorrow. That is why I asked you to call."

Nicholas nodded, mulling things over in his mind. "How long were you and your husband married?"

"Four years."

"I see. Then...how did I come to meet you?"

"You met Lady Duplesse at her wedding, Nicholas," Lady Longworth informed her son quietly.

There was no resentment in the woman's voice, and Lavinia glanced at her hesitantly. "I truly wish it had been sooner, Lady Longworth," Lavinia told her softly.

She was amazed to see a thawing in the blue eyes and the appearance of a tentative smile. "Yes, I realize that now, Lady Duplesse." She turned to look almost gratefully, Lavinia thought, at her son. "It would seem that I have, indeed, been given another chance to realize that."

THE EVENING PASSED pleasantly enough, but by the end of it, Lavinia was more than ready to leave. It had been a strain on everyone, especially Nicholas. She had watched him all evening as he struggled to remember the names his mother mentioned, the places they had been and the things they had done as a family.

Still, it was not a complete loss, Lavinia reflected. At least she and Lady Longworth appeared to have made some headway with their own relationship.

"You are uncommonly quiet, my lord," Lavinia said in the carriage on the way home.

Nicholas breathed a heavy sigh. "It is so strange, seeing someone like . . . my mother. Knowing that there should be so many memories, yet having none. And I could see it was difficult for her." His next remark surprised her. "We were not close, were we."

Lavinia glanced at him sharply. He hadn't phrased it as a question. "Why would you say that, Nicholas?"

"Because I felt it. I felt . . . the reserve. It shouldn't have been there, but it was."

"Perhaps she just did not know what to say to you."

Nicholas shook his head sadly. "No, Lavinia. People I meet on the street do not know what to say to me. Acquaintances I see in the Park do not know what to say to me. My mother did not know *how* to speak to me, and therein lies the difference." He offered her a weak smile. "I may not remember much about my own life, but I do know the way it should be between a mother and son."

Lavinia had to fight the urge to pull him into her arms and comfort him. There was so much loneliness in him. So much emptiness. And loving him the way she did it made it that much harder to bear. It tore at her soul, making her feel empty as well. There was so much she wanted him to know, and so much she wanted to tell him.

"Nicholas, how would you like to go down to the country for a while?"

Nicholas glanced at her in surprise. "The country?"

"Yes, I think it might be a good idea."

"Do I have a house in the country?" Nicholas enquired.

Lavinia managed a laugh. "Yes, of course you do, but actually, I was thinking of my own. I have a house in Kent. I haven't been there in years, but it could be made ready for us in a few days." As she was speaking, Lavinia found herself warming to the idea. "Perhaps it would be good for you to get out of London for a while."

Nicholas sighed. "I confess, I am growing weary of people staring at me as though I were an imbecile."

Lavinia rushed to his defence. "They are not looking at you that way at all, Nicholas. It is merely that they are...unsure as to how to approach you."

Unexpectedly, he lifted her hand to his lips and pressed a kiss into her soft palm. "Would that they all had your tact and patience, Lavinia."

Lavinia felt the tears spring to her eyes. "Ah, but they do not love you the way I do," she replied, striving for a bantering tone.

The look he turned towards her was laden with sadness. "Am I not beginning to wear on your patience, too, Lavinia? God knows, you have reason to feel that way."

"You could never try my patience, Nicholas. I *love* you. Nothing in the world is more important to me than you. You must believe that."

He nodded slowly, and then his eyes darkened as he looked at her. He suddenly felt an inexplicable longing to be close to her.

"Lavinia, I have no wish to embarrass you, but...were we ever...that is, did we ever..." The words trailed off.

Lavinia knew what he was trying to say, and resisted the urge to smile. "No, we...never did. Why would you ask?"

"Because I cannot help but be strongly aware of you...as a woman, and I simply wondered if there was...a reason for it."

Lavinia was thankful the darkness of the carriage hid her flaming cheeks. "No, Nicholas, we were never...intimate, though there were times when we came rather close."

He smiled at her in the darkness. "How close?"

She laughed unsteadily. "Very close, though you always stopped before things went too far."

She heard him sigh. "Always the gentleman, eh?"

"Well, perhaps not...all the time," Lavinia admitted, blushing hotly. "There was...one occasion where I had to tell you to behave."

Nicholas turned, his smile widening. "Really?"

"Twice, in fact."

"Good Lord, twice? Whatever was I doing?"

"Nicholas, I really don't think—"

"No, you must tell me, Lavinia," he said, endeavouring to keep a straight face. "After all, the doctor did say that it was impossible to tell what might prompt me into remembering."

Lavinia glanced down at her hands. "Really, Nicholas, I hardly think something as...trivial as this would initiate a complete return of your memory."

His laugh was low and disturbingly sensual. "Why don't you try me?"

Lavinia's cheeks grew warmer. "Well, if you must know...it was on the day after you...proposed to me."

"The day after?"

"Yes. We had just come back from dinner at the Clarendon Hotel, where you had taken me to celebrate our betrothal. You had engaged a private chamber."

"How romantic of me," Nicholas said with a chuckle.

"Oh, yes, it was certainly that. Needless to say, I was very impressed, Lord Longworth."

"I am delighted to hear it. So how did I blot my copybook after starting out so well?"

"When you brought me home, I invited you in for a glass of brandy."

"All very honest and above-board," Nicholas observed.

"Yes, it was. Except that one glass stretched to two, and given that you had already imbibed rather freely at dinner, well, you ended up being a little more...amorous than usual."

His mouth quirked with humour. "Is that when you were forced to tell me to behave?"

"Yes, I'm afraid it was. You became rather...fascinated with the beadwork on my gown. Especially on the...bodice of my gown."

Unbidden, Nicholas's dark eyes dropped to the soft swell of Lavinia's breasts, now safely hidden beneath her elegant pelisse. A delightful picture formed in his mind. "I take it you were wearing a low-cut gown?" He was surprised to hear the huskiness in his voice.

Lavinia bit her lip and tried not to laugh. "Shockingly low, I'm afraid. And you were rather intent on seeing how the beads were attached to the...inside of the fabric."

Nicholas purposely cleared his throat, wondering why he couldn't clear away the image in his mind. He shifted uncomfortably in his seat, aware of a tightening in his lower body. "I hope I apologized for my disreputable behaviour the next morning."

This time, Lavinia couldn't help but laugh. "Yes, you certainly did. In fact, you were so busy apologizing I never did get a chance to tell you that I . . . really wasn't annoyed at all."

Nicholas stared at her in astonishment. "You weren't?"

"No. Now," Lavinia said, suddenly sounding prim, "I do believe we were talking about going down to the country, were we not?"

Nicholas let out his breath. "Yes," he muttered faintly, "I do believe we were."

LAVINIA WAS DELIGHTED at how well Nicholas responded to Martine the following afternoon. She had feared that an awkwardness might develop between them, but it was only moments before she realized that she had absolutely no cause for concern. Martine accepted Nicholas's reserve and quickly broke it down. There was no discomfort or embarrassment at all. In fact, Nicholas appeared far more at ease in the company of the seventeen-year-old French girl than he did with many of his tonnish friends.

Lavinia had received an invitation to her good friend Lady Renton's musicale while Nicholas was still in France. The invitation had been extended to both of them, of course, and Lavinia thought it might be a good opportunity for Nicholas to attend his first social function since returning to London. But when she mentioned it to him that afternoon, she was not overly surprised when he demurred.

"You are not angry, I hope?" he asked quickly.

Lavinia shook her head. "No, of course not. There will be other functions, Nicholas."

"Will Lady Renton be offended?" he enquired tactfully.

"Not in the least. Caroline is a close friend of mine. She will not expect a long explanation, nor will I feel obliged to give one."

"I am relieved." Nicholas hesitated. "Is there perhaps another gentleman you might like to have accompany you?"

Lavinia laughed in delight and relief. "No, and I am happy to say that one of the advantages of being a widow is that I am allowed a great deal more freedom than I ever had before. It is not necessary that I be escorted to every function."

And it was true enough. Lavinia went to the musicale quite comfortably on her own. She probably would not have gone at all, except for the fact that her dear friend Lady Renton was holding it. The two had been friends since school, and had spent a great deal of time since Lavinia's return catching up on their years apart. Lady Renton—Caroline Abbott before her marriage—was one of the few people Lavinia had troubled to keep in touch with, even during her time in France.

"And you say he remembers nothing?" Lady Renton asked after the Italian tenor finished singing and the two friends had strolled into the ballroom, where refreshments were being served.

"Nothing. Names, faces—they mean nothing to him," Lavinia told her sadly. "I don't know that he even remembers places. He did not seem to recognize my parlour."

Lady Renton laughed. "Dear me, perhaps you should have taken him up to your boudoir, Livie. That might have jogged his memory."

"Caroline!" Lavinia gasped, blushing and laughing all at once. "Nicholas has never been in my...boudoir."

"No? Pity. Handsome man like that. I thought you might not have been able to resist the temptation. After all, my dear, you are a widow."

"I know, Caroline, but that does not give me licence to act disrespectfully."

"Tosh, Livie, how disrespectful would it have been?" Caroline's face was surprisingly compassionate. "Everyone knows how dreadfully in love the two of you were. How can you feel that kind of love and not wish to..."

Lavinia blushed again. "I'm not saying I did not wish to, Caroline," she admitted, biting her lip. "I am merely saying that we never...did."

"Hmm. Well, more's the pity," Caroline observed. "It might have helped jog his memory. Great things have been known to happen in the midst of passion, you know."

"I shall try to remember that," Lavinia said drily.

"Excuse me, Lady Renton, but I wonder if I might have a word."

Both ladies turned at the sound of a deep, masculine voice, and Lavinia found herself looking into the faces of two men she could not recall having seen before.

One was quite tall and very elegantly, though not foppishly, dressed. He appeared to Lavinia somewhat older than many of the men present, and yet was still exceedingly handsome. The man standing beside him was equally welldressed. His chestnut brown hair was cropped short in the back and brushed forward in the current style.

"Ah, Lord Rushton, Lord Havermere, how good of you both to come," Caroline said warmly. "I was not sure you were returned to London."

The man identified as Lord Havermere bowed. "We are only recently returned, my lady, having spent the last few weeks at my estate in the north of Scotland. But we were most grateful for your invitation."

"And I am delighted you could come." Caroline turned towards Lavinia. "May I introduce my good friend, Lady Duplesse. Lavinia, Lord Havermere, and Lord Rushton."

Lord Rushton smiled in an urbane manner. "So we finally meet, Lady Duplesse. I knew your husband."

Lavinia glanced at him in surprise. "You did?"

"Yes, although it was many years ago. We attended the Sorbonne together."

"You do not look old enough to have been a classmate of my husband's, Lord Rushton."

Rushton's voice was perfectly cultured, though somewhat lacking in inflection. "You flatter me, Lady Duplesse. I assure you, only a few years separated us in age."

"I understand you are engaged to be married, Lady Duplesse," Lord Havermere said now.

Lavinia managed a smile. "Yes, I am."

"Is your fiancé here this evening?"

"Sadly, he was feeling a trifle indisposed."

"Lady Duplesse is engaged to Lord Longworth, my lord," Caroline said quickly. "He is only recently returned to London after suffering an illness on the Continent. He has not yet taken up the rounds of Society."

"Ah, yes, now I remember," Havermere said. He turned back towards Lavinia. "Something about an accident in France."

"Yes."

"Dreadful shame. I understand he was very ill. And something about him...losing his memory, if I remember correctly?"

"Yes, that's right."

"What a pity," Lord Rushton remarked. "Has he no memory at all?"

"None, I'm afraid."

"Dear me, what an inconvenience," Havermere remarked in a sympathetic tone. "I can't imagine what it must be like not to remember places and names. Please extend our condolences, Lady Duplesse."

"Yes, thank you, I shall."

"Oh, Lavinia, will you excuse me?" Caroline said suddenly. "I see Lady Stanton gesturing madly. No doubt we have run out of some delicacy she is partial to. Gentlemen, please do continue to enjoy yourselves."

"We are sure to, Lady Renton," Lord Havermere replied smoothly.

When Caroline had gone, Lavinia turned to find Lord Rushton watching her speculatively. "My lord?"

"Forgive me, Lady Duplesse. I did not mean to stare. I was just thinking what a shame it is, Lord Longworth losing his memory like that, coming back to London and finding everything suddenly a mystery."

Lavinia smiled bravely. "Indeed, it is a shame, but he is managing extremely well."

"I am sure he is. And you say he remembers nothing at all of what happened?"

"Nothing."

Lord Havermere shook his head. "Do the doctors hold out any hope?"

"They cannot say. Apparently, Nicholas was very ill. He nearly died. I suppose we should be thankful that it was only his memory he lost."

"Yes, of course," Havermere replied. "Still, it must be a comfort to him that he was able to take care of that blackguard Leclerc before being wounded himself."

It was on the tip of Lavinia's tongue to ask him how he knew about Leclerc, but then she remembered that the account of the incident had been well detailed in the newspaper. No doubt everyone in London knew what had happened on that terrible night in France.

"Nasty business," Rushton was continuing, as if following her thoughts. "For myself, I shall be glad when the war is over. All this cloak-and-dagger nonsense—it leaves one wondering whom you can really trust, does it not, Lady Duplesse?"

Lavinia could not explain why the presence of the two men made her feel ill at ease. There was really nothing objectionable about either of them. They were both well spoken and very distinguished looking. So what was it about them that made Lavinia want to put as much distance between herself and them as possible?

CHAPTER SIX

LAVINIA DECIDED THAT they would go down to the country in a week's time. She felt the days in between would give the staff at the house in Kent time to get ready, as well as give Nicholas plenty of time to accustom himself to the idea. She told Edward Kingsley of her intention, and was relieved to receive his overwhelming approval.

"I think it's a splendid idea," Edward replied honestly. "Nicholas is trying too hard here. Every time he looks at something new, he is forcing himself to remember. Truth is, he's putting more strain on himself than is good for him."

"I thought much the same," Lavinia confided. "I am hoping that the peace and quiet of Rose Cottage will bring some peace to his soul. Lord knows, he seems to have little enough of it now."

And it was true. Rather than becoming more accustomed to his lack of memory, Nicholas was growing more distressed by it. He found himself falling into a temper far faster than before. He became impatient with himself and with those around him. And he knew why.

The suspicion that something had gone wrong in France would not leave him. It remained like a troublesome thorn in his side—there, but just out of reach. He knew now, after having spoken at length with Lord Osborne, exactly what he had gone over to do and why. He now understood that this man Leclerc had planned to return to England, and that he had threatened to kill certain people once he arrived. Nicholas had gone to France to stop him.

Further, he knew that Leclerc and the Englishman with him, Ferris, had been directly responsible for the death of Lavinia's first husband, and that Lavinia herself had been targeted by Leclerc.

But what he could not get out of his head, no matter how hard he tried, was that something had gone wrong—that someone else had been there that night. And that it was not the Frenchman, Leclerc, who had shot him in the road and left him there for dead.

"MARTINE, ARE YOU ready?" Lavinia called, tapping on the girl's door. "It is almost time to leave." Opening the door, she paused on the threshold in delight. "Oh, Martine, you look lovely! You will surely be the belle of the ball tonight."

Martine blushed with pleasure and fingered her delicate white India-muslin gown appreciatively. "It is lovely, *non?*"

"It and you are beautiful," Lavinia said, advancing into the room. "Thank you, Hélène, you have done a marvellous job with Martine's hair."

"Thank you, *madame.*"

"Is Nicholas here yet?" Martine asked softly.

"Not yet, but he will be here any minute now."

Nicholas had resolutely avoided all functions to which he received invitations, saying that he preferred quiet evenings spent with Lavinia. But this time, Martine had not allowed him to say no. She had bullied him until Lavinia feared he would either shout at her or give in. Thankfully, he had not shouted.

"Now, you must help Nicholas tonight, Martine," Lavinia said as they walked down the curving staircase together. "This is not going to be easy for him."

"Poor Nicholas. I hope he will get his memory back soon."

"So do I," Lavinia said sincerely. "So do I."

"Are you still to be married?"

Lavinia tried to hide the pensive shimmer in her eyes. "I do not know, Martine. Everything is still very . . . confused in Nicholas's mind. It would not be fair to push him into something for which he is not ready. Marriage is a very serious business."

"But you still love him, yes?"

"Of course. I will always love him, no matter what happens," she admitted. "But I cannot expect the man to marry someone for whom he has no feelings, simply because of a prior arrangement."

"Then you must make him fall in love with you again," Martine declared with touching naiveté. "You made it happen once. You can make it happen again."

"Dear me, Martine, the things you say!" Lavinia said, laughing.

Nicholas arrived just after eight o'clock, and Lavinia caught her breath at the sight of him. Impeccably attired in formal evening clothes, he cut a dashing figure. He may not have regained his memory, but he had certainly regained his health and his exceptional good looks. Even his eyes seemed to have found some of their old sparkle, very obvious now as he watched her approach in the gown of sapphire-blue satin.

"You look a vision, Lavinia," he said, bowing over her hand. "I am honoured to be escorting such a beautiful woman."

Lavinia curtsied graciously. "It is I who am honoured by the escort of such a handsome gentleman, my lord. I vow the ladies will be watching me with envy tonight."

"Mmm, those who are not pitying you," Nicholas said with a sudden return of bitterness.

Lavinia refused to allow him to sink into the depression that so coloured his moods of late. "None of them will be pitying me, I can assure you."

"Nicholas!"

They both turned at the sound of Martine's voice in the doorway. Immediately, Nicholas's features relaxed into an easy grin. *"Ma belle, vous êtes très jolie."*

"Nicholas," Lavinia chided him.

"Hmm? Oh yes, excuse me," he said with a devilish grin. "I'm not supposed to be encouraging your French, am I. Then let me say, in English, how very pretty you look. The gentlemen will be very busy vying for your regard."

Martine sparkled under his praise. "Thank you, Nicholas. But I already know it will be *maman* who sparkles. Does she not look beautiful?"

Nicholas levelled a smiling glance in her direction, and was about to voice his agreement, when suddenly a flash of another night edged up from his subconscious. A blue gown. The memory of Martine's words... of his looking at Lavinia's throat, and of seeing..."

"The necklace," he said abruptly. "Where is the necklace?"

"Oh, I did not think to wear..." Lavinia gasped, her hand going to her throat even as she stared at him in shock. "Nicholas! You remember... the necklace?"

Martine glanced at her mother with an expression of delight. *"Oui,* the diamonds, yes. With sapphires. You remembered!"

"Yes, to match...your engagement ring," Nicholas said, his excitement mounting.

"Nicholas, you do remember!" Lavinia cried. "You remembered the necklace you bought for me! It was part of my betrothal gift!"

Nicholas felt a shudder of exhilaration. Dear God, was it possible? Was it happening at last?

"Yes, I remember," he said, quickly. "I remember that...there was a necklace. That you were wearing it...with this gown the...last time."

"At our betrothal party. Do you remember that, Nicholas?"

He tried. He tried harder than he had ever tried before. He felt both Martine and Lavinia urging him to dig back and pull the memories out of his mind.

But he couldn't. It had come like a brief flash of lightning, and it had gone just as swiftly. He remembered the necklace, and he remembered Lavinia wearing it . . . but he remembered nothing beyond that.

"No, there is . . . nothing else," he said bitterly. "Damn! It lasted for but a moment."

Lavinia refused to allow the significance of the moment to pale. "But it was a moment, Nicholas," she whispered, holding his hand tightly in hers. "A moment that will lead to others. The important thing now is that there is room for hope. You have just proven that."

IT WAS PERHAPS because of the remarkable occurrence of his remembering the necklace that Nicholas set off for the ball in a spirit of considerable optimism. The fact that he had remembered anything—even something as inconsequential as a necklace—proved that there was indeed hope. And it was perhaps his unusual vivacity—more evident than upon any occasion since his return to London—that caused people to gravitate towards him, drawn as they had always been by his irresistible wit and charm.

"Well, Lord Longworth, I am delighted to see you in such a good mood this evening," Lady Wolverton commented with delight. "Is there a reason for this return of high spirits?"

Nicholas shook his head, having decided not to tell anyone about what had happened. "None at all, Lady Wolverton. I simply came to the realization today that there is no point in bemoaning the fact that I can remember nothing, but rather that I should be thankful that I am alive, as Lavinia keeps pointing out." He turned and glanced at his radiant fiancée with a pride he did not need to pretend. "She is a very special lady, and I am very lucky to have her."

Lady Wolverton beamed. "Does this mean that we may still be hearing wedding bells in the near future?"

"I think it is a little too early for that, Lady Wolverton," Lavinia said self-consciously. "There is still much that Lord Longworth and I need to understand. After all, it is like getting to know someone again for the first time."

"Well, if the two of you end up looking as happy as you did the first time, I shouldn't imagine the nuptials will be all that far off. I shan't soon forget that beautiful toast you gave to Lavinia at your betrothal party, Lord Longworth. I must admit, it near moved me to tears. Or perhaps this young lady will beat you both to the altar," Lady Wolverton said, smiling benevolently on Martine. "You are a most popular young lady with the gentlemen, Miss Duplesse. No doubt you will receive a number of offers before the end of the Season."

Martine blushed in a charming fashion. "Thank you, Lady Wolverton, but I should prefer to see *maman* settled first."

Lady Wolverton shook her head. "Charming, utterly charming. She is a credit to you, Lavinia. I even heard Sally Jersey remarking on her the other day. I vow it will not be long before you receive her vouchers for Almack's."

"That would, of course, be delightful," Lavinia said, knowing that the all-important vouchers were mandatory for any hopeful young lady's success in Society.

"Ah, now there is a face I have not seen in a long time," Lady Wolverton commented suddenly, glancing over Lavinia's shoulder. "Such a handsome man. And so very distinguished. Lord Rushton!" she called.

Lavinia kept the smile on her face, though she could not explain the tiny shiver that coursed through her body.

"Dear me, you cannot be cold, Lavinia," Lady Wolverton whispered as the gentleman approached. "It is warm enough in here to poach an egg. Ah, my dear Lord Rushton, how good of you to come. Do you know Lady Duplesse?"

Rushton bowed, his eyes lingering appreciatively on Lavinia's face. "Yes. We met at Lady Renton's musicale. Good evening, Lady Duplesse."

"Lord Rushton. May I present my fiancé, Lord Longworth."

Nicholas turned and extended his hand to the new arrival. "Rushton."

"Longworth. I understand you had something of an accident in France," Rushton said. "Feeling better now?"

"Yes, much better, thank you."

As they were speaking, another gentleman drifted over to join them. "Evening, all," he said genially.

"Lord Havermere, how delightful to see you again," Lady Wolverton gushed. "We were just talking about Lord Longworth's unfortunate accident in France."

"Dear me, yes, I heard all about it," Havermere said, clearly concerned. "What frightful business. Do you remember much of what happened, Lord Longworth?"

Nicholas shook his head. "Not a thing, I'm afraid. The doctors told me it was probably as a result of the head injury I suffered."

"Dashed nuisance. No memory at all, then?"

"None."

"Do they hold out any hope that it will come back?" Lady Wolverton enquired anxiously.

Nicholas managed to keep his frustration at bay. "Very little."

During the conversation, Rushton's attention strayed, and he now stood smiling down at Martine. "Well, well, never tell me that this beautiful young woman is Miss Martine Duplesse?"

Martine's surprise was evident. "You know me?"

"Indeed." Rushton pressed a quick kiss to the back of her hand. *"Enchanté, mademoiselle."*

Martine gasped, her eyes lighting up. *"Vous parlez français, monsieur?"*

"Martine, English please," Lavinia reminded her.

Rushton glanced in amusement at Lavinia. "Surely you do not object to your stepdaughter speaking French, Lady Duplesse? It is her native tongue, after all."

"Martine is allowed to speak French at home, Lord Rushton, but at social functions I prefer that she use English," Lavinia said calmly. "I feel it is important that she become fully conversant with the language of the country she is living in. Do you think that wrong?"

"Not at all. I have always thought it is a sign of respect to speak the language of the country one is in. It has always stood me in good stead."

"Do you speak other languages, Lord Rushton?" Martine asked, intrigued.

"A few."

Lavinia regarded him narrowly. "You speak French like a native. Have you spent much time abroad?"

Rushton smiled obliquely. "Not recently. As I am sure you will agree, France is very dangerous just now, and I consider myself an Englishman, first and last. But that is not to say that I do not enjoy what Paris has to offer. Just as I enjoy the pleasures of many other European cities. Venice, Rome, Florence, to name but a few."

Martine fairly devoured him with her eyes. "Ah, but you are so well travelled, *monsieur*. How exciting it must be to see all those places."

"Before the war, I was able to travel freely on the Continent, visiting the other great cities. Places like Salzburg and Vienna." Rushton's eyes were warm as they lingered on the girl's face. "Sadly, we are much more restricted now."

"Vienna!" Martine sighed rapturously. "I should so love to go there. *La cité de la musique.*"

"The city of music," Havermere translated, displaying his own knowledge of the language.

"Yes, there is much music," Rushton said. "Music inspired by the great composers. Perhaps one day you will see these wonderful places, Miss Duplesse."

Martine's eyes were glowing as they rested on the man's face. "*J'espère*... that is, I hope so, *monsieur*. And soon."

"Well, not too soon, perhaps," Lady Wolverton spoke up. "I am sure a number of English gentlemen would like to have the opportunity of meeting you first, my dear. Speaking of which, would you mind if I introduced Martine to Lady Trevor's son, Lavinia? He has been most anxious to meet her." Lady Wolverton leaned a little closer. "Quite taken with her already, I fancy, as are a number of them."

Lavinia carefully hid her smile. "Yes, by all means, Lady Wolverton."

To this point, Nicholas had been content to stand back and listen. But when he happened to glance towards the door and see Edward, he touched Lavinia's shoulder gently. "Lavinia, would you excuse me for a moment? I have just seen Edward come in."

Lavinia nodded. "Yes, of course. I shall find you directly."

When he was gone, Lavinia turned to find Lord Rushton watching her, the same speculative look in his eye as she had seen at Lady Renton's musicale.

"Did you wish to ask me something, Lord Rushton?" Lavinia enquired candidly, aware of Lord Havermere watching them both.

"Not at all, Lady Duplesse. I was merely thinking what a charming young lady your stepdaughter is. Is she happy living in London after growing up in France?"

"She is adjusting well."

He nodded, watching Martine across the length of the floor. "Beautiful. As her mother was."

Lavinia started. "I wasn't aware you knew Genevieve Duplesse that well."

"I knew your whole family. Or rather, your husband's."

Rushton's eyes were veiled, and it seemed to Lavinia that there was a great deal he wasn't telling her. She was just about to ask, when his next question forestalled her.

"I wonder, Lady Duplesse, if you might allow me to call upon Miss Duplesse tomorrow. I should like to take her driving in the Park."

Lavinia felt a knot form in the pit of her stomach, and hoped her alarm was not evident. "Unfortunately, my daughter and I are getting ready to go down to the country for a while, my lord. As such, there are a great many things we have to attend to. I'm sure you understand."

Rushton bowed graciously. If he had detected the slight note of reserve in her voice, he gave no sign. "But of course. Perhaps I may call upon her when you return."

"If that is to her liking," Lavinia told him carefully.

"Your servant, *madame.*"

"Lady Duplesse," Havermere said, moving off with Rushton.

Not until the two men were well away did Lavinia let out the breath she had unconsciously been holding. Hearing Martine's approach, she was careful to greet her with a bright smile. "Are you having a good time, my dear?"

"*Oui,* a very good time, *maman.*" Martine glanced shyly at Rushton's retreating back. "Lord Rushton is a most handsome gentleman, is he not? And so distinguished."

Lavinia's smile was forced. "Yes, but then, he is a lot older than you, Martine. In fact, he is almost your father's age. But now, what did you think of Lady Trevor's son?"

Martine nodded, though with a definite lack of enthusiasm. "He is a nice boy."

Lavinia did not miss the implication. "He may be a boy, Martine, but rather a boy than a man jaded by life," she murmured, more to herself than to her stepdaughter.

Unfortunately, Martine heard. "Lord Rushton did not sound jaded to me. In fact, I found him very interesting indeed. And so handsome, yes?"

Lavinia did not reply. Yes, Lord Rushton was handsome. Too handsome. His were the type of looks that caused impressionable young women to do foolish things. Still, if it were only his looks that disturbed her, Lavinia would not have minded nearly so much.

ACROSS THE ROOM, Nicholas sipped his champagne and glanced out over the jostling crowd. "Do you know, Edward, it is amazing. All these people, and no more than ten to whom I could put a name. And then only with Lavinia's assistance."

Edward gave his friend a lopsided grin. "Count yourself fortunate, Nicholas. I myself would be happy to recognize so few."

Nicholas glanced at him shrewdly. "Not a lover of these affairs, eh?"

Edward shrugged. "Not particularly. Still, it's all part of the game, I suppose, but one, I admit, I've never found much time for." His own eyes darkened. "What I saw during my time in France made all this appear very frivolous to me. I only went back into Society for my sister's sake. And for Laura's, of course."

"Your sister Charlotte?" Nicholas said, recalling what Lavinia had told him.

"Yes. She is now married to the Earl of Marwood. Splendid fellow. But then, you knew him well."

Nicholas blinked. "I did?"

"One of your closest friends. You stood up for him at his wedding."

"Did I, by Jove? And how did I come to know you?"

"Osborne sent you to France to help me escape."

"Dear me, what an exciting life I've led," Nicholas commented sardonically. "What I wouldn't give to remember it

all." Glancing about the room, Nicholas noticed Havermere and Rushton still standing beside Lavinia. "Edward,
do you know those two gentlemen talking to Lavinia?"

Edward peered across the room. "Rushton and Havermere, you mean?"

"Yes. What do you know about them?"

"Not a great deal. Havermere has an estate up in Scotland, where I believe he spends most of the year. As for
Rushton, he keeps pretty much to himself."

"Are they good friends?"

"They seem to be. They're often at each other's estates.
Apparently, they've been in Scotland for the past month. I
hear the salmon fishing is very good."

"What about Rushton?" Nicholas asked. "Is he married?"

"No. Seems to like the ladies well enough, but never
bothers with any particular one for any length of time.
Havermere is definitely more the lady's man. He's kept a
string of mistresses in Kensington. Why?"

"I don't know. There's just something about Rushton
that bothers me. Damned if I know what it is, though."

Edward glanced at the man again. "Can't recall having
heard any unsavoury rumours about him. He used to spend
a lot of time in France, though he's kept a pretty low pro-
file these last few years. I believe his mother was a French
aristocrat. His father was, of course, English."

"And Havermere?"

"Bit of a dandy, I suppose, but an affable-enough fellow. Born in London, spent part of his childhood in France,
I believe, and travelled extensively with his tutor."

Nicholas watched the two for a moment, his eyes going
back to Rushton. The man's manners were impeccable. He
was attentive to a fault. Nicholas's gaze narrowed as he saw
Rushton's eyes linger on Martine. "I don't like the way he's
looking at Martine."

"I shouldn't worry about it," Edward replied casually. "Probably just wishing he were a good deal younger. Lavinia's stepdaughter is a devilishly pretty girl."

"Who is a devilishly pretty girl, Edward?" Laura asked with a hint of amusement in her voice.

"No one you need worry about, my love. I was just telling Nicholas that Martine Duplesse is a diamond."

"Oh, yes, I agree with you there," Laura said with a charming laugh. "And such a sweet thing. I overheard some of the tabbies talking amongst themselves earlier. It would appear they are most upset with her."

"They are?" Nicholas frowned. "But why?"

"It seems that they want very much to dislike her, but are finding it exceedingly difficult to do so."

Nicholas laughed, and suddenly felt as though a weight had been lifted from his shoulders. Perhaps it wouldn't turn out so badly after all, he reflected stoically. Lord Osborne had told him that he had accomplished in France what he had set out to do. Lavinia was still in love with him, Martine was cutting a dash in Society and he was beginning to feel at home again in the glittering world that was London. Would it not be simpler just to give in and enjoy what he had?

It would, if it were not for this damned nagging suspicion that something had gone dreadfully wrong in France.

CHAPTER SEVEN

THE DAY BEFORE they set off for the country, an event took place that caused Lavinia considerable distress and which lingered in her mind for some time after. She and Laura had spent the better part of the morning idly browsing through the shops for some last-minute purchases. Martine had not accompanied them, saying that she wished to remain at home to write some letters. But when Lavinia and Laura returned, it was to learn that Martine was not at home, and that a gentleman had called and taken her driving. Lavinia paused in the act of removing her gloves. "Which gentleman, Habinger?"

"Lord Rushton, my lady."

"Rushton!"

The note of annoyance in her voice was unmistakable, and Laura glanced at her in surprise. "Is there something wrong with Lord Rushton, Lavinia?"

"Wrong? No, not exactly," she said quickly, still unable to pinpoint what it was about Rushton that disturbed her. "It is just that I am not...pleased by his attentions towards Martine. The man is old enough to be her father."

Laura shrugged gracefully. "I am sure it is naught but a passing fancy, Lavinia. You said yourself that Martine is interested in travelling. Perhaps it is Lord Rushton's knowledge of other cities she finds fascinating."

Recalling the look in Martine's eyes the evening she and Lord Rushton had met, however, Lavinia wasn't so sure. There was something about the older man that fascinated

her stepdaughter, and whether it was indeed his sophistica-
tion, or the air of mystery that surrounded him, Lavinia
knew that his impression upon Martine had been a strong
one.

She was suddenly very glad that they would be leaving for
Rose Cottage on the morrow. Perhaps the journey by carriage would provide a good opportunity for the two of them
to have a mother-daughter chat. She also decided to speak
to Lord Rushton when he and Martine returned.

"When are you and Edward coming down?" Lavinia
asked, changing the subject as they moved into the parlour.

"Well, to be perfectly honest," Laura replied, "Edward
thought we should give you and Nicholas some time alone
together."

Lavinia saw her friend's cheeks colour and she laughed.
"Laura, it is very good of you, but it is really not necessary. Besides, Nicholas and I will hardly be alone, what with
Martine and a full retinue of servants travelling down with
us."

"No, but you know what I mean," Laura said, her eyes
twinkling. "In answer to your question, however, I shall
probably arrive on Thursday, and I believe Edward is planning to follow on the Saturday."

"Good. Then I shall arrange some entertainments for the
weekend," Lavinia said brightly. "There are some people in
the area I like very much and have not seen these last few
years. It will be a good excuse to have them to visit." She
glanced at Laura warmly. "I should not like you and Edward to be bored while you are with us."

"Nonsense! How could I possibly be bored?" Laura said
quickly. "After these last few months I should be quite
happy to escape to the peace and quiet of the country for a
while. It will also give me time to prepare for our wedding."

Lavinia glanced at her, unable to prevent a fleeting touch
of envy. "Are you excited?"

"Dreadfully! I cannot wait to be married to Edward."
Laura slid a shy glance towards Lavinia. "Is that...terribly
bold of me to say?"

"Gracious, not in the least," Lavinia assured her. "I
should far rather hear you say that you were excited about
the wedding than apprehensive about it."

Laura's pretty face clouded momentarily. "Will it trouble you, Lavinia, coming to our wedding?"

She knew what her friend was referring to, and shook her
head. "No. While Nicholas and I have been forced to delay
our own wedding, it does not mean I would resent going to
yours. But you are a dear for asking. I hope very much that
ours will still take place."

"Do you think some time in the country will help him?"

"I do hope so," Lavinia admitted. "Nicholas has been
under so much strain since his return. He's pushing himself
to remember, and when he doesn't, I fear it only increases
the pressure that much more. I am hoping that in the country he will be able to forget about what happened. He's
never met the people I will be introducing him to, so he
won't have to force himself to try to remember them."

Just then, Lavinia heard the sound of the front door
opening, followed by Martine's pretty laughter. She rose and
went out immediately. Lord Rushton was standing in the
hall just behind the girl.

"Oh, *maman!* We had such a lovely time!" Martine's
eyes were shining. "Lord Rushton has been telling me the
most wonderful stories of his travels. I almost felt as though
I were there myself."

Lavinia forced a pleasant smile to her lips, even though
her heart was sinking. Her stepdaughter's face was positively glowing.

"Run along upstairs and change, my dear. Your tea will
be ready soon."

Martine's smile faded a little at the unexpected sharpness
in her mother's voice. *"Oui, maman."* She turned towards

the gentleman standing silently behind them. *"Merci, monsieur.* I enjoyed the drive very much."

Rushton bowed gallantly. "It was my pleasure, Miss Duplesse. I look forward to having the opportunity again."

With another quick glance at Lavinia, Martine ran lightly up the stairs. When she had gone, Lavinia turned back towards Lord Rushton, her own smile disappearing. "I would prefer in future, Lord Rushton, that you ask my permission before taking my stepdaughter out."

Rushton eyed her speculatively. "Your daughter is no longer a schoolroom miss, Lady Duplesse. She is of an age to receive visits from gentlemen."

"I did not say that she was not," Lavinia said quietly. "But she is still very new to English ways and I will not allow her to entertain or be entertained, by gentlemen without my knowledge."

"I can assure you, Lady Duplesse, my intentions were strictly honourable. In fact, it was a rather spur-of-the-moment idea on my part. When I realized that you were leaving for the country soon, I merely thought that most of your arrangements would have been taken care of and that Miss Duplesse might have some time on her hands." He smiled in a charming fashion. "She did not seem unhappy to see me."

"Still, I would have preferred that you ask me first, Lord Rushton. Martine is young and impressionable. She is not in the least sophisticated, and I will not see her hurt. Do I make myself clear?"

Rushton regarded the woman in front of him with an expression akin to amusement. Her anger had heightened the colour in her cheeks and caused her eyes to flash with azure fire. She was an incredibly beautiful woman, and Rushton wondered that he had never noticed it before. She was like a lioness protecting her cub. Still, he was also aware that in the jungle, only the fittest survived.

He bowed mockingly. "Quite clear, Lady Duplesse. I take it you are warning me to stay away from her?"

"I think it might be better, my lord," Lavinia agreed quietly. "I hardly need point out that you are considerably older than my stepdaughter. No doubt you would soon grow tired of her youthful ways."

"On the contrary, I find the young lady's naiveté refreshing. However, I will endeavour to respect your wishes. Although perhaps it is Miss Duplesse you should be speaking with, rather than myself."

Lavinia did not care for the insinuation, but understood him well enough. "I shall speak with my stepdaughter, Lord Rushton. Of that you may be sure."

Rushton bowed again, a faintly contemptuous glitter in his eye. "Young ladies can be powerfully stubborn when they want to be."

"Good day, Lord Rushton!"

Her anger seemed to have no effect on him whatsoever, and he turned to leave with that same mocking smile hovering about his lips. After the door closed, Lavinia clenched her hands into fists.

She had made an enemy today. And the fact that it was a man she had not been able to trust from the moment she'd met him did nothing in the least to allay her fears.

She would watch Martine very carefully from now on.

ROSE COTTAGE was a beautiful country house of graceful proportions and comfortable size. A fifteenth-century manor house with additions made early in the seventeenth century, it had drawn its name from the magnificent rose gardens that surrounded it. The house had long been in Lavinia's family, and yet it was the one place she had never shown François. He had expressed no desire to explore the English countryside, preferring to return to France as soon as possible after their wedding.

Looking back now, Lavinia was relieved. The house held no unpleasant memories for her. It was as calming and as restful as it had always been. Happily, Nicholas felt its tranquillity at once.

"It is so peaceful here," he murmured as Lavinia led him down one of the many intimate walks that wound through the extensive gardens. "A man could be completely at rest here."

Lavinia smiled and tucked her arm into his. "I certainly hope so, Nicholas. That was my reason for wanting to bring you."

Nicholas turned and looked into her face. "Was I so admirable a man that I inspired this kind of devotion in you, Lavinia?"

Her smile was as gentle as a mother's toward a newborn babe. "There has never been anyone like you in my life, Nicholas. Even without your memory, you are still the man I fell in love with. Your character has not changed, only your knowledge of the past. You are as good and as loving as you always were."

He stared down into her eyes. "I want so much to remember, Lavinia," he whispered desperately. "I want to feel again, to live and breathe as the man I was. I want to remember how much I loved you."

"And I truly hope you will, my darling," Lavinia replied huskily, moved as always by his nearness. "We can stay here for as long as you wish."

Nicholas laughed throatily. "Are you not afraid of being branded a loose woman, Lavinia Duplesse?" he teased her. "There are those who will comment upon our staying so long together in the country."

"Let them say what they will," she replied calmly. "I am doing nothing wrong. We are suitably chaperoned by my stepdaughter and the servants, and Edward and Laura will be joining us shortly, as well as other guests."

"Other guests?" Nicholas looked wary. "You did not tell me anyone else would be coming from London."

"No, not from London," Lavinia assured him. "These are friends of mine who live in the area. Friends I have not seen in a long time."

"Will they not be...surprised to find you here with me?" Nicholas asked.

"No. They did not know François, though they heard of his death." Lavinia's voice was matter-of-fact. "And they knew that I was to be married again. They will know soon enough that you have had an accident, if they have not already heard."

Momentarily, a look of unhappiness settled on Nicholas's handsome features. "Yes, is there anyone who does not know that Viscount Longworth is starting all over again— that his memory was wiped clean by a stray bullet?"

Lavinia heard the bitterness in his voice, and her heart went out to him. "Oh, Nicholas, you must put the anger aside. You are alive, my darling, and that is all that matters. And there is hope. Or have you forgotten the necklace?"

At the mention of his one brief moment of lucidity, Nicholas sighed. "No, I have not forgotten. I cling to it like a drowning man to a raft. But the knowledge that there have been no more such occurrences frightens me." He grasped her hands with feverish intensity. "I tried so hard to hold on to that moment, Lavinia—to see beyond the necklace, to remember something else that had happened that night, anything at all. But there was nothing."

"Of course not, because you were trying too hard," Lavinia chastised him. "The memory of the necklace came to you when you were not even thinking of it. That is how it will happen, Nicholas, I feel sure of it," she said earnestly as they began to walk again. "When you least expect it, something will come into your mind. That is why I wanted you to come here with me. Here," she said, glancing around at the beautiful surroundings, "all is peace and tranquillity. Here, there are no memories for you to struggle with. Here, your mind will be clear."

Nicholas abruptly halted and drew Lavinia into the circle of his arms. "And here, there is no one to disturb my time with you."

His voice, deep and sensual, sent a shiver of desire through her. "There is Martine," she reminded him softly.

"Mmm." He nuzzled his lips gently against her cheek. "Dear Martine, who would very much like to see me fall in love with her mother again."

Lavinia blushed, but did not bother denying what they both knew to be the truth. She glanced up at him, doubt and concern reflected in her eyes. "Oh, Nicholas, it is the dearest wish of my heart that you could. But if it does not happen, I will not hold you. You are free to go at any time. You know that, don't you?" she whispered.

Nicholas looked down into her eyes and saw no duplicity there. She meant every word she said. She was willing to let him go altogether, rather than have him stay out of a sense of obligation.

"I know, Lavinia," he breathed softly. "And you may rest assured that, if I stay, it will be only for the right reasons. But I would be lying if I did not tell you that I already feel myself extremely drawn to you."

Lavinia strove for a bantering tone, which was very difficult, given the tempting proximity of his lips. "You are drawn to me because you have not been exposed to any other attractive ladies. I wonder if you would not choose a younger lady, were you to be given the choice."

Nicholas laughed. "They would have to be very special young ladies indeed to compare to you. The more time I spend with you, the more I am convinced that you are truly a remarkable woman...."

His lips met hers, and Lavinia groaned softly as she willingly returned his kiss. Lifting her arms, she twined her fingers in his dark curls. Her heart soared as he pulled her closer against his firm body, moulding her to him. In that one kiss she communicated everything to him: her love, her longing, her need.

Yes, her need. A need that urged him to reach up and tentatively touch the aching fullness of her breasts through the silkiness of her gown. A need that inspired her gasp of pleasure as his thumb caresses grew more impassioned.

But it was a need that would never be fully satisfied in the garden of her home, Lavinia realized tremulously. Hopefully, there would come a time when the two of them could be together, but this was not it. She drew back out of his arms, even as he went to unfasten her bodice.

"Lavinia...." His voice was rough with desire. They were both breathing unsteadily.

"No, Nicholas, I cannot. Not now. Not like this..."

Her voice throbbed with suppressed emotion, and suddenly, Nicholas knew how hard this was for her. She was drawing on reserves far deeper than his.

He hung his head in shame, dropping his hands. "Forgive me, Lavinia, I...don't know what came over me. I should never have done that."

Summoning a shaky smile, she pressed her finger against his lips, silencing him. "No, my darling, do not apologize. I wanted it as much as you. More, perhaps," she admitted huskily, knowing how badly she had wanted him to go on touching her. "But perhaps it is better that we...take our time. I would not want you to think...ill of me."

Nicholas shook his head fiercely. "I could never think ill of you. And I would never doubt that anything which happened between us could happen for any but the right reasons."

Lavinia laughed shakily. "Nevertheless, we are still, for all intents and purposes, a betrothed couple, Lord Longworth," she said with mock primness. "And it would not do to allow our emotions to sweep us headlong down a path from which there could be no return.''

Nicholas laughed, and the tension eased. "Dear me, Lady Duplesse, such philosophical thoughts. I never dreamed you to be so profound.''

"Oh, I assure you, there are many things you do not know about me, Lord Longworth.'' She smiled as they turned back towards the house. "Not yet, at any rate.''

THE FIRST THREE DAYS at Rose Cottage were delightful in their simplicity. Lavinia spent as much time in Nicholas's company as he seemed to want, and divided the rest of her hours between Martine and her other pastimes. Thankfully, her stepdaughter, who had displayed an uncustomary stiffness with Lavinia after the incident with Lord Rushton, soon regained her normal *joie de vivre* and began enjoying her holiday in the English countryside.

The three of them rode together every day, setting out from the stables just after breakfast and sometimes not returning until early afternoon. Lavinia had the cook prepare a hamper of food for the groom to carry. When they came upon a particularly lovely vista, the groom would simply unfurl the blanket, set out the plates and cutlery and unpack the simple, yet delicious meal Cook had provided.

As the days passed, Lavinia was delighted to see the last remaining traces of anxiety pass from Nicholas's face. He laughed frequently, and Lavinia often caught his eyes on her when she turned to look at him.

Even Martine noticed his increased attention. "I think Nicholas is falling in love with you, *maman*,'' she said one afternoon as the two of them sat in companionable silence in the conservatory. "He follows you with his eyes.''

Lavinia tried not to show how happy that made her. "I hope you are right, Martine, but it is still early yet.''

"He is looking better though, *non?*''

"Yes, much better. I think Rose Cottage agrees with him."

Martine smiled secretly. "I think it is *l'amour* that agrees with him."

Lavinia blushed and returned her attention to her book. But the pages of her novel did not hold her attention. It was true, she and Nicholas did seem to be growing closer. He always had a gentle smile for her, a tender word. And lately, his kisses had been growing more impassioned, reminding her of the way he had kissed her just before he had gone to France.

Oh, dear God, let it be as it was, Lavinia prayed silently. *Bring him back to me just the way he was.*

NICHOLAS SAT WITH his hands resting on the pommel of his saddle and gazed down at Rose Cottage, aware of an undeniable feeling of contentment. A thin plume of smoke rose from one of the largest chimneys, and he could imagine Lavinia curled up in front of the fire with a novel. Martine was probably beside her, lost in the pages of her own book, looking for all the world like a kitten curled up cosily beside her mother.

Nicholas sighed. Did he have a place in that picture? At times he thought he did. When he was with Lavinia, everything felt so right. But when he was away from her, the doubts came crowding in. Who was he? What had happened in his life to this point? And what had happened that night in France that had changed the course of his destiny?

Suddenly, the anger that always accompanied such thoughts surrounded Nicholas, obliterating his happiness and plunging him into gloom. Though he had been less inclined to suffer these fits of depression since coming to Rose Cottage, he had still not been able to escape them altogether.

Why could he not accept that it was Leclerc who had shot him that night? Why did he keep thinking that there was more? What else could have happened?

Nicholas groaned in frustration. Lavinia was right. The harder he tried to remember, the more the truth eluded him. Sometimes at night he felt vague stirrings of memory coming back to haunt him. He caught glimpses of the man he had been, faces of people he'd known—elusive, dancing shadows that hovered on the very brink of his awareness. But as soon as he tried to reach out and touch them, they disappeared like moonbeams in the first light of dawn.

But at least they came, Nicholas told himself. He'd have to be content with that. And most of the time he was, always knowing that tomorrow was another day, and possibly one day closer to recovery.

CONTRARY TO LAURA'S original plans, she and Edward arrived together on the Friday. Waving aside their apologies for the last-minute change, Lavinia had the butler deal with the luggage and then happily welcomed her guests.

"Lavinia, your house is simply breathtaking," Laura exclaimed, sighing enviously as they toured the main floor. "How can you bear to be away from it?"

"The time I spend away from it makes me appreciate it all the more when I am here," Lavinia explained simply. "Come, let us retire to the drawing-room. From there, you have the view onto the rose gardens."

Martine joined them just as tea was being served. "Good afternoon, Mademoiselle Beaufort, Monsieur Kingsley."

"Good day, Martine. Are you enjoying your holiday at Rose Cottage?" Edward enquired.

"*Ah, oui, c'est très—,*" The girl broke off, seeing Lavinia's raised eyebrow, then continued with enthusiasm, "It is very beautiful. Has *maman* told you about the *soirée* yet?"

Laura glanced at her hostess. "No, she hasn't. Have you planned it then, Lavinia?"

"Yes. I have already sent out invitations and everyone has accepted."

"Oh, how marvellous. It will be like old times, will it not, Edward?"

"Yes, or rather, almost," he said. His gaze slid to Nicholas, who had been sitting quietly, listening to the ladies chat. "Any improvement, my friend?"

Nicholas flushed, but then, realizing he was with his closest friends, he let his features relax. "No, I'm afraid not. I sometimes catch brief glimpses of people or places, but nothing stays with me."

"Still, there was the incident with the necklace," Laura reminded him. "That was very positive."

Nicholas nodded. He had agreed to let Lavinia tell Edward and Laura about the breakthrough, but no one else. "Yes. Unfortunately, there hasn't been a reoccurrence. I keep hoping, of course."

"Never mind," Edward said in a tone of encouragement. "It has not been all that long since the accident, and the doctors did say that if your memory were to return, it might not be for a while."

"Yes, I know. It's just that I find myself growing anxious for it to happen. Was I always so impatient?"

"Always! Impatient and stubborn," Edward told him, laughing.

"Dear me, what an unlovable cad," Nicholas replied with a mock frown. "Can't think why anyone would be in a hurry to have the old Nicholas back."

"I can."

His gaze swivelled round to Lavinia's, and he saw the answer reflected in her eyes. "Apart from you, that is, my dear," he amended softly.

Lavinia smiled, and quickly turned her attention to the refreshments. Perhaps God had heard her prayer after all.

CHAPTER EIGHT

"*MAMAN*, MAY I go into town?" Martine asked Lavinia the following afternoon. "I should like to get some new ribbon for my bonnet."

Lavinia nodded. "Yes, of course, Martine. One of the grooms can drive you."

"Oh, that's all right," the girl said quickly. "I can drive the curricle myself. Nicholas has been teaching me."

"Has he indeed?" Lavinia slid an amused glance towards Laura, who was sitting in a winged-back chair doing needlework. "Well, in that case, I suppose it would be all right. But take Hélène with you."

"Yes, *maman*."

"And do not be late."

"No, *maman*."

As Martine scurried out, Laura shook her head. "Dear me, that girl is so full of life. Does she not wear you out?"

"At times," Lavinia admitted. "She forgets to behave like a properly reared young lady sometimes, but I tend to let her get away with it. I was inclined to such boisterousness in my own youth. Besides, she was such a serious girl when I met her. François did not approve of frivolity in young ladies."

"Well, she has certainly blossomed under your care. Has there been any further mention of Lord Rushton?"

"No, thank goodness!" Lavinia replied. "And I have not brought the subject up. I may be an ostrich sticking my head in the sand, but I should rather like to think that out of sight is out of mind. Besides, I did ask Lord Rushton to stay away from her, and I hope he is gentleman enough to comply.''

"Well, as you say, Lavinia, Martine is an impressionable girl. No doubt her head will be turned many times before she meets the young man who will finally capture her heart as well as her head.''

"I hope so.'' A frown marred the smooth line of Lavinia's forehead. "Martine has always been so intense, so... passionate in her approach to life. When she takes to something, it becomes the centre of her world—for as long as it remains with her. Then it is discarded, as another new passion moves in to take its place.'' She levelled a meaningful glance at Laura. "I can only hope it is that way with Lord Rushton.''

"You think she is infatuated with him?''

Lavinia nodded, her eyes troubled. "Yes, I do. I can tell you, Laura, I was very glad we left for the country when we did. As far as I am concerned, the less Martine sees of that man, the better!''

THE GUESTS LAVINIA HAD invited for dinner that evening were a delightful couple, and Nicholas warmed to them immediately. Anthony Hewitt, a tall, solidly built man close in age to Nicholas and Edward, was as well informed on sports and current affairs as any London gentleman. He travelled to Town frequently, but he preferred the comfort of his large country property in Kent.

His wife Pamela, on the other hand, was a soft-spoken young woman who looked hardly old enough to be the mother of two healthy children and the mistress of such a sprawling estate. She watched her husband with pride, and it was clear that a mutual bond of love and affection bound them together. Dinner was a light-hearted affair, punctuated with much laughter and many shared remembrances of earlier days.

"Oh, yes, Lavinia was a dreadful child," Anthony Hewitt confided as the dinner plates were being cleared away. "Pushed me into the lake once, then took off like a frightened colt. I didn't see her again for days."

"Do you blame me?" Lavinia retaliated. "I saw you waiting for me down by the gate, Anthony Hewitt, and I knew what you were going to do. I purposely stayed in the house."

Nicholas looked at his fiancée with an expression of amazement. "Lavinia, I would never have imagined you doing such a thing. Why on earth did you push Anthony into the lake in the first place?"

"Because he teased me," Lavinia replied. "And because he called me names."

"Anthony, you didn't!" Pamela Hewitt gasped.

"I certainly did," her husband replied without a trace of remorse. "I used to call her Misfit, because she was forever getting into scrapes. Scrapes for which *I* was always blamed."

"Aha, now the truth comes out," Pamela said. "I knew you would be involved somehow."

"I was not in the least involved," Anthony protested. "It wasn't my fault that Lavinia fell off her horse when she tried to jump bareback over the gate."

"It certainly was!" Lavinia replied, laughing. "*You* were the one who dared me to do it in the first place!"

Amidst the laughter that ensued, Lavinia did not at first notice that Martine was unusually quiet, nor that her attention seemed to be far away. But later, when the ladies retired, leaving the gentlemen to their port and cigars, she drew her stepdaughter aside. "Martine, are you feeling all right? You were very quiet during the meal."

"Yes, *maman*, I am fine. I am just a little tired," she replied diffidently

"Are you sure?" Lavinia studied the girl's face intently. "You're looking a little flushed. Not coming down with something, are you?"

"No, *maman.*"

"Well, if you're sure," Lavinia said hesitantly. "By the way, I did not see you when you came in this afternoon. You were gone quite a while. Did you find your ribbon?"

She was surprised to see the girl's cheeks grow pink. "Yes. And then I... went to the baker's and... had a biscuit."

"A biscuit. So that's why you didn't eat very much at dinner," Lavinia said, suddenly realizing why the girl had blushed; obviously, she had not intended to tell her about the treat she'd indulged in.

"I know I should not have, but I was... hungry." Martine glanced at Lavinia intently. "You're not angry, are you?"

"No, of course not," Lavinia said, surprised at the girl's apprehension. "Good heavens, if you cannot indulge yourself with a treat once in a while, what fun would there be in going out?"

Martine's expression noticeably relaxed. "Thank you, *maman.*"

"Are you going to join us for tea?"

"If it is all right with you, I would rather... go up to my room."

Lavinia smiled. Obviously, all the fresh air she'd had was wearing her stepdaughter out. "Of course. Off you go then. I shall see you in the morning. Don't forget, we are going to see the cathedral tomorrow."

"No, I had not forgotten. Good night."

"Good night, Martine."

Lavinia watched the girl climb the stairs and then turned to rejoin her guests, blissfully unaware of the storm that was brewing under her very nose.

LONG AFTER THE HEWITTS left and Edward and Laura retired to their respective rooms, Lavinia found herself propped up in bed, flipping through the pages of a magazine. She was not in the least tired, nor had she been for the last few nights. Given that her days were filled with activities, and her evenings with entertaining, she should have fallen into bed every night quite exhausted. And yet, again tonight, she was too restless to settle down.

The moon shining in through her window beckoned to her, and tossing aside the magazine, Lavinia rose. Slipping a robe over her nightgown, she quietly opened the door and made her way downstairs to the conservatory. Once there, she opened the door and stepped out into the night air. It was cool, but not unpleasantly so. The moon lit a brilliant path through the night, illuminating the flagstone walk as clearly as though it were day.

"You couldn't sleep either, I see."

The voice startled her, and Lavinia jumped at the sight of a shadowy figure seated on the bench ahead of her. "Nicholas! What are you doing out here so late?"

He rose as she approached, his voice a throaty whisper. "I might ask you the same thing. This is hardly the recommended strolling hour."

Lavinia chuckled, pulling her robe closely about her. She was well aware that the nearly transparent muslin did little to hide the contours of her figure.

Nicholas noticed her action. "Are you cold?"

She shook her head. She had begun to shiver but not as a result of the cold. "No."

"You are not frightened of me, I hope."

Lavinia laughed, the sound as soft as raindrops falling on a leaf. "Not in the way you might be thinking, my lord, though I confess I am very... aware of you."

Nicholas chuckled. "Yes, no doubt as much as I am aware of you in that flimsy night covering. Do you always walk about dressed so provocatively, Lady Duplesse?'' he teased.

Lavinia was thankful for the darkness that hid her blush. "Odious creature, of course not. At least, not when there are gentlemen about. I simply felt the need for...a walk. A bit of air." Her brows drew together. "I found I was not the least bit sleepy tonight."

She heard Nicholas sigh. "No, I fear sleep did not come easily to me, either. Perhaps it was the wine."

"Yes, perhaps."

"Shall we walk?"

Lavinia nodded and fell into step beside him. "What did you think of the Hewitts?"

"I think that if all your friends are as charming as they, I shall never want to leave Kent," Nicholas replied with eloquent simplicity. "They made me feel most welcome this evening."

"They were comfortable with you."

"How did you know?"

"Because Anthony was more gregarious than usual. He would never have related all those childhood pranks if he didn't like you."

Nicholas suddenly started to laugh. "I admit, it conjured up some interesting pictures. Did you really push him into the pond?"

"I most certainly did," Lavinia replied. "He made me so angry, I couldn't help myself. But I ran as fast as my legs would carry me once I realized what I'd done."

"Dearest Lavinia, I can just imagine what you looked like, running like the wind with your hair flying out behind you. Or did you wear it in braids?"

"Oh, no, it was loose most of the time," Lavinia admitted. "I could never sit still long enough for Nanny to braid it. She often told my mother I was quite hopeless."

Nicholas reached for her hand and drew her towards him. "Did she? And what would she say about you now, I wonder?"

Lavinia felt the warmth emanating from his body as he pulled her closer. "I cannot imagine that she would think me all that improved. I am quite shamelessly compromising myself by being out here all alone with you."

"Yes, you are. *And* with a man who has no memory of you," Nicholas reminded her.

Lavinia tilted her head back and gazed into his eyes. "He may have no memory of me from the past, but has he no thoughts of me in the present?"

Nicholas looked at her with an expression akin to wonder. "You are in my thoughts constantly. In fact, I'm surprised that there is room for anything else. I wake thinking of you, I go to sleep thinking of you, and when we are together like this, I am filled with a sense of peace that pushes away all the uncertainties, all the pain. Without you, I feel as though I am only... half a man. You are part of me, Lavinia, and that frightens me."

"Frightens you?" Lavinia searched his face. "But why, my darling? Why would that frighten you?"

His burning eyes held her still. "Because if I were to lose you now, if you were suddenly to grow tired and leave me, I think I would be far worse off than a man without a memory. I would be a man... without a heart."

Lavinia felt a shudder run through her body at the intensity of his words. "I am not going to leave you, Nicholas. I will *never* leave you, even if you never regain your memory. I will love you just the way you are!"

"Lavinia!" He bent his head to kiss her—and then abruptly froze.

Lavinia felt him tense. "Nicholas, what's wrong?"

He didn't answer. He only stood, staring into space with a burning, faraway look in his eyes.

"Nicholas!" Lavinia shook him gently. "Nicholas, answer me, please! What is wrong?"

It seemed an eternity before he whispered, "There was...another man."

She gasped, feeling a shiver of fear. "Oh, my God!"

"An image of him just...appeared...in my mind," Nicholas said haltingly. "A man. An Englishman."

Lavinia struggled to understand. "You mean a man other than Ferris?"

"There were...three men." Nicholas set her gently away from him, his face twisted in concentration. "I can see them. Leclerc, Ferris and...another man who came later. A man on...horseback."

"Did he shoot Leclerc?"

Nicholas hesitated. "No. I shot Leclerc. But the other man...shot Ferris." He glanced at her in astonishment. "And then...he shot me!"

Lavinia blanched. "Dear God! But why, Nicholas? Who was he?"

"I don't know. Damn, I can't remember...what he looked like." Nicholas pressed his hands to his temples. "I just remember him being on a horse. He came out of the darkness. I remember hearing...the sound of his pistol, just before I felt the pain in my side."

"His voice, Nicholas—do you remember if he said anything to you?"

Nicholas struggled to recapture the memory, but just as with the necklace, this, too, was a brief flash and then gone. "No. That's all. Damn it! I can't remember anything else."

Lavinia felt her legs begin to tremble. "I think I would...like to sit down," she said quietly.

As if recalled from a dream, Nicholas quickly nodded. "Yes, of course. Forgive me, Lavinia. I've frightened you." He took her arm and led her to the bench. "I should not have said anything."

"No, it is better that you did," she insisted, grateful for the cool stone seat beneath her. "But it frightens me, Nicholas. Who was this man? Why did he shoot you?"

He shook his head. "I don't know. He might have been a thief, I suppose," he said, recalling how the papers had described the accident as an attempted robbery.

"Nicholas, I am frightened," Lavinia said. "What if...it wasn't a robbery? What if he was trying to..."

She couldn't finish, couldn't bring herself to say the dreadful words. Slowly, her tears began to fall. Nicholas didn't speak, either. He merely sat down on the bench beside her and pulled her into his arms, holding her tightly until she stopped crying. But even as he did, he was painfully aware of one thing.

His feeling that something had gone wrong was not incorrect. There *had* been another man on that lonely stretch of road that night—someone who had stalked him and waited until the moment was right to shoot him down. Someone who had thought him dead and had left him that way.

Someone who was very much alive and was no doubt looking for him again!

NICHOLAS DID NOT GO back to bed that night. The memory of what he had seen banished all thought of sleep. Like a child waking to a new day, he felt as though he were on the verge of a tremendous discovery, and though his memory had not returned, he was aware of having discovered a new purpose in life. And the first person he sought to tell was Edward. He found him in the breakfast-room, enjoying a quiet cup of coffee.

"Nicholas, good morning," Edward greeted him. "I thought I was the only one who rose at this ridiculous hour."

"You might be any other morning, but not today, my friend. I did not sleep all night." Nicholas sat down in the chair beside him. "Edward, I remembered something. Something terribly important."

Edward hesitated in the act of lifting the cup to his lips. The tension in Nicholas's voice was palpable. "What?"

"There was another man on the road that night. A stranger shot Ferris—and then shot me."

"Bloody hell!" Edward put down his cup with such a bang it was amazing the fine china did not shatter. "Are you sure?"

"As sure as I can be. It came to me clearly, and completely without warning."

"Do you remember who it was? Was it someone you knew?"

Nicholas shook his head. "That's the frustrating part. I can't remember anything beyond that. I know that I had my pistol trained on Leclerc and Ferris when I heard the sound of a shot and saw Ferris go down. I remember seeing Leclerc pull a small pistol out of his pocket and aim it at me."

"Then it was Leclerc who shot you."

"No. I fired first. I know I hit him. And he told me—" Nicholas broke off, his face twisting "—he told me he was . . . not really Leclerc. But before I had a chance to ask him what he meant, he died. That's when I heard the sound of a pistol cocking, and then a bullet hit me in the side."

Edward searched his friend's grim face. "You know what this means, don't you?"

Nicholas felt an icy hand clutch at his stomach. "Yes. It means that there is a murderer loose in London, and that we have absolutely no idea who he is."

AFTER NICHOLAS'S startling revelation in the moonlit garden, Lavinia knew that the mood of happiness and tranquillity they had begun to feel at Rose Cottage was gone forever. The knowledge that another person had been involved in the murders—and that he was still walking free—changed everything.

For the sake of those who were not aware of the alarming news, however, she was determined to maintain an outward mien of normalcy. It would be difficult, especially given that Nicholas and Edward were planning to return to London as soon as possible to apprise Lord Osborne of the situation.

"Must you go, Nicholas?" Lavinia asked in a forlorn voice. "I am so afraid for you."

"Lord Osborne has to be made aware of this development, Lavinia," Nicholas replied gently.

"But what can you tell him? Yes, I understand that another man was there the night of the shooting, and that he is now walking freely about London, but how is that going to help you? You have no idea who he is, and until you are able to remember, of what possible use can the information be?"

Edward glanced at Nicholas and sighed. "She's right, Nicholas. We're not much further ahead than we were before."

"Maybe not, but does it not make sense to warn the people who were on that list so that they can at least take suitable precautions," Nicholas pointed out.

"Yes, I go along with that," Edward said. "But there's no need for both of us to leave, my friend. I can just as easily go to London and give Osborne the news. Then it will be up to him to advise the appropriate people." Edward shot Nicholas a meaningful glance. "Seems a pity to leave three such lovely young ladies here in the country—all on their own."

Icy fingers of fear wrapped around Nicholas's heart as he realized what Edward was saying. Lavinia was one of the seven people on Leclerc's list!

A cold, black anger swept through him as he realized the danger she was in, and how relatively little he was able to do about it. Keeping his voice as emotionless as possible, he said, "Yes, perhaps you have a point, Edward. Both of us need not go to London, and under the circumstances, it would be a pity to spoil Lavinia's plans. I think it more expedient, however, that I be the one to go to London to speak with Lord Osborne.''

"Nicholas, do you think that wise?" Lavinia objected. "You still don't know who you're dealing with."

"No, but then neither does Edward," Nicholas pointed out. "And if this signals the return of at least part of my memory, perhaps my being in London will help it along. That way, if I have another flash of insight while I'm there, I will be able to communicate with Osborne immediately. Edward, you wouldn't mind staying here with the ladies, would you? Seems a pity to cut short everyone's holiday needlessly.''

Edward nodded, fully understanding the implications in what Nicholas was saying. If there was a chance that Nicholas's memory was finally returning, he would be far better off in London than here. And under no circumstances could Lavinia be left alone now. "I wouldn't mind at all. I say, Lavinia, didn't you mention something about going to see the cathedral in Canterbury today?''

"Well, yes, but under the circumstances—"

"Good, then I shall accompany you," Edward said before she had a chance to finish. "Haven't been to Canterbury in an age. Charming place, as I recall.''

"I've always thought so," Nicholas agreed.

"But, Nicholas—"

"Yes, splendid idea," Edward carried on. "That way, the ladies will not have to postpone their outing, and you can post up to London, have your meeting and perhaps return in time for the weekend.''

"But—"

"I wouldn't have to miss Lavinia's soirée."

"Gentlemen—"

"Yes, I think that would be an excellent plan."

"Gentlemen!"

Two pair of eyes swivelled towards her. "Yes, Lavinia?" Nicholas said.

"If you don't mind, Nicholas, I should like to have a small say in this matter."

He smiled at her indulgently. "But of course, my dear. We never said that you should not."

Lavinia looked at him in astonishment. "But you never allowed me to say *anything!*"

"Edward and I were just settling the arrangements in our own minds first," Nicholas told her calmly. "Do you not think my going to London and Edward escorting you to Canterbury to be a good idea?"

"I think it an excellent idea," Lavinia snapped. "I just wish someone had troubled to ask me about it first!"

IT HAD BEEN YEARS since Lavinia had been to the ancient cathedral city of Canterbury, and she was looking forward to the outing. Or at least she had been, until the plans had altered so dramatically. Her pleasure was definitely curtailed at not having Nicholas with her to share it. He had already set out for London, leaving before Martine or Laura were up. Lavinia understood his concern, of course. It was imperative that Osborne be made aware of the situation as soon as possible, hopefully before Leclerc had opportunity to strike. But that had not made her parting from Nicholas any the less painful.

Still, at least Lavinia could console herself with the knowledge that he had promised to return as soon as possible. And knowing that he was going for a good reason helped to ease the sorrow.

After Nicholas left, Lavinia and Edward returned to the breakfast parlour. Lavinia poured herself a fresh cup of coffee and then sighed. "Oh, Edward, I can't help but feel that Nicholas is putting himself in terrible danger by going up to London."

Edward nodded. "Unfortunately, other people's lives are in more danger by his not going."

Lavinia glanced at him narrowly. "That was how you tried to justify his mission to France, and look how badly that turned out."

"I know, but you saw for yourself how difficult it was to stop him. Nicholas takes his responsibilities very seriously. He knew the dangers inherent in his going to find Leclerc, but he also knew he was the best man available for the job. And whether we like it or not, right now Nicholas may be the only one with the ability to solve this case."

"But he *doesn't* have the ability, Edward," Lavinia cried, rising to her feet in frustration. "Not yet. Not fully. He's had only two brief glimpses into the past, neither of which have been complete. And look how long it was between the first and the second recollections. What if he goes weeks again without remembering anything, all the while being stalked by a man who wants to kill him? What protection has he against such a murderer?"

"No more than anyone, I'm afraid," Edward replied softly. "But you have to understand the gravity of the situation from Nicholas's point of view, Lavinia. If his memory is beginning to return, he is the *only* man who can find the real Leclerc. And he knows that. So do you. You know better than anyone the depths of Nicholas's loyalty."

"Yes, I do," Lavinia admitted wearily, sinking back into her chair. "And believe me, that is the only reason that allows me to accept what he is doing now."

"What are you going to tell Martine?"

Lavinia sighed. "The same thing I'm going to tell Laura. That Nicholas had some business to attend to, but that he will be back in time for the weekend."

"The soirée is this weekend, isn't it?"

Lavinia nodded. "I sent an invitation to your sister and her husband, but I haven't heard anything. They should be back any time now, I would think."

Edward chuckled. "Actually, I expected them last week. They must be having a grand time."

"They deserve it, after everything they went through," Lavinia said, recalling the misunderstandings and problems that had plagued Edward's sister and her fiancé before their wedding.

"Quite true," Edward acknowledged. "But given this most recent development, I'm not at all unhappy that they are still out of London. I hope they stay away another month. Marwood is also on Leclerc's list."

Lavinia's cheeks blanched. "Do you intend to try to get in touch with him?"

Edward poured himself another cup of coffee. "I already have."

Lavinia glanced out through the window, marvelling at how tranquil the countryside could be, untouched by the turmoil around them. "I wish to God Nicholas had never gone to France in the first place!" she said emphatically. "Everything would be so different now."

"I don't know that it would have been, Lavinia," Edward said heavily. "Clearly, the man who shot Nicholas is as good as they come. And I have a sneaking suspicion that, had Nicholas not gone, the blackguard would be in London regardless. Our only hope is that Nicholas's memory will return fully. He's the only one who can identify the killer now."

The sound of footsteps approaching the door effectively put an end to the conversation. "Well, good morning, Lavinia, Edward," Laura said brightly. "Dear me, everyone's up already, I see. I confess, I slept like a baby again. This truly is the most peaceful place." She glanced around the room. "But where is Lord Longworth?"

"Nicholas had to return to London for a day or two, my dear," Edward informed her in a deliberately offhand manner. "Something to do with the estate. Tiresome business, but that is one of the joys of being a landowner."

"Oh dear, what a pity." Laura's face fell. "And we were to have gone to Canterbury today."

"And so we shall," Lavinia said briskly. "Except that Edward will have to act as our sole escort."

"Well, I can't think that it will trouble him unduly," Laura replied lightly. "Just think, Edward, the welfare of three lovely ladies is in your hands today."

Edward purposely did not meet Lavinia's eyes. Thank God neither of the ladies knew how true those innocent-sounding words really were.

CHAPTER NINE

NICHOLAS MADE EXCELLENT time to London. The traffic was light, and his curricle, drawn by a fleet pair of blacks, covered the distance between Rose Cottage and Town in no time at all.

Nicholas's thoughts as he raced towards London were mixed. He was pleased at having been given yet another tantalizing glimpse into his past, and the fact that it had happened so soon after he'd remembered the necklace was promising.

On the other hand, the realization that the man who had shot him and left him for dead was still on the loose terrified him. Everyone believed the danger had ended with the deaths of the other two men that night in France. Clearly, those men had been but pawns in a brutal killer's game.

Arriving in London, Nicholas went immediately to Whitehall, where he was shown into Osborne's office.

"Lord Osborne, I hope you will forgive my rather unexpected arrival."

Osborne waved his apology aside. "Think nothing of it, Longworth. Am I to assume from your hasty arrival that something of moment has taken place? Has your memory returned?"

"Not in full," Nicholas admitted. "But there have been two occasions where things have come back to me. One of which is the reason I am here. I remembered something about the shooting."

He saw Osborne tense. "Go on."

"There was another man there, my lord. I cannot recall anything about him, other than that he was mounted and that he shot at me from the darkness."

There was a brief, ominous silence as the import of Nicholas's words sank in. "Did he shoot Leclerc?" Osborne asked finally.

"No, I shot Leclerc, or rather the man we suspected of being Leclerc. The stranger shot Ferris. And me."

"My God!" Osborne sank down heavily in his chair. "Then it's true."

Nicholas was alarmed at the note of fear in the war minister's voice. "What's true?"

"That the man you shot was not the man we were looking for. Two nights ago, Lord Winchester was set upon and killed on the way home from his club. There were no witnesses, no clues, no suspects. He was shot at close range." Osborne glanced at Nicholas, his eyes dulled with worry. "You know what this means."

Nicholas nodded, his own worst suspicions confirmed. "That the man we seek *is* in London and that he's begun to carry out his threat as stated in the letter."

Osborne nodded. "Precisely. And as such, we have no time to waste. I take it you've told Kingsley."

"Yes, but not Lavinia. I thought it better not to frighten her. Edward is with her, though, and is taking every precaution."

"Good. What about Marwood?"

"As far as I know, he and Charlotte are still abroad. Edward has tried to reach him, but feels sure they will contact him as soon as they arrive back in London. He will arrange to meet them once they land."

"Fine. Then I'll contact Lord Sullivan," Osborne said. "He's the only other person on the list who isn't aware of what's happened. I'll warn him to take extra precautions for his safety until we apprehend this bastard." Osborne glanced at Nicholas again. "And you say you have absolutely no idea who the man was."

"God help me, I wish I did," he said fervently. "I can only hope it will come to me as unexpectedly as the other flashes did."

"Yes, I hope so too, Nicholas," Osborne muttered. "And without too much delay. There is a killer walking amongst us, my friend, and right now, you are the only one who knows who he is."

"That poses another problem, my lord," Nicholas said slowly.

"What's that?"

"There is a very good chance that this man knows I am alive. The fact that I have lost my memory may buy me some time, but not much. While I live, his continued safety depends on my not being able to remember what happened. Therefore, I can only conclude that whoever he is, he is likely to keep close tabs on me—to ensure that my memory doesn't return before he has taken care of me and everyone else named in the letter."

"What are you saying?"

"I am saying that if my memory does return, for the safety of all concerned, *no one* must know it but you and me."

IT WAS A STYLISH PARTY that set off from Rose Cottage a little later that morning. Lavinia had ordered the landau brought round, and with the top folded back, the passengers were given an unobstructed view of the countryside on the drive to the old cathedral town.

Lavinia was wearing a new gown of sky-blue muslin with a matching three-quarter-length pelisse, while Martine looked delightful in a jonquil-yellow carriage gown and a demure bonnet. Laura, in deference to her favourite colour, sported an elegant ensemble in peach sarcenet with a dainty parasol of peach-and-white stripe. Edward, as the only gentleman, declined to join them in the carriage, and chose instead to accept Lavinia's offer of a spirited mount to ride alongside.

It was a lovely day, and the ride to Canterbury was a leisurely one. They reached St. Dunstan's Street on the outskirts of the city by noon, and after enjoying lunch at a very pleasant inn, they carried on through Westgate, along St. Peter's Street past the church and eventually down to the spacious cathedral grounds. Lavinia ordered the coachman to bring the carriage to a halt.

"I think a little stroll would be a good idea, don't you?"

At the chorus of agreement, she and the other ladies descended. Edward handed his horse's reins to the groom, and the party began their leisurely stroll through the grounds, Lavinia and Martine in the lead, Laura and Edward following a few paces behind.

"Oh, *c'est magnifique!* How beautiful it is!" Martine exclaimed at her first sight of the cathedral through Christ Church Gate. "And you say it is very old?"

"Yes, indeed. In fact, parts of the city date back to Roman times. Sections of the King's School and areas around it were originally monastic."

"But it is so very large. Will we be able to see it all today?"

Lavinia laughed, enjoying her stepdaughter's enthusiasm. "I hardly think so, Martine. Not and do it any justice. But we can always come back another day."

"Yes, I should like that."

The foursome continued to wander, pointing out areas of interest and generally enjoying the feeling of timelessness associated with places of great antiquity. Eventually, Laura and Edward wandered off on their own, leaving Lavinia and Martine to make their way towards The Oaks, a pretty area to the right of the cathedral.

Sitting down in the shade of a huge oak tree, Lavinia found her thoughts returning to Nicholas. She couldn't help but wonder how he was feeling. Poor man, she mused sadly. What a weight of guilt he must be carrying. He was blaming himself for having failed in his mission.

And yet he hadn't failed. He had taken care of the man they'd suspected of being Leclerc, just as he had set out to do. How was he to know that the true danger was from another person altogether?

"Well, good afternoon, Lady Duplesse, Miss Duplesse. What a pleasant coincidence this is."

Lavinia went very still, aware that what little pleasure she felt for the day had abruptly vanished. Lord Rushton was strolling across the lawn towards them.

Unfortunately, Martine was clearly not in the least displeased. "Lord Rushton!" she said brightly. *"Qu'est ce que vous—"*

"Martine!" Lavinia chided her.

"But *maman,* Lord Rushton speaks French so fluently—"

"I am well aware of that, Martine, but you are in England now, and I would thank you to remember to speak English."

Lavinia knew that her voice was sharp, but she couldn't help it. Lord Rushton seemed to bring out the worst in her. She lifted her eyes to the man in front of her. "Good afternoon, Lord Rushton. What are you doing here?"

If Rushton noticed that her voice was decidedly cool, he gave no indication of it. "I am simply enjoying the pleasure of the day, like yourselves."

"Indeed." Lavinia's smile was reserved. "I am surprised to find you so far from London."

"It is not really all that far," Rushton observed. "Besides, London is so quiet these days."

"Have you come to see the cathedral?" Martine asked, mindful of her stepmother's censure.

Rushton smiled at her with a trace of condescension. "I have seen the cathedral many times, Miss Duplesse. It holds little wonder for me now. Though seeing it through your eyes could add a new element of enjoyment. May I join you?"

Lavinia stiffened. She desperately wanted to say no, but to do so would appear the height of bad manners. After all, what could she object to? The man merely wanted to walk with them.

"If that is your wish, Lord Rushton," Lavinia said finally. "Though I fear you may find our company and our conversation sadly lacking."

"On the contrary, Lady Duplesse, how could I find the company of two such beautiful and charming ladies the least bit tiresome?"

Lavinia inclined her head at the compliment, but her feeling of disquiet remained. Especially when they began strolling again and Rushton seemed inclined to monopolize Martine's attention. He had a tendency to draw the girl away, whispering things to her and causing her to blush. When he bent his head a little too close to hers, however, Lavinia decided enough was enough.

"Come, Martine, I think we should be heading back to the carriage. Mr. Kingsley and Miss Beaufort will be looking for us."

Martine returned at once, but Lavinia could see that the girl was disappointed—and a little annoyed.

"Is Lord Longworth not with you today, Lady Duplesse?" Rushton said conversationally.

"No, I fear he had to return to London unexpectedly."

"Oh? Nothing serious, I hope. Or has he perhaps regained his memory?"

Lavinia was not sure if she detected a sudden watchfulness in his gaze. "Unfortunately, nothing has changed in that regard, my lord. He simply needed to attend to some matters concerning the estate. He promised to return as soon as he could." Lavinia lowered her voice so that Martine, walking slightly ahead of them, could not hear. "And I would remind you, Lord Rushton, that I do not approve of your attentions towards my stepdaughter. I would be grateful if you would not attempt to approach her again."

Rushton swept her a mocking bow, but made no reply. He took a last glance at Martine, who had turned to look back at them in surprise, before pivoting on his heel and walking towards the cathedral.

"*Maman,* why are you so upset?" Martine asked when Lavinia reached her side.

"I am not upset," she replied, striving for composure. "But let us hurry. Laura and Mr. Kingsley will surely be waiting for us by now."

Lavinia said very little on the ride back to Rose Cottage. Fortunately, Martine more than made up for her stepmother's silence, filling the two-hour drive with chatter about the cathedral, the town, the old Roman buildings and their unexpected meeting with Lord Rushton. Laura cast a quick glance at Lavinia when the man's name was first mentioned, but did not ask about the incident until they were back at the house.

"Lavinia, what was Lord Rushton doing in Canterbury?"

"I don't know. He tried to say it was nothing more than a coincidence, but I have trouble believing that. And I certainly don't like the way he looks at Martine." Lavinia drew a deep breath, forcing herself to calm down. "Hopefully, after today, though, we won't be troubled by him again."

Laura moved a step closer to her. "Did you say something to Lord Rushton?"

"Yes, I did, and I would rather that you not tell Nicholas. He has enough on his plate right now. Besides, I'm probably just being . . . over-sensitive."

"If you are concerned about the man's intentions—"

"Laura, I want you to promise."

Her friend hesitated, clearly loath to commit to such a promise when she didn't know the extent of Lord Rushton's transgression.

"Oh, very well," she relented finally. "But if he troubles you again, I think it only right that you tell Nicholas."

"If he troubles me again, I shall," Lavinia said. "But hopefully he received my message quite clearly this afternoon!"

NICHOLAS DECIDED NOT to return to the country immediately, feeling it might be worth his while to spend a little time in London in an attempt to discover anything he could pertaining to Lord Winchester's murder. The clubs, of course, were buzzing with the news. It was generally accepted that Winchester had been set upon by a gang of footpads and killed during a robbery attempt. The fact that his purse, watch and fob were missing corroborated the story. Only a handful of people had been put wise to the true nature of Winchester's death.

It was for this reason that Nicholas retired to his club two nights later. He had hoped that through casual conversation, or even selective eavesdropping, he might learn something that would benefit him in his search. This . . . mystery man had to show himself sometime, and Nicholas knew it would take only a small slip for the blackguard to expose himself. Unfortunately, time was on the other man's side—time and anonymity.

"Lord Longworth, I thought I saw you come in." Lord Havermere approached Nicholas's table in a leisurely fashion. "Still no luck with the memory?"

Nicholas shook his head and put down the paper he had been perusing. "Not a bit. I begin to think the doctors were wrong. I don't think my memory is going to come back at all." He indicated the vacant chair opposite him. "Would you care to join me?"

"If you will allow me to buy you a drink?"

Nicholas inclined his head. "I wouldn't say no to a cognac, thank you."

Havermere signalled for the waiter. As he did, Nicholas studied the other man's face. "You seem in good spirits tonight, Havermere. Have you been lucky at cards or at love?"

"Neither. But then, I don't trouble myself with one and don't bother about the other. Although," Havermere said with a wink, "I might be persuaded to take Mademoiselle Chaufrière were she available."

Nicholas looked at him blankly. "Mademoiselle Chaufrière? Is she an actress?"

Havermere laughed. "My good man, she is the most exquisite Cyprian in London. Are you telling me you don't remember her, either?"

Nicholas smiled sheepishly. "I'm afraid I wouldn't know her if I fell over her."

"Dear me, you really have lost your memory. Well, it's probably just as well. A costly expense, a mistress." Havermere smiled urbanely. "Especially for a man contemplating marriage. Speaking of which, this memory loss must be a dashed nuisance with regards to your lovely fiancée."

"How do you mean?"

"Well, one minute ready to marry the woman, the next not even remembering who she is. Bit of a turnabout, I should think."

Nicholas's smile could have meant anything. "I just have to start over again, as they say. Fortunately, Lavinia is being most patient with me."

Havermere's smile was smug. "You mean in giving you time to fall in love with her again?"

Resentment sharpened Nicholas's voice. "That's not what I meant."

"Now, now, Longworth, there's no need to fly up in the boughs," Havermere said quickly. "All I'm saying is that when a man loses his memory, the good memories as well as the bad are lost, are they not?''

''The feelings that inspired the good memories can be recreated,'' Nicholas said. ''Which is why Lavinia and I decided not to break off our betrothal. We are giving ourselves time for those feelings to develop.''

''And if they do not?''

Nicholas's face was carefully expressionless. ''I have every reason to believe that they will.''

Havermere shrugged eloquently. ''Love takes a long time to grow.''

''I have time enough, Havermere.''

''Yes, I suppose.'' Havermere poured out two glasses of cognac. ''You are a fortunate man, Longworth.''

Nicholas smiled, but his eyes were cool. ''All things considered, yes, I suppose I am.''

''The stepdaughter, Martine, is charming. And so devoted to her stepmother. She reminds me of her father, though. Did you know François Duplesse?''

''If I did, I don't remember.''

''But of course, I keep forgetting,'' Havermere said with a laugh. ''Forgive me. It's just so hard to imagine not being able to remember anything. People, places, even voices.''

''As I said, a complete blank.''

They made desultory conversation for a few more minutes. Then, as the clock in the hall struck twelve, Havermere looked up in surprise. ''Dear me, is it that time already? I must take myself off. Told Rushton I'd meet him at The Club House before midnight.''

Nicholas glanced at the man. ''The Club House?''

''Yes. On Bennet Street.'' Havermere winked. ''One of the less-respectable places for a gentleman to be seen, but there's always something of interest going on. You never know who you're going to bump into.'' He smiled down at Nicholas as he stood up. ''Lovely chatting with you, old boy. Do keep me informed as to the memory. Oh, please stay and have another cognac, on me.''

Nicholas picked up his newspaper as soon as Havermere left. But when the door closed behind him, he slowly lowered it again. The man had been pumping him. No, more than that, he had been testing him, trying to trip him up on his knowledge of the Cyprian, and of François Duplesse.

But why? Why would Lord Havermere be interested in trying to find out how much he was able to remember? And why the sudden interest in Lavinia? Nicholas hadn't failed to note the admiration in Havermere's voice when he'd spoken of her. Admiration and . . . desire?

Jealousy slammed into Nicholas's stomach like a blow from an iron fist. Bloody hell! Was it possible that Havermere was interested in Lavinia? Was he hoping that Lavinia might tire of him, and eventually start looking for someone else? Was that why he had been testing him? Baiting him?

Nicholas felt his mood veer sharply towards anger. The more he thought about it, the more sense it made. It would certainly explain the watchfulness in Havermere's eyes—and his questions regarding Nicholas's memory. No doubt Havermere hoped his memory might never return, and that eventually Lavinia would get tired of waiting. Maybe Havermere saw himself as the one she might eventually turn to!

He picked up the bottle of cognac Havermere had so graciously provided and poured himself another glass. "In a pig's bloody eye!" he swore softly.

TRUE TO HIS WORD, Nicholas did return before the weekend. He found Lavinia and her guests in the drawing-room, playing cards. Martine was reading a book on the settee and was the first to spot him. "Nicholas, you're back!"

Lavinia glanced up from her cards. Resisting the urge to rush headlong into his arms, she gracefully rose and held out her hand to him. "Nicholas, was everything all right in London?"

"Everything was...much as I expected." His smile slipped for no more than a moment, long enough for Edward to realize that something was wrong.

"Well, we have missed you."

"Oh, yes, Nicholas, we had such a lovely time in Canterbury," Martine said. "I must tell you all about it."

"And you will, my dear, but perhaps not right now," Lavinia said gently. She had noticed the worry in her fiancé's eyes the moment he had stepped into the room. "I think perhaps Nicholas is tired after his journey."

He smiled at her gratefully. "Yes, I confess I am weary. It seems I am not as recovered from my injuries as I would like to think."

Martine was all contrition. "Oh, *pardon,* Nicholas, *je ne pensais pas—*"

"Martine," Lavinia reminded her.

"Oh, bother!" the girl groaned, using a very English expression indeed. "I was just so eager to tell you about it."

"And tell me you shall, Martine, for I am anxious to hear," Nicholas said kindly. "I know, we shall discuss it over breakfast, you and I. Would you like that?"

"Oh, yes, I would like that very much."

"Good." Nicholas turned to greet Lavinia. "And how is my favourite hostess?"

Lavinia laughed, and blushed prettily. "Very well, now that all her guests are returned."

"Yes, and in good time for the soirée, too," Laura observed.

"I told you I would be back in time," Nicholas said. "Edward, I wonder if I might have a word with you. I bumped into an old friend of yours while I was in Town. He wanted me to pass along a message for you."

"Did he indeed? Well, I am consumed with curiosity." Edward rose and bowed to the ladies. "If you will excuse me."

"Ladies," Nicholas said.

When they had gone, Laura turned to Lavinia with a long-suffering smile. "I vow, it is just the same with those two as it was with Edward and Lord Marwood. Always disappearing together somewhere, always talking about things."

"What things?"

"Oh, I don't know. Things we're not supposed to know about. Matters concerning Lord Osborne, most of the time," Laura admitted. "Charlotte did warn me that I would have to get used to it if I hoped to marry Edward. Of course, at the time, I never thought I would be fortunate enough to... That is, I had no idea he felt...that way," she finished, blushing.

Lavinia smiled. "Well, he obviously did. But I do know what you mean about the two of them disappearing. Just once, I would like to be a fly on the wall when Edward and Nicholas are discussing business."

"WINCHESTER KILLED?" Edward repeated in a shocked. voice. "But how did it happen? And when?"

"A few nights ago. Made to look like a robbery. One bullet fired at close range." Nicholas sighed. "Winchester never had a chance, poor blighter."

"Why are they calling it robbery?"

"His purse was taken, as well as his gold watch and fob. The killer obviously wanted everyone to think it was a simple robbery."

Edward drew a heavy breath. "Then it's begun."

"So it would seem. Osborne has warned Sullivan, and with Winchester dead, that just leaves Osborne, Marwood and the three of us."

"I hope to God Charlotte and Devon decide to prolong their wedding trip," Edward muttered. "Not a pleasant thought, coming back to find that someone is trying to kill you."

"We'll just have to get word to Marwood as soon as he does return. As for the rest of us, I think we had better keep in very close contact."

"Nicholas, do you think it's wise not to tell Lavinia of the danger she's in? I mean, I understand that you don't want her to worry, but surely she has a right to protect herself. You can't do that for her."

"I can to the best of my ability."

"Yes, but you're not with her all the time," Edward pointed out. "It would be a lot easier if you were married, of course, but given that you're not..."

"Yes, I know." Nicholas thought about it for a few minutes. "And you're right. I suppose it is only fitting that she know. I've asked Osborne to have one of his men keep an eye on her house in London. I want to know everyone who goes in and out of there."

"I think that's a good idea." Edward took a sip of brandy from the glass he had brought in with him. "Anything else of interest happen while you were gone?"

"Yes, now that you ask," Nicholas said, unable to prevent the chill from entering his voice. "I went to the club the other night, hoping to stumble across something, when Havermere came up and started chatting to me. He left around midnight for a place called The Club House."

"The Club House!" Edward frowned. "I say, that's a bit seedy for the likes of Havermere. Didn't think he'd be the type to frequent the hells."

"Well, I don't know about that. He said he was meeting Rushton."

"Rushton?" Edward sat up. "Now that is a coincidence. Lavinia told me that she and Martine bumped into him in Canterbury the other day."

Nicholas glanced at him quickly. "What would Rushton be doing in Canterbury?"

"I don't know. Why don't you ask Lavinia?"

Nicholas's hand closed tightly around the stem of his glass. "Yes, I think perhaps I shall."

CHAPTER TEN

NICHOLAS DECIDED NOT TO broach the subject of Lord Rushton with Lavinia that night. He was surprisingly tired after the trip from London and turned in early. But once again his sleep was restless, punctuated by dreams of faceless people, all of whom spoke in low, monotone voices. He tossed endlessly, trying to find escape from the images, but they were always there, waiting for him when he drifted off again.

Consequently, when he awoke the next morning, he had dark shadows under his eyes and was in a less-than-amiable frame of mind. Recalling that he had promised to talk with Martine, however, he reluctantly rose, and with his valet's help, eventually made his way downstairs, hoping to enjoy a fortifying cup of coffee before she arrived.

Martine was already there. "Good morning, Nicholas," she greeted him brightly. "I have been waiting for you."

Nicholas regarded her in wry amusement. "My dear girl, it is far too early to be about. You should still be abed."

"You are not."

"Of course not, but gentlemen generally do not linger in their beds as long as ladies."

"Well, I do not linger in bed, either," Martine asserted. "I knew we were to talk this morning. Would you like me to pour you some coffee?"

Nicholas smiled ruefully. "Yes, thank you, that would be lovely."

He watched as she handled the silver pot with a grace not unlike Lavinia's. "There you are," she said, handing him the cup.

"Thank you, Martine. Now, tell me about your trip to Canterbury."

"Oh, it was so lovely, Nicholas. The cathedral, the Roman wall. It has such a sense of history, *n'est-ce pas?*"

"Does that surprise you?"

Martine tilted her head to one side. "No. I know that England is a very old country. It is like France in that way. Have you seen Versailles, Nicholas?"

"I'm afraid I don't know, Martine. I assume it is very impressive."

"*Oui,* it is. And I felt that same kind of emotion when I saw the cathedral, which is so very beautiful. There were many young ladies sketching."

"What else happened on your trip, Martine?" Nicholas asked casually. "I understand you met someone."

He noted the colour deepening in the girl's cheeks. "Yes, we saw . . . Lord Rushton."

Nicholas took a sip of coffee. "And how did that come about?"

"*Maman* and I were sitting on a bench and he walked right up to us. Isn't that a coincidence—that he would be there on the very same day?"

"A coincidence indeed." Nicholas set his cup on the table. "Did Lord Rushton say why he was in Canterbury?"

"He mentioned that he liked to get away from Town now and then. He said London was very quiet just now."

Quiet? A prominent peer killed in a supposed robbery and Rushton called that quiet? Interesting.

"Tell me, Martine, did Lord Rushton talk to Lavinia at all?"

Martine's smile faded. "Yes, but I do not think *maman* likes Lord Rushton, Nicholas. I heard them talking just before he left and I think she was angry."

"Did you hear what they were talking about?"

"No. I was walking a little ahead of them. But when I turned around, I saw Lord Rushton bow and then walk away."

Nicholas phrased his next question carefully. "Martine, apart from the time you met Lord Rushton in London, and the other day at Canterbury, have you seen the gentleman any other time?"

Nicholas knew he had his answer when the girl's face flushed crimson. "I see you have. When, Martine?"

"I did not do anything wrong, Nicholas."

"I'm not saying you did, my dear, but I would like to know how it is you and Lavinia keep running into Lord Rushton. Where did you see him the other time?"

Martine bit her lip. "He was . . . in the village. I told *maman* I wanted to get some ribbon for my bonnet."

"I see. So you met him there. Did he arrange that?"

Martine nodded guiltily. "Yes. Before we left London."

Nicholas tried not to show his anger. He didn't like what he was hearing. "Martine, does Lord Rushton . . . ask you anything about Lavinia, or myself?"

"Oh yes, Nicholas, he is most concerned about you. He always asks how you are feeling, and if your memory has returned."

Nicholas felt the hair on the back of his neck rise. "You didn't tell him about the necklace, did you?"

Martine blushed. "I nearly did, but then I remembered that you said not to tell anyone in case it got their hopes up."

"That's right, Martine. I wouldn't want to raise anyone's hopes needlessly." *Or suspicions.* "For that reason, it is very important that we keep the information to ourselves, all right?"

"Yes, Nicholas, I promise."

"That's my girl."

"Nicholas?"

"Yes?"

"Have you remembered . . . anything else?"

Nicholas shook his head, convinced that it was better for everyone that she not know. "I'm afraid not, Martine. But I am still hopeful."

The door to the breakfast parlour opened and they both turned as Lavinia entered. "So this is where the two of you are," she said. "I looked in your room, Martine, but Hélène said you had already gone down. I might have known you were meeting a gentleman."

"I just wanted to tell Nicholas about our trip. And now that I have, may I be excused?"

"Where are you off to now?"

"The big white cat in the stable has had kittens, and Jim said he would show them to me."

"Jim?" Nicholas enquired.

Lavinia chuckled. "My old groom. All right, Martine, off you go."

Martine dashed out of the room, leaving Nicholas and Lavinia behind to smile at each other. "One minute an elegant young lady, the next, a giggling girl off to see kittens." Lavinia shook her head. "I never quite know where I am with her."

"I suppose that's one of the joys of motherhood."

"Mmm, I'm afraid I didn't have much of a run up to it, though," Lavinia admitted. "By the time I came on the scene, most of Martine's growing up had already been done."

Nicholas laced his fingers together on the table. "She still needs you, Lavinia. She's not as sure of herself as she likes to make out."

"Yes, I know. But then, at other times, she seems so dreadfully mature that I really feel quite helpless beside her. Lately, I have begun to feel that there is a distance growing between us. She isn't telling me . . . everything that's going on in her life." Lavinia fingered the lace edge of the tablecloth and glanced at Nicholas. "Nicholas, what do you think of...Lord Rushton?"

"Rushton?" Nicholas schooled his expression to one of neutrality. "Why do you ask?"

"Because I think that Martine is...intrigued by him," she said carefully.

"Do you mean infatuated?"

Lavinia blushed. She should have known better. Nicholas—even without his memory—was a very astute man. "Yes, I suppose. I know they haven't had much to do with each other, but—"

"On the contrary, Lavinia, they've had more contact than you think." Nicholas proceeded to tell Lavinia what Martine had confided.

"Nicholas, I don't like this," Lavinia said, unable to hide her concern any longer. "It bothers me that the man always seems to be laying in wait for her."

"Is that what you think he's doing?" Nicholas enquired.

"Yes. And I'm afraid I've not been very subtle about my own reservations towards him."

He drew a long breath. "Lavinia, what do you know about Rushton?"

"Next to nothing," she admitted. "He claims to have known François and his family, but it must have been long before I married him. I never heard François mention the man."

"And did Martine remember ever having seen him about the house?"

"No, but she was probably quite young when Lord Rushton was visiting."

"But why does he seem so interested in her all of a sudden? And why does he keep on asking her about my memory?"

Lavinia sighed. "I can only think that his interest in Martine stems from the fact that she is an extremely pretty girl and of marriageable age, though it pains me to think so in this case. As for his interest in you, I assume it arises from the same thing. He knows how close the two of you are. Perhaps he hopes to work his way into her heart by affecting an interest in you."

Unfortunately, Nicholas knew that affecting an interest was all it really was. He no more thought Lord Rushton was genuinely concerned about his welfare than he believed that the man's bumping into Lavinia and Martine in Canterbury the other day had been a coincidence. Too many incidents involving the mysterious Lord Rushton were being labelled "coincidental" for his liking.

NICHOLAS'S FEELINGS OF uncertainty grew. He recognized that his insecurities were getting far too strong a hold on him. There had been no more elusive flashes of memory. Even his dreams were growing more nebulous. For the first time since his return to London, Nicholas truly began to fear that his memory lapse would turn out to be permanent.

"Lavinia, I think I should...go back to London for a while."

The suggestion came like a bolt out of the blue, catching Lavinia totally unawares. They had gone out for an early afternoon ride to enjoy the weather and had dismounted to walk in companionable silence, though Lavinia was well aware that Nicholas's mind was far from restful. She could read the play of emotions on his face like an open book.

"Go back to London?" she repeated. "But why? Are you tired of Rose Cottage?"

He shook his head. "I don't think anyone could ever tire of this place," he admitted softly. "No, it has nothing to do with Rose Cottage. Or with you," he said, before she had a chance to suggest it.

"Then why do you wish to leave?"

Nicholas stopped walking, forcing Lavinia to do the same. "I don't know exactly. I just sense that something should be happening. I feel that by staying out here in the countryside, I'm missing something, that I'm not going to be able to make it happen."

"Make what happen, Nicholas?" Lavinia asked. Then her face went pale. "Have you had another flashback?"

"No. There's been nothing. But I can't help but feel that it's just there beyond my reach, waiting for me to grab it." He turned and looked at her earnestly. "I know why you wanted me to come here, Lavinia, and believe me, I thought it was a good idea, too. But it hasn't worked—not the way we wanted it to. Now I think it's time to try another tactic."

Lavinia stared at him in puzzlement. "What other tactic?"

"One I probably should have used earlier," Nicholas admitted. "But I can't do it here. I have to go back to London."

"Then I will come back with you," she said immediately.

"Oh, no, you won't." Nicholas was adamant. "You're far safer in the country."

"Safer?" Lavinia glanced at him and chuckled. "Why wouldn't I be safe in Town?"

Nicholas bit his lip. That had been an unfortunate slip. He still wasn't sure he wanted Lavinia to know she was on Leclerc's list. "Look, Lavinia, I understand what you're trying to do, but this is something I think I'm going to have to do for myself. You've done everything humanly possible. Now it's my turn."

Lavinia glanced at him with huge, worried eyes. "And what about...us, Nicholas? Is it time to do something about that, too?"

Nicholas turned and gazed into her eyes, seeing the hurt, the worry, the pain clouding them. He shook his head.

"No. My relationship with you hasn't been given a chance to develop. Not while I've been so busy trying to reestablish who *I* am. I want to give us all the time we deserve."

Lavinia smiled sadly. "Perhaps there is no need, Nicholas. You said you fell in love with me at first sight. If it is taking you so long to make up your mind this time, perhaps I already have my answer."

They rode back to Rose Cottage in silence. Watching her, Nicholas couldn't help but feel that she had just taken the first, tiny step away from him. The thought caused him more pain than he could have imagined possible.

NICHOLAS MET WITH EDWARD later that same night. He knew his friend was planning on returning to London in two days. But when Nicholas told him that he would be leaving, too, there was no mistaking the surprise on Edward's face.

"But why?" he asked, puzzled at the abrupt turn of events. "Has something happened?"

"No, but I now realize that nothing is going to as long as I remain here." He ran his fingers through his dark hair in frustration. "There's a killer walking free in London, Edward. A killer that only I can recognize. I'm never going to be able to identify him by sitting here in Kent. There's nothing else for it. I *must* return to London."

"That's all very well, my friend, but the problem is you *can't* recognize him. You wouldn't know him if he walked up and slapped you across the face."

Nicholas shook his head. "Not at the moment, no. But I refuse to believe the situation won't change. If there hadn't been those two instances, I would feel more inclined to believe there's no hope. But I know differently. If something has come back to me from the past, other things will, too!"

"All right. What do you intend to do?"

"I intend to be as visible as possible," Nicholas told him. "I intend to go back to London and be seen in public as much as I can. The more I hear, the more I'll learn. And the more I learn, the more likely I'll be to stumble upon something that will trigger my memory."

"You realize that we're going to have to change some plans," Edward said. "We can't both go back to London and leave the ladies here."

"No. I originally told Lavinia that she should stay here, but I think it better that we all return to London together. Lavinia has planned this soirée for Saturday night, and I'm not going to disappoint her by leaving. But I think we had best be prepared to leave Sunday, or Monday at the latest."

Edward nodded in agreement. "All right, if you're sure. But it may look rather obvious if we all leave together. Perhaps Laura and I should leave Sunday, then you can follow with Lavinia and Martine early in the week."

"Good idea. We have to move very carefully now, Edward. Until we know exactly who we're dealing with, we can't afford to take any chances. If the murderer gets even a hint that we're on to him, the results could be devastating!"

LAVINIA SAT in her bedroom and put the finishing touches on her toilette, trying to ignore the words of doubt the voice in the back of her mind was whispering.

Something is going on. Something terrible is about to happen. Someone is going to get hurt.

Yes, something was happening, and it had to do with Nicholas. Just as she had felt a premonition the night he had been shot, so Lavinia felt tension mounting again. The only difference was that this time the sensation of danger was not focused. This time, it seemed to be all around her, and try as she might, she could not shake the feeling.

She turned at the sound of a knock on her door. "Come in, Martine." The door swung open, but it was not her stepdaughter who stood on the threshold. "Nicholas!"

Nicholas took in the sight of Lavinia sitting at her dressing-table, noting the elegantly upswept hairstyle, the richness of the emerald-green gown and the compassion and intelligence in the bright blue eyes. He couldn't help but marvel that this beautiful woman was actually bothering to wait for him.

She could have had her pick from among dozens of men, all of whom she knew, all of whom knew her. And many, Nicholas was quickly finding out, would have been very happy to take his place at her side—Havermere first and foremost. It was not an encouraging thought.

"Have you nothing to say to me this evening, my lord?" Lavinia flashed a slow, seductive smile. "Does my appearance not meet with your approval?"

Nicholas took a deep breath. "I fear that nothing I could say would seem sufficient. You quite literally defy words."

A warmth flashed in her eyes. "How is it, Nicholas, that even when you do not use traditional words of flattery, I feel that I have been complimented far more than if you had?"

He laughed, the sound a throaty, masculine chuckle. "Because hopefully, I am able to communicate more by the manner in which I say things than by the words I use."

"Yes, I would say you succeed quite admirably at that." Lavinia reached for her fan and looped its silk cord around her wrist. "Shall we go?" She saw the momentary hesitation in his eyes. "Nicholas? Is something wrong?"

"Wrong? No, of course not," he said, abruptly changing his mind. He had been about to tell her that they would all be leaving when the weekend was over, but decided against it. There would be time enough when the evening was done. "Come, my dear, your guests await."

Lavinia slipped her hand through his arm. "On the contrary, Nicholas, *our* guests await."

With Martine's help, the servants had decorated Rose Cottage so that it resembled something out of a fairy tale. Hundreds of candles illuminated the entry and main reception rooms, while lengths of rose-coloured silk draping the walls cast a warm glow over everything. It was a cosy, intimate feeling, and Nicholas knew that it was a reflection of Lavinia herself.

As for his fiancée, Nicholas found himself watching her frequently throughout the course of the evening. His eyes returned to her time and again, drawn by the sound of her laughter, held by the richness of her beauty.

When she eventually returned to his side, she was touched by the admiration she saw on his face. "Are you having a good time?"

"I am, because you are a consummate hostess, Lavinia Duplesse," Nicholas murmured. He tucked her hand into his arm and led her out through the French doors onto the terrace, where hundreds of tiny candles glowed like stars. "There is a tremendous feeling of warmth in this house tonight, and it is all because of you."

Lavinia tried not to show how much his words moved her. "You give me far too much credit, my dear. It is simply that you are enjoying yourself. You feel no pressure, and you know you are with friends."

Nicholas glanced back towards the crowded room. "Yes, you are fortunate to have gathered such a congenial group of people around you. I have not heard one unkind remark about anyone tonight." He chuckled ruefully. "I did not think it was possible."

Lavinia's laughter was as clear and light as a bell. "Oh Nicholas, not everyone is out to impress, or to criticize. I should almost think that that is one of the few benefits of your condition—you are forming all your opinions again."

"Lavinia, there you are," Anthony Hewitt said. "I thought I heard your voice. And Lord Longworth, good evening."

"Evening, Hewitt. A pleasure to see you again."

The two men shook hands warmly. "Actually, it was you I wanted to see, Lord Longworth. I understand you are recently returned from London. No doubt you heard about that nasty bit of business with Lord Winchester."

Lavinia turned to Anthony in surprise. "Oh? What happened?"

"You didn't hear about the robbery?"

Nicholas quickly spoke up. "It need not concern you, Lavinia. Unfortunately, footpads and thieves are as common as streetwalkers in London after dark."

"Thieves are one thing, Longworth," Anthony agreed, "but murderers are another altogether."

Lavinia blanched. "Murderers! Dear Lord, has someone been killed?"

"Yes. Poor old Winchester. Set upon by a gang of thieves. Had his purse and watch taken, and then was shot dead. I tell you, it is no longer safe to walk the streets," Hewitt commented ruefully. "The next time I go up to London, I shall make damn sure I don't step out of my... Lavinia! Are you all right?"

Nicholas turned, and grabbed his fiancée's arm just as she swayed forward. "Lavinia!"

"I'm... all right," she said weakly, avoiding his eyes.

"Perhaps you would like to go and lie down for a while," Nicholas suggested.

She looked at him then, her gaze probing. "Yes, I think that might be a good idea. I am sure it is just the excitement of the evening."

"Hewitt, will you excuse us?"

"Yes, of course. I hope it wasn't something I said, Lavinia," he added belatedly. "I didn't mean to upset you."

Lavinia managed a weak smile. "No, you did not. And I'm fine. Really. Nicholas, why don't you stay here with Anthony. I'll just take a few moments alone. Pray do not tell anyone."

"Of course not." He escorted her as far as the bottom of the stairs. "Are you sure you can manage on your own?"

She heard the genuine note of concern in his voice, but shook her head. She was beginning to realize why she had sensed danger before. "Quite sure." She turned and met his gaze. "Though I wish you had been truthful with me earlier."

Nicholas felt the weight of his deception more fully. "I did not wish to alarm you."

Lavinia nodded, and then slowly turned and made her way upstairs. So, there was more going on than Nicholas had told her about. It didn't surprise her. It explained why he had been so quiet since his return from London. It explained why he had closeted himself with Edward the moment he'd returned. And it explained the look of concern she had glimpsed in his eyes earlier.

A murderer was stalking British agents in London. He'd already killed Winchester, and had promised to kill more. And as long as Nicholas's memory was gone, the villain could waltz undetected through the drawing-rooms of Society. He could laugh and share a joke with anyone—before pulling out a pistol and cold-bloodedly shooting them dead. And only Nicholas knew who he was.

Dear God, was it any wonder the poor man was suffering so?

THE SOIRÉE WAS OVER. The last of the guests had gone. Martine had retired to her room, leaving Laura, Edward, Nicholas and Lavinia in the drawing-room. Their faces reflected the gravity of the situation.

"So this is why you want us to return to London," Lavinia said quietly. She spoke without noticeable inflection and directed her question towards Nicholas, who nodded tersely.

"I think it best," he answered. "Osborne has warned Sullivan of the danger, and they are both taking extra precautions. But as they have voiced their intention of remaining in London, it seems likely that the murderer will stay there, too."

"Then why do you need to be there?" Laura's voice shook as she turned to Edward. "Surely it would be safer for you and Nicholas if you were distanced from the others."

"On the contrary, Laura," Edward replied, "we probably stand a better chance of catching the man if we are all in the same area. We can observe other peoples' movements."

"Staying in London didn't help Lord Winchester," Laura retaliated stubbornly.

"No, but then Winchester was completely unsuspecting," Nicholas said in a saddened voice. "What gentleman has not walked through the London streets after dark at some time or other?"

"When would you like us to be ready to leave?" Lavinia enquired.

Nicholas silently blessed his fiancée's level-headedness. "Edward and I have already discussed this. We don't want to make it look too obvious, so he and Laura will return tomorrow. I thought perhaps you, Martine and I could return Tuesday."

Lavinia nodded. "We'll be ready."

"Well, in that case, I think I had better turn in," Laura said. "Tomorrow will be a busy day. I shall have my maid start packing first thing."

Nicholas smiled. "Thank you, Laura. And I am sorry to have brought this idyllic stay to such an abrupt end."

"Well, at least we were able to enjoy it for a while," Laura said charitably. "Good night all."

"Good night." Edward slowly rose, stretching his long limbs. "I suppose I'd best turn in, too. We can make the rest of the arrangements in the morning."

Nicholas nodded. "Yes. Good night, Edward."

When they were alone, Lavinia turned her gaze on Nicholas. "You didn't tell me the truth, did you?"

He studied her carefully. "What do you mean?"

She rose and made her way to his side, sinking down on the carpet by his feet, just as she had done the first time he had seen her upon his return from France. "You didn't tell me the names of all of the people on Leclerc's list."

At his look of dismay, she smiled rather sadly. "You shouldn't be surprised, Nicholas. One of the things you used to admire most about me was my intuitiveness, and I fear that has not changed. My name is on that list, too, isn't it?"

When he didn't answer, Lavinia gave a brief, mirthless laugh. "Of course it is. It would have to be, being that I was married to François. They tried to get me after they killed my husband, but I managed to escape. Why should I think that this man would not want to settle the score with me now?"

Nicholas reached for her hands and raised them both to his lips. "I didn't want to frighten you, Lavinia. And until Winchester was killed, I wasn't even sure we had any reason to be concerned. But as soon as Osborne told me, I knew that the danger existed. And until we find this man, I can't afford to have you here where I can't protect you."

"You don't have to explain, Nicholas, I understand why we have to return. But it doesn't mean I feel any better about it. Do you realize the kind of danger you're putting yourself in?"

"Yes." Nicholas met her gaze directly. "But as long as I have no recollection of what happened, I pose no immediate threat to the killer. He's playing a game of cat and mouse. He knows I can't get away, but he's not ready to kill me just yet."

"Dear God, don't say that!" Lavinia shut her eyes.

"But it's true. That is why I told Osborne that, even if my memory does return, no one must know but him and me. It's the only way to ensure my safety, and ultimately yours."

Lavinia searched his face. "Has your memory returned, Nicholas? Surely you can tell me."

He shook his head. "No, it hasn't," he growled. "In truth, I don't know that it ever will. There hasn't been anything since the last time. Not a flash, not a premonition, not even a—a feeling that I was getting closer to recapturing my past. Don't you see, Lavinia, that's another reason why I have to go back. I have to make something happen. I have to force the issue!''

"But you can't force it!" she cried. "You've already seen that. The harder you try, the more elusive your memory becomes."

"Then I have to stop relying on my memory," he told her quietly. "I was a good agent before this happened. I have to believe that part of my ability came from within, from my own instincts and reactions. I have to confront this devil and the only place I can do that is in London. I know he's there, Lavinia. And one way or another, I'll track him down. For all of our sakes, I have to!''

EDWARD AND LAURA LEFT around noon the following day. Nicholas, Martine and Lavinia waved them off, and then returned to the house to continue their own packing. Martine had been saddened to learn that they would be returning to London, but had accepted it with the perpetual optimism of youth.

"You're not too disappointed, I hope, Martine," Lavinia said as they walked back to the house.

"Not really. I love Rose Cottage, and I look forward to coming back here again, but I am anxious to get back to London, too." The girl's eyes shone brightly. "There is so much to see and do in Town. Parties to go to, shops to buy pretty things in."

"And the company of handsome young gentlemen?" Lavinia asked. She was amused to see the blush that suffused her stepdaughter's cheeks. Thankfully, there had been no more mention of Lord Rushton. But Martine was growing up quickly. "Never mind, I will not tease you. But I am glad you are not unhappy about leaving here."

"Are you sorry to leave, *maman?*" Martine asked.

Lavinia glanced at the ivy-covered walls of Rose Cottage and nodded. "Yes, I am. This is a peaceful place, and I feel its serenity like a soothing balm. I feel that . . . nothing bad could ever happen here." She shook her head, wishing she could say the same for London.

By Wednesday night, Rose Cottage was just a memory. Lavinia and Martine were once again settled in the town house in London, and Nicholas had returned to his bachelor premises. He had gone to see Lord Osborne immediately upon his return. Edward was already there, waiting for him. But the news was not good.

"Sullivan's dead," Osborne told him without preamble.

"Dead!" Nicholas gasped. "But what in blazes happened? I thought you were going to warn him."

"I did. He was killed during a hunt. Apparently, he fell from his horse and broke his neck."

"So he wasn't murdered."

Edward drummed his fingers on the desk. "We don't know that for sure, Nicholas. It could have been disguised to look like an accident. I doubt our killer will want to make things too obvious."

"Humph. Damn difficult to make a murder look innocent," Osborne grumbled.

"Difficult, but not impossible." Nicholas studied the fine painting of a race horse on the wall behind Osborne's desk. Strange that he hadn't noticed it the last time he'd been here. "When you think about it, even something as simple as a riding fatality could be made to look like an accident."

Osborne raised an eyebrow. "You're not making me feel any better about this, Longworth."

"Sorry, my lord, but when you consider that the man is a trained killer, you realize he'd hardly resort to obvious means to dispatch his victims."

"Well, I suppose there's nothing we can do but maintain a careful watch and ensure that none of us on that list are left alone at any time," Edward said. "Not even in our homes."

"Yes, I've no doubt that this man is capable of breaking into houses," Nicholas observed grimly.

"If that's the case, I wonder if it's a good idea for Lavinia and Martine to be left alone in theirs," Osborne said suddenly. "Seems to me it would be a good deal safer to have them living somewhere else for a while."

Nicholas cursed himself for not having thought of that sooner.

"Damn it, you're right. But where? I'd move them into my place, but I hate to think what the Town would say."

"You and Lavinia could always get married," Edward suggested.   Nicholas glanced at him in astonishment. "Married?"

"Well, think about it. It's a perfect solution. You and Lavinia seem to be getting on extremely well, and you certainly like Martine."

"Yes, but—"

"And the banns have already been read. You could be married immediately. Then you could move both of them into your house, giving them the extra protection they need."

"I say, that's not a bad idea," Osborne said suddenly. "And it could work both ways. You could protect Lavinia, and Lavinia could protect you."

"Protect me?" Nicholas stared at him. "How in the world could she protect me?"

"Simply by being there, my friend," Edward explained. "Right now you live alone with just a valet, a cook and a butler in the house. If you were married, Lavinia would be there with you, too. All the time."

"It would also allow the two of you to be seen together," Osborne said. "Whenever Lavinia went out in the evening, it would be with you. And in the daytime, you could have a footman accompany her. But at least you would know that every night she would be coming back to your house."

Nicholas's mind was in turmoil. Marry Lavinia? He'd been so caught up in trying to regain his memory that he'd never really stopped to think about how far their relationship had developed. Did he love the woman enough to spend the rest of his life with her?

More important, was he willing to take the chance that she might not be alive if he *didn't* marry her?

"YOU'RE ASKING ME to...marry you?" Lavinia stared at Nicholas in shock. "But...are you sure?"

"It is something I have given a lot of thought to, Lavinia, and I think it would be a good idea." Nicholas tried not to smile at the look of surprise on her face. "Or perhaps you have had a change of heart yourself."

Lavinia swallowed and quickly shook her head. "N-no, my feelings on the matter have not...changed, Nicholas. It's just that I am somewhat...surprised to hear that you've come to this decision so abruptly, that's all. Dear me, this is most unexpected."

Nicholas smiled and walked towards the settee where she sat. "I understand that the banns have already been read."

"Yes, of course. Before you went away, in fact." Lavinia felt herself blush. "I wasn't going to say anything but...we were to have been married in just a few days time."

"How marvellous. Then we still can be."

"What?" she gasped.

"Well, I see no point in waiting. Do you?"

Lavinia could hardly believe this was happening. "Well, no, I suppose not, but—"

"And then, as soon as we are married, you and Martine can come to live with me," he informed her.

That brought Lavinia up short. "Live with you? But...where?"

"Where? Where do you think? At my house, of course."

"That's very good of you, Nicholas, but I hardly think there will be room enough for everyone. You are living in bachelor's quarters, after all."

Nicholas thought for a moment. "Well, there is the house in Mayfair. I'm sure mother would not mind."

"Perhaps, but I rather doubt she would welcome all of us on such short notice." Lavinia hesitated a moment. "Would you consider living here?"

"Here?" Nicholas glanced around him. He thought for a moment. It might not be a bad idea at that. There was a good deal more traffic on this road than on his own. More difficult for someone to break in unobserved.

"Yes, that might not be a bad idea. At least temporarily. We would, of course, look for something more suitable at the first opportunity."

Lavinia looked into his face and shook her head. "Why, Nicholas? Why all of a sudden like this? It has something to do with this man, doesn't it?" she enquired softly.

"Lavinia, it has nothing to do with—"

"You want to...protect me, don't you? And the best way for you to do that is to have me living with you. Is that right, Nicholas? Is that what prompted this sudden declaration of marriage?"

Nicholas hesitated, not sure of the answer himself. "It is not the only reason, no. But would it be such a bad reason if it were?"

Lavinia shrugged gracefully. "It would not be the worst reason I have heard, of course, but neither would it be the best." She studied his face with loving eyes. "Do you remember how you proposed to me the first time?"

He shook his head wistfully. "Sadly, I do not."

"You were terribly romantic." Lavinia's eyes softened as her memory slipped back to a scene he could not visualize. "I had been back from France only two days. You arrived on the morning of the third day with four perfect red roses."

"Four?"

"Mmm. One for each year you'd been in love with me."

"Romantic devil," he muttered.

"Then you took me into the garden behind the house here. It's not much of a garden, really," Lavinia admitted, "but it was a beautiful day, and the sun was shining brightly. You told me that…every day we had been apart, your heart had broken a little more, but that…you had been able to live with it because every day that passed also meant we were one day closer to the time we would be together."

"I said that?" he whispered huskily.

"Yes. And then you went down on your knee and asked me to marry you."

"Which knee?"

"The right one."

Nicholas sank slowly down, bending his right knee to the floor. "I have no roses, Lavinia, and this is not the garden. But will you…marry me?"

Lavinia felt the sting of tears in her eyes. She had wanted so desperately for this to happen, for Nicholas to say, "Will you marry me?" so that she could put the past behind her and go forward once again. She had dreamed that she would hear the words. And yet, now that she had, they brought her hollow pleasure.

"No, Nicholas. I will not marry you. Not until I know that you are asking for the right reasons. I understand that you want to…protect me, and that it would be easier for you to do so if I were living under your roof—or you under mine. But marriage is for the rest of our lives, dearest," she said, willing him to understand. "Once this man is apprehended, you will still be married to me. And perhaps, knowing that you weren't ready to make the decision when you did, you will end up resenting me."

"No, that could never happen," Nicholas told her vehemently. "I want you, Lavinia. I love you!"

The words were out almost before he realized it, but as soon as he'd said them, Nicholas knew them to be the truth.

He did love her. And he did want her to marry him. Not just for now, but for always. But his momentary hesitation had told Lavinia something else. She shook her head sadly. "You may say that you love me, Nicholas, but it is not in the way you did before, my darling. You cannot love me as totally as you did then. Not when so many other things are weighing on your mind, distracting you."

He shook his head. "I don't understand."

"Nicholas, when you fell in love with me all those years ago, it was because, on the day we met, you knew that there could be no one else in the world for you. Just as I realized that, even as I married another man, I could never love anyone but you. You felt no pressure to fall in love with me. No sense of decency, or obligation."

"My asking you to marry me now has nothing to do with obligation or decency," Nicholas retorted, the rich timbre of his voice striking an answering need in Lavinia's heart. "I'm asking you to marry me because I love you, damn it!"

"No, not totally," Lavinia replied with quiet emphasis. "Part of you is saying that you love me, but another part is telling you that you *should* love me. That you are obligated to love me because of what we meant to each other before your accident. I don't want there to be any sense of obligation, Nicholas. I've had a taste of what it is to love you without reservation, and I cannot accept anything less. I would rather wait—or not marry you at all—than have you look back and feel you've made a mistake."

Nicholas stared down at the floor, the silence lengthening between them. "I don't know what to say," he said finally. "I didn't expect you to say no."

"And I haven't. Not exactly," Lavinia said with a return of her engaging smile. "I'm just saying...not yet. When all of this is over and you are not feeling pressured to do something because you feel you should, ask me again, Nicholas. And even if your memory has not returned, I will give you my answer. I promise."

Nicholas rose and, taking her hands in his, drew her up beside him. "You are an incredible woman, Lavinia Duplesse. And a very sensible one."

"Dear me, how unflattering." Lavinia strove for lightness in her voice, even as her tears trembled dangerously close to the surface. "I remember my governess once telling me that to be sensible was of more value to a lady than being beautiful. I remember disagreeing with her most heartily, even then."

"Ah, but you have the benefit of being both, my dear," Nicholas said. "You are beautiful *and* sensible. And the combination is most attractive." He turned to go, and paused. "Lavinia?"

"Yes?"

"I will ask again."

She nodded. "I certainly hope so, my lord."

CHAPTER ELEVEN

KNOWING THAT LAVINIA and Martine were to stay in their own house only strengthened Nicholas's desire to find the man who had murdered Sullivan and Winchester. He knew he had to be in London for it was here he had sworn to carry out his threats. There was no reason for him to be anywhere else.

Nicholas saw Lavinia every day, stopping by her house frequently to ensure that she and Martine were all right. He took to attending most of the functions he was invited to, and every one that Lavinia was. He would not allow her or Martine to go anywhere on their own, and made sure that one of his own footmen was always present to escort the ladies wherever they went.

Lavinia, meanwhile, tried to keep herself busy. Part of her regretted having turned down Nicholas's proposal. She had waited so long to be with him again, and the knowledge that, by her own choice, she wasn't with him struck her as being somewhat absurd. On the other hand, she knew that it would not have been fair to Nicholas. Not now, when he had so many other things to worry about.

It went without saying that she had wanted to say yes, and for a moment, she almost had. But in her heart of hearts, she'd known what had prompted Nicholas to offer her marriage. Only when he came to her out of love would she accept his proposal. And if he didn't, well, that was something she would have to deal with. She told Lady Renton as much when they went driving the following afternoon.

"Livie, you are too noble for your own good," Caroline chided her. "The man asked you to marry him and you said no?"

"He only asked because he felt obligated to," Lavinia informed her friend, careful not to mention the protection aspect. "I think he feels guilty."

"And so he should after all the love and attention you have showered on him," Caroline observed. "Dear me, you should hear what some of the dowagers are saying. You're setting a very bad example for the rest of us, my dear."

"I beg your pardon?"

"Indeed. Your loyalty to Nicholas in spite of his continued loss of memory has earned you a great deal of respect, and some husbands of my acquaintance are advising their wives to take a page from your book."

"Never!"

"Yes, indeed."

"Not Lord Renton, I hope," Lavinia said sincerely.

"No, not William. He seems happy enough with the attention he gets," Caroline said fondly. "But there are others who fare dreadfully in comparison to you, my dear."

Lavinia started to laugh, a sound that quickly died at the approach of a familiar gentleman mounted on a big black horse. She stiffened and averted her gaze, praying that Caroline would drive on. Contrarily, Lady Renton, not knowing of Lavinia's aversion to the man, drew the carriage to a halt. "Good afternoon, Lord Rushton," she greeted him cordially.

"Lady Renton, I have been watching you traverse the Park. I must say you handle the ribbons as well as any gentleman of my acquaintance, and better than many."

"Your flattery is most appreciated, Lord Rushton," Caroline replied with an engaging grin. "Perhaps you would be good enough to pass on your views to my husband the next time you see him. He is constantly telling me that I will never make a competent whip."

Rushton smiled smoothly. "I shall be sure to." He turned and swept Lavinia a courtly bow. "And Lady Duplesse. Returned from the countryside so soon? I had expected you to linger there longer."

Lavinia's voice was courteous, but distant. "The countryside is delightful, Lord Rushton, but it does not offer the scope of amusements to be found in Town."

"I see. And was Miss Duplesse also eager to return?"

Lavinia clenched her hands together in the folds of her pelisse. "She is happy in either place. There are still many youthful pleasures for her to enjoy in the country."

"Yes, so I observed. I enjoyed seeing the two of you in Canterbury that day. The cathedral seemed to make a strong impression on Martine."

Lavinia's smile was cool. "*Miss Duplesse* is at an impressionable age, my lord, and is often swept away by a momentary fancy. She will grow out of it in time."

"I hope she does not grow out of it too soon, Lady Duplesse. She is a charming and spirited creature. It would be a shame to see that enthusiasm curbed. But tell me, how do your own plans go on?" he asked conversationally. "Have you and Lord Longworth set the date yet?"

Her smile was chilly. "Not yet."

"Then I take it there has been no change in his condition?"

"None. In fact," Lavinia added, "I believe Lord Longworth fears there will not be any."

Rushton's eyes glowed with a strange intensity. "Then perhaps the two of you will not be getting married after all."

Lavinia stiffened. "That is between myself and my fiancé."

"But of course. Well, I shall detain you no longer. Enjoy your ride."

Doffing his hat, Rushton moved off, a lingering smile on his lips.

"Is it my imagination or do the two of you strike sparks?" Caroline observed drolly.

"It is not your imagination," Lavinia muttered. "In fact, were there loose tinder around, no doubt we should cause a blazing fire. I do not like that man above half!"

"That is quite obvious, my dear." Caroline whipped up the horses. "Unfortunately, it is also quite obvious that, regardless of your own feelings for the man, Lord Rushton is very interested in both you *and* Martine. Your Lord Longworth might do well to sit up and take notice!"

AT THE THEATRE the following evening, Martine peered excitedly through her quizzing glass at the rows of well-filled boxes lining the walls, while Lavinia sat quietly at her side and thought about her meeting with Lord Rushton. In truth, she was quite disturbed by it, just as she had been by every encounter they had had. It was almost as though he were toying with her. Her and Martine.

"Oh look, *maman,* is that not Lady Skifton down there?" Martine passed the quizzing glass to Lavinia. "The one in the purple velvet?"

Lavinia studied the box almost directly across from them and nodded. She didn't need a lorgnette to identify the woman; the lady's tremendous size gave her away. "Yes, I believe so."

Martine tittered. "The box does not look large enough to hold her and Lord Skifton both. However did she become so big, I wonder?"

Lavinia smiled. "Lady Skifton has a healthy appetite."

"But surely Lord Skifton cannot find her attractive any more."

"I don't know that he is overly concerned. They deal well enough together." Lavinia purposely did not mention that Lord Skifton had no need to deal with his wife, having kept a string of mistresses in a discreet house in Kensington for the last ten years.

Martine raised the glass to her eyes again and slowly swept the audience with her gaze. "Lady Renton looks beautiful tonight. I see her there in the box next to... Oh!"

Lavinia heard the muffled exclamation, and turned to see that the girl's cheeks had flushed a bright pink. She was staring rather intently through the glass. "What's wrong, Martine? Did you see a handsome gentleman looking at you?" Lavinia teased.

"No, of course not." The girl's laugh was a touch too bright, and she quickly put down the glasses. "When is Nicholas coming?"

At that moment, the velvet curtain behind them moved and Nicholas entered, along with Laura and Edward. "Look who I bumped into downstairs."

"But what a lovely surprise!" Lavinia happily brushed Laura's cheek with her own. "I did not know you were coming tonight."

"Neither did I until this afternoon." Laura sat down in the seat next to her. "Edward planned it as a bit of a surprise. Hello, Martine."

"Good evening, Miss Beaufort, Mr. Kingsley." Martine's face lit up as she turned to greet Nicholas. "Oh, Nicholas, this is so exciting. Thank you so very much for inviting me."

"It was my pleasure." Nicholas and Edward sat down in the seats directly behind their ladies. "I thought it might be an enjoyable performance. I understand Kean is not one to disappoint his audiences."

Lavinia turned and smiled into Nicholas's eyes. "You have made her night," she whispered.

Nicholas bent forward slightly and pressed his lips to the curve of Lavinia's bare neck as the lights began to dim. "Just as you have made mine, dear lady. You look beautiful."

Lavinia blushed and quickly turned around, aware that the curtain was rising.

As expected, Kean gave a brilliant performance. Martine was entranced, as much by the ugly actor's rich speaking voice as she was by his amazing stage presence. After a particularly stirring scene in the second half, Nicholas leaned forward. "Would you like me to fetch some lemonade?"

Lavinia turned gratefully. "Oh, yes, that would be most appreciated, Nicholas. Thank you."

"I'll come with you, shall I?" Edward offered. "More ladies here than you can carry drinks for, I'm afraid."

Downstairs, Edward and Nicholas made their way through the crowd of bejewelled matrons, dazzling dandies and bored theatre-goers who came as much to be seen themselves as for seeing the play. Nicholas nodded to some acquaintances and glanced around.

"Quite the crowd, eh, Nicholas?" Edward observed drily.

"Indeed. Is it always thus?"

"Pretty much so, though Kean's performances do tend to pack them in more than usual."

Nicholas nodded, and the two men jostled their way closer to the area where lemonade was being served. It was while he was waiting that he heard a group of gentlemen somewhere behind him discussing the entertainment.

"Well, of course, it's all a play on good versus evil. And if that's the case, we know who has to win," one voice observed.

"Yes, but the hero is such a lacklustre character," another said critically. "Indeed, I almost wish the villain would triumph, even though you know the fellow's going to die at the end."

"Personally, I've always found villains to be much more colourful figures," a third voice said mockingly. "In fact, I've often wondered whether it isn't better to live a villain than to die a hero."

Nicholas froze. *Better to live a villain than to die a hero.* Those words. Why did they seem so . . . familiar? And that voice?

He whipped around, suddenly aware that his vision was blurring. His mind was being inundated with names, with faces.

Better to die a hero than to live a coward. No, not a statement, he realized, shaking his head, trying to clear the mists that were closing in around him. A question.

Is it more noble to die a hero or to live a coward?

A question put to him by—

Nicholas gasped, and abruptly felt sweat breaking out on his forehead. In one blinding moment it all came back— everything a murderer's bullet had wiped from his mind that fateful night in France. His family, his work, Lavinia, his life—all were brought rushing back by a single question, a question casually overheard in the midst of a crowded theatre lobby.

A question put to him by the very man who had shot him from his horse and left him in the road to die!

"*MAMAN*, WHERE HAS Nicholas gone?" Martine enquired.

"To get some lemonade for us." Lavinia turned and smiled at her stepdaughter. "Are you thirsty?"

"Yes, very much. May I . . . go and look for him?"

"I don't know if that is a good idea, Martine. The lobby is no doubt extremely crowded."

Martine's eyes were unusually bright. "Please, *maman*, it will be all right. Nicholas will be there."

Lavinia glanced at Laura. "What do you think?"

"I don't see that she will come to any harm. As she says, Nicholas and Edward are both downstairs."

Lavinia nodded. "All right then, Martine, but make sure you find them right away and stay with them until they return."

"Yes, *maman*."

When Martine had gone, Lavinia started to laugh. "Do you know, Laura, I remember my first evening at the theatre. I was so excited, I couldn't sleep the whole night before.''

"What did you see?"

"I've no idea," Lavinia admitted. "I was so busy watching the people in the audience that I scarcely paid five minutes attention to what was happening on stage."

The curtain twitched a few minutes later and Edward reappeared. "Did I miss anything?"

Laura shook her head, accepting the glass of lemonade he handed her. "Not really."

Lavinia smiled, and waited for Nicholas and Martine to enter. When they did not, she frowned. "Edward, are Nicholas and Martine not with you?"

"No, I lost track of Nicholas when I went up to get the refreshments. I thought perhaps he'd already come back. Has he not returned?"

"No. Nor has Martine. Did you see her downstairs?"

Edward looked at her sharply. "She came down? When?"

"A little while ago. She went to look for you and Nicholas. And now neither of them are here," Lavinia replied, panic beginning to tinge her voice. "Edward, where are they?"

He was already out of his seat. "Calm yourself, Lavinia. I'll go back down and find them. Don't either of you leave this box."

Edward disappeared through the curtain, leaving Lavinia to look after him nervously. "Laura, what could have happened to them?"

"You don't know that anything has happened to them, Lavinia," Laura replied reassuringly. "It was crowded downstairs. Martine may have become disoriented when she was looking for Nicholas."

"But where did Nicholas go? Why didn't he tell Edward he was coming back up here, if that's what he was planning to do?"

Lavinia stood up. Laura stared at her. "Lavinia, where are you going?"

"To look for them."

"But Edward told us—"

"I know what Edward told us, but I'm worried. I can't just sit here and wait."

"Oh, all right. But I'm coming, too," Laura said.

"No, you stay here in case Martine returns. She'll be worried if she comes back and there is no one here. You can just tell her that I . . . had to get a breath of fresh air."

Grudgingly, Laura sat down, her face clearly worried. "You *will* hurry back?"

"Just as soon as I find them."

Lavinia turned and quit the box, making her way down to the crowded lobby. Dear Lord, how was she to find anyone in this throng? She anxiously scanned the faces of the people below, but Martine was nowhere to be seen. Nor was Nicholas.

"Lady Duplesse, you look a trifle upset. Could I be of some assistance?"

Lavinia turned and found herself looking into Lord Havermere's smiling, urbane face. "Oh, Lord Havermere, I was just . . . looking for my stepdaughter. Have you seen her, by any chance?"

"Yes, as a matter of fact, I have. I saw her talking to Lord Rushton just outside the theatre."

"Rushton!" The knot of fear in Lavinia's stomach tightened. "But what were they doing outside?"

"I don't know. Perhaps I could show you where I last saw them."

Lavinia quickly scanned the crowded lobby once more. It was getting even worse now. The performance was over and people were beginning to pour from the interior. In a few minutes she wouldn't be able to find anyone. "Yes, all right," she agreed reluctantly.

With Havermere clearing the way, she made her way outside, to where a crowd was already milling about. The street was filled to overflowing with carriages, both private and for hire. Lavinia struggled to see around the hordes of people jostling for position.

"Down here a little, I think, Lady Duplesse," Havermere said. "I believe I just caught a glimpse of Lord Rushton's coat."

By now Lavinia's fears had intensified. They were farther away from the theatre. It was darker here, and there were not so many people around.

"Lord Havermere, perhaps I should—" She got no further. Finding herself beside a closed carriage, she suddenly felt a large hand close over her mouth as her arms were grabbed and pinned behind her back. The door of the carriage opened and she was shoved unceremoniously inside. Havermere shouted something to the coachman and then sprang in behind her, slamming the door.

They set off so quickly that Lavinia was thrown against him. She felt his hands close around her arms. Before she had a chance to say anything, Havermere had extracted a length of cord from under the seat and was tying it securely around her wrists.

"What are you doing?" Lavinia demanded. "Let me out this instant or I shall scream!"

"You're not in a position to be ordering anyone about, my dear Lady Duplesse," Havermere said smoothly. "And I wouldn't bother to scream. At the moment, I have the upper hand and you are going to do exactly as I tell you."

"What do you mean? Why should I do anything you tell me to?"

"Because if you don't, I guarantee you will not see your precious Martine alive again."

NICHOLAS OPENED HIS EYES to find himself lying face down on the floor. He groaned and gingerly lifted a hand to the lump on the back of his head. He hadn't even seen it coming. He'd been so intent on following Havermere that he hadn't noticed the man hiding behind the curtain.

Slowly, Nicholas eased himself into a sitting position and waited for the room to stop spinning. He was obviously still in the theatre, judging from the assortment of stage props stacked around him. This must have been where the man deposited him after knocking him out.

Nicholas remembered it all now—the reason he'd gone to France, the inn he'd stayed at; ambushing the carriage carrying Leclerc and the other Englishman. And the man on the black horse who had ridden up through the darkness and shot him—a man whose face he had only glimpsed through shadows—but whose voice he would remember until the day he died.

Havermere. Havermere was the one who had shot him and left him there in the ditch to die. It was Havermere who had taunted him with the very words that had exposed him tonight, and it was probably he who had cold-bloodedly killed Winchester and Sullivan. Not Rushton, as Nicholas had begun to suspect, but Rushton's good friend Lord Havermere, the man who had questioned him so closely about Lavinia...

Lavinia! He remembered her, too. Everything about her. The love and the compassion they had felt for one another. The years of longing when they'd lived apart. His good friend Devon Marwood, risking his life to bring her out of France. Their reunion when she had finally returned to England. Even the proposal she had had to tell him about only a few days ago.

He remembered it all. And now that he had, it was time to put things right. To take care of things properly. But first, he had to get back to the box. Lavinia was probably beside herself with worry. He'd have to warn them all.

The moment he stepped out of the room however, Nicholas knew it wasn't going to be that easy. He must have been unconscious longer than he'd thought.

The theatre was in complete darkness, the doors locked and barred. There wasn't a soul in the place.

LAVINIA HAD NO IDEA where Havermere was taking her. All of the carriage windows were covered. But that really didn't matter at the moment. All that mattered was that he had Martine, and that he would not hesitate to kill her if he thought it necessary.

"Why?" Lavinia asked quietly. "Why are you doing this? What have Martine and I done to you?"

"The two of you have done nothing," Havermere replied. "I simply intend to use you to facilitate my next . . . accident."

"Accident?"

"Yes. Lord Sullivan met with a most unfortunate one when he was out hunting. And then there was poor Winchester, viciously set upon on his way home after a pleasant evening of gambling. Such a pity, but—" Havermere grinned evilly. "—accidents will happen."

Stark, black fear settled in the pit of Lavinia's stomach, stopping the breath in her throat. Havermere was the murderer! It was Havermere who had shot Nicholas that night in France and left him for dead, just as it was Havermere who had arranged poor Lord Winchester's murder and now, by the sounds of it, Lord Sullivan's.

"Why so silent all of a sudden, Lavinia?" Havermere asked, breaking into her thoughts. "Nothing to say?"

She shivered. "How can anyone be so evil?"

"My dear Lavinia, this is war, and war is business. A business fought between countries."

"But you're dealing with innocent peoples' lives!"

"An expendable commodity." Havermere's voice was totally expressionless. "Besides, Winchester and Sullivan were hardly innocent. They knew what they were getting into when they went into the service. Just as François did."

Lavinia felt a wave of revulsion and nausea. "You killed my husband."

"Actually, no." Havermere studied his smooth leather gloves impassively. "I did not kill your husband. I merely gave the order that he be killed. The man Longworth shot on that country road in France did the actual work for me. Speaking of which, I nearly forgot about that accident— another one of mine. Two gentlemen and a cleric shot dead in a midnight robbery on a deserted country road. Quite original, I thought. Pity I slipped up, though," Havermere remarked as though he were discussing the state of the weather.

"You're the one!" Lavinia flung the words at him, her suspicions confirmed. "You're the one who shot Nicholas and left him to die."

Havermere smiled coldly. "Yes, most negligent on my part. I don't usually leave loose ends. They have a nasty way of turning up again. That's why I put a bullet in his head as well as his side, or so I thought. Fortunately, Nicholas hasn't been able to do me any harm. He was very lucky to have suffered that memory loss. Otherwise I would have had to kill him right away. Perhaps I should have done so regardless. It would have saved me all this bother now, though I admit it's been rather amusing to watch him stumbling around Town, acting like a backward schoolboy."

"You disgust me!" Lavinia whispered in a voice resonant with hatred.

"Really. Then I take it you would not welcome my presence as a husband."

Lavinia blanched. "About as much as I would welcome the devil's! Where is Martine?" she demanded in a choked voice.

"Oh, you needn't worry, she is quite safe. Rushton told her—"

"Rushton! What has Rushton to do with this?" Lavinia demanded.

"Quite a lot, actually. I doubt I would have been able to get out of France had he not arranged for the boat to meet me at Calais."

"Rushton... helped you? But why?"

"Because while his interest in Napoleon's cause was not the same as mine, it was sufficient to sway his loyalties away from England. His mother was just one of many French aristocrats who had her family's lands and properties confiscated. Rushton hoped that with the success of Bonaparte, he would have a chance at reclaiming those lands. Sadly, it would appear now that such is not to be the case."

"What has Rushton done with Martine?"

"Oh, you needn't worry. He hasn't hurt her. He simply told her that he was escorting her to Rose Cottage as per your instructions."

"*My* instructions! And she believed him?"

"She would have no reason not to. I understand the two of them have become quite close over the last little while." Havermere chuckled unpleasantly. "She even sneaked out of the theatre to meet him this evening. And of course, Rushton would have no wish to hurt his future bride."

"His *bride?* Don't be ridiculous, I would never allow Martine to marry Lord Rushton!"

"I wouldn't sound so sure if I were you, my dear." Havermere was clearly unconcerned. "She is of marriageable age, and Rushton finds her quite charming. She is young, yes, and terribly naive, but she will learn." His eyes glowed as he turned to look at her. "Just as you could learn to love me."

Lavinia shuddered. "I could no more learn to love you than I could a toad!"

The smile abruptly faded from Havermere's face, to be replaced by an ugly, menacing sneer. "That will be quite enough. I have been very tolerant with you thus far, Lavinia, but there is nothing to say that my charity has to continue. I am quite capable of making your death look as accidental as Sullivan's.''

Lavinia swallowed. "Why have you kidnapped me?''

"Kidnapped? I have not kidnapped you, my dear. I am merely providing a ride back to the country for you. To Rose Cottage.''

"Then what is it you want?''

"What I want is quite simple.'' The mien of the sophisticated gentleman was back in place. "You will write a letter to Lord Longworth telling him that you and Martine have returned to the house in Kent for a few days because you believe you know the identity of the killer and now fear for your safety in London. To that end, you will also ask him to come and see you as soon as possible.''

"So that you can kill him there?''

"Not at all,'' Havermere informed her in the tone of a tutor to his pupil. "I don't intend that he will ever reach Kent. You see, there will be an unfortunate incident with a footpad on the road. And this time, poor Lord Longworth will not survive.''

"You cannot mean this!''

"Ah, but I do, my dear. I have been patient long enough, but now I have reason to believe that Longworth suspects who I am. Rushton discovered him following me in the theatre this evening. And being that you also know, I cannot risk your getting together with him again. As soon as we reach our first stop, you will write the letter for me so that it can be delivered to your precious fiancé.''

"No!''

He continued as if she hadn't spoken. "You will also write one to your friend Miss Beaufort, telling her that everything is fine and that you and Martine have decided to return to Kent. After all, she was most taken with the house, as I recall Martine telling Rushton. She will certainly not find it strange that you have returned. Then we will continue down to Rose Cottage, where Martine is anxiously awaiting your arrival. She will be delighted to see that I have brought her mama to her."

"I will tell her exactly what you and Rushton have done," Lavinia said in a low voice.

"On the contrary, you will tell her nothing," Havermere said coldly. "Because if you do, it will not only be Lord Longworth who meets with an accident, but the charming Miss Beaufort, as well."

"Dear God! Laura!"

"Yes, it is always so helpful when people have friends."

"But she has nothing to do with this! Or with you!"

"Indirectly, she has," Havermere tossed back. "She will be marrying Edward Kingsley, a rather exceptional British agent, and one who has caused me no end of irritation. That is reason enough to kill her—if you force me to."

Lavinia fought to stem the rising tide of nausea. "You cannot possibly get away with this. People will come looking. Edward will—"

"Kingsley will do nothing, because after I take care of Lord Longworth tonight, I will return to London and tell Mr. Kingsley that the two of you are enjoying a lover's rendezvous. Hence, there will be no reason for him to be suspicious. And, after all, he would hardly wish to disturb a pair of lovers, would he?"

"Edward won't believe you."

"He will, at first. But he'll be dead before he has time to figure it out and tell anyone else."

"You're mad!" Lavinia gasped.

"Not in the least. In fact, I am extremely sane. And the idea is, I think, quite a good one."

"You seem to have forgotten one thing."

"Oh?"

"What about me?" Lavinia asked quietly. "I know all about your plans. Do you think I will sit by and watch you get away with them?"

"Not for a moment," Havermere said with an engaging smile. "Once Nicholas is taken care of, there will be an unfortunate fire at Rose Cottage. Luckily, Rushton will be in the area and manage to save poor Martine, thereby ensuring her devotion to him. But I'm afraid he will not be able to reach her stepmother's room in time. A most tragic loss."

Lavinia swallowed again, closing her eyes against the face of a madman. He had it all planned. "And the others?" she asked in a strangled voice.

"They will be dealt with in my own time and in my own way. Now, my dear, I suggest you start thinking about what you are going to say in the letter to your dear fiancé. Because once we reach our first stop, you will have a very short time to write it before my man arrives to take it back to London."

"I won't do it." Lavinia returned his steady regard. "I will not lure Nicholas to his death."

"Then you condemn Martine to hers," Havermere said emotionlessly. "Rushton will get over it. I only promised Martine to him as a reward for his services. And it really doesn't matter, because Longworth will die anyway. But if you agree, Lavinia, you can at least know that Martine will live. Is it not better to know that she will survive, rather than see *everyone* dispatched?"

Lavinia turned away from the repulsive sight of his face, horrified by the choices he had given her, but knowing deep in her heart that he had given her no choice at all.

CHAPTER TWELVE

THE FIRST PLACE Nicholas went after leaving the theatre was to Lavinia's house. He wasn't surprised to find that neither she nor Martine were there. Upon questioning Lavinia's maid, he discovered that neither lady had returned home from the theatre.

Thankfully, he was more successful at his second stop. "Nicholas! Where the hell have you been?" Edward demanded after ushering his friend inside. "I searched everywhere in that damn theatre for you."

"Unfortunately, you forgot the prop room," Nicholas informed him ruefully. "Seems the murderer was correct in assuming it would be a safe hiding-place for me. But never mind that. Where's Lavinia?"

"I don't know. After I lost track of you downstairs, I went back to the box, assuming you'd already gone up. Lavinia and Laura were there, but you weren't."

"Where was Martine?"

"Apparently, she'd gone to look for you. I told the ladies I was going back down and ordered them to stay put. But when I returned, Lavinia was gone and Laura was having fits!"

"And Lavinia never came back?"

"Neither of them did. When I couldn't find you in the theatre, I left to take Laura home, hoping you would eventually turn up here. If you hadn't appeared within the next fifteen minutes, I was on my way to Osborne."

"It wouldn't have made any difference. He's already got both of them."

"Who?"

"Havermere. It's been Havermere all along. Havermere was the man who shot me in France."

"But how do you—" Edward gasped. "Good Lord, your memory's come back?"

"With stunning clarity."

"But how? When?"

"I overheard Havermere and Rushton talking at the theatre earlier. Something Havermere said took me back to that night, and that's when it all came flooding in, like a huge dam breaking. I began to remember faces, names. And I remembered his voice. That's when I realized that Havermere was the man who'd shot me." "What happened then?"

"I started to follow him, but I was hit from behind."

"Bloody hell, when I think we had him right in the palm of our hand and let him slip away."

"I know, my friend, I know. And it sickens me to think that he has Lavinia and Martine."

"So what now?"

"I shall go to see Lord Osborne and let him know what's happened. Then we wait."

"What? Sit back and do nothing? Are you mad?"

"I'm afraid we don't have much choice," Nicholas said grimly. "As much as I would like to tear London apart brick by brick searching for them, it would be a complete waste of time. Havermere could be hiding them almost anywhere. I'm afraid we're going to have to wait for him to make the first move."

"What about your memory? Are you going to tell anyone?"

"No!" Nicholas all but shouted the word. "As far as everyone else is concerned, nothing has changed. Only you and Osborne will know differently. Lavinia's and Martine's lives may very well depend on it."

"SO IT WAS HAVERMERE all along." Lord Osborne slammed his fist down on the desk in his library, where Nicholas had been ushered by a sleepy servant. "Damn! When I think of the times we could have had him."

"It doesn't matter now, my lord," Nicholas said. "What matters is that he has Lavinia and Martine, and that he will use them to get to me."

"Yes, you're right, of course. What do you want me to do?"

"Nothing, for the moment. I'm afraid we're totally at Havermere's mercy," Nicholas admitted. "We don't know where he's hiding the ladies or precisely what he intends to do. My guess is he will contact us as soon as he's ready. And the moment he does, we must be prepared to move."

The manner of contact did not turn out precisely as Nicholas had expected, however. A few hours later, a letter was delivered to the back kitchen of Nicholas's house by a young lad who disappeared into the night the moment he left it.

"Shall I give chase, sir?" his butler offered, handing Nicholas the missive.

Nicholas shook his head. "No. I doubt the boy will be able to tell us anything." Havermere was far too clever to be exposed so easily.

Nicholas quickly broke the seal. His hand began to tremble as he recognized Lavinia's elegant writing.

My dearest Nicholas,
Pray forgive my hasty departure from the theatre, but I thought it best that Martine and I leave London as soon as possible. I now know the identity of the man who shot you, and realize that the safest place for us is at Rose Cottage. Please come as soon as you can. We

only have a mere few hours before he finds us.

Yours,
Lavinia

Nicholas read the letter twice over before he saw it:
... *have a mere few hours*...

He closed his eyes, fighting down a wave of intense anger. *Havermere.* Havermere was using Lavinia to lure him to Rose Cottage. Her carefully worded letter was a warning that he would be walking into a trap.

Nicholas crushed the letter into a ball. Very well, the game was in motion; his opponent had made the first move. Now it was up to Nicholas to play along until he got the opportunity to take the upper hand. And he fully intended to do so, as quickly and as quietly as possible. But if anything were to happen to Lavinia or Martine in the meantime, nothing on earth would stop him from bringing the game to a swift and brutal conclusion. Nothing!

"IT'S A TRAP," Edward said when he'd finished reading the letter. "He's obviously going to be waiting for you at the cottage."

Nicholas nodded. "Of course. And he's using Lavinia as bait."

"Do you think she and Martine are even there?"

Nicholas shrugged. "I don't know. The problem is, I can't afford to take any chances until I know for sure. I have to play along."

Edward put the letter on the table. "When are you leaving?"

"As soon as I've seen Osborne. I expect he will offer to provide me with backup if I want it."

"And do you?"

Nicholas grinned. "I was thinking about taking along the best man I know. Are you available?"

Edward smiled in a conspiratorial fashion. "Just try to stop me."

AS SOON AS HE'D BEEN to see Lord Osborne, Nicholas set out. He was far too agitated to wait until dawn. The sooner he reached Rose Cottage, the sooner he could see to Martine's and Lavinia's safety.

At the thought of the beautiful and brave woman who had risked so much to see him well again, Nicholas offered up a silent prayer for her safety. Through everything that had happened, Lavinia had stuck with him, encouraging him, loving him. And now it was his turn to show Lavinia how deeply he cared. Because long before his memory had returned, Nicholas knew that he had fallen totally and quite hopelessly in love with Lavinia Duplesse—again.

Rounding a bend in the road, he suddenly came upon the sight of a carriage stopped dead in the middle of the road. The horses were still hitched, but the back wheel was badly smashed. Nicholas reined in, his dark eyebrows slanting in a frown. The door to the carriage was thrown open, yet there did not appear to be anyone within. Spilling out over the steps was a cloak. A lady's cloak.

Lavinia's cloak!

Nicholas dismounted and cautiously approached the carriage. His gaze intent on the vehicle, he did not at first notice the shadowy figure on horseback standing just inside the trees. It wasn't until he heard the familiar sound of a pistol being cocked that he realized he had stumbled into his trap a little sooner than expected.

"So, my friend, I find you on a deserted stretch of road again."

Nicholas swallowed, and drawing on whatever acting skills he possessed, turned around and looked in the direction of the horseman, feigning surprise. "Who goes there?"

"Do you not recognize me, Nicholas?"

"Havermere? Is that you? For God's sake, man, this is no time to be playing games. There's been an accident here."

"So it would appear."

Nicholas turned away from Havermere and started walking towards the carriage. With every step he half expected to feel the thud of a bullet in his back. But there was nothing else he could do. If he reached for his pistol, Havermere would shoot him down. He had to pretend that he was not aware of the danger. His life—and Lavinia's—depended on his acting totally believable. "Will you not lend me a hand?"

"I hardly think it necessary. There don't appear to be any passengers within."

"But surely that is a lady's cloak."

"It may well be. But tell me, Nicholas, what are you doing out on the road so late?"

"I am on my way to see Lavinia." Nicholas threw the words back over his shoulder. "She sent me a letter asking me to come."

"And being the dutiful fiancé, you came at once, eh?"

"Do you find it so strange that I would wish to be with her?"

Havermere appeared to be enjoying himself. "Not at all. She is a beautiful woman. In fact, what would you say were I to tell you that I was thinking of asking Lavinia for her hand in marriage?"

Nicholas was thankful for the darkness, which hid his rage. "I would wonder why you were wasting your time, when you know the lady is already betrothed to me."

"Yes, but if you were to leave again...unexpectedly, Lavinia would be left all alone once more."

"Fortunately, I do not intend to leave."

The wind suddenly picked up. Nicholas heard a faint rustling in the grass. "But come, Havermere, the middle of the night is hardly the time to be discussing marriage possibilities."

"No, Nicholas, indeed it is not, and I confess this polite social chit-chat is beginning to bore me. I would have liked it better had you regained your memory. There is really no sport in killing a man who doesn't even know why he is going to die."

Nicholas quickly calculated the distance between himself and the carriage. No more than two steps. "What are you talking about?"

"Oh, really, Nicholas, this is growing quite tedious. Do you not know that it was I who shot you in France that night?"

"You! But—"

"Throw down your weapon, Havermere!" Edward's voice reverberated through the darkness like a pistol shot.

Havermere whirled round in the saddle. "What the—"

In the split second Havermere's attention was diverted, Nicholas threw himself under the carriage. He heard Havermere's muffled oath, and then the sound of a shot. The bullet landed in the dirt only inches from where he lay. But it was the only shot Havermere was to get. Cocking his own pistol, Nicholas rolled out from under the carriage and, getting to his feet on the other side, took aim and fired.

The bullet hit Havermere in the upper body, knocking him out of the saddle. Nicholas watched his adversary land heavily on the dirt road, and then tensed as the injured man raised his hand, still clutching his pistol.

"I wouldn't do that if I were you," Edward warned in a silken voice. He emerged from the bushes just behind Havermere's horse, his own weapon aimed directly at the scoundrel's chest. "I wouldn't think twice about shooting a cold-blooded murderer like you."

Havermere's face contorted with anger and pain. "Kingsley! By God, I should have killed you when I had the chance. You've caused me nothing but trouble."

"And very glad I am to hear it." Edward kicked Havermere's pistol away with his foot. "Now, my lord, face down on the road, if you don't mind. Nice piece of shooting, Nicholas."

"Thank you." Nicholas looked up at the sound of a second carriage arriving. The door opened and Lord Osborne stepped down, flanked by two armed guards, their pistols trained on the man lying in the road.

"So, Havermere, it ends like this." Osborne stared down at the wounded man in disgust. "You should have known better than to take on my two best men."

By now, Havermere was saying very little, but Nicholas wasn't finished with him. "Where are they, my lord?"

Havermere's lips pulled back in a malevolent smile. "Go to hell!"

"On the contrary, hell is more likely somewhere you will be going if you don't answer my question in the next three seconds." Nicholas cocked his pistol and placed the end of the barrel against Havermere's temple. "Like Kingsley said, it would give me great pleasure to avenge François's murder right here and now, not to mention Baker's, Winchester's and God knows how many others'. Now, I shall ask you one last time. Where are they!"

Havermere laughed, but it was little more than a rasp. "They're where I told you they would be. At the cottage."

Nicholas gave him a cold, hard look. "They had better be, Havermere. And for your sake, they had better both be safe, or you're going to wish my first bullet had killed you right off."

Without waiting to hear anything more, Nicholas swung up into the saddle and headed in the direction of Rose Cottage. There was only one thought in his mind now—to find Lavinia and Martine as soon as possible. And if Havermere had done anything to harm them, by God, he'd tear him apart with his bare hands!

NICHOLAS SAW A FAINT light emanating from the drawing-room window as soon as the cottage came into view. He also saw a carriage waiting in the drive, and abruptly drew his stallion to a halt.

Someone other than Lavinia and Martine was inside the house!

Nicholas swore softly under his breath. He hadn't expected Havermere to post a guard. Obviously, he was working in league with someone—and Nicholas had a pretty strong suspicion as to who that person might be.

He pulled the pistol from his belt and silently slid out of the saddle. Creeping through the darkness like an avenging angel, he made his way round to the back of the cottage and cautiously peered in through the leaded window. What he saw made his mouth narrow into a tight, angry line.

Lavinia was sitting on a chair with her wrists and ankles bound. Seated a few feet away, with his back to the window and a pistol held loosely in his hand, was Rushton.

Nicholas crouched back down below the window and struggled to contain his anger. *Rushton.* He might have known that bastard would be in on this. No wonder he'd been hanging around Martine and asking questions, trying to discover the extent of Nicholas's injuries. No wonder he and Havermere had appeared to be such good friends.

Nicholas frowned, anger hardening his features into a stony mask. He was tempted to burst into the room and open fire, but he knew he couldn't risk it. Lavinia might be wounded in the exchange. No, he would have to remain calm and think the situation through—luckily, something that took only minutes to do. Rushton might have Lavinia, but Martine was nowhere in sight. Which meant that he had probably locked her upstairs in her room, inadvertently giving Nicholas the advantage he needed.

Tucking the pistol securely into his belt, Nicholas approached the rose-draped trellis that covered the back of the cottage. Finding it sturdy enough to hold his weight, he quickly began to climb. In a matter of minutes he had reached the window to Martine's room, and seconds later had eased open the casement and slipped quietly inside.

"Nicholas!" Martine flung herself into his arms, sobbing.

Nicholas gathered the trembling girl to him and held her close. "Hush, Martine, hush. Everything is going to be all right now."

"Oh, Nicholas, I was so afraid," she whispered tearfully against his jacket. "Lord Rushton...forced me to get into the carriage at the theatre. He—he said that...*maman* was coming, and that we were to...wait for her here. But I haven't seen her. Is *maman* here, Nicholas? Is she all right?"

"Lavinia is downstairs in the drawing-room, Martine, and she's all right, but—"

"But...Lord Rushton is...with her?"

Nicholas sighed. "Yes, and I'm going to need your help in getting her away. We're going to have to create a diversion."

Martine sniffed again, then wiped away her tears. She nodded, suddenly looking very grown-up indeed. "Tell me what you want me to do, Nicholas."

IN THE DRAWING-ROOM below, Lavinia sat in the chair and stared at the floor in front of her. She tried not to think about what might have happened to Nicholas. It seemed an eternity since she had last seen him. Where was he? Was he all right? Had he seen and understood the message hidden in her letter?

"I am going to marry her, you know," Rushton said, suddenly breaking into Lavinia's thoughts. "For all your warning me away from Martine, I will have her in the end. You can't stop me now."

Lavinia kept her eyes on the floor, unwilling to look at him. "She will never agree to marry you. I shall tell her what kind of monster you really are, and she will never go to you."

But Rushton only laughed softly. "No, Lavinia, not this time. You won't have a chance to say anything to her. And she won't hate me. She will be eternally grateful to me for having saved her life, even though I won't be able to save yours when this place goes up in— What the hell?" Rushton broke off at the sound of a loud crash, followed by a high-pitched scream.

Lavinia looked towards the stairs in horror. "Martine!"

Rushton was already moving. He grabbed the oil lamp from the table, and ignoring Lavinia's cries, raised his pistol and made for the stairs.

In the bedroom above, Nicholas waited patiently behind the door. "Lie perfectly still, Martine," he whispered to the girl who lay stretched out on the floor as if unconscious. "We have to make Lord Rushton believe that you've been injured."

It wasn't an unlikely conclusion, given the way the shattered fragments of the cheval-glass lay all around her—the mirror Nicholas had smashed with one good blow from the warming pan and then sent crashing to the floor.

Nicholas heard the sound of Rushton's footsteps on the stairs and pressed his body back against the wall, holding the barrel of his pistol tightly in his hand. He would have only one chance at this.

Abruptly, the door flew open. Rushton paused on the threshold of the room and stared down at the girl lying seemingly unconscious on the floor.

Nicholas tensed, his fingers clenching the pistol. As Rushton moved forward, he stepped out from behind the door and brought the butt of the weapon down hard on the back of Rushton's head. The man groaned and crumpled limply to the floor, unconscious.

Nicholas expelled the breath he hadn't even realized he'd been holding, and then dropped his pistol on the bed. It was over.

"Nicholas?" Martine whispered, her voice muffled against the floor. "Can I get up now?"

"Yes, Martine, you can." He carefully lifted the girl out of the wreckage of broken glass and sat her down on the bed. "Lord Rushton won't be troubling us any more."

"Is *maman* all right?" She asked in a whisper.

"That's what I intend to find out as soon as I take care of our friend here."

Nicholas quickly secured Rushton's ankles and wrists, using strong lengths of cotton torn from the sheets on Martine's bed. Nodding in satisfaction, he returned to Martine, still sitting on the bed, and handed her his pistol. "Now, I need you to stay here and guard our prisoner for a few minutes while I see to Lavinia. Can you do that, Martine?"

She nodded, a fierce look on her face. "I shall be fine, Nicholas. If Lord Rushton moves, I shall shoot him!"

"Dear me, you needn't go quite that far," Nicholas murmured with a smile as he bent to pick up Rushton's weapon. "Just keep the pistol trained on him. He won't be coming round for a while yet, and when he does, he certainly won't be going anywhere." Nicholas gave Martine a reassuring wink. "You just watch him for me, and I'll be back in a matter of minutes."

LAVINIA HEARD THE SOUND of footsteps coming down the stairs and strained her eyes towards the door. She held her breath as the light from the lamp drew closer. "Martine?" she whispered fearfully.

But it wasn't her stepdaughter who appeared on the threshold of the room and then strode forward, his face set in rigid lines as he looked down at the woman he loved. "Lavinia!"

"Nicholas? Oh, dear God, Nicholas, you're safe!" Lavinia cried, the feeling of relief so strong it nearly made her swoon. "But what happened? Where is Martine? I heard the crash—"

"Martine is safe, my darling. It was just a trick to lure Rushton away from you. He is safely bound and gagged upstairs." Nicholas swiftly untied the ropes restraining her, aware that his hands were shaking. "Thanks to your letter, I realized that I would be walking into a trap. As a result, Edward and I planned our own midnight ambush. Havermere is now in Osborne's custody and on his way back to London."

"Nicholas!" It was the only word Lavinia uttered before she fell into Nicholas's open arms and felt herself being crushed against his heart. She clung to him, drawing on his strength, relishing the closeness of his strong, hard body. "I was so afraid for you, Nicholas."

"I know, darling, I know, but it's all right now," he murmured huskily against her hair, holding her as though he would never let her go. "Everything's going to be all right. We're safe now, and we're going to stay that way. Because I'm never going away again, do you hear, Lavinia?" Nicholas whispered fervently. "I am never, ever going to leave you again!"

WHEN LAVINIA CAME downstairs the following morning, her cheeks were pale, but otherwise her face bore little evidence of the strain of the previous day and night. And what a night it had been. Shortly after she had been freed, Edward and one of Osborne's men had unexpectedly arrived at the cottage, to make sure that everything was all right. Rushton had been taken away, and Edward had returned to London, anxious to comfort an overwrought Laura. Martine had gone to bed, exhausted, and was, it seemed, still sleeping peacefully.

"Thank God she is young and resilient," Lavinia said now as she and Nicholas stood quietly by the window, looking out into the peaceful garden. "She will forget all about this, just as she did about François's death."

Nicholas heard Lavinia's heavy sigh and turned to regard her in silence. In the demure sprigged-muslin gown, and with her hair caught back in a loose cluster of curls, she barely looked older than Martine. Only the nervous fluttering of her hands betrayed her lingering memories of the frightening events.

"Lavinia, I wonder if you might like to join me for a walk in the garden."

Lavinia glanced up at him in surprise. "What . . . now?"

"Why not?" Taking her hand, he opened the French doors that led onto the terrace and guided her towards the sunny garden. "Can you think of a better time?"

Lavinia frowned as he led her outside to the very bench where they had sat just a few nights ago. "A better time for what?" She watched in confusion as Nicholas picked up a pair of garden shears. "Nicholas, what are you doing?"

"I'm trying to remember what you told me the other day. Now, sit there and don't say a word."

Nicholas slowly made his way through the garden, taking care to cut the five most perfect roses he could find. "As I recall, you told me that the first time I proposed to you, I gave you four roses—one for each year I'd been in love with you. Well," he said, returning to her side and holding out the blooms, "now I give you five."

Lavinia blushed as she accepted the fragrant flowers. "Nicholas, this really isn't necessary—"

"It most certainly is." His eyes on her face, Nicholas bent his right knee and slowly sank to the ground. "And then you told me that I went down on my knee like this, and said that every day we had been apart, my heart broke a little more, but that every day also brought us closer to the time when we would finally be together. Isn't that right?"

Lavinia's lips curved into a loving smile. "Yes."

"But I said something else, too. Something you forgot to tell me."

Lavinia started. "I did?"

"You forgot to tell me, my darling, that I promised to love you for as long as I was capable of drawing breath, and that I would hold you in my arms until the strength left my body and there were no more sunrises. Do *you* remember that?" he asked with infinite gentleness.

Lavinia stared at him, hardly daring to believe what she was hearing. "Nicholas . . . ?"

"And do you remember what you answered?" Nicholas continued, his smile growing broader by the minute. "You said that—"

"I said that . . . if you couldn't . . . hold me any more, there would be no more . . . need for sunrises. Oh, Nicholas! Your memory!" Lavinia laughed as the tears sprang to her eyes and spilled over her lashes. "It's come back. You've remembered! You've truly remembered!"

"Every last detail, my darling," Nicholas told her, joyfully pulling her into his arms. "Everything about who I am, why I went to France and how much I loved you. But there is something else I have to tell you that is even more important than my memory returning, or how much I used to love you," he went on urgently.

Lavinia's eyes gleamed with emotion. "There is?"

Nicholas's gaze grew infinitely tender as he set her slightly away from him and smiled down into her beautiful blue eyes. "I need to tell you that I love you more than I ever imagined possible. To tell you that, even had my memory not come back, it wouldn't have made any difference. Because I love you, Lavinia. Not for what we had, or what you once meant to me, but because of what you mean to me now. You are the *only* woman I have ever loved, my darling, and you are the only woman I ever will—with or without a memory."

"Oh . . . Nicholas!"

He kissed her then, tasting the saltiness of tears mingled with the honeyed sweetness of her lips. He ran his mouth over the softness of her cheek, the smooth line of her jaw, pressing his lips to the fluttering pulse at the base of her throat before returning once more to her lips. He held her as if she were the most precious treasure imaginable, because to him she was a treasure, one more valuable than all the gold and jewels in the world. She was his Lavinia, the woman he had promised to love until there were no more sunrises.

"And now, my lady," Nicholas whispered huskily, "if I haven't forgotten anything else, I shall ask you the question I was told to ask again. Darling Lavinia, will you marry me?"

Lavinia opened her mouth, choking on a sob that abruptly turned into a laugh. "Yes! Oh, yes, please." She tightened her arms around his neck and held him with all the strength she possessed. "And as soon as possible, if you don't mind. Before either one of us has a chance to forget another blessed thing!"

About the Author

Born in Sri Lanka, Stephanie Laurens has
lived mostly in Australia. After qualifying
as a scientist, she and her husband travelled
extensively through the Far and Middle East,
as well as throughout Europe and England. Four
years in London gave her the settings for her
Regency romances. Now settled once more in
Australia, she lives with her husband, two young
children, a mindless but lovable dog and a cat
with a crooked leg.

FOUR IN HAND
Stephanie Laurens

CHAPTER ONE

THE RATTLE OF THE curtain rings sounded like thunder. The head of the huge four-poster bed remained wreathed in shadow yet Max was aware that for some mysterious reason Masterton was trying to wake him. Surely it couldn't be noon already?

Lying prone amid his warm sheets, his stubbled cheek cushioned in softest down, Max contemplated faking slumber. But Masterton knew he was awake. And knew that he knew, so to speak. Sometimes, the damned man seemed to know his thoughts before he did. And he certainly wouldn't go away before Max capitulated and acknowledged him.

Raising his head, Max opened one very blue eye. His terrifyingly correct valet was standing, entirely immobile, plumb in his line of vision. Masterton's face was impassive. Max frowned.

In response to this sign of approaching wrath, Masterton made haste to state his business. Not that it was *his* business, exactly. Only the combined vote of the rest of the senior staff of Delmere House had induced him to disturb His Grace's rest at the unheard-of hour of nine o'clock. He had every reason to know just how dangerous such an undertaking could be. He had been in the service of Max Rotherbridge, Viscount Delmere, for nine years. It was highly unlikely his master's recent elevation to the estate of His Grace the Duke of Twyford had in any way altered his temper. In fact, from what Masterton had seen, his master had had more to try his temper in dealing with his unexpected inheritance than in all the rest of his thirty-four years.

"Hillshaw wished me to inform you that there's a young lady to see you, Your Grace."

It was still a surprise to Max to hear his new title on his servants' lips. He had to curb an automatic reaction to look about him for whomever they were addressing. A lady. His frown deepened. "No." He dropped his head back into the soft pillows and closed his eyes.

"*No*, Your Grace?"

The bewilderment in his valet's voice was unmistakable. Max's head ached. He had been up until dawn. The evening had started badly, when he had felt constrained to attend a ball given by his maternal aunt, Lady Maxwell. He rarely attended such functions. They were too tame for his liking; the languishing sighs his appearance provoked among all the sweet young things were enough to throw even the most hardened reprobate entirely off his stride. And while he had every claim to that title, seducing débutantes was no longer his style. Not at thirty-four.

He had left the ball as soon as he could and repaired to the discreet villa wherein resided his latest mistress. But the beautiful Carmelita had been in a petulant mood. Why were such women invariably so grasping? And why did they imagine he was so besotted that he'd stand for it? They had had an almighty row, which had ended with him giving the luscious ladybird her congé in no uncertain terms.

From there, he had gone to White's, then Boodles. At that discreet establishment, he had found a group of his cronies and together they had managed to while the night away. And most of the morning, too. He had neither won nor lost. But his head reminded him that he had certainly drunk a lot.

He groaned and raised himself on his elbows, the better to fix Masterton with a gaze which, despite his condition, was remarkably lucid. Speaking in the voice of one instructing a dimwit, he explained. "If there's a woman to see me, she can't be a lady. No lady would call here."

Max thought he was stating the obvious but his hench-man stared woodenly at the bedpost. The frown, which had temporarily left his master's handsome face, returned.

Silence.

Max sighed and dropped his head on to his hands. "Have you seen her, Masterton?"

"I did manage to get a glimpse of the young lady when Hillshaw showed her into the library, Your Grace."

Max screwed his eyes tightly shut. Masterton's insistence on using the term "young lady" spoke volumes. All of Max's servants were experienced in telling the difference between ladies and the sort of female who might be expected to call at a bachelor's residence. And if both Masterton and Hillshaw insisted the woman downstairs was a young lady, then a young lady she must be. But it was inconceivable that any young lady would pay a nine o'clock call on the most notorious rake in London.

Taking his master's silence as a sign of commitment to the day, Masterton crossed the large chamber to the wardrobe. "Hillshaw mentioned that the young lady, a Miss Twinning, Your Grace, was under the impression she had an appointment with you."

Max had the sudden conviction that this was a nightmare. He rarely made appointments with anyone and certainly not with young ladies for nine o'clock in the morning. And particularly not with unmarried young ladies. "Miss Twinning?" The name rang no bells. Not even a rattle.

"Yes, Your Grace." Masterton returned to the bed, various garments draped on his arm, a deep blue coat lovingly displayed for approval. "The Bath superfine would, I think, be most appropriate?"

Yielding to the inevitable with a groan, Max sat up.

ONE FLOOR BELOW, Caroline Twinning sat calmly reading His Grace of Twyford's morning paper in an armchair by his library hearth. If she felt any qualms over the propriety of her present position, she hid them well. Her charmingly candid countenance was free of all nervousness and, as she scanned a frankly libellous account of a garden party enlivened by the scandalous propensities of the ageing Duke of Cumberland, an engaging smile curved her generous lips. In truth, she was looking forward to her meeting with the Duke. She and her sisters had spent a most enjoyable eighteen months, the wine of freedom a heady tonic after their previously monastic existence. But it was time and more for them to embark on the serious business of securing their futures. To do that, they needs must enter the *ton*, that glittering arena thus far denied them. And, for them, the Duke of Twyford undeniably held the key to that particular door.

Hearing the tread of a masculine stride approach the library door, Caroline raised her head, then smiled confidently. Thank heavens the Duke was so easy to manage.

By the time he reached the ground floor, Max had exhausted every possible excuse for the existence of the mysterious Miss Twinning. He had taken little time to dress, having no need to employ extravagant embellishments to distract attention from his long and powerful frame. His broad shoulders and muscular thighs perfectly suited the prevailing fashion. His superbly cut coats looked as though they had been moulded on to him and his buckskin breeches showed not a crease. The understated waistcoat, perfectly tied cravat and shining top-boots which completed the picture were the envy of many an aspiring exquisite. His hair, black as night, was neatly cropped to frame a dark face on which the years had left nothing more than a trace of worldly cynicism. Disdaining the ornamentation common to the times, His Grace of Twyford wore no ring other than a gold signet on his left hand and displayed no fobs or seals. In spite of this, no one setting eyes on him could imagine he was other than he was—one of the most fashionable and wealthy men in the *ton*.

He entered his library, a slight frown in the depths of his midnight-blue eyes. His attention was drawn by a flash of movement as the young lady who had been calmly reading

his copy of the morning *Gazette* in his favourite armchair by
the hearth folded the paper and laid it aside, before rising to
face him. Max halted, blue eyes suddenly intent, all trace of
displeasure vanishing as he surveyed his unexpected visitor.
His nightmare had transmogrified into a dream. The vision
before him was unquestionably a houri. For a number of
moments he remained frozen in rapturous contemplation.
Then, his rational mind reasserted itself. Not a houri. Hou-
ris did not read the *Gazette*. At least, not in his library at
nine o'clock in the morning. From the unruly copper curls
clustering around her face to the tips of her tiny slippers,
showing tantalisingly from under the simply cut and outrageously fashionable gown, there was nothing with which he
could find fault. She was built on generous lines, a tall Ju-
noesque figure, deep-bosomed and wide-hipped, but all in
the most perfect proportions. Her apricot silk gown did
justice to her ample charms, clinging suggestively to a figure of Grecian delight. When his eyes returned to her face,
he had time to take in the straight nose and full lips and the
dimple that peeked irrepressibly from one cheek before his
gaze was drawn to the finely arched brows and long lashes
which framed her large eyes. It was only when he looked
into the cool grey-green orbs that he saw the twinkle of
amusement lurking there. Unused to provoking such a response, he frowned.

"Who, exactly, are you?" His voice, he was pleased to
find, was even and his diction clear.

The smile which had been hovering at the corners of those
inviting lips finally came into being, disclosing a row of
small pearly teeth. But instead of answering his question, the
vision replied, "I was waiting for the Duke of Twyford."

Her voice was low and musical. Mentally engaged in
considering how to most rapidly dispense with the formali-
ties, Max answered automatically. "I am the Duke."

"You?" For one long moment, utter bewilderment was
writ large across her delightful countenance.

For the life of her, Caroline could not hide her surprise. How could this man, of all men, be the Duke? Aside from the fact he was far too young to have been a crony of her father's, the gentleman before her was unquestionably a rake. And a rake of the first order, to boot. Whether the dark-browed, harsh-featured face with its aquiline nose and firm mouth and chin or the lazy assurance with which he had entered the room had contributed to her reading of his character, she could not have said. But the calmly arrogant way his intensely blue eyes had roved from the top of her curls all the way down to her feet, and then just as calmly returned by the same route, as if to make sure he had missed nothing, left her in little doubt of what sort of man she now faced. Secure in the knowledge of being under her guardian's roof, she had allowed the amusement she felt on seeing such decided appreciation glow in the deep blue eyes to show. Now, with those same blue eyes still on her, piercingly perceptive, she felt as if the rug had been pulled from beneath her feet.

Max could hardly miss her stunned look. "For my sins," he added in confirmation.

With a growing sense of unease, he waved his visitor to a seat opposite the huge mahogany desk while he moved to take the chair behind it. As he did so, he mentally shook his head to try to clear it of the thoroughly unhelpful thoughts that kept crowding in. Damn Carmelita!

Caroline, rapidly trying to gauge where this latest disconcerting news left her, came forward to sink into the chair indicated.

Outwardly calm, Max watched the unconsciously graceful glide of her walk, the seductive swing of her hips as she sat down. He would have to find a replacement for Carmelita. His gaze rested speculatively on the beauty before him. Hillshaw had been right. She was unquestionably a lady. Still, that had never stopped him before. And, now he came to look more closely, she was not, he thought, that young. Even better. No rings, which was odd. Another twinge of pain from behind his eyes lent a harshness to his voice. "Who the devil are you?"

The dimple peeped out again. In no way discomposed, she answered, "My name is Caroline Twinning. And, if you really are the Duke of Twyford, then I'm very much afraid I'm your ward."

Her announcement was received in perfect silence. A long pause ensued, during which Max sat unmoving, his sharp blue gaze fixed unwaveringly on his visitor. She bore this scrutiny for some minutes, before letting her brows rise in polite and still amused enquiry.

Max closed his eyes and groaned. "Oh, God."

It had only taken a moment to work it out. The only woman he could not seduce was his own ward. And he had already decided he very definitely wanted to seduce Caroline Twinning. With an effort, he dragged his mind back to the matter at hand. He opened his eyes. Hopefully, she would put his reaction down to natural disbelief. Encountering the grey-green eyes, now even more amused, he was not so sure. "Explain, if you please. Simple language only. I'm not up to unravelling mysteries at the moment."

Caroline could not help grinning. She had noticed twinges of what she guessed to be pain passing spasmodically through the blue eyes. "If your head hurts that much, why don't you try an ice-pack? I assure you I won't mind."

Max threw her a look of loathing. His head felt as if it was splitting, but how dared she be so lost to all propriety as to notice, let alone mention it? Still, she was perfectly right. An ice-pack was exactly what he needed. With a darkling look, he reached for the bell pull.

Hillshaw came in answer to his summons and received the order for an ice-pack without noticeable perturbation. "Now, Your Grace?"

"Of course now! What use will it be later?" Max winced at the sound of his own voice.

"As Your Grace wishes." The sepulchral tones left Max in no doubt of his butler's deep disapproval.

As the door closed behind Hillshaw, Max lay back in the chair, his fingers at his temples, and fixed Caroline with an unwavering stare. "You may commence."

She smiled, entirely at her ease once more. "My father was Sir Thomas Twinning. He was an old friend of the Duke of Twyford—the previous Duke, I imagine."

Max nodded. "My uncle. I inherited the title from him. He was killed unexpectedly three months ago, together with his two sons. I never expected to inherit the estate, so am unfamiliar with whatever arrangements your parent may have made with the last Duke."

Caroline nodded and waited until Hillshaw, delivering the requested ice-pack on a silver salver to his master, withdrew. "I see. When my father died eighteen months ago, my sisters and I were informed that he had left us to the guardianship of the Duke of Twyford."

"Eighteen months ago? What have you been doing since then?"

"We stayed on the estate for a time. It passed to a distant cousin and he was prepared to let us remain. But it seemed senseless to stay buried there forever. The Duke wanted us to join his household immediately, but we were in mourning. I persuaded him to let us go to my late stepmother's family in New York. They'd always wanted us to visit and it seemed the perfect opportunity. I wrote to him when we were in New York, telling him we would call on him when we returned to England and giving him the date of our expected arrival. He replied and suggested I call on him today. And so, here I am."

Max saw it all now. Caroline Twinning was yet another part of his damnably awkward inheritance. Having led a life of unfettered hedonism from his earliest days, a rakehell ever since he came on the town, Max had soon understood that his lifestyle required capital to support it. So he had ensured his estates were all run efficiently and well. The Delmere estates he had inherited from his father were a model of modern estate management. But his uncle Henry had never had much real interest in his far larger holdings. After the tragic boating accident which had unexpectedly foisted on to him the responsibilities of the dukedom of Twyford, Max had found a complete overhaul of all his uncle's numerous estates was essential if they were not to sap the strength from his more prosperous Delmere holdings. The last three months had been spent in constant upheaval, with the old Twyford retainers trying to come to grips with the new Duke and his very different style. For Max, they had been three months of unending work. Only this week, he had finally thought that the end of the worst was in sight. He had packed his long-suffering secretary, Joshua Cummings, off home for a much needed rest. And now, quite clearly, the next chapter in the saga of his Twyford inheritance was about to start.

"You mentioned sisters. How many?"

"My half-sisters, really. There are four of us, altogether."

The lightness of the answer made Max instantly suspicious. "How old?"

There was a noticeable hesitation before Caroline answered, "Twenty, nineteen and eighteen."

The effect on Max was electric. "Good Lord! They didn't accompany you here, did they?"

Bewildered, Caroline replied, "No. I left them at the hotel."

"Thank God for that," said Max. Encountering Caroline's enquiring gaze, he smiled. "If anyone had seen them entering here, it would have been around town in a flash that I was setting up a harem."

The smile made Caroline blink. At his words, her grey eyes widened slightly. She could hardly pretend not to understand. Noticing the peculiar light in the blue eyes as they rested on her, it seemed a very good thing she was the Duke's ward. From her admittedly small understanding of the morals of his type, she suspected her position would keep her safe as little else might.

Unbeknown to her, Max was thinking precisely the same thing. And resolving to divest himself of his latest inherited responsibility with all possible speed. Aside from having no wish whatever to figure as the guardian of four young ladies of marriageable age, he needed to clear the obstacles from his path to Caroline Twinning. It occurred to him that her explanation of her life history had been curiously glib and decidedly short on detail. "Start at the beginning. Who was your mother and when did she die?"

Caroline had come unprepared to recite her history, imagining the Duke to be cognizant of the facts. Still, in the circumstances, she could hardly refuse. "My mother was Caroline Farningham, of the Staffordshire Farninghams."

Max nodded. An ancient family, well-known and well-connected.

Caroline's gaze had wandered to the rows of books lining the shelves behind the Duke. "She died shortly after I was born. I never knew her. After some years, my father married again, this time to the daughter of a local family who were about to leave for the colonies. Eleanor was very good to me and she looked after all of us comfortably, until she died six years ago. Of course, my father was disappointed that he never had a son and he rarely paid any attention to the four of us, so it was all left up to Eleanor."

The more he heard of him, the more Max was convinced that Sir Thomas Twinning had had a screw loose. He had clearly been a most unnatural parent. Still, the others were only Miss Twinning's half-sisters. Presumably they were not all as ravishing as she. It occurred to him that he should ask for clarification on this point but, before he could properly phrase the question, another and equally intriguing matter came to mind.

"Why was it none of you was presented before? If your father was sufficiently concerned to organize a guardian for you, surely the easiest solution would have been to have handed you into the care of husbands?"

Caroline saw no reason not to satisfy what was, after all, an entirely understandable curiosity. "We were never presented because my father disapproved of such...oh, frippery pastimes! To be perfectly honest, I sometimes thought he disapproved of women in general."

Max blinked.

Caroline continued, "As for marriage, he had organized that after a fashion. I was supposed to have married Edgar Mulhall, our neighbour." Involuntarily, her face assumed an expression of distaste.

Max was amused. "Wouldn't he do?"

Caroline's gaze returned to the saturnine face. "You haven't met him or you wouldn't need to ask. He's..." She wrinkled her nose as she sought for an adequate description. "Righteous," she finally pronounced.

At that, Max laughed. "Clearly out of the question."

Caroline ignored the provocation in the blue eyes. "Papa had similar plans for my sisters, only, as he never noticed they were of marriageable age and I never chose to bring it to his attention, nothing came of them either."

Perceiving Miss Twinning's evident satisfaction, Max made a mental note to beware of her manipulative tendencies. "Very well. So much for the past. Now to the future. What was your arrangement with my uncle?"

The grey-green gaze was entirely innocent as it rested on his face. Max did not know whether to believe it or not.

"Well, it was really his idea, but it seemed a perfectly sensible one to me. He suggested we should be presented to the *ton*. I suspect he intended to find us suitable husbands and so bring his guardianship to an end." She paused, thinking. "I'm not aware of the terms of my father's will, but I assume such arrangements terminate should we marry?"

"Very likely," agreed Max. The throbbing in his head had eased considerably. His uncle's plan had much to recommend it, but, personally, he would much prefer not to have any wards at all. And he would be damned if he would have

Miss Twinning as his ward—that would cramp his style far too much. There were a few things even reprobates such as he held sacred and guardianship was one.

He knew she was watching him but made no further comment, his eyes fixed frowningly on his blotter as he considered his next move. At last, looking up at her, he said, "I've heard nothing of this until now. I'll have to get my solicitors to sort it out. Which firm handles your affairs?"

"Whitney and White. In Chancery Lane."

"Well, at least that simplifies matters. They handle the Twyford estates as well as my others." He laid the ice-pack down and looked at Caroline, a slight frown in his blue eyes. "Where are you staying?"

"Grillon's. We arrived yesterday."

Another thought occurred to Max. "On what have you been living for the last eighteen months?"

"Oh, we all had money left us by our mothers. We arranged to draw on that and leave our patrimony untouched."

Max nodded slowly. "But who had you in charge? You can't have travelled halfway around the world alone."

For the first time during this strange interview, Max saw Miss Twinning blush, ever so slightly. "Our maid and coachman, who acted as our courier, stayed with us."

The airiness of the reply did not deceive Max. "Allow me to comment, Miss Twinning, as your potential guardian, that such an arrangement will not do. Regardless of what may have been acceptable overseas, such a situation will not pass muster in London." He paused, considering the proprieties for what was surely the first time in his life. "At least you're at Grillon's for the moment. That's safe enough."

After another pause, during which his gaze did not leave Caroline's face, he said, "I'll see Whitney this morning and settle the matter. I'll call on you at two to let you know how things have fallen out." A vision of himself meeting a beautiful young lady and attempting to converse with her within the portals of fashionable Grillon's, under the fas-

cinated gaze of all the other patrons, flashed before his eyes.
"On second thoughts, I'll take you for a drive in the Park.
That way," he continued in reply to the question in her grey-
green eyes, "we might actually get a chance to talk."

He tugged the bell pull and Hillshaw appeared. "Have the
carriage brought around. Miss Twinning is returning to
Grillon's."

"Yes, Your Grace."

"Oh, no! I couldn't put you to so much trouble," said
Caroline.

"My dear child," drawled Max, "my wards would certainly not go about London in hacks. See to it, Hillshaw."

"Yes, Your Grace." Hillshaw withdrew, for once in perfect agreement with his master.

Caroline found the blue eyes, which had quizzed her
throughout this exchange, still regarding her, a gently
mocking light in their depths. But she was a lady of no little courage and smiled back serenely, unknowingly sealing
her fate.

Never, thought Max, had he met a woman so attractive.
One way or another, he would break the ties of guardianship. A short silence fell, punctuated by the steady ticking
of the long case clock in the corner. Max took the opportunity afforded by Miss Twinning's apparent fascination
with the rows of leather-bound tomes at his back to study
her face once more. A fresh face, full of lively humour and
a brand of calm self-possession which, in his experience, was
rarely found in young women. Undoubtedly a woman of
character.

His sharp ears caught the sound of carriage wheels in the
street. He rose and Caroline perforce rose, too. "Come,
Miss Twinning. Your carriage awaits."

Max led her to the front door but forbore to go any further, bowing over her hand gracefully before allowing Hillshaw to escort her to the waiting carriage. The less chance
there was for anyone to see him with her the better. At least
until he had solved this guardianship tangle.

As soon as the carriage door was shut by the majestic Hillshaw, the horses moved forward at a trot. Caroline lay back against the squabs, her gaze fixed unseeingly on the nearside window as the carriage traversed fashionable London. Bemused, she tried to gauge the effect of the unexpected turn their futures had taken. Imagine having a guardian like that!

Although surprised at being redirected from Twyford House to Delmere House, she had still expected to meet the vague and amenable gentleman who had so readily acquiesced, albeit by correspondence, to all her previous suggestions. Her mental picture of His Grace of Twyford had been of a man in late middle age, bewigged as many of her father's generation were, distinctly past his prime and with no real interest in dealing with four lively young women. She spared a small smile as she jettisoned her preconceived image. Instead of a comfortable, fatherly figure, she would now have to deal with a man who, if first impressions were anything to go by, was intelligent, quick-witted and far too perceptive for her liking. To imagine the new Duke would not know to a nicety how to manage four young women was patently absurd. If she had been forced to express an opinion, Caroline would have said that, with the present Duke of Twyford, managing women was a speciality. Furthermore, given his undoubted experience, she strongly suspected he would be highly resistant to feminine cajoling in any form. A frown clouded her grey-green eyes. She was not entirely sure she approved of the twist their fates had taken. Thinking back over the recent interview, she smiled. He had not seemed too pleased with the idea himself.

For a moment, she considered the possibility of coming to some agreement with the Duke, essentially breaking the guardianship clause of her father's will. But only for a moment. It was true she had never been presented to the *ton* but she had cut her social eyeteeth long ago. While the idea of unlimited freedom to do as they pleased might sound tempting, there was the undeniable fact that she and her half-sisters were heiresses of sorts. Her father, having an extremely repressive notion of the degree of knowledge which could be allowed mere females, had never been particularly forthcoming regarding their eventual state. Yet there had never been any shortage of funds in all the years Caroline could remember. She rather thought they would at least be comfortably dowered. Such being the case, the traps and pitfalls of society, without the protection of a guardian, such as the Duke of Twyford, were not experiences to which she would willingly expose her sisters.

As the memory of a certain glint in His grace of Twyford's eye and the distinctly determined set of his jaw drifted past her mind's eye, the unwelcome possibility that he might repudiate them, for whatever reasons, hove into view. Undoubtedly, if there was any way to overset their guardianship, His Grace would find it. Unaccountably, she was filled with an inexplicable sense of disappointment.

Still, she told herself, straightening in a purposeful way, it was unlikely there was anything he could do about it. And she rather thought they would be perfectly safe with the new Duke of Twyford, as long as they *were* his wards. She allowed her mind to dwell on the question of whether she really wanted to be safe from the Duke of Twyford for several minutes before giving herself a mental shake. Great heavens! She had only just met the man and here she was, mooning over him like a green girl! She tried to frown but the action dissolved into a sheepish grin at her own susceptibility. Settling more comfortably in the corner of the luxurious carriage, she fell to rehearsing her description of what had occurred in anticipation of her sisters' eager questions.

WITHIN MINUTES of Caroline Twinning's departure from Delmere House, Max had issued a succession of orders, one of which caused Mr. Hubert Whitney, son of Mr. Josiah Whitney, the patriarch of the firm Whitney and White, Solicitors, of Chancery Lane, to present himself at Delmere House just before eleven. Mr. Whitney was a dry, desic-

cated man of uncertain age, very correctly attired in dusty
black. He was his father's son in every way and, now that
his sire was no longer able to leave his bed, he attended to all
his father's wealthier clients. As Hillshaw showed him into
the well-appointed library, he breathed a sigh of relief, not
for the first time, that it was Max Rotherbridge who had
inherited the difficult Twyford estates. Unknown to Max,
Mr. Whitney held him in particular esteem, frequently
wishing that others among his clients could be equally
straightforward and decisive. It really made life so much
easier.

Coming face-to-face with his favourite client, Mr. Whitney was immediately informed that His Grace, the Duke of
Twyford, was in no way amused to find he was apparently
the guardian of four marriageable young ladies. Mr. Whitney was momentarily at a loss. Luckily, he had brought with
him all the current Twyford papers and the Twinning documents were among these. Finding that his employer did not
intend to upbraid him for not having informed him of a cir-
cumstance which, he was only too well aware, he should
have brought forward long ago, he applied himself to as-
sessing the terms of the late Sir Thomas Twinning's will.
Having refreshed his memory on its details, he then turned
to the late Duke's will.

Max stood by the fire, idly watching. He liked Whitney.
He did not fluster and he knew his business.

Finally, Mr. Whitney pulled the gold pince-nez from his
face and glanced at his client. "Sir Thomas Twinning pre-
deceased your uncle, and, under the terms of your uncle's
will, it's quite clear you inherit all his responsibilities."

Max's black brows had lowered. "So I'm stuck with this
guardianship?"

Mr. Whitney pursed his lips. "I wouldn't go so far as to
say that. The guardianship could be broken, I fancy, as it's
quite clear Sir Thomas did not intend you, personally, to be
his daughters' guardian." He gazed at the fire and sol-

emnly shook his head. "No one, I'm sure, could doubt that."

Max smiled wryly.

"However," Mr. Whitney continued, "should you succeed in dissolving the guardianship clause, then the young ladies will be left with no protector. Did I understand you correctly in thinking they are presently in London and plan to remain for the Season?"

It did not need a great deal of intelligence to see where Mr. Whitney's discourse was heading. Exasperated at having his usually comfortably latent conscience pricked into life, Max stalked to the window and stood looking out at the courtyard beyond, hands clasped behind his straight back. "Good God, man! You can hardly think I'm a suitable guardian for four sweet young things!"

Mr. Whitney, thinking the Duke could manage very well if he chose to do so, persevered. "There remains the question of who, in your stead, would act for them."

The certain knowledge of what would occur if he abandoned four inexperienced, gently reared girls to the London scene, to the mercies of well-bred wolves who roamed its streets, crystallised in Max's unwilling mind. This was closely followed by the uncomfortable thought that he was considered the leader of one such pack, generally held to be the most dangerous. He could hardly refuse to be Caroline Twinning's guardian, only to set her up as his mistress. No. There was a limit to what even he could face down. Resolutely thrusting aside the memory, still vivid, of a pair of grey-green eyes, he turned to Mr. Whitney and growled, "All right, dammit! What do I need to know?"

Mr. Whitney smiled benignly and started to fill him in on the Twinning family history, much as Caroline had told it. Max interrupted him. "Yes, I know all that! Just tell me in round figures—how much is each of them worth?"

Mr. Whitney named a figure and Max's brows rose. For a moment, the Duke was entirely bereft of speech. He moved towards his desk and seated himself again.

"Each?"

Mr. Whitney merely inclined his head in assent. When the Duke remained lost in thought, he continued, "Sir Thomas was a very shrewd businessman, Your Grace."

"So it would appear. So each of these girls is an heiress in her own right?"

This time, Mr. Whitney nodded decisively.

Max was frowning.

"Of course," Mr. Whitney went on, consulting the documents on his knee, "you would only be responsible for the three younger girls."

Instantly he had his client's attention, the blue eyes oddly piercing. "Oh? Why is that?"

"Under the terms of their father's will, the Misses Twinning were given into the care of the Duke of Twyford until they attained the age of twenty-five or married. According to my records, I believe Miss Twinning to be nearing her twenty-sixth birthday. So she could, should she wish, assume responsibility for herself."

Max's relief was palpable. But hard on its heels came another consideration. Caroline Twinning had recognised his interest in her—hardly surprising as he had taken no pains to hide it. If she knew he was not her guardian, she would keep him at arm's length. Well, try to, at least. But Caroline Twinning was not a green girl. The aura of quiet self-assurance which clung to her suggested she would not be an easy conquest. Obviously, it would be preferable if she continued to believe she was protected from him by his guardianship. That way, he would have no difficulty in approaching her, his reputation notwithstanding. In fact, the more he thought of it, the more merits he could see in the situation. Perhaps, in this case, he could have his cake and eat it too? He eyed Mr. Whitney. "Miss Twinning knows nothing of the terms of her father's will. At present, she believes herself to be my ward, along with her half-sisters. Is there any pressing need to inform her of her change in status?"

Mr. Whitney blinked owlishly, a considering look suffusing his face as he attempted to unravel the Duke's motives for wanting Miss Twinning to remain as his ward. Particularly after wanting to dissolve the guardianship altogether. Max Rotherbridge did not normally vacillate.

Max, perfectly sensible of Mr. Whitney's thoughts, put forward the most acceptable excuses he could think of. "For a start, whether she's twenty-four or twenty-six, she's just as much in need of protection as her sisters. Then, too, there's the question of propriety. If it was generally known she was not my ward, it would be exceedingly difficult for her to be seen in my company. And as I'll still be guardian to her sisters, and as they'll be residing in one of my establishments, the situation could become a trifle delicate, don't you think?"

It was not necessary for him to elaborate. Mr. Whitney saw the difficulty clearly enough. It was his turn to frown. "What you say is quite true." Hubert Whitney had no opinion whatever in the ability of the young ladies to manage their affairs. "At present, there is nothing I can think of that requires Miss Twinning's agreement. I expect it can do no harm to leave her in ignorance of her status until she weds."

The mention of marriage brought a sudden check to Max's racing mind but he resolutely put the disturbing notion aside for later examination. He had too much to do today.

Mr. Whitney was continuing, "How do you plan to handle the matter, if I may make so bold as to ask?"

Max had already given the thorny problem of how four young ladies could be presented to the *ton* under his protection, without raising a storm, some thought. "I propose to open up Twyford House immediately. They can stay there. I intend to ask my aunt, Lady Benborough, to stand as the girls' sponsor. I'm sure she'll be only too thrilled. It'll keep her amused for the Season."

Mr. Whitney was acquainted with Lady Benborough. He rather thought it would. A smile curved his thin lips.

The Duke stood, bringing the interview to a close.

Mr. Whitney rose. "That seems most suitable. If there's anything further in which we can assist Your Grace, we'll be only too delighted."

Max nodded in response to this formal statement. As Mr. Whitney bowed, prepared to depart, Max, a past master of social intrigue, saw one last hole in the wall and moved to block it. "If there's any matter you wish to discuss with Miss Twinning, I suggest you do it through me, as if I was, in truth, her guardian. As you handle both our estates, there can really be no impropriety in keeping up appearances. For Miss Twinning's sake."

Mr. Whitney bowed again. "I foresee no problems, Your Grace."

CHAPTER TWO

AFTER MR. WHITNEY LEFT, Max issued a set of rapid and comprehensive orders to his majordomo Wilson. In response, his servants flew to various corners of London, some to Twyford House, others to certain agencies specializing in the hire of household staff to the élite of the *ton*. One footman was despatched with a note from the Duke to an address in Half Moon Street, requesting the favour of a private interview with his paternal aunt, Lady Benborough.

As Max had intended, his politely worded missive intrigued his aunt. Wondering what had prompted such a strange request from her reprehensible nephew, she immediately granted it and settled down to await his coming with an air of pleasurable anticipation.

Max arrived at the small house shortly after noon. He found his aunt attired in a very becoming gown of purple sarsenet with a new and unquestionably modish wig perched atop her commanding visage. Max, bowing elegantly before her, eyed the wig askance.

Augusta Benborough sighed. "Well, I suppose I'll have to send it back, if that's the way you feel about it!"

Max grinned and bent to kiss the proffered cheek. "Definitely not one of your better efforts, Aunt."

She snorted. "Unfortunately, I can hardly claim you know nothing about it. It's the very latest fashion, I'll have you know." Max raised one laconic brow. "Yes, well," continued his aunt, "I dare say you're right. Not quite my style."

As she waited while he disposed his long limbs in a chair opposite the corner of the chaise where she sat, propped up by a pile of colourful cushions, she passed a critical glance over her nephew's elegant figure. How he contrived to look so precise when she knew he cared very little how he appeared was more than she could tell. She had heard it said that his man was a genius. Personally, she was of the opinion it was Max's magnificent physique and dark good looks that carried the day.

"I hope you're going to satisfy my curiosity without a great deal of roundaboutation."

"My dear aunt, when have I ever been other than direct?"

She looked at him shrewdly. "Want a favour, do you? Can't imagine what it is but you'd better be quick about asking. Miriam will be back by one and I gather you'd rather not have her listening." Miriam Alford was a faded spinster cousin of Lady Benborough's who lived with her, filling the post of companion to the fashionable old lady. "I sent her to Hatchard's when I got your note," she added in explanation.

Max smiled. Of all his numerous relatives, his Aunt Benborough, his father's youngest sister, was his favourite. While the rest of them, his mother included, constantly tried to reform him by ringing peals over him, appealing to his sense of what was acceptable, something he steadfastly denied any knowledge of, Augusta Benborough rarely made any comment on his lifestyle or the numerous scandals this provoked. When he had first come on the town, it had rapidly been made plain to his startled family that in Max they beheld a reincarnation of the second Viscount Delmere. If even half the tales were true, Max's great-grandfather had been a thoroughly unprincipled character, entirely devoid of morals. Lady Benborough, recently widowed, had asked Max to tea and had taken the opportunity to inform him in no uncertain terms of her opinion of his behaviour. She had then proceeded to outline all his faults, in detail. However,

as she had concluded by saying that she fully expected her
tirade to have no effect whatsoever on his subsequent conduct, nor could she imagine how anyone in their right mind
could think it would, Max had borne the ordeal with an
equanimity which would have stunned his friends. She had
eventually dismissed him with the words, "Having at least
had the politeness to hear me out, you may now depart and
continue to go to hell in your own fashion and with my good
will."

Now a widow of many years' standing, she was still a
force to be reckoned with. She remained fully absorbed in
the affairs of the *ton* and continued to be seen at all the
crushes and every gala event. Max knew she was as shrewd
as she could hold together and, above all, had an excellent
sense of humour. All in all, she was just what he needed.

"I've come to inform you that, along with all the other
encumbrances I inherited from Uncle Henry, I seem to have
acquired four wards."

"*You?*" Lady Benborough's rendering of the word was
rather more forceful than Miss Twinning's had been.

Max nodded. "Me. Four young ladies, one, the only one
I've so far set eyes on, as lovely a creature as any other likely
to be presented this Season."

"Good God! Who was so besotted as to leave four young
girls in your care?" If anything, her ladyship was outraged
at the very idea. Then, the full impact of the situation struck
her. Her eyes widened. "Oh, good lord!" She collapsed
against her cushions, laughing uncontrollably.

Knowing this was an attitude he was going to meet increasingly in the next few weeks, Max sighed. In an even
tone suggestive of long suffering, he pointed out the obvious. "They weren't left to me but to my esteemed and now
departed uncle's care. Mind you, I can't see that he'd have
been much use to 'em either."

Wiping the tears from her eyes, Lady Benborough considered this view. "Can't see it myself," she admitted.
"Henry always was a slow-top. Who are they?"

"The Misses Twinning. From Hertfordshire." Max proceeded to give her a brief résumé of the life history of the Twinnings, ending with the information that it transpired all four girls were heiresses.

Augusta Benborough was taken aback. "And you say they're beautiful to boot?"

"The one I've seen, Caroline, the eldest, most definitely is."

"Well, if anyone should know it's you!" replied her ladyship testily. Max acknowledged the comment with the slightest inclination of his head.

Lady Benborough's mind was racing. "So, what do you want with me?"

"What I would *like*, dearest Aunt," said Max, with his sweetest smile, "is for you to act as chaperon to the girls and present them to the *ton*." Max paused. His aunt said nothing, sitting quite still with her sharp blue eyes, very like his own, fixed firmly on his face. He continued. "I'm opening up Twyford House. It'll be ready for them tomorrow. I'll stand the nonsense—all of it." Still she said nothing. "Will you do it?"

Augusta Benborough thought she would like nothing better than to be part of the hurly-burly of the marriage game again. But four? All at once? Still, there was Max's backing, and that would count for a good deal. Despite his giving the distinct impression of total uninterest in anything other than his own pleasure, she knew from experience that, should he feel inclined, Max could and would perform feats impossible for those with lesser clout in the fashionable world. Years after the event, she had learned that, when her youngest son had embroiled himself in a scrape so hideous that even now she shuddered to think of it, it had been Max who had rescued him. And apparently for no better reason than it had been bothering her. She still owed him for that.

But there were problems. Her own jointure was not particularly large and, while she had never asked Max for relief, turning herself out in the style he would expect of his wards' chaperon was presently beyond her slender means. Hesitantly, she said, "My own wardrobe..."

"Naturally you'll charge all costs you incur in this business to me," drawled Max, his voice bored as he examined through his quizzing glass a china cat presently residing on his aunt's mantelpiece. He knew perfectly well his aunt managed on a very slim purse but was too wise to offer direct assistance which would, he knew, be resented, not only by the lady herself but also by her pompous elder son.

"Can I take Miriam with me to Twyford House?"

With a shrug, Max assented. "Aside from anything else, she might come in handy with four charges."

"When can I meet them?"

"They're staying at Grillon's. I'm taking Miss Twinning for a drive this afternoon to tell her what I've decided. I'll arrange for them to move to Twyford House tomorrow afternoon. I'll send Wilson to help you and Mrs. Alford in transferring to Mount Street. It would be best, I suppose, if you could make the move in the morning. You'll want to familiarize yourself with the staff and so on." Bethinking himself that it would be wise to have one of his own well-trained staff on hand, he added, "I suppose I can let you have Wilson for a week or two, until you settle in. I suggest you and I meet the Misses Twinning when they arrive—shall we say at three?"

Lady Benborough was entranced by the way her nephew seemed to dismiss complications like opening and staffing a mansion overnight. Still, with the efficient and reliable Wilson on the job, presumably it would be done. Feeling a sudden and unexpected surge of excitement at the prospect of embarking on the Season with a definite purpose in life, she drew a deep breath. "Very well. I'll do it!"

"Good!" Max stood. "I'll send Wilson to call on you this afternoon."

His aunt, already engrossed in the matter of finding husbands for the Twinning chits, looked up. "Have you seen the other three girls?"

Max shook his head. Imagining the likely scene should they be on hand this afternoon when he called for Miss Twinning, he closed his eyes in horror. He could just hear the *on-dits*. "And I hope to God I don't see them in Grillon's foyer either!"

Augusta Benborough laughed.

WHEN HE CALLED AT Grillon's promptly at two, Max was relieved to find Miss Twinning alone in the foyer, seated on a chaise opposite the door, her bonnet beside her. He was not to know that Caroline had had to exert every last particle of persuasion to achieve this end. And she had been quite unable to prevent her three sisters from keeping watch from the windows of their bedchambers.

As she had expected, she had had to describe His Grace of Twyford in detail for her sisters. Looking up at the figure striding across the foyer towards her, she did not think she had done too badly. What had been hardest to convey was the indefinable air that hung about him—compelling, exciting, it immediately brought to mind a whole range of emotions well-bred young ladies were not supposed to comprehend, let alone feel. As he took her hand for an instant in his own, and smiled down at her in an oddly lazy way, she decided she had altogether underestimated the attractiveness of that sleepy smile. It was really quite devastating.

Within a minute, Caroline found herself on the box seat of a fashionable curricle drawn by a pair of beautiful but restive bays. She resisted the temptation to glance up at the first-floor windows where she knew the other three would be stationed. Max mounted to the driving seat and the diminutive tiger, who had been holding the horses' heads, swung up behind. Then they were off, tacking through the traffic towards Hyde Park.

Caroline resigned herself to silence until the safer precincts of the Park were reached. However, it seemed the Duke was quite capable of conversing intelligently while negotiating the chaos of the London streets.

"I trust Grillon's has met with your approval thus far?"

"Oh, yes. They've been most helpful," returned Caroline. "Were you able to clarify the matter of our guardianship?"

Max was unable to suppress a smile at her directness. He nodded, his attention temporarily claimed by the off-side horse which had decided to take exception to a monkey dancing on the pavement, accompanied by an accordion player.

"Mr. Whitney has assured me that, as I am the Duke of Twyford, I must therefore be your guardian." He had allowed his reluctance to find expression in his tone. As the words left his lips, he realised that the unconventional woman beside him might well ask why he found the role of protector to herself and her sisters so distasteful. He immediately went on the attack. "And, in that capacity, I should like to know how you have endeavoured to come by Parisian fashions?"

His sharp eyes missed little and his considerable knowledge of feminine attire told him Miss Twinning's elegant pelisse owed much to the French. But France was at war with England and Paris no longer the playground of the rich.

Initially stunned that he should know enough to come so close to the truth, Caroline quickly realised the source of his knowledge. A spark of amusement danced in her eyes. She smiled and answered readily, "I assure you we did not run away to Brussels instead of New York."

"Oh, I wasn't afraid of that!" retorted Max, perfectly willing to indulge in plain speaking. "If you'd been in Brussels, I'd have heard of it."

"Oh?" Caroline turned a fascinated gaze on him.

Max smiled down at her.

Praying she was not blushing, Caroline strove to get the conversation back on a more conventional course. "Actually, you're quite right about the clothes, they are Parisian. But not from the Continent. There were two *couturières* from Paris on the boat going to New York. They asked if they could dress us, needing the business to become known in America. It was really most fortunate. We took the opportunity to get quite a lot made up before we returned— we'd been in greys for so long that none of us had anything suitable to wear."

"How did you find American society?"

Caroline reminded herself to watch her tongue. She did not delude herself that just because the Duke was engaged in handling a team of high-couraged cattle through the busy streets of London he was likely to miss any slip she made. She was rapidly learning to respect the intelligence of this fashionable rake. "Quite frankly, we found much to entertain us. Of course, our relatives were pleased to see us and organised a great many outings and entertainments." No need to tell him they had had a riotous time.

"Did the tone of the society meet with your approval?"

He had already told her he would have known if they had been in Europe. Did he have connections in New York? How much could he know of their junketing? Caroline gave herself a mental shake. How absurd! He had not known of their existence until this morning. "Well, to be sure, it wasn't the same as here. Many more cits and half-pay officers about. And, of course, nothing like the *ton*."

Unknowingly, her answer brought some measure of relief to Max. Far from imagining his new-found wards had been indulging in high living abroad, he had been wondering whether they had any social experience at all. Miss Twinning's reply told him that she, at least, knew enough to distinguish the less acceptable among society's hordes.

They had reached the gates of the Park and turned into the carriage drive. Soon, the curricle was bowling along at a steady pace under the trees, still devoid of any but the earliest leaves. A light breeze lifted the ends of the ribbons on Caroline's hat and playfully danced along the horses' dark manes.

Max watched as Caroline gazed about her with interest. "I'm afraid you'll not see many notables at this hour. Mostly nursemaids and their charges. Later, between three and five, it'll be crowded. The Season's not yet begun in earnest, but by now most people will have returned to town. And the Park is the place to be seen. All the old biddies come here to exchange the latest *on-dits* and all the young ladies promenade along the walks with their beaux."

"I see." Caroline smiled to herself, a secret smile as she imagined how she and her sisters would fit into this scene.

Max saw the smile and was puzzled. Caroline Twinning was decidedly more intelligent than the women with whom he normally consorted. He could not guess her thoughts and was secretly surprised at wanting to know them. Then, remembered one piece of vital information he had yet to discover. "Apropos of my uncle's plan to marry you all off, satisfy my curiosity, Miss Twinning. What do your sisters look like?"

This was the question she had been dreading. Caroline hesitated, searching for precisely the right words with which to get over the difficult ground. "Well, they've always been commonly held to be well to pass."

Max noted the hesitation. He interpreted her careful phrasing to mean that the other three girls were no more than average. He nodded, having suspected as much, and allowed the subject to drop.

They rounded the lake and he slowed his team to a gentle trot. "As your guardian, I've made certain arrangements for your immediate future." He noticed the grey eyes had flown to his face. "Firstly, I've opened Twyford House. Secondly, I've arranged for my aunt, Lady Benborough, to act as your chaperon for the Season. She's very well-connected and will know exactly how everything should be managed. You may place complete confidence in her advice. You will remove from Grillon's tomorrow. I'll send my man, Wilson, to assist you in the move to Twyford House. He'll call for you at two tomorrow. I presume that gives you enough time to pack?''

Caroline assumed the question to be rhetorical. She was stunned. He had not known they existed at nine this morning. How could he have organised all that since ten?

Thinking he may as well clear all the looming fences while he was about it, Max added, ''As for funds, I presume your earlier arrangements still apply. However, should you need any further advances, as I now hold the purse-strings of your patrimonies, you may apply directly to me.''

His last statement succeeded in convincing Caroline that it would not be wise to underestimate this Duke. Despite having only since this morning to think about it, he had missed very little. And, as he held the purse-strings, he could call the tune. As she had foreseen, life as the wards of a man as masterful and domineering as the present Duke of Twyford was rapidly proving to be was definitely not going to be as unfettered as they had imagined would be the case with his vague and easily led uncle. There were, however, certain advantages in the changed circumstances and she, for one, could not find it in her to repine.

More people were appearing in the Park, strolling about the lawns sloping down to the river and gathering in small groups by the carriageway, laughing and chatting.

A man of slight stature, mincing along beside the carriage drive, looked up in startled recognition as they passed. He was attired in a bottle-green coat with the most amazing amount of frogging Caroline had ever seen. In place of a cravat, he seemed to be wearing a very large floppy bow around his neck. ''Who on earth was that quiz?'' she asked.

''That quiz, my dear ward, is none other than Walter Millington, one of the fops. In spite of his absurd clothes, he's unexceptionable enough but he has a sharp tongue so it's wise for young ladies to stay on his right side. Don't laugh at him.''

Two old ladies in an ancient landau were staring at them with an intensity which in lesser persons would be considered rude.

Max did not wait to be asked. "And those are the Misses Berry. They're as old as bedamned and know absolutely everyone. Kind souls. One's entirely vague and the other's sharp as needles."

Caroline smiled. His potted histories were entertaining.

A few minutes later, the gates came into view and Max headed his team in that direction. Caroline saw a horseman pulled up by the carriage drive a little way ahead. His face clearly registered recognition of the Duke's curricle and the figure driving it. Then his eyes passed to her and stopped. At five and twenty, Caroline had long grown used to the effect she had on men, particularly certain sorts of men. As they drew nearer, she saw that the gentleman was impeccably attired and had the same rakish air as the Duke. The rider held up a hand in greeting and she expected to feel the curricle slow. Instead, it flashed on, the Duke merely raising a hand in an answering salute.

Amused, Caroline asked, "And who, pray tell, was that?"

Max was thinking that keeping his friends in ignorance of Miss Twinning was going to prove impossible. Clearly, he would be well-advised to spend some time planning the details of this curious seduction, or he might find himself with rather more competition than he would wish. "That was Lord Ramsleigh."

"A friend of yours?"

"Precisely."

Caroline laughed at the repressive tone. The husky sound ran tingling along Max's nerves. It flashed into his mind that Caroline Twinning seemed to understand a great deal more than one might expect from a woman with such a decidedly restricted past. He was prevented from studying her face by the demands of successfully negotiating their exit from the Park.

They were just swinging out into the traffic when an elegant barouche pulled up momentarily beside them, heading into the Park. The thin, middle-aged woman, with a severe, almost horsy countenance, who had been languidly lying against the silken cushions, took one look at the curricle and sat bolt upright. In her face, astonishment mingled freely with rampant curiosity. "Twyford!"

Max glanced down as both carriages started to move again. "My lady." He nodded and then they were swallowed up in the traffic.

Glancing back, Caroline saw the elegant lady remonstrating with her coachman. She giggled. "Who was she?"

"That, my ward, was Sally, Lady Jersey. A name to remember. She is the most inveterate gossip in London. Hence her nickname of Silence. Despite that, she's kind-hearted enough. She's one of the seven patronesses of Almack's. You'll have to get vouchers to attend but I doubt that will be a problem."

They continued in companionable silence, threading their way through the busy streets. Max was occupied with imagining the consternation Lady Jersey's sighting of them was going to cause. And there was Ramsleigh, too. A wicked smile hovered on his lips. He rather thought he was going to spend a decidedly amusing evening. It would be some days before news of his guardianship got around. Until then, he would enjoy the speculation. He was certain he would not enjoy the mirth of his friends when they discovered the truth.

"Oooh, Caro! Isn't he magnificent?" Arabella's round eyes, brilliant and bright, greeted Caroline as she entered their parlour.

"Did he agree to be our guardian?" asked the phlegmatic Sarah.

And, "Is he nice?" from the youngest, Lizzie.

All the important questions, thought Caroline with an affectionate smile, as she threw her bonnet aside and subsided into an armchair with a whisper of her stylish skirts. Her three half-sisters gathered around eagerly. She eyed them fondly. It would be hard to find three more attractive young ladies, even though she did say so herself. Twenty-year-old Sarah, with her dark brown hair and dramatically pale face, settling herself on one arm of her chair. Arabella on her other side, chestnut curls rioting around her heart-shaped and decidedly mischievous countenance, and Lizzie, the youngest and quietest of them all, curling up at her feet, her grey-brown eyes shining with the intentness of youth, the light dusting of freckles on the bridge of her nose persisting despite the ruthless application of Denmark lotion, crushed strawberries and every other remedy ever invented.

"Commonly held to be well to pass." Caroline's own words echoed in her ears. Her smile grew. "Well, my loves, it seems we are, incontrovertibly and without doubt, the Duke of Twyford's wards."

"When does he want to meet us?" asked Sarah, ever practical.

"Tomorrow afternoon. He's opening up Twyford House and we're to move in then. He resides at Delmere House, where I went this morning, so the properties will thus be preserved. His aunt, Lady Benborough, is to act as our chaperon—she's apparently well-connected and willing to sponsor us. She'll be there tomorrow."

A stunned silence greeted her news. Then Arabella voiced the awe of all three. "Since ten this morning?"

Caroline's eyes danced. She nodded.

Arabella drew a deep breath. "Is he . . . masterful?"

"Very!" replied Caroline. "But you'll be caught out, my love, if you think to sharpen your claws on our guardian. He's a deal too shrewd, and experienced besides." Studying the pensive faces around her, she added. "Any flirtation between any of us and Max Rotherbridge would be doomed to failure. As his wards, we're out of court, and he won't stand any nonsense, I warn you."

"Hmm." Sarah stood and wandered to the windows before turning to face her. "So it's as you suspected? He won't be easy to manage?"

Caroline smiled at the thought and shook her head decisively. "I'm afraid, my dears, that any notions we may have had of setting the town alight while in the care of a complaisant guardian have died along with the last Duke." One slim forefinger tapped her full lower lip thoughtfully. "However," she continued, "provided we adhere to society's rules and cause him no trouble, I doubt our new guardian will throw any rub in our way. We did come to London to find husbands, after all. And that," she said forcefully, gazing at the three faces fixed on hers, "is, unless I miss my guess, precisely what His Grace intends us to do."

"So he's agreed to present us so we can find husbands?" asked Lizzie.

Again Caroline nodded. "I think it bothers him, to have four wards." She smiled in reminiscence, then added, "And from what I've seen of the *ton* thus far, I suspect the present Duke as our protector may well be a distinct improvement over the previous incumbent. I doubt we'll have to fight off the fortune-hunters."

Some minutes ticked by in silence as they considered their new guardian. Then Caroline stood and shook out her skirts. She took a few steps into the room before turning to address her sisters.

"Tomorrow we'll be collected at two and conveyed to Twyford House, which is in Mount Street." She paused to let the implication of her phrasing sink in. "As you love me, you'll dress demurely and behave with all due reticence. No playing off your tricks on the Duke." She looked pointedly at Arabella, who grinned roguishly back. "Exactly so! I think, in the circumstances, we should make life as easy as possible for our new guardian. I feel sure he could have broken the guardianship if he had wished and can only be thankful he chose instead to honour his uncle's obligations. But we shouldn't try him too far." She ended her motherly admonitions with a stern air, deceiving her sisters not at all.

As the other three heads came together, Caroline turned to gaze unseeingly out of the window. A bewitching smile curved her generous lips and a twinkle lit her grey-green eyes. Softly, she murmured to herself, "For I've a definite suspicion he's going to find us very trying indeed!"

THUP, THUP, THUP. The tip of Lady Benborough's thin cane beat a slow tattoo, muffled by the pile of the Aubusson carpet. She was pleasantly impatient, waiting with definite anticipation to see her new charges. Her sharp blue gaze had already taken in the state of the room, the perfectly organised furniture, everything tidy and in readiness. If she had not known it for fact, she would never have believed that, yesterday morn, Twyford House had been shut up, the knocker off the door, every piece of furniture shrouded in Holland covers. Wilson was priceless. There was even a bowl of early crocus on the side-table between the long windows. These stood open, giving access to the neat courtyard, flanked by flowerbeds bursting into colourful life. A marble fountain stood at its centre, a Grecian maiden pouring water never-endingly from an urn.

Her contemplation of the scene was interrupted by a peremptory knock on the street door. A moment later, she heard the deep tones of men's voices and relaxed. Max. She would never get used to thinking of him as Twyford—she had barely become accustomed to him being Viscount Delmere. Max was essentially Max—he needed no title to distinguish him.

The object of her vagaries strode into the room. As always, his garments were faultless, his boots beyond compare. He bowed with effortless grace over her hand, his blue eyes, deeper in shade than her own but alive with the same intelligence, quizzing her. "A vast improvement, Aunt."

It took a moment to realise he was referring to her latest wig, a newer version of the same style she had favoured for the past ten years. She was not sure whether she was pleased or insulted. She compromised and snorted. "Trying to turn me up pretty, heh?"

"I would never insult your intelligence so, ma'am," he drawled, eyes wickedly laughing.

Lady Benborough suppressed an involuntary smile in response. The trouble with Max was that he was such a thorough-going rake that the techniques had flowed into all spheres of his life. He would undoubtedly flirt outrageously with his old nurse! Augusta Benborough snorted again. "Wilson's left to get the girls. He should be back any minute. Provided they're ready, that is."

She watched as her nephew ran a cursory eye over the room before selecting a Hepplewhite chair and elegantly disposing his long length in it.

"I trust everything meets with your approval?"

She waved her hand to indicate the room. "Wilson's been marvellous. I don't know how he does it."

"Neither do I," admitted Wilson's employer. "And the rest of the house?"

"The same," she assured him, then continued, "I've been considering the matter of husbands for the chits. With that sort of money, I doubt we'll have trouble even if they have spots and squint."

Max merely inclined his head. "You may leave the fortune-hunters to me."

Augusta nodded. It was one of the things she particularly appreciated about Max—one never needed to spell things out. The fact that the Twinning girls were his wards would certainly see them safe from the attentions of the less desirable elements. The new Duke of Twyford was a noted Corinthian and a crack shot.

"Provided they're immediately presentable, I thought I might give a small party next week, to start the ball rolling.

But if their wardrobes need attention, or they can't dance, we'll have to postpone it.''

Remembering Caroline Twinning's stylish dress and her words on the matter, Max reassured her. ''And I'd bet a monkey they can dance, too.'' For some reason, he felt quite sure Caroline Twinning waltzed. It was the only dance he ever indulged in; he was firmly convinced that she waltzed.

Augusta was quite prepared to take Max's word on such matters. If nothing else, his notorious career through the bedrooms and bordellos of England had left him with an unerring eye for all things feminine. ''Next week, then,'' she said. ''Just a few of the more useful people and a smattering of the younger crowd.''

She looked up to find Max's eye on her.

''I sincerely hope you don't expect to see *me* at this event?''

''Good Lord, no! I want all attention on your wards, not on their guardian!''

Max smiled his lazy smile.

''If the girls are at all attractive, I see no problems at all in getting them settled. Who knows? One of them might snare Wolverton's boy.''

''That milksop?'' Max's mind rebelled at the vision of the engaging Miss Twinning on the arm of the future Earl of Wolverton. Then he shrugged. After all, he had yet to meet the three younger girls. ''Who knows?''

''Do you want me to keep a firm hand on the reins, give them a push if necessary or let them wander where they will?''

Max pondered the question, searching for the right words to frame his reply. ''Keep your eye on the three younger girls. They're likely to need some guidance. I haven't sighted them yet, so they may need more than that. But, despite her advanced years, I doubt Miss Twinning will need any help at all.''

His aunt interpreted this reply to mean that Miss Twinning's beauty, together with her sizeable fortune, would be sufficient to overcome the stigma of her years. The assessment was reassuring, coming as it did from her reprehensible nephew, whose knowledge was extensive in such matters. As her gaze rested on the powerful figure, negligently at ease in his chair, she reflected that it really was unfair he had inherited only the best from both his parents. The combination of virility, good looks and power of both mind and body was overwhelming; throw the titles in for good measure and it was no wonder Max Rotherbridge had been the target of so many matchmaking mamas throughout his adult life. But he had shown no sign whatever of succumbing to the demure attractions of any débutante. His preference was, always had been, for women of far more voluptuous charms. The litany of his past mistresses attested to his devotion to his ideal. They had all, every last one, been well-endowed. Hardly surprising, she mused. Max was tall, powerful and vigorous. She could not readily imagine any of the delicate debs satisfying his appetites. Her wandering mind dwelt on the subject of his latest *affaire*, aside, of course, from his current *chère amie*, an opera singer, so she had been told. Emma, Lady Mortland, was a widow of barely a year's standing but she had returned to town determined, it seemed, to make up for time lost through her marriage to an ageing peer. If the *on-dits* were true, she had fallen rather heavily in Max's lap. Looking at the strikingly handsome face of her nephew, Augusta grinned. Undoubtedly, Lady Mortland had set her cap at a Duchess's tiara. Deluded woman! Max, for all his air of unconcern, was born to his position. There was no chance he would offer marriage to Emma or any of her ilk. He would certainly avail himself of their proffered charms. Then when he tired of them, he would dismiss them, generously rewarding those who had the sense to play the game with suitable grace, callously ignoring those who did not.

The sounds of arrival gradually filtered into the drawing-room. Max raised his head. A spurt of feminine chatter drifted clearly to their ears. Almost immediately, silence was restored. Then, the door opened and Millwade, the new butler, entered to announce, "Miss Twinning."

Caroline walked through the door and advanced into the room, her sunny confidence cloaking her like bright sunshine. Max, who had risen, blinked and then strolled forward to take her hand. He bowed over it, smiling with conscious charm into her large eyes.

Caroline returned the smile, thoroughly conversant with its promise. While he was their guardian, she could afford to play his games. His strong fingers retained their clasp on her hand as he drew her forward to meet his aunt.

Augusta Benborough's mouth had fallen open at first sight of her eldest charge. But by the time Caroline faced her, she had recovered her composure. No wonder Max had said she would need no help. Great heavens! The girl was... well, no sense in beating about the bush—she was devilishly attractive. Sensually so. Responding automatically to the introduction, Augusta recognised the amused comprehension in the large and friendly grey eyes. Imperceptibly, she relaxed.

"Your sisters?" asked Max.

"I left them in the hall. I thought perhaps..." Caroline's words died on her lips as Max moved to the bell pull. Before she could gather her wits, Millwade was in the room, receiving his instructions. Bowing to the inevitable, Caroline closed her lips on her unspoken excuses. As she turned to Lady Benborough, her ladyship's brows rose in mute question. Caroline smiled and, with a swish of her delicate skirts, sat beside Lady Benborough. "Just watch," she whispered, her eyes dancing.

Augusta Benborough regarded her thoughtfully, then turned her attention to the door. As she did so, it opened again. First Sarah, then Arabella, then Lizzie Twinning entered the room.

A curious hiatus ensued as both Max Rotherbridge and his aunt, with more than fifty years of town bronze between them, started in patent disbelief at their charges. The three girls stood unselfconsciously, poised and confident, and then swept curtsies, first to Max, then to her ladyship.

Caroline beckoned and they moved forward to be presented, to a speechless Max, who had not moved from his position beside his chair, and then to a flabbergasted Lady Benborough.

As they moved past him to make their curtsy to his aunt, Max recovered the use of his faculties. He closed his eyes. But when he opened them again, they were still there. He was not hallucinating. There they were: three of the loveliest lovelies he had ever set eyes on—four if you counted Miss Twinning. They were scene-stealers, every one—the sort of young women whose appearance suspended conversations, whose passage engendered rampant curiosity, aside from other, less nameable emotions, and whose departure left onlookers wondering what on earth they had been talking about before. All from the same stable, all under one roof. Nominally his. Incredible. And then the enormity, the mind-numbing, all-encompassing reality of his inheritance struck him. One glance into Miss Twinning's grey eyes, brimming with mirth, told him she understood more than enough. His voice, lacking its customary strength and in a very odd register, came to his ears. "Impossible!"

His aunt Augusta collapsed laughing.

CHAPTER THREE

"No!" Max shook his head stubbornly, a frown of quite dramatic proportions darkening his handsome face.

Lady Benborough sighed mightily and frowned back. On recovering her wits, she had sternly repressed her mirth and sent the three younger Twinnings into the courtyard. But after ten minutes of carefully reasoned argument, Max remained adamant. However, she was quite determined her scapegrace nephew would not succeed in dodging his responsibilities. Aside from anything else, the situation seemed set to afford her hours of entertainment and, at her age, such opportunities could not be lightly passed by. Her lips compressed into a thin line and a martial light appeared in her blue eyes.

Max, recognising the signs, got in first. "It's impossible! Just *think* of the talk!"

Augusta's eyes widened to their fullest extent. "Why should you care?" she asked. "Your career to date would hardly lead one to suppose you fought shy of scandal." She fixed Max with a penetrating stare. "Besides, while there'll no doubt be talk, none of it will harm anyone. Quite the opposite. It'll get these girls into the limelight!"

The black frown on Max's face did not lighten.

Caroline wisely refrained from interfering between the two principal protagonists, but sat beside Augusta, looking as innocent as she could. Max's gaze swept over her and stopped on her face. His eyes narrowed. Caroline calmly returned his scrutiny.

There was little doubt in Max's mind that Caroline Twinning had deliberately concealed from him the truth about her sisters until he had gone too far in establishing himself as their guardian to pull back. He felt sure some retribution was owing to one who had so manipulated him but, staring into her large grey-green eyes, was unable to decide which of the numerous and varied punishments his fertile imagination supplied would be the most suitable. Instead, he said, in the tones of one goaded beyond endurance, "'Commonly held to be well to pass', indeed!"

Caroline smiled.

Augusta intervened. "Whatever you're thinking of, Max, it won't do! You're the girls' guardian—you told me so yourself. You cannot simply wash your hands of them. I can see it'll be a trifle awkward for you," her eyes glazed as she thought of Lady Mortland, "but if you don't concern yourself with them, who will?"

Despite his violent response to his first sight of all four Twinning sisters, perfectly understandable in the circumstances, Max had not seriously considered giving up his guardianship of them. His behaviour over the past ten minutes had been more in the nature of an emotional rearguard action in an attempt, which his rational brain acknowledged as futile, to resist the tide of change he could see rising up to swamp his hitherto well-ordered existence. He fired his last shot. "Do you seriously imagine that someone with my reputation will be considered a suitable guardian for four...?" He paused, his eyes on Caroline, any number of highly apt descriptions revolving in his head. "Excessively attractive virgins?" he concluded savagely.

Caroline's eyes widened and her dimple appeared.

"On the contrary!" Augusta answered. "Who better than you to act as their guardian? Odds are you know every ploy ever invented and a few more besides. And if you can't keep the wolves at bay, then no one can. I really don't know why you're creating all this fuss."

Max did not know either. After a moment of silence, he turned abruptly and crossed to the windows giving on to the courtyard. He had known from the outset that this was one battle he was destined to lose. Yet some part of his mind kept suggesting in panic-stricken accents that there must be some other way. He watched as the three younger girls—his wards, heaven forbid!—examined the fountain, prodding and poking in an effort to find the lever to turn it on. They were a breathtaking sight, the varied hues of their shining hair vying with the flowers, their husky laughter and the unconsciously seductive way their supple figures swayed this way and that causing him to groan inwardly. Up to the point when he had first sighted them, the three younger Twinnings had figured in his plans as largely irrelevant entities, easily swept into the background and of no possible consequence to his plans for their elder sister. One glimpse had been enough to scuttle that scenario. He was trapped—a guardian in very truth. And with what the Twinning girls had to offer he would have no choice but to play the role to the hilt. Every man in London with eyes would be after them!

Lady Benborough eyed Max's unyielding back with a frown. Then she turned to the woman beside her. She had already formed a high opinion of Miss Twinning. What was even more to the point, being considerably more than seven, Augusta had also perceived that her reprehensible nephew was far from indifferent to the luscious beauty. Meeting the grey-green eyes, her ladyship raised her brows. Caroline nodded and rose.

Max turned as Caroline laid her hand on his arm. She was watching her sisters, not him. Her voice, when she spoke, was tactfully low. "If it would truly bother you to stand as our guardian, I'm sure we could make some other arrangement." As she finished speaking, she raised her eyes to his.

Accustomed to every feminine wile known to woman, Max nevertheless could see nothing in the lucent grey eyes to tell him whether the offer was a bluff or not. But it only took a moment to realise that if he won this particular argument, if he succeeded in withdrawing as guardian to the Twinning sisters, Caroline Twinning would be largely removed from his orbit. Which would certainly make his seduction of her more difficult, if not impossible. Faced with those large grey-green eyes, Max did what none of the habitués of Gentleman Jackson's boxing salon had yet seen him do. He threw in the towel.

HAVING RESIGNED himself to the inevitable, Max departed, leaving the ladies to become better acquainted. As the street door closed behind him, Lady Benborough turned a speculative glance on Caroline. Her lips twitched. "Very well done, my dear. Clearly you need no lessons in how to manage a man."

Caroline's smile widened. "I've had some experience, I'll admit."

"Well, you'll need it all if you're going to tackle my nephew." Augusta grinned in anticipation. From where she sat, her world looked rosy indeed. Not only did she have four rich beauties to fire off, and unlimited funds to do it with, but, glory of glories, for the first time since he had emerged from short coats her reprehensible nephew was behaving in a less than predictable fashion. She allowed herself a full minute to revel in the wildest of imaginings, before settling down to extract all the pertinent details of their backgrounds and personalities from the Twinning sisters. The younger girls returned when the tea-tray arrived. By the time it was removed, Lady Benborough had satisfied herself on all points of interest and the conversation moved on to their introduction to the *ton*.

"I wonder whether news of your existence has leaked out yet," mused her ladyship. "Someone may have seen you at Grillon's."

"Lady Jersey saw me yesterday with Max in his curricle," said Caroline.

"Did she?" Augusta sat up straighter. "In that case, there's no benefit in dragging our heels. If Silence already has the story, the sooner you make your appearance, the better. We'll go for a drive in the Park tomorrow." She ran a knowledgeable eye over the sisters' dresses. "I must say, your dresses are very attractive. Are they all like that?"

Reassured on their wardrobes, she nodded. "So there's nothing to stop us wading into the fray immediately. Good!" She let her eyes wander over the four faces in front of her, all beautiful yet each with its own allure. Her gaze rested on Lizzie. "You—Lizzie, isn't it? You're eighteen?"

Lizzie nodded. "Yes, ma'am."

"If that's so, then there's no reason for us to be missish," returned her ladyship. "I assume you all wish to find husbands?"

They all nodded decisively.

"Good! At least we're all in agreement over the objective. Now for the strategy. Although your sudden appearance all together is going to cause a riot. I rather think that's going to be the best way to begin. At the very least, we'll be noticed."

"Oh, we're *always* noticed!" returned Arabella, hazel eyes twinkling.

Augusta laughed. "I dare say." From any other young lady, the comment would have earned a reproof. However, it was impossible to deny the Twinning sisters were rather more than just beautiful, and as they were all more than green girls it was pointless to pretend they did not fully comprehend the effect they had on the opposite sex. To her ladyship's mind, it was a relief not to have to hedge around the subject.

"Aside from anything else," she continued thoughtfully, "your public appearance as the Duke of Twyford's wards will make it impossible for Max to renege on his decision." Quite why she was so very firmly set on Max fulfilling his obligations she could not have said. But his guardianship would keep him in contact with Miss Twinning. And that, she had a shrewd suspicion, would be a very good thing.

THEIR DRIVE in the Park the next afternoon was engineered by the experienced Lady Benborough to be tantalisingly brief. As predicted, the sight of four ravishing females in the Twyford barouche caused an immediate impact. As the carriage sedately bowled along the avenues, heads rapidly came together in the carriages they passed. Conversations between knots of elegant gentlemen and the more dashing of ladies who had descended from their carriages to stroll about the well-tended lawns halted in midsentence as all eyes turned to follow the Twyford barouche.

Augusta, happily aware of the stir they were causing, sat on the maroon leather seat and struggled to keep the grin from her face. Her charges were attired in a spectrum of delicate colours, for all the world like a posy of gorgeous blooms. The subtle peach of Caroline's round gown gave way to the soft turquoise tints of Sarah's. Arabella had favoured a gown of the most delicate rose muslin while Lizzie sat, like a quiet bluebell, nodding happily amid her sisters. In the soft spring sunshine, they looked like refugees from the fairy kingdom, too exquisite to be flesh and blood. Augusta lost her struggle and grinned widely at her fanciful thoughts. Then her eyes alighted on a landau drawn up to the side of the carriageway. She raised her parasol and tapped her coachman on the shoulder. "Pull up over there."

Thus it happened that Emily, Lady Cowper and Maria, Lady Sefton, enjoying a comfortable cose in the afternoon sunshine, were the first to meet the Twinning sisters. As the Twyford carriage drew up, the eyes of both experienced matrons grew round.

Augusta noted their response with satisfaction. She seized the opportunity to perform the introductions, ending with, "Twyford's wards, you know."

That information, so casually dropped, clearly stunned both ladies. *"Twyford's?"* echoed Lady Sefton. Her mild

eyes, up to now transfixed by the spectacle that was the
Twinning sisters, shifted in bewilderment to Lady Benborough's face. "How on *earth*...?"

In a few well-chosen sentences, Augusta told her. Once
their ladyships had recovered from their amusement, both
at once promised vouchers for the girls to attend Almack's.

"My dear, if your girls attend, we'll have to lay on more
refreshments. The gentlemen will be there in droves," said
Lady Cowper, smiling in genuine amusement.

"Who knows? We might even prevail on Twyford himself to attend," mused Lady Sefton.

While Augusta thought that might be stretching things a
bit far, she was thankful for the immediate backing her two
old friends had given her crusade to find four fashionable
husbands for the Twinnings. The carriages remained together for some time as the two patronesses of Almack's
learned more of His Grace of Twyford's wards. Augusta
was relieved to find that all four girls could converse with
ease. The two younger sisters prettily deferred to the elder
two, allowing the more experienced Caroline, ably sec-
onded by Sarah, to dominate the responses.

When they finally parted, Augusta gave the order to return to Mount Street. "Don't want to rush it," she explained to four enquiring glances. "Much better to let them
come to us."

TWO DAYS LATER, the *ton* was still reeling from the discovery of the Duke of Twyford's wards. Amusement, from the
wry to the ribald, had been the general reaction. Max had
gritted his teeth and borne it, but the persistent demands of
his friends to be introduced to his wards sorely tried his
temper. He continued to refuse all such requests. He could
not stop their eventual acquaintance but at least he did not
need directly to foster it. Thus, it was in a far from benign
mood that he prepared to depart Delmere House on that
fine April morning, in the company of two of his particular

cronies, Lord Darcy Hamilton and George, Viscount Pilborough.

As they left the parlour at the rear of the house and entered the front hallway, their conversation was interrupted
by a knock on the street door. They paused in the rear of the
hall as Hillshaw moved majestically past to answer it.

"I'm not at home, Hillshaw," said Max.

Hillshaw regally inclined his head. "Very good, Your
Grace."

But Max had forgotten that Hillshaw had yet to experience the Misses Twinning *en masse*. Resistance was impossible and they came swarming over the threshold, in a
frothing of lace and cambrics, bright smiles, laughing eyes
and dancing curls.

The girls immediately spotted the three men, standing
rooted by the stairs. Arabella reached Max first. "Dear
guardian," she sighed languishingly, eyes dancing, "are you
well?" She placed her small hand on his arm.

Sarah, immediately behind, came to his other side. "We
hope you are because we want to ask your permission for
something." She smiled matter-of-factly up at him.

Lizzie simply stood directly in front of him, her huge eyes
trained on his face, a smile she clearly knew to be winning
suffusing her countenance. "Please?"

Max raised his eyes to Hillshaw, still standing dumb by
the door. The sight of his redoubtable henchman rolled up
by a parcel of young misses caused his lips to twitch. He
firmly denied the impulse to laugh. The Misses Twinning
were outrageous already and needed no further encouragement. Then his eyes met Caroline's.

She had hung back, watching her sisters go through their
paces, but as his eyes touched her, she moved forward, her
hand outstretched. Max, quite forgetting the presence of all
the others, took it in his.

"Don't pay any attention to them, Your Grace; I'm afraid
they're sad romps."

"Not *romps*, Caro," protested Arabella, eyes fluttering over the other two men, standing mesmerized just behind Max.

"It's just that we heard it was possible to go riding in the Park but Lady Benborough said we had to have your permission," explained Sarah.

"So, here we are and can we?" asked Lizzie, big eyes beseeching.

"No," said Max, without further ado. As his aunt had observed, he knew every ploy. And the opportunities afforded by rides in the Park, where chaperons could be present but sufficiently remote, were endless. The first rule in a seduction was to find the opportunity to speak alone to the lady in question. And a ride in the Park provided the perfect setting.

Caroline's fine brows rose at his refusal. Max noticed that the other three girls turned to check their elder sister's response before returning to the attack.

"Oh, you can't mean that! How shabby!"

"Why on earth not?"

"We all ride well. I haven't been out since we were home."

Both Arabella and Sarah turned to the two gentlemen still standing behind Max, silent auditors to the extraordinary scene. Arabella fixed Viscount Pilborough with pleading eyes. "Surely there's nothing unreasonable in such a request?" Under the Viscount's besotted gaze, her lashes fluttered almost imperceptibly, before her lids decorously dropped, veiling those dancing eyes, the long lashes brushing her cheeks, delicately stained with a most becoming blush.

The Viscount swallowed. "Why on earth not, Max? Not an unreasonable request at all. Your wards would look very lovely on horseback."

Max, who was only too ready to agree on how lovely his wards would look in riding habits, bit back an oath. Ignoring Miss Twinning's laughing eyes, he glowered at the hapless Viscount.

Sarah meanwhile had turned to meet the blatantly admiring gaze of Lord Darcy. Not as accomplished a flirt as Arabella, she could nevertheless hold her own, and she returned his warm gaze with a serene smile. "Is there any real reason why we shouldn't ride?"

Her low voice, cool and strangely musical, made Darcy Hamilton wish there were far fewer people in Max's hall. In fact, his fantasies would be more complete if they were not in Max's hall at all. He moved towards Sarah and expertly captured her hand. Raising it to his lips, he smiled in a way that had thoroughly seduced more damsels than he cared to recall. He could well understand why Max did not wish his wards to ride. But, having met this Twinning sister, there was no way in the world he was going to further his friend's ambition.

His lazy drawl reached Max's ears. "I'm very much afraid, Max, dear boy, that you're going to have to concede. The opposition is quite overwhelming."

Max glared at him. Seeing the determination in his lordship's grey eyes and understanding his reasons only too well, he knew he was outnumbered on all fronts. His eyes returned to Caroline's face to find her regarding him quizzically. "Oh, very well!"

Her smile warmed him and at the prompting lift of her brows he introduced his friends, first to her, and then to her sisters in turn. The chattering voices washed over him, his friends' deeper tones running like a counterpoint in the cacophony. Caroline moved to his side.

"You're not seriously annoyed by us riding, are you?"

He glanced down at her. The stern set of his lips reluctantly relaxed. "I would very much rather you did not. However," he continued, his eyes roving to the group of her three sisters and his two friends, busy with noisy plans for their first ride that afternoon, "I can see that's impossible."

Caroline smiled. "We won't come to any harm, I assure you."

"Allow me to observe, Miss Twinning, that gallivanting about the London *ton* is fraught with rather more difficulty than you would have encountered in American society, nor yet within the circle to which you were accustomed in Hertfordshire."

A rich chuckle greeted his warning. "Fear not, dear guardian," she said, raising laughing eyes to his. Max noticed the dimple, peeking irrepressibly from beside her soft mouth. "We'll manage."

NATURALLY, MAX FELT obliged to join the riding party that afternoon. Between both his and Darcy Hamilton's extensive stables, they had managed to assemble suitable mounts for the four girls. Caroline had assured him that, like all country misses, they could ride very well. By the time they gained the Park, he had satisfied himself on that score. At least he need not worry over them losing control of the frisky horses and being thrown. But, as they were all as stunning as he had feared they would be, elegantly gowned in perfectly cut riding habits, his worries had not noticeably decreased.

As they ambled further into the Park, by dint of the simple expedient of reining in his dappled grey, he dropped to the rear of the group, the better to keep the three younger girls in view. Caroline, riding by his side, stayed with him. She threw him a laughing glance but made no comment.

As he had expected, they had not gone more than two hundred yards before their numbers were swelled by the appearance of Lord Tulloch and young Mr. Mitchell. But neither of these gentlemen seemed able to interrupt the rapport which, to Max's experienced eye, was developing with alarming rapidity between Sarah Twinning and Darcy Hamilton. Despite his fears, he grudgingly admitted the Twinning sisters knew a trick or two. Arabella flirted outrageously but did so with all gentlemen, none being able to claim any special consideration. Lizzie attracted the quieter men and was happy to converse on the matters currently holding the interest of the *ton*. Her natural shyness and understated youth, combined with her undeniable beauty, was a heady tonic for these more sober gentlemen. As they ventured deeper into the Park, Max was relieved to find Sarah giving Darcy no opportunity to lead her apart. Gradually, his watchfulness relaxed. He turned to Caroline.

"Have you enjoyed your first taste of life in London?"

"Yes, thank you," she replied, grey eyes smiling. "Your aunt has been wonderful. I can't thank you enough for all you've done."

Max's brow clouded. As it happened, the last thing he wanted was her gratitude. Here he was, thinking along lines not grossly dissimilar from Darcy's present preoccupation, and the woman chose to thank him. He glanced down at her as she rode beside him, her face free of any worry, thoroughly enjoying the moment. Her presence was oddly calming.

"What plans to you have for the rest of the week?" he asked.

Caroline was slightly surprised by his interest but replied readily. "We've been driving in the Park every afternoon except today. I expect we'll continue to appear, although I rather think, from now on, it will be on horseback." She shot him a measuring glance to see how he would take that. His face was slightly grim but he nodded in acceptance. "Last evening, we went to a small party given by Lady Malling. Your aunt said there are a few more such gatherings in the next week which we should attend, to give ourselves confidence in society."

Max nodded again. From the corner of his eye, he saw Sarah avoid yet another of Darcy's invitations to separate from the group. He saw the quick frown which showed fleetingly in his friend's eyes. Serve him right if the woman drove him mad. But, he knew, Darcy was made of sterner stuff. The business of keeping his wards out of the arms of his friends was going to be deucedly tricky. Returning to contemplation of Miss Twinning's delightful countenance, he asked, "Has Aunt Augusta got you vouchers for Almack's yet?"

"Yes. We met Lady Sefton and Lady Cowper on our first drive in the Park."

Appreciating his aunt's strategy, Max grinned. "Trust Aunt Augusta."

Caroline returned his smile. "She's been very good to us."

Thinking that the unexpected company of four lively young women must have been a shock to his aunt's system, Max made a mental note to do anything in his power to please his aunt Benborough.

They had taken a circuitous route through the Park and only now approached the fashionable precincts. The small group almost immediately swelled to what, to Max, were alarming proportions, with every available gentleman clamouring for an introduction to his beautiful wards. But, to his surprise, at a nod from Caroline, the girls obediently brought their mounts closer and refused every attempt to draw them further from his protective presence. To his astonishment, they all behaved with the utmost decorum, lightened, of course, by their natural liveliness but nevertheless repressively cool to any who imagined them easy targets. Despite his qualms, he was impressed. They continued in this way until they reached the gates of the Park, by which time the group had dwindled to its original size and he could relax again.

He turned to Caroline, still by his side. "Can you guarantee they'll always behave so circumspectly, or was that performance purely for my benefit?" As her laughing eyes met his, he tried to decide whether they were greeny-grey or greyish-green. An intriguing question.

"Oh, we're experienced enough to know which way to jump, I assure you," she returned. After a pause, she continued, her voice lowered so only he could hear. "In the circumstances, we would not willingly do anything to bring disrepute on ourselves. We are very much aware of what we owe to you and Lady Benborough."

Max knew he should be pleased at this avowal of good intentions. Instead, he was aware of a curious irritation. He would certainly do everything in his power to reinforce her expressed sentiment with respect to the three younger girls, but to have Caroline Twinning espousing such ideals was not in keeping with his plans. Somehow, he was going to have to convince her that adherence to all the social strictures was not the repayment he, at least, would desire. The unwelcome thought that, whatever the case, she might now consider herself beholden to him, and would, therefore, grant him his wishes out of gratitude, very nearly made him swear aloud. His horse jibbed at the suddenly tightened rein and he pushed the disturbing thought aside while he dealt with the grey. Once the horse had settled again, he continued by Caroline's side as they headed back to Mount Street, a distracted frown at the back of his dark blue eyes.

AUGUSTA BENBOROUGH flicked open her fan and plied it vigorously. Under cover of her voluminous skirts, she slipped her feet free of her evening slippers. She had forgotten how stifling the small parties, held in the run-up to the Season proper, could be. Every bit as bad as the crushers later in the Season. But there, at least, she would have plenty of her own friends to gossip with. The mothers and chaperons of the current batch of débutantes were a generation removed from her own and at these small parties they were generally the only older members present. Miriam Alford had elected to remain at Twyford House this evening, which left Augusta with little to do but watch her charges. And even that, she mused to herself, was not exactly riveting entertainment.

True, Max was naturally absent, which meant her primary interest in the entire business was in abeyance. Still, it was comforting to find Caroline treating all the gentlemen who came her way with the same unfailing courtesy and no hint of partiality. Arabella, too, seemed to be following that line, although, in her case, the courtesy was entirely cloaked

in a lightly flirtatious manner. In any other young girl, Lady
Benborough would have strongly argued for a more demure style. But she had watched Arabella carefully. The girl
had quick wits and a ready tongue. She never stepped beyond what was acceptable, though she took delight in sailing close to the wind. Now, convinced that no harm would
come of Arabella's artful play, Augusta nodded benignly as
that young lady strolled by, accompanied by the inevitable
gaggle of besotted gentlemen.

One of their number was declaiming,

> " 'My dearest flower,
> More beautiful by the hour,
> To you I give my heart.' "

Arabella laughed delightedly and quickly said, "My dear
sir, I beg you spare my blushes! Truly, your verses do me
more credit than I deserve. But surely, to do them justice,
should you not set them down on parchment?" Anything
was preferable to having them said aloud.

The budding poet, young Mr. Rawlson, beamed.
'*Nothing* would give me greater pleasure, Miss Arabella.
I'll away and transcribe them immediately. And dedicate
them to your inspiration!" With a flourishing bow, he departed precipitately, leaving behind a silence pregnant with
suppressed laughter.

This was broken by a snigger from Lord Shannon. "Silly
puppy!"

As Mr. Rawlson was a year or two older than Lord
Shannon, who himself appeared very young despite his attempts to ape the Corinthians, this comment itself caused
some good-natured laughter.

"Perhaps, Lord Shannon, you would be so good as to
fetch me some refreshment?" Arabella smiled sweetly on the
hapless youngster. With a mutter which all interpreted to

mean he was delighted to be of service to one so fair, the young man escaped.

With a smile, Arabella turned to welcome Viscount Pilborough to her side.

Augusta's eyelids drooped. The temperature in the room seemed to rise another degree. The murmuring voices washed over her. Her head nodded. With a start, she shook herself awake. Determined to keep her mind active for the half-hour remaining, she sought out her charges. Lizzie was chattering animatedly with a group of débutantes much her own age. The youngest Twinning was surprisingly innocent, strangely unaware of her attractiveness to the opposite sex, still little more than a schoolgirl at heart. Lady Benborough smiled. Lizzie would learn soon enough; let her enjoy her girlish gossiping while she might.

A quick survey of the room brought Caroline to light, strolling easily on the arm of the most eligible Mr. Willoughby.

"It's so good of you to escort your sister to these parties, sir. I'm sure Miss Charlotte must be very grateful." Caroline found conversation with the reticent Mr. Willoughby a particular strain.

A faint smile played at the corners of Mr. Willoughby's thin lips. "Indeed, I believe she is. But really, there is very little to it. As my mother is so delicate as to find these affairs quite beyond her, it would be churlish of me indeed to deny Charlotte the chance of becoming more easy in company before she is presented."

With grave doubts over how much longer she could endure such ponderous conversation without running amok, Caroline seized the opportunity presented by passing a small group of young ladies, which included the grateful Charlotte, to stop. The introductions were quickly performed.

As she stood conversing with a Miss Denbright, an occupation which required no more than half her brain, Caroline allowed her eyes to drift over the company. Other than Viscount Pilborough, who was dangling after Arabella in an entirely innocuous fashion, and Darcy Hamilton, who was pursuing Sarah in a far more dangerous way, there was no gentleman in whom she felt the least interest. Even less than her sisters did she need the opportunity of the early parties to gain confidence. Nearly eighteen months of social consorting in the ballrooms and banquet halls in New York had given them all a solid base on which to face the London *ton*. And even more than her sisters, Caroline longed to get on with it. Time, she felt, was slipping inexorably by. Still, there were only four more days to go. And then, surely their guardian would reappear? She had already discovered that no other gentleman's eyes could make her feel quite the same breathless excitement as the Duke of Twyford's did. He had not called on them since that first ride in the Park, a fact which had left her with a wholly resented feeling of disappointment. Despite the common sense on which she prided herself, she had formed an irritating habit of comparing all the men she met with His domineering Grace and inevitably found them wanting. Such foolishness would have to stop. With a small suppressed sigh, she turned a charming smile on Mr. Willoughby, wishing for the sixteenth time that his faded blue eyes were of a much darker hue.

Satisfied that Caroline, like Lizzie and Arabella, needed no help from her, Lady Benborough moved her gaze on, scanning the room for Sarah's dark head. When her first survey drew no result, she sat up straighter, a slight frown in her eyes. Darcy Hamilton was here, somewhere, drat him. He had attended every party they had been to this week, a fact which of itself had already drawn comment. His attentions to Sarah were becoming increasingly marked. Augusta knew all the Hamiltons. She had known Darcy's father and doubted not the truth of the 'like father, like son' adage. But surely Sarah was too sensible to... She wasted no time in completing that thought but started a careful, methodical and entirely well-disguised visual search. From her present position, on a slightly raised dais to one side, she commanded a view of the whole room. Her gaze passed over the alcove set in the wall almost directly opposite her but then returned, caught by a flicker of movement within the shadowed recess.

There they were, Sarah and, without doubt, Darcy Hamilton. Augusta could just make out the blur of colour that was Sarah's green dress. How typical of Darcy. They were still in the room, still within sight, but, in the dim light of the alcove, almost private. As her eyes adjusted to the poor light, Augusta saw to her relief that, despite her fears and Darcy's reputation, they were merely talking, seated beside one another on a small setee. Still, to her experienced eye, there was a degree of familiarity in their pose, which, given that it must be unconscious, was all too revealing. With a sigh, she determined to have a word, if not several words, with Sarah, regarding the fascinations of men like Darcy Hamilton. She would have to do it, for Darcy's proclivities were too well-known to doubt.

She watched as Darcy leaned closer to Sarah.

"My dear," drawled Darcy Hamilton, "do you have any idea of the temptation you pose? Or the effect beauty such as yours has on mere men?"

His tone was lazy and warm, with a quality of velvety smoothness which fell like a warm cloak over Sarah's already hypersensitized nerves. He had flung one arm over the back of the settee and long fingers were even now twining in the soft curls at her nape. She knew she should move but could not. The sensations rippling down her spine were both novel and exhilarating. She was conscious of a ludicrous desire to snuggle into that warmth, to invite more soft words. But the desire which burned in his lordship's grey eyes was already frighteningly intense. She determinedly ignored the small reckless voice which urged her to encourage him and instead replied, "Why, no. Of course not."

Darcy just managed to repress a snort of disgust. Damn the woman! Her voice had held not the thread of a quaver. Calm and steady as a rock when his own pulses were well and truly racing. He simply did not believe it. He glanced

down into her wide brown eyes, guileless as ever, knowing
that his exasperation was showing. For a fleeting instant, he
saw a glimmer of amusement and, yes, of triumph in the
brown depths. But when he looked again, the pale face was
once again devoid of emotion. His grey eyes narrowed.

Sarah saw his intent look and immediately dropped her
eyes.

Her action confirmed Darcy's suspicions. By God, the
chit was playing with him! The fact that Sarah could only be
dimly aware of the reality of the danger she was flirting with
was buried somewhere in the recesses of his mind. But, like
all the Hamiltons, for him, desire could easily sweep aside
all reason. In that instant, he determined he would have her,
no matter what the cost. Not here, not now—neither place
nor time was right. But some time, somewhere, Sarah
Twinning would be his.

Augusta's attention was drawn by the sight of a mother
gathering her two daughters and preparing to depart. As if
all had been waiting for this signal, it suddenly seemed as if
half the room was on their way. With relief, she turned to see
Darcy lead Sarah from the alcove and head in her direction. As Caroline approached, closely followed by Lizzie
and Arabella, Augusta Benborough wriggled her aching toes
back into her slippers and rose. It was over. And in four
days' time the Season would begin. As she smiled benignly
upon the small army of gentlemen who had escorted her
charges to her side, she reminded herself that, with the exception of Darcy Hamilton, there was none present tonight
who would make a chaperon uneasy. Once in wider society,
she would have no time to be bored. The Twinning sisters
would certainly see to that.

CHAPTER FOUR

EMMA, LADY MORTLAND, thought Max savagely, had no right to the title. He would grant she was attractive, in a blowsy sort of way, but her conduct left much to be desired. She had hailed him almost as soon as he had entered the Park. He rarely drove there except when expediency demanded. Consequently, her ladyship had been surprised to see his curricle, drawn by his famous match bays, advancing along the avenue. He had been forced to pull up or run the silly woman down. The considerable difficulty in conversing at any length with someone perched six feet and more above you, particularly when that someone displayed the most blatant uninterest, had not discouraged Lady Mortland. She had done her best to prolong the exchange in the dim hope, Max knew, of gaining an invitation to ride beside him. She had finally admitted defeat and archly let him go, but not before issuing a thickly veiled invitation which he had had no compunction in declining. As she had been unwise enough to speak in the hearing of two gentlemen of her acquaintance, her resulting embarrassment was entirely her own fault. He knew she entertained hopes, totally unfounded, of becoming his Duchess. Why she should imagine he would consider taking a woman with the morals of an alley cat to wife was beyond him.

As he drove beneath the trees, he scanned the carriages that passed, hoping to find his wards. He had not seen them since that first ride in the Park, a feat of self-discipline before which any other he had ever accomplished in his life paled into insignificance. Darcy Hamilton had put the idea into his head. His friend had returned with him to Delmere House after that first jaunt, vociferous in his complaints of the waywardness of Sarah Twinning. The fact that she was Max's ward had not subdued him in the least. Max had not been surprised; Darcy could be ruthlessly singleminded when hunting. It had been Darcy who had suggested that a short absence might make the lady more amenable and had departed with the firm resolve to give the Twinning girls the go-by for at least a week.

That had been six days ago. The Season was about to get under way and it was time to reacquaint himself with his wards. Having ascertained that their horses had not left his stable, he had had the bays put to and followed them to the Park. He finally spied the Twyford barouche drawn up to the side of the avenue. He pulled up alongside.

"Aunt Augusta," he said as he nodded to her. She beamed at him, clearly delighted he had taken the trouble to find them. His gaze swept over the other occupants of the carriage in an appraising and approving manner, then came to rest on Miss Twinning. She smiled sunnily back at him. Suddenly alert, Max's mind returned from where it had wandered and again counted heads. There was a total of five in the carriage but Miriam Alford was there, smiling vaguely at him. Which meant one of his wards was missing. He quelled the urge to immediately question his aunt, telling himself there would doubtless be some perfectly reasonable explanation. Perhaps one was merely unwell. His mind reverted to its main preoccupation.

Responding automatically to his aunt's social chatter, he took the first opportunity to remark, "But I can't keep my horses standing, ma'am. Perhaps Miss Twinning would like to come for a drive?"

He was immediately assured that Miss Twinning would and she descended from the carriage. He reached down to help her up beside him and they were off.

Caroline gloried in the brush of the breeze on her face as the curricle bowled along. Even reined in to the pace accepted in the Park, it was still infinitely more refreshing than the funereal plod favoured by Lady Benborough. That was undoubtedly the reason her spirits had suddenly soared. Even the sunshine seemed distinctly brighter.

"Not riding today?" asked Max.

"No. Lady Benborough felt we should not entirely desert the matrons."

Max smiled. "True enough. It don't do to put people's backs up unnecessarily."

Caroline turned to stare at him. "Your philosophy?" Augusta had told her enough of their guardian's past to realise this was unlikely.

Max frowned. Miss Caroline Twinning was a great deal too knowing. Unprepared to answer her query, he changed the subject. "Where's Sarah?"

"Lord Darcy took her up some time ago. Maybe we'll see them as we go around?"

Max suppressed the curse which rose to his lips. How many friends was he going to have left by the end of this Season? Another thought occurred. "Has she been seeing much of him?"

A deep chuckle answered this and his uneasiness grew. "If you mean has he taken to haunting us, no. On the other hand, he seems to have the entrée to all the salons we've attended this week."

He should, he supposed, have anticipated his friend's duplicity. Darcy was, after all, every bit as experienced as he. Still, it rankled. He would have a few harsh words to say to his lordship when next they met. "Has he been ... particularly attentive towards her?"

"No," she replied in a careful tone, "not in any unacceptable way."

He looked his question and she continued, "It's just that she's the only lady he pays any attention to at all. If he's not with Sarah, he either leaves or retires to the card tables or simply watches her from a distance."

The description was so unlike the Darcy Hamilton he knew that it was on the tip of his tongue to verify they were talking about the same man. A sneaking suspicion that Darcy might, just might, be seriously smitten awoke in his mind. One black brow rose.

They paused briefly to exchange greetings with Lady Jersey, then headed back towards the barouche. Coming to a decision, Max asked, "What's your next major engagement?"

"Well, we go to the first of Almack's balls tomorrow, then it's the Billingtons' ball the next night."

The start of the Season proper. But there was no way he was going to cross the threshold of Almack's. He had not been near the place for years. Tender young virgins were definitely not on his menu these days. He did not equate that description with Miss Twinning. Nor, if it came to that, to her sisters. Uncertain what to do for the best, he made no response to the information, merely inclining his head to show he had heard.

Caroline was silent as the curricle retraced its journey. Max's questions had made her uneasy. Lord Darcy was a particular friend of his—surely Sarah was in no real danger with him? She stifled a small sigh. Clearly, their guardian's attention was wholly concentrated on their social performance. Which, of course, was precisely what a guardian should be concerned with. Why, then, did she feel such a keen sense of disappointment?

They reached the barouche to find Sarah already returned. One glance at her stormy countenance was sufficient to answer Max's questions. It seemed Darcy's plans had not prospered. Yet.

As he handed Caroline to the ground and acknowledged her smiling thanks, it occurred to him she had not expressed any opinion or interest in his week-long absence. So much for that tactic. As he watched her climb into the barouche, shapely ankles temporarily exposed, he realised he had made no headway during their interlude. Her sister's affair with his friend had dominated his thoughts. Giving his horses the office, he grimaced to himself. Seducing a young woman while acting as guardian to her three younger sisters was clearly going to be harder going than he had imagined.

CLIMBING THE STEPS to Twyford House the next evening, Max was still in two minds over whether he was doing the right thing. He was far too wise to be overly attentive to Caroline, yet, if he did not make a push to engage her interest, she would shortly be the object of the attentions of a far larger circle of gentlemen, few of whom would hesitate to attend Almack's purely because they disliked being mooned over by very young women. He hoped, in his capacity as their guardian, to confine his attentions to the Twinning sisters and so escape the usual jostle of matchmaking mamas. They should have learned by now that he was not likely to succumb to their daughters' vapid charms. Still, he was not looking forward to the evening.

If truth were told, he had been hearing about his wards on all sides for the past week. They had caught the fancy of the *ton*, starved as it was of novelty. And their brand of beauty always had attraction. But what he had not heard was worrying him more. There had been more than one incident when, entering a room, he had been aware of at least one conversation abruptly halted, then smoothly resumed. Another reason to identify himself more closely with his wards. He reminded himself that three of them were truly his responsibility and, in the circumstances, the polite world would hold him responsible for Miss Twinning as well. His duty was clear.

Admitted to Twyford House, Max paused to exchange a few words with Millwade. Satisfied that all was running smoothly, he turned and stopped, all thought deserting him. Transfixed, he watched the Twinning sisters descend the grand staircase. Seen together, gorgeously garbed for the ball, they were quite the most heart-stopping sight he had beheld in many a year. His eyes rested with acclaim on each in turn, but stopped when they reached Caroline. The rest of the company seemed to dissolve in a haze as his eyes roamed appreciatively over the clean lines of her eau-de-Nil silk gown. It clung suggestively to her ripe figure, the neckline scooped low over her generous breasts. His hands burned with the desire to caress those tantalising curves. Then his eyes locked with hers as she crossed the room to his side, her hand extended to him. Automatically, he took it in his. Then she was speaking, smiling up at him in her usual confiding way.

"Thank you for coming. I do hope you'll not be too bored by such tame entertainment." Lady Benborough, on receiving Max's curt note informing them of his intention to accompany them to Almack's, had crowed with delight. When she had calmed, she had explained his aversion to the place. So it was with an unexpected feeling of guilt that Caroline had come forward to welcome him. But, gazing into his intensely blue eyes, she could find no trace of annoyance or irritation. Instead, she recognised the same emotion she had detected the very first time they had met. To add to her confusion, he raised her hand to his lips, his eyes warm and entirely too knowing.

"Do you know, I very much doubt that I'll be bored at all?" her guardian murmured wickedly.

Caroline blushed vividly. Luckily, this was missed by all but Max in the relatively poor light of the hall and the bustle as they donned their cloaks. Both Lady Benborough and Miriam Alford were to go, cutting the odds between chaperons and charges. Before Max's intervention, the coach would have had to do two trips to King Street. Now, Caroline found that Augusta and Mrs. Alford, together with Sarah and Arabella, were to go in the Twyford coach while she and Lizzie were to travel with Max. Suddenly suspicious of her guardian's intentions, she was forced to accept the arrangement with suitable grace. As Max handed her into the carriage and saw her settled comfortably, she told herself she was a fool to read into his behaviour anything other than an attempt to trip her up. He was only amusing himself.

As if to confirm her supposition, the journey was unremarkable and soon they were entering the hallowed precincts of the Assembly Rooms. The sparsely furnished halls were already well filled with the usual mix of débutantes and unmarried young ladies, carefully chaperoned by their mamas in the hope of finding a suitable connection among the unattached gentlemen strolling through the throng. It was a social club to which it was necessary to belong. And it was clear from their reception that, at least as far as the gentlemen were concerned, the Twinning sisters definitely belonged. To Max's horror, they were almost mobbed.

He stood back and watched the sisters artfully manage their admirers. Arabella had the largest court with all the most rackety and dangerous blades. A more discerning crowd of eminently eligible gentlemen had formed around Sarah while the youthful Lizzie had gathered all the more earnest of the younger men to her. But the group around Caroline drew his deepest consideration. There were more than a few highly dangerous roués in the throng gathered about her but all were experienced and none was likely to attempt anything scandalous without encouragement. As he watched, it became clear that all four girls had an innate ability to choose the more acceptable among their potential partners. They also had the happy knack of dismissing the less favoured with real charm, a not inconsiderable feat. The more he watched, the more intrigued Max became. He was about to seek clarification from his aunt, standing beside him, when that lady very kindly answered his unspoken query.

"You needn't worry, y'know. Those girls have got heads firmly on their shoulders. Ever since they started going about, I've been bombarded with questions on who's eligible and who's not. Even Arabella, minx that she is, takes good care to know who she's flirting with."

Max looked his puzzlement.

"Well," explained her ladyship, surprised by his obtuseness, "they're all set on finding husbands, of course!" She glanced up at him, eyes suddenly sharp, and added, "I should think you'd be thrilled—it means they'll be off your hands all the sooner."

"Yes. Of course," Max answered absently.

He stayed by his wards until they were claimed for the first dance. His sharp eyes had seen a number of less than desirable gentlemen approach the sisters, only to veer away as they saw him. If nothing else, his presence had achieved that much.

Searching through the crowd, he finally spotted Darcy Hamilton disappearing into one of the salons where refreshments were laid out.

"Going to give them the go-by for at least a week, huh?" he growled as he came up behind Lord Darcy.

Darcy choked on the lemonade he had just drunk.

Max gazed in horror at the glass in his friend's hand. "No! Bless me, Darcy! You turned temperate?"

Darcy grimaced. "Have to drink something and seemed like the best of a bad lot." His wave indicated the unexciting range of beverages available. "Thirsty work, getting a dance with one of your wards."

"Incidentally—" intoned Max in the manner of one about to pass judgement.

But Darcy held up his hand. "No. Don't start. I don't need any lectures from you on the subject. And you don't need to bother, anyway. Sarah Twinning has her mind firmly set on marriage and there's not a damned thing I can do about it."

Despite himself, Max could not resist a grin. "No luck?"

"None!" replied Darcy, goaded. "I'm almost at the stage of considering offering for her but I can't be sure she wouldn't reject me, and *that* I couldn't take."

Max, picking up a glass of lemonade himself, became thoughtful.

Suddenly, Darcy roused himself. "Do you know what she told me yesterday? Said I spent too much time on horses and not enough on matters of importance. *Can* you believe it?"

He gestured wildly and Max nearly hooted with laughter. Lord Darcy's stables were known the length and breadth of England as among the biggest and best producers of quality horseflesh.

"I very much doubt that she appreciates your interest in the field," Max said placatingly.

"Humph," was all his friend vouchsafed.

After a pause, Darcy laid aside his glass. "Going to find Maria Sefton and talk her into giving Sarah permission to waltz with me. One thing she won't be able to refuse." With a nod to Max, he returned to the main hall.

For some minutes, Max remained as he was, his abstracted gaze fixed on the far wall. Then, abruptly, he replaced his glass and followed his friend.

"YOU WANT ME to give *your ward* permission to waltz with you?" Lady Jersey repeated Max's request, clearly unable to decide whether it was as innocuous as he represented or whether it had an ulterior motive concealed within and if so, what.

"It's really not such an odd request," returned Max, unperturbed. "She's somewhat older than the rest and, as I'm here, it seems appropriate."

"Hmm." Sally Jersey simply did not believe there was not more to it. She had been hard-pressed to swallow her astonishment when she had seen His Grace of Twyford enter the room. And she was even more amazed that he had not left as soon as he had seen his wards settled. But he was, after all, Twyford. And Delmere and Rotherbridge, what was more. So, if he wanted to dance with his ward . . . She shrugged. "Very well. Bring her to me. If you can separate her from her court, that is."

Max smiled in a way that reminded Lady Jersey of the causes of his reputation. "I think I'll manage," he drawled, bowing over her hand.

CAROLINE WAS surprised that Max had remained at the Assembly Rooms for so long. She lost sight of him for a while, and worked hard at forcing herself to pay attention to her suitors, for it was only to be expected their guardian would seek less tame entertainment elsewhere. But then his tall figure reappeared at the side of the room. He seemed to be scanning the multitude, then, over a sea of heads, his eyes met hers. Caroline fervently hoped the peculiar shock which went through her was not reflected in her countenance. After a moment, unobtrusively, he made his way to her side.

Under cover of the light flirtation she was engaged in with an ageing baronet, Caroline was conscious of the sudden acceleration of her heartbeat and the constriction that seemed to be affecting her breathing. Horrendously aware of her guardian's blue eyes, she felt her nervousness grow as he approached despite her efforts to remain calm.

But, when he gained her side and bowed over her hand in an almost bored way, uttering the most commonplace civilities and engaging her partner in a discussion of some sporting event, the anticlimax quickly righted her mind for her.

Quite how it was accomplished she could not have said, but Max succeeded in excusing them to her court, on the grounds that he had something to discuss with his ward. Finding herself on his arm, strolling apparently randomly down the room, she turned to him and asked, "What was it you wished to say to me?"

He glanced down at her and she caught her breath. That devilish look was back in his eyes as they rested on her, warming her through and through. What on earth was he playing at?

"Good heavens, my ward. And I thought you up to all the rigs. Don't you know a ruse when you hear it?"

The tones of his voice washed languorously over Caroline, leaving a sense of relaxation in their wake. She made a grab for her fast-disappearing faculties. Interpreting his remark to mean that his previously bored attitude had also been false, Caroline was left wondering what the present reality meant. She made a desperate bid to get their interaction back on an acceptable footing. "Where are we going?"

Max smiled. "We're on our way to see Lady Jersey."

"Why?"

"Patience, sweet Caroline," came the reply, all the more outrageous for its tone. "All will be revealed forthwith."

They reached Lady Jersey's side where she stood just inside the main room.

"There you are, Twyford!"

The Duke of Twyford smoothly presented his ward. Her ladyship's prominent eyes rested on the curtsying Caroline, then, as the younger woman rose, widened with a suddenly arrested expression. She opened her mouth to ask the question burning the tip of her tongue but caught His Grace's eye and, reluctantly swallowing her curiosity, said, "My dear Miss Twinning. Your guardian has requested you to be given permission to waltz and I have no hesitation in granting it. And, as he is here, I present the Duke as a suitable partner."

With considerable effort, Caroline managed to school her features to impassivity. Luckily, the musicians struck up at that moment, so that she barely had time to murmur her thanks to Lady Jersey before Max swept her on to the floor, leaving her ladyship, intrigued, staring after them.

Caroline struggled to master the unnerving sensation of being in her guardian's arms. He was holding her closer than strictly necessary, but, as they twirled down the room, she realised that to everyone else they presented a perfect picture of the Duke of Twyford doing the pretty by his eldest ward. Only she was close enough to see the disturbing glint in his blue eyes and hear the warmth in his tone as he said,

"My dear ward, what a very accomplished dancer you are. Tell me, what other talents do you have that I've yet to sample?"

For the life of her, Caroline could not tear her eyes from his. She heard his words and understood their meaning but her brain refused to react. No shock, no scandalized response came to her lips. Instead, her mind was completely absorbed with registering the unbelievable fact that, despite their relationship of guardian and ward, Max Rotherbridge had every intention of seducing her. His desire was clear in the heat of his blue, blue gaze, in the way his hand at her back seemed to burn through the fine silk of her gown, in the gentle caress of his long fingers across her knuckles as he twirled her about the room under the long noses of the biggest gossips in London.

Mesmerized, she had sufficient presence of mind to keep a gentle smile fixed firmly on her face but her thoughts were whirling even faster than her feet. With a superhuman effort, she forced her lids to drop, screening her eyes from his. "Oh, we Twinnings have many accomplishments, dear guardian." To her relief, her voice was clear and untroubled. "But I'm desolated to have to admit that they're all hopelessly mundane."

A rich chuckle greeted this. "Permit me to tell you, my ward, that, for the skills I have in mind, your qualifications are more than adequate." Caroline's eyes flew to his. She could hardly believe her ears. But Max continued before she could speak, his blue eyes holding hers, his voice a seductive murmur. "And while you naturally lack experience, I assure you that can easily, and most enjoyably, be remedied."

It was too much. Caroline gave up the struggle to divine his motives and made a determined bid to reinstitute sanity. She smiled into the dark face above hers and said, quite clearly, "This isn't happening."

For a moment, Max was taken aback. Then, his sense of humour surfaced. "No?"

"Of course not," Caroline calmly replied. "You're my guardian and I'm your ward. Therefore, it is simply not possible for you to have said what you just did."

Studying her serene countenance, Max recognised the strategy and reluctantly admired her courage for adopting it. As things stood, it was not an easy defence for him to overcome. Reading in the grey-green eyes a determination not to be further discomposed, Max, too wise to push further, gracefully yielded.

"So what do you think of Almack's?" he asked.

Relieved, Caroline took the proffered olive branch and their banter continued on an impersonal level.

At the end of the dance, Max suavely surrendered her to her admirers, but not without a glance which, if she had allowed herself to think about it, would have made Caroline blush. She did not see him again until it was time for them to quit the Assembly Rooms. In order to survive the evening, she had sternly refused to let her mind dwell on his behaviour. Consequently, it had not occurred to her to arrange to exchange her place in her guardian's carriage for one in the Twyford coach. When Lizzie came to tug at her sleeve with the information that the others had already left, she perceived her error. But the extent of her guardian's foresight did not become apparent until they were halfway home.

She and Max shared the forward facing seat with Lizzie curled up in a corner opposite them. On departing King Street, they preserved a comfortable silence—due to tiredness in Lizzie's case, from being too absorbed with her thoughts in her case and, as she suddenly realised, from sheer experience in the case of her guardian.

They were still some distance from Mount Street when, without warning, Max took her hand in his. Surprised, she turned to look up at him, conscious of his fingers moving gently over hers. Despite the darkness of the carriage, his eyes caught hers. Deliberately, he raised her hand and kissed her fingertips. A delicious tingle raced along Caroline's nerves, followed by a second of increased vigour as he turned her hand over and placed a lingering kiss on her wrist. But they were nothing compared to the galvanising shock that hit her when, without giving any intimation of his intent, he bent his head and his lips found hers.

From Max's point of view, he was behaving with admirable restraint. He knew Lizzie was sound asleep and that his manipulative and normally composed eldest ward was well out of her depth. Yet he reined in his desires and kept the kiss light, his lips moving gently over hers, gradually increasing the pressure until she parted her lips. He savoured the warm sweetness of her mouth, then, inwardly smiling at the response she had been unable to hide, he withdrew and watched as her eyes slowly refocused.

Caroline, eyes round, looked at him in consternation. Then her shocked gaze flew to Lizzie, still curled in her corner.

"Don't worry. She's sound asleep." His voice was deep and husky in the dark carriage.

Caroline, stunned, felt oddly reassured by the sound. Then she felt the carriage slow.

"And you're safe home," came the gently mocking voice.

In a daze, Caroline helped him wake Lizzie and then Max very correctly escorted them indoors, a smile of wicked contentment on his face.

ARABELLA STIFLED a wistful sigh and smiled brightly at the earnest young man who was guiding her around the floor in yet another interminable waltz. It had taken only a few days of the Season proper for her to sort through her prospective suitors. And come to the unhappy conclusion that none matched her requirements. The lads were too young, the men too old. There seemed to be no one in between. Presumably many were away with Wellington's forces, but surely there were those who could not leave the important business of keeping England running? And surely not all of them were old? She could not describe her ideal man, yet was sure she would instantly know when she met him. She was convinced she would feel it, like a thunderbolt from the blue. Yet no male of her acquaintance increased her heartbeat one iota.

Keeping up a steady and inconsequential conversation with her partner, something she could do half asleep, Arabella sighted her eldest sister, elegantly waltzing with their guardian. Now there was a coil. There was little doubt in Arabella's mind of the cause of Caroline's bright eyes and slightly flushed countenance. She looked radiant. But could a guardian marry his ward? Or, more to the point, was their guardian intent on marriage or had he some other arrangement in mind? Still, she had complete faith in Caroline. There had been many who had worshipped at her feet with something other than matrimony in view, yet her eldest sister had always had their measure. True, none had affected her as Max Rotherbridge clearly did. But Caroline knew the ropes, few better.

"I'll escort you back to Lady Benborough."

The light voice of her partner drew her thoughts back to the present. With a quick smile, Arabella declined. "I think I've torn my flounce. I'll just go and pin it up. Perhaps you could inform Lady Benborough that I'll return immediately?" She smiled dazzlingly upon the young man. Bemused, he bowed and moved away into the crowd. Her flounce was perfectly intact but she needed some fresh air and in no circumstances could she have borne another half-hour of that particular young gentleman's serious discourse.

She started towards the door, then glanced back to see Augusta receive her message without apparent perturbation. Arabella turned back to the door and immediately collided with a chest of quite amazing proportions.

"Oh!"

For a moment, she thought the impact had winded her. Then, looking up into the face of the mountain she had met,

she realised it wasn't that at all. It was the thunderbolt she
had been waiting for.

Unfortunately, the gentleman seemed unaware of this
momentous happening. "My apologies, m'dear. Didn't see
you there."

The lazy drawl washed over Arabella. He was tall, very
tall, and seemed almost as broad, with curling blond hair
and laughing hazel eyes. He had quite the most devastating
smile she had ever seen. Her knees felt far too weak to support her if she moved, so she stood still and stared, mouth-
ing she knew not what platitudes.

The gentleman seemed to find her reaction amusing. But,
with a polite nod and another melting smile, he was gone.

Stunned, Arabella found herself standing in the doorway
staring at his retreating back. Sanity returned with a thump.
Biting back a far from ladylike curse, she swept out in search
of the withdrawing-room. The use of a borrowed fan and
the consumption of a glass of cool water helped to restore
her outward calm. Inside, her resentment grew.

No gentleman simply excused himself and walked away
from her. That was her role. Men usually tried to stay by her
side as long as possible. Yet this man had seemed disinclined to linger. Arabella was not vain but wondered what
was more fascinating than herself that he needs must move
on so abruptly. Surely he had felt that strange jolt just as she
had? Maybe he wasn't a ladies' man? But no. The memory
of the decided appreciation which had glowed so warmly in
his hazel eyes put paid to that idea. And, now she came to
think of it, the comprehensive glance which had roamed
suggestively over most of her had been decidedly impertinent.

Arabella returned to the ballroom determined to bring her
large gentleman to heel, if for no better reason than to assure herself she had been mistaken in him. But frustration
awaited her. He was not there. For the rest of the evening,
she searched the throng but caught no glimpse of her quarry.

Then, just before the last dance, another waltz, he appeared in the doorway from the card-room.

Surrounded by her usual court, Arabella was at her effervescent best. Her smile was dazzling as she openly debated, laughingly teasing, over who to bestow her hand on for this last dance. Out of the corner of her eye, she watched the unknown gentleman approach. And walk past her to solicit the hand of a plain girl in an outrageously overdecorated pink gown.

Arabella bit her lip in vexation but managed to conceal it as severe concentration on her decision. As the musicians struck up, she accepted handsome Lord Tulloch as her partner and studiously paid him the most flattering attention for the rest of the evening.

CHAPTER FIVE

MAX WAS WORRIED. Seriously worried. Since that first night at Almack's, the situation between Sarah Twinning and Darcy Hamilton had rapidly deteriorated to a state which, from experience, he knew was fraught with danger. As he watched Sarah across Lady Overton's ballroom, chatting with determined avidity to an eminently respectable and thoroughly boring young gentleman, his brows drew together in a considering frown. If, at the beginning of his guardianship, anyone had asked him where his sympathies would lie, with the Misses Twinning or the gentlemen of London, he would unhesitatingly have allied himself with his wards, on the grounds that four exquisite but relatively inexperienced country misses would need all the help they could get to defend their virtue successfully against the highly knowledgeable rakes extant within the *ton*. Now, a month later, having gained first-hand experience of the tenacious perversity of the Twinning sisters, he was not so sure.

His behaviour with Caroline on the night of their first visit to Almack's had been a mistake. How much of a mistake had been slowly made clear to him over the succeeding weeks. He was aware of the effect he had on her, had been aware of it from the first time he had seen her in his library at Delmere House. But in order to make any use of that weapon, he had to have her to himself. A fact, unfortunately, that she had worked out for herself. Consequently, whenever he approached her, he found her surrounded either by admirers who had been given too much encourage-

ment for him to dismiss easily or one or more of her far too
perceptive sisters. Lizzie, it was true, was not attuned to the
situation between her eldest sister and their guardian. But
he had unwisely made use of her innocence, to no avail as it
transpired, and was now unhappily certain he would get no
further opportunity by that route. Neither Arabella nor
Sarah was the least bit perturbed by his increasingly blatant
attempts to be rid of them. He was sure that, if he was ever
goaded into ordering them to leave their sister alone with
him, they would laugh and refuse. And tease him unmercifully about it, what was more. He had already had to withstand one episode of Arabella's artful play, sufficiently
subtle, thank God, so that the others in the group had not
understood her meaning.

His gaze wandered to where the third Twinning sister held
court, seated on a chaise surrounded by ardent swains, her
huge eyes wickedly dancing with mischief. As he watched,
she tossed a comment to one of the circle and turned, her
head playfully tilted, to throw a glance of open invitation
into the handsome face of a blond giant standing before her.
Max stiffened. Hell and the devil! He would have to put a
stop to that game, and quickly. He had no difficulty in recognising the large frame of Hugo, Lord Denbigh. Although a few years younger than himself, in character and
accomplishments there was little to choose between them.
Under his horrified gaze, Hugo took advantage of a momentary distraction which had succeeded in removing attention temporarily from Arabella to lean forward and
whisper something, Max could guess what, into her ear. The
look she gave him in response made Max set his jaw grimly.
Then, Hugo extended one large hand and Arabella, adroitly
excusing herself to her other admirers, allowed him to lead
her on to the floor. A waltz was just starting up.

Knowing there was only so much Hugo could do on a
crowded ballroom floor, Max made a resolution to call on
his aunt and wards on the morrow, firmly determined to
acquaint them with his views on encouraging rakes. Even as

the idea occurred, he groaned. How on earth could he tell Arabella to cease her flirtation with Hugo on the grounds he was a rake when he was himself trying his damnedest to seduce her sister and his best friend was similarly occupied with Sarah? He had known from the outset that this crazy situation would not work.

Reminded of what had originally prompted him to stand just inside the door between Lady Overton's ballroom and the salon set aside for cards and quietly study the company, Max returned his eyes to Sarah Twinning. Despite her assured manner, she was on edge, her hands betraying her nervousness as they played with the lace on her gown. Occasionally, her eyes would lift fleetingly to the door behind him. While to his experienced eye she was not looking her best, Darcy, ensconced in the card-room, was looking even worse. He had been drinking steadily throughout the evening and, although far from drunk, was fast attaining a dangerous state. Suffering from Twinning-induced frustration himself, Max could readily sympathise. He sincerely hoped his pursuit of the eldest Miss Twinning would not bring him so low. His friendship with Darcy Hamilton stretched back over fifteen years. In all that time he had never seen his friend so affected by the desire of a particular woman. Like himself, Darcy was an experienced lover who liked to keep his affairs easy and uncomplicated. If a woman proved difficult, he was much more likely to shrug and, with a smile, pass on to greener fields. But with Sarah Twinning, he seemed unable to admit defeat.

The thought that he himself had no intention of letting the elder Miss Twinning escape and was, even now, under the surface of his preoccupation with his other wards, plotting to get her into his arms, and, ultimately, into his bed, surfaced to shake his self-confidence. His black brows rose a little, in self-mockery. One could hardly blame the girls for keeping them at arm's length. The Twinning sisters had never encouraged them to believe they were of easy virtue, nor that they would accept anything less than marriage.

Their interaction, thus far, had all been part of the game. By
rights, it was they, the rakes of London, who should now
acknowledge the evident truth that, despite their bountiful
attractions, the Twinnings were virtuous females in search
of husbands. And, having acknowledged that fact, to desist from their pursuit of the fair ladies. Without conscious
thought on his part, his eyes strayed to where Caroline stood
amid a group, mostly men, by the side of the dance floor.
She laughed and responded to some comment, her copper
curls gleaming like rosy gold in the bright light thrown down
by the chandeliers. As if feeling his gaze, she turned and,
across the intervening heads, their eyes met. Both were still.
Then, she smoothly turned back to her companions and
Max, straightening his shoulders, moved further into the
crowd. The trouble was, he did not think that he, any more
than Darcy, could stop.

Max slowly passed through the throng, stopping here and
there to chat with acquaintances, his intended goal his aunt,
sitting in a blaze of glorious purple on a chaise by the side
of the room. But before he had reached her, a hand on his
arm drew him around to face the sharp features of Emma
Mortland.

"Your Grace! It's been such an age since we've...talked."
Her ladyship's brown eyes quizzed him playfully.

Her arch tone irritated Max. It was on the tip of his
tongue to recommend she took lessons in flirting from Arabella before she tried her tricks on him. Instead, he took her
hand from his sleeve, bowed over it and pointedly returned
to her, "As you're doubtless aware, Emma, I have other
claims on my time."

His careless use of her first name was calculated to an-
noy but Lady Mortland, having seen his absorption with his
wards, particularly his eldest ward, over the past weeks, was
fast coming to the conclusion that she should do everything
in her power to bring Twyford to his knees or that tiara
would slip through her fingers. As she was a female of little
intelligence, she sincerely believed the attraction that had

brought Max Rotherbridge to her bed would prove sufficient to induce him to propose. Consequently, she coyly
glanced up at him through her long fair lashes and sighed
sympathetically. "Oh, my dear, *I know*. I do *feel* for you.
This business of being guardian to four country girls must
be such a bore to you. But surely, as a diversion, you could
manage to spare us some few hours?"

Not for the first time, Max wondered where women such
as Emma Mortland kept their intelligence. In their pock-
ets? One truly had to wonder. As he looked down at her, his
expression unreadable, he realized that she was a year or so
younger than Caroline. Yet, from the single occasion on
which he had shared her bed, he knew the frills and furbe-
lows she favoured disguised a less than attractive figure,
lacking the curves that characterized his eldest ward. And
Emma Mortland's energies, it seemed, were reserved for
scheming. He had not been impressed. As he knew that a
number of gentlemen, including Darcy Hamilton, had likewise seen her sheets, he was at a loss to understand why she
continued to single him out. A caustic dismissal was about
to leave his lips when, amid a burst of hilarity from a group
just behind them, he heard the rich tones of his eldest ward's
laugh.

On the instant, a plan, fully formed, came into his head
and, without further consideration, he acted. He allowed a
slow, lazy smile to spread across his face. "How well you
read me, my sweet," he drawled to the relieved Lady Mortland. Encouraged, she put her hand tentatively on his arm.
He took it in his hand, intending to raise it to his lips, but to
his surprise he could not quite bring himself to do so. Instead, he smiled meaningfully into her eyes. With an ease
born of countless hours of practice, he instituted a conversation of the risqué variety certain to appeal to Lady Mortland. Soon, he had her gaily laughing and flirting freely with
her eyes and her fan. Deliberately, he turned to lead her on
to the floor for the waltz just commencing, catching, as he
did, a look of innocent surprise on Caroline's face.

Grinning devilishly, Max encouraged Emma to the limits of acceptable flirtation. Then, satisfied with the scene he had created, as they circled the room, he raised his head to see the effect the sight of Lady Mortland in his arms was having on Caroline. To his chagrin, he discovered his eldest ward was no longer standing where he had last seen her. After a frantic visual search, during which he ignored Emma entirely, he located Caroline, also dancing, with the highly suitable Mr. Willoughby. That same Mr. Willoughby who, he knew, was becoming very particular in his attentions. Smothering a curse, Max half-heartedly returned his attention to Lady Mortland.

He had intended to divest himself of the encumbrance of her ladyship as soon as the dance ended but, as the music ceased, he realized they were next to Caroline and her erstwhile partner. Again, Emma found herself the object of Max's undeniable, if strangely erratic charm. Under its influence, she blossomed and bloomed. Max, with one eye on Caroline's now unreadable countenance, leaned closer to Emma to whisper an invitation to view the beauties of the moonlit garden. As he had hoped, she crooned her delight and, with an air of anticipated pleasure, allowed him to escort her through the long windows leading on to the terrace.

"COUNT ME OUT." Darcy Hamilton threw his cards on to the table and pushed back his chair. None of the other players was surprised to see him leave. Normally an excellent player, tonight his lordship had clearly had his mind elsewhere. And the brandy he had drunk was hardly calculated to improve matters, although his gait, as he headed for the ballroom, was perfectly steady.

In the ballroom, Darcy paused to glance about. He saw the musicians tuning up and then sighted his prey.

Almost as if she sensed his approach, Sarah turned as he came up to her. The look of sudden wariness that came into her large eyes pricked his conscience and, consequently, his temper. "My dance, I think."

It was not, as he well knew, but before she could do more than open her mouth to deny him Darcy had swept her on to the floor.

They were both excellent dancers and, despite their current difficulties, they moved naturally and easily together. Which was just as well, as their minds were each completely absorbed in trying to gauge the condition of the other. Luckily, they were both capable of putting on a display of calmness which succeeded in deflecting the interest of the curious.

Sarah, her heart, as usual, beating far too fast, glanced up under her lashes at the handsome face above her, now drawn and slightly haggard. Her heart sank. She had no idea what the outcome of this strange relationship of theirs would be, but it seemed to be causing both of them endless pain. Darcy Hamilton filled her thoughts, day in, day out. But he had steadfastly refused to speak of marriage, despite the clear encouragement she had given him to do so. He had sidestepped her invitations, offering, instead, to introduce her to a vista of illicit delights whose temptation was steadily increasing with time. But she could not, would not accept. She would give anything in the world to be his wife but had no ambition to be his mistress. Lady Benborough had, with all kindness, dropped her a hint that he was very likely a confirmed bachelor, too wedded to his equestrian interests to be bothered with a wife and family, satisfied instead with mistresses and the occasional *affaire*. Surreptitiously studying his rigid and unyielding face, she could find no reason to doubt Augusta's assessment. If that was so, then their association must end. And the sooner the better, for it was breaking her heart.

Seeing her unhappiness reflected in the brown pools of her eyes, Darcy inwardly cursed. There were times he longed to hurt her, in retribution for the agony she was putting him through, but any pain she felt seemed to rebound, ten times amplified, back on him. He was, as Lady Benborough had rightly surmised, well satisfied with his bachelor life. At least, he had been, until he had met Sarah Twinning. Since then, nothing seemed to be right any more. Regardless of the response he knew he awoke in her, she consistently denied any interest in the delightful pleasures he was only too willing to introduce her to. Or rather, held the prospect of said pleasures like a gun at his head, demanding matrimony. He would be damned if he would yield to such tactics. He had long ago considered matrimony, the state of, in a calm and reasoned way, and had come to the conclusion that it held few benefits for him. The idea of being driven, forced, pushed into taking such a step, essentially by the strength of his own raging desires, horrified him, leaving him annoyed beyond measure, principally with himself, but also, unreasonably he knew, with the object of said desires. As the music slowed and halted, he looked down at her lovely face and determined to give her one last chance to capitulate. If she remained adamant, he would have to leave London until the end of the Season. He was quite sure he could not bear the agony any longer.

As Sarah drew away from him and turned towards the room, Darcy drew her hand through his arm and deftly steered her towards the long windows leading on to the terrace. As she realized his intention, she hung back. With a few quick words, he reassured her. "I just want to talk to you. Come into the garden."

Thus far, Sarah had managed to avoid being totally private with him, too aware of her inexperience to chance such an interview. But now, looking into his pale grey eyes and seeing her own unhappiness mirrored there, she consented with a nod and they left the ballroom.

A stone terrace extended along the side of the house, the balustrade broken here and there by steps leading down to the gardens. Flambeaux placed in brackets along the walls threw flickering light down into the avenues and any number of couples could be seen, walking and talking quietly amid the greenery.

Unhurriedly, Darcy led her to the end of the terrace and then down the steps into a deserted walk. They both breathed in the heady freshness of the night air, calming their disordered senses and, without the need to exchange words, each drew some measure of comfort from the other's presence. At the end of the path, a secluded summer-house stood, white paintwork showing clearly against the black shadows of the shrubbery behind it.

As Darcy had hoped, the summer-house was deserted. The path leading to it was winding and heavily screened. Only those who knew of its existence would be likely to find it. He ushered Sarah through the narrow door and let it fall quietly shut behind them. The moonlight slanted through the windows, bathing the room in silvery tints. Sarah stopped in the middle of the circular floor and turned to face him. Darcy paused, trying to decide where to start, then crossed to stand before her, taking her hands in his. For some moments, they stood thus, the rake and the maid, gazing silently into each other's eyes. Then Darcy bent his head and his lips found hers.

Sarah, seduced by the setting, the moonlight and the man before her, allowed him to gather her, unresisting, into his arms. The magic of his lips on hers was a more potent persuasion than any she had previously encountered. Caught by a rising tide of passion, she was drawn, helpless and uncaring, beyond the bounds of thought. Her lips parted and gradually the kiss deepened until, with the moonlight washing in waves over then, he stole her soul.

It was an unintentionally intimate caress which abruptly shook the stars from her eyes and brought her back to earth with an unsteady bump. Holding her tightly within one arm, Darcy had let his other hand slide, gently caressing, over her hip, intending to draw her more firmly against him. But the feel of his hand, scorching through her thin evening dress, sent shock waves of such magnitude through Sarah's pliant body that she pulled back with a gasp. Then, as horrified realization fell like cold water over her heated flesh, she tore herself from his arms and ran.

For an instant, Darcy, stunned both by her response and by her subsequent reaction, stood frozen in the middle of the floor. A knot of jonquil ribbon from Sarah's dress had caught on the button of his cuff and impatiently he shook it free, then watched, fascinated, as it floated to the ground. The banging of the wooden door against its frame had stilled. Swiftly, he crossed the floor and, opening the door, stood in the aperture, listening to her footsteps dying in the spring night. Then, smothering a curse, he followed.

Sarah instinctively ran away from the main house, towards the shrubbery which lay behind the summer-house. She did not stop to think or reason, but just ran. Finally, deep within the tall clipped hedges and the looming bushes, her breath coming in gasps, she came to a clearing, a small garden at the centre of the shrubbery. She saw a marble bench set in an arbour. Thankfully, she sank on to it and buried her face in her hands.

Darcy, following, made for the shrubbery, her hurrying footsteps echoing hollowly on the gravel walks giving him the lead. But once she reached the grassed avenues between the high hedges, her feet made no sound. Penetrating the dark alleys, he was forced to go slowly, checking this way and that to make sure he did not pass her by. So quite fifteen minutes had passed before he reached the central garden and saw the dejected figure huddled on the bench.

In that time, sanity of sorts had returned to Sarah's mind. Her initial horror at her weakness had been replaced by the inevitable reaction. She was angry. Angry at herself, for being so weak that one kiss could overcome all her defences; angry at Darcy, for having engineered that little scene. She was busy whipping up the necessary fury to face the prospect of not seeing him ever again, when he materialized at her side. With a gasp, she came to her feet.

Relieved to find she was not crying, as he had thought, Darcy immediately caught her hand to prevent her flying from him again.

Stung by the shock his touch always gave her, intensified now, she was annoyed to discover, Sarah tried to pull her hand away. When he refused to let her go, she said, her voice infused with an iciness designed to freeze, "Kindly release me, Lord Darcy."

On hearing her voice, Darcy placed the emotion that was holding her so rigid. The knowledge that she was angry, nay, furious, did nothing to improve his own temper, stirred to life by her abrupt flight. Forcing his voice to a reasonableness he was far from feeling, he said, "If you'll give me your word you'll not run away from me, I'll release you."

Sarah opened her mouth to inform him she would not so demean herself as to run from him when the knowledge that she just had, and might have reason to do so again, hit her. She remained silent. Darcy, accurately reading her mind, held on to her hand.

After a moment's consideration, he spoke. "I had intended, my dear, to speak to you of our...curious relationship."

Sarah, breathing rapidly and anxious to end the interview, immediately countered, "I really don't think there's anything to discuss."

A difficult pause ensued, then, "So you would deny there's anything between us?"

The bleakness in his voice shook her, but she determinedly put up her chin, turning away from him as far as their locked hands would allow. "Whatever's between us is neither here nor there," she said, satisfied with the lightness she had managed to bring to her tone.

Her satisfaction was short-lived. Taking advantage of her movement, Darcy stepped quickly behind her, the hand still holding hers reaching across her, his arm wrapping around her waist and drawing her hard against him. His other hand came to rest on her shoulder, holding her still. He knew the shock it would give her, to feel his body against hers, and heard with grim satisfaction the hiss of her indrawn breath.

Sarah froze, too stunned to struggle, the sensation of his hard body against her back, his arm wound like steel about her waist, holding her fast, driving all rational thought from her brain. Then his breath wafted the curls around her ear. His words came in a deep and husky tone, sending tingling shivers up and down her spine.

"Well, sweetheart, there's very little between us now. So, perhaps we can turn our attention to our relationship?"

Sarah, all too well aware of how little there was between them, wondered in a moment of startling lucidity how he imagined that would improve her concentration. But Darcy's attention had already wandered. His lips were very gently trailing down her neck, creating all sorts of marvellous sensations which she tried very hard to ignore.

Then, he gave a deep chuckle. "As I've been saying these weeks past, my dear, you're wasted as a virgin. Now, if you were to become my mistress, just think of all the delightful avenues we could explore."

"I don't want to become your mistress!" Sarah almost wailed, testing the arm at her waist and finding it immovable.

"No?" came Darcy's voice in her ear. She had the impression he considered her answer for a full minute before he continued, "Perhaps we should extend your education a trifle, my dear. So you fully appreciate what you're turning down. We wouldn't want you to make the wrong decision for lack of a few minutes' instruction, would we?"

Sarah had only a hazy idea of what he could mean but his lips had returned to her throat, giving rise to those strangely heady swirls of pleasure that washed through her, sapping her will. "Darcy, stop! You know you shouldn't be doing this!"

He stilled. "Do I?"

Into the silence, a nightingale warbled. Sarah held her breath.

But, when Darcy spoke again, the steel threading his voice, so often sensed yet only now recognised, warned her of the futility of missish pleas.

"Yes. You're right. I know I shouldn't." His lips moved against her throat, a subtle caress. "But what I want to do is make love to you. As you won't allow that, then this will have to do for now."

Sarah, incapable of further words, simply shook her head, powerless to halt the spreading fires he was so skilfully igniting.

Afterwards, Darcy could not understand how it had happened. He was as experienced with women as Max and had never previously lost control as he did that night. He had intended to do no more than reveal to the perverse woman her own desires and give her some inkling of the pleasures they could enjoy together. Instead, her responses were more than he had bargained for and his own desires stronger than he had been prepared to admit. Fairly early in the engagement, he had turned her once more into his arms, so he could capture her lips and take the lesson further. And further it had certainly gone, until the moon sank behind the high hedges and left them in darkness.

How THE HELL WAS HE to get rid of her? Max, Lady Mortland on his arm, had twice traversed the terrace. He had no intention of descending to the shadowy avenues. He had no intention of paying any further attention to Lady Mortland at all. Lady Mortland, on the other hand, was waiting for his attentions to begin and was rather surprised at his lack of ardour in keeping to the terrace.

They were turning at the end of the terrace, when Max, glancing along, saw Caroline come out of the ballroom, alone, and walk quickly to the balustrade and peer over. She was clearly seeking someone. Emma Mortland, prattling on at his side, had not seen her. With the reflexes necessary for being one of the more successful rakes in the *ton*, Max whisked her ladyship back into the ballroom via the door they were about to pass.

Finding herself in the ballroom once more, with the Duke of Twyford bowing over her hand in farewell, Lady Mortland put a hand to her spinning head. "Oh! But surely..."

"A guardian is never off duty for long, my dear," drawled Max, about to move off.

"Perhaps I'll see you in the Park, tomorrow?" asked Emma, convinced his departure had nothing to do with inclination.

Max smiled. "Anything's possible."

He took a circuitous route around the ballroom and exited through the same door he had seen his ward use. Gaining the terrace, he almost knocked her over as she returned to the ballroom, looking back over her shoulder towards the gardens.

"Oh!" Finding herself unexpectedly in her guardian's arms temporarily suspended Caroline's faculties.

From her face, Max knew she had not been looking for him. He drew her further into the shadows of the terrace, placing her hand on his arm and covering it comfortingly with his. "What is it?"

Caroline could not see any way of avoiding telling him. She fell into step beside him, unconsciously following his lead. "Sarah. Lizzie saw her leave the ballroom with Lord Darcy. More than twenty minutes ago. They haven't returned."

In the dim light, Max's face took on a grim look. He had suspected there would be trouble. He continued strolling towards the end of the terrace. "I know where they'll be. There's a summer-house deeper in the gardens. I think you had better come with me."

Caroline nodded and, unobtrusively, they made their way to the summer-house.

Max pushed open the door, then frowned at the empty room. He moved further in and Caroline followed. "Not here?"

Max shook his head, then bent to pick up a knot of ribbon from the floor.

Caroline came to see and took it from him. She crossed to the windows, turning the small cluster this way and that to gauge the colour.

"Is it hers?" asked Max as he strolled to her side.

"Yes. I can't see the colour well but I know the knot. It's a peculiar one. I made it myself."

"So they were here."

"But where are they now?"

"Almost certainly on their way back to the house," answered Max. "There's nowhere in this garden suitable for the purpose Darcy would have in mind. Presumably, your sister convinced him to return to more populated surroundings." He spoke lightly, but, in truth, was puzzled. He could not readily imagine Sarah turning Darcy from his purpose, not in his present mood, not in this setting. But he was sure there was nowhere else they could go.

"Well, then," said Caroline, dusting the ribbon, "we'd better go back, too."

"In a moment," said Max.

His tone gave Caroline an instant's warning. She put out a hand to fend him off. "No! This is *absurd*—you know it is."

Despite her hand, Max succeeded in drawing her into his arms, holding her lightly. "Absurd, is it? Well, you just keep on thinking how absurd it is, while I enjoy your very sweet lips." And he proceeded to do just that.

As his lips settled over hers, Caroline told herself she should struggle. But, for some mystical reason, her body remained still, her senses turned inward by his kiss. Under gentle persuasion, her lips parted and, with a thrill, she felt his gentle exploration teasing her senses, somehow drawing her deeper. Time seemed suspended and she felt her will weakening as she melted into his arms and they locked around her.

Max's mind was ticking in double time, evaluating the amenities of the summer-house and estimating how long they could remain absent from the ballroom. He decided neither answer was appropriate. Seduction was an art and should not be hurried. Besides, he doubted his eldest ward was quite ready to submit yet. Reluctantly, he raised his head and grinned wolfishly at her. "Still absurd?"

Caroline's wits were definitely not connected. She simply stared at him uncomprehendingly.

In face of this response, Max laughed and, drawing her arm through his, steered her to the door. "I think you're right. We'd better return."

SANITY RETURNED to Sarah's mind like water in a bucket, slowing filling from a dripping tap, bit by bit, until it was full. For one long moment, she allowed her mind to remain blank, savouring the pleasure of being held so gently against him. Then, the world returned and demanded her response. She struggled to sit up and was promptly helped to her feet. She checked her gown and found it perfectly tidy, bar one knot of ribbon on her sleeve which seemed to have gone missing.

Darcy, who had returned to earth long before, had been engaged in some furious thinking. But, try as he might, he could not imagine how she would react. Like Max, it had been a long time since young virgins had been his prey. As she stood, he tried to catch a glimpse of her face in the dim light but she perversely kept it averted. In the end, he caught her hands and drew her to stand before him. "Sweetheart, are you all right?"

Strangely enough, it was the note of sincerity in his voice which snapped Sarah's control. Her head came up and, even in the darkness, her eyes flashed fire. "Of course I'm not all right! How *dare* you take advantage of me?"

She saw Darcy's face harden at her words and, in fury at his lack of comprehension, she slapped him.

For a minute, absolute silence reigned. Then a sob broke from Sarah as she turned away, her head bent to escape the look on Darcy's face.

Darcy, slamming a door on his emotions, so turbulent that even he had no idea what he felt, moved to rescue them both. In a voice totally devoid of all feeling, he said, "We had better get back to the house."

In truth, neither had any idea how long they had been absent. In silence, they walked side by side, careful not to touch each other, until, eventually, the terrace was reached. Sarah, crying but determined not to let the tears fall, blinked hard, then mounted the terrace steps by Darcy's side. At the top, he turned to her. "It would be better, I think, if you went in first."

Sarah, head bowed, nodded and went.

CAROLINE AND MAX regained the ballroom and both glanced around for their party. Almost immediately, Lizzie appeared by her sister's side on the arm of one of her youthful swains. She prettily thanked him and dismissed him before turning to her sister and their guardian. "Sarah came back just after you left to look for her. She and Lady Benborough and Mrs. Alford have gone home."

"Oh?" It was Max's voice which answered her. "Why?"

Lizzie cast a questioning look at Caroline and received a nod in reply. "Sarah was upset about something."

Max was already scanning the room when Lizzie's voice reached him. "Lord Darcy came in a little while after Sarah. He's left now, too."

With a sigh, Max realized there was nothing more to be done that night. They collected Arabella and departed Overton House, Caroline silently considering Sarah's problem and Max wondering if he was going to have to wait until his friend solved his dilemma before he would be free to settle his own affairs.

CHAPTER SIX

MAX TOOK A LONG SIP of his brandy and savoured the smooth warmth as it slid down his throat. He stretched his legs to the fire. The book he had been trying to reach rested open, on his thighs, one strong hand holding it still. He moved his shoulders slightly, settling them into the comfort of well padded leather and let his head fall back against the chair.

It was the first night since the beginning of the Season that he had had a quiet evening at home. And he needed it. Who would have thought his four wards would make such a drastic change in a hitherto well-ordered existence? Then he remembered. He had. But he had not really believed his own dire predictions. And the only reason he was at home to-night was because Sarah, still affected by her brush with Darcy the night before, had elected to remain at home and Caroline had stayed with her. He deemed his aunt Augusta and Miriam Alford capable of chaperoning the two younger girls between them. After the previous night, it was unlikely they would allow any liberties.

Even now, no one had had an accounting of what had actually taken place between Darcy and Sarah. But, knowing Darcy, his imagination had supplied a quantity of detail. He had left Delmere House at noon that day with the full intention of running his lordship to earth and demanding an explanation. He had finally found him at Manton's Shooting Gallery, culping wafer after wafer with grim precision. One look at his friend's face had been enough to cool his temper. He had patiently waited until Darcy, having dispatched all the wafers currently in place, had thrown the pistol down with an oath and turned to him.

"Don't ask!"

So he had preserved a discreet silence on the subject and together they had rolled about town, eventually ending in Cribb's back parlour, drinking Blue Ruin. Only then had Darcy reverted to the topic occupying both their minds. "I'm leaving town."

"Oh?"

His lordship had run a hand through his perfectly cut golden locks, disarranging them completely, in a gesture Max had never, in all their years together, seen him use. "Going to Leicestershire. I need a holiday."

Max had nodded enigmatically. Lord Darcy's principal estates lay in Leicestershire and always, due to the large number of horses he raised, demanded attention. But in general, his lordship managed to run his business affairs quite comfortably from town.

"No, by God! I've got a better idea. I'll go to Ireland. It's further away."

As Max knew, Lord Darcy's brother resided on the family estates in Ireland. Still, he had said nothing, patiently waiting for what he had known would come.

Darcy had rolled his glass between his hands, studying the swirling liquid with apparent interest. "About Sarah."

"Mmm?" Max had kept his own eyes firmly fixed on his glass.

"I didn't."

"Oh?"

"No. But I'm not entirely sure she knows what happened." Darcy had drained his glass, using the opportunity to watch Max work this out.

Finally, comprehension had dawned. A glimmer of a smile had tugged at the corners of His Grace of Twyford's mouth. "Oh."

"Precisely. I thought I'd leave it in your capable hands."

"Thank you!" Max had replied. Then he had groaned and dropped his head into his hands. "How the hell do you imagine I'm going to find out what she believes and then explain it to her if she's wrong?" His mind had boggled at the awful idea.

"I thought you might work through Miss Twinning," Darcy had returned, grinning for the first time that day.

Relieved to see his friend smile, even at his expense, Max had grinned back. "I've not been pushing the pace quite as hard as you. Miss Twinning and I have some way to go before we reach the point where such intimate discussion would be permissible."

"Oh, well," Darcy had sighed. "I only hope you have better luck than I."

"Throwing in the towel?"

Darcy had shrugged. "I wish I knew." A silence had ensued which Darcy eventually broke. "I've got to get away."

"How long will you be gone?"

Another shrug. "Who knows? As long as it takes, I suppose."

He had left Darcy packing at Hamilton House and returned to the comfort of his own home to spend a quiet evening in contemplation of his wards. Their problems should really not cause surprise. At first sight, he had known what sort of men the Twinning girls would attract. And there was no denying they responded to such men. Even Arabella seemed hell-bent on tangling with rakes. Thankfully, Lizzie seemed too quiet and gentle to take the same road—three rakes in any family should certainly be enough.

Family? The thought sobered him. He sat, eyes on the flames leaping in the grate, and pondered the odd notion.

His reverie was interrupted by sounds of an arrival. He glanced at the clock and frowned. Too late for callers. What now? He reached the hall in time to see Hillshaw and a footman fussing about the door.

"Yes, it's all right, Hillshaw, I'm not an invalid, you know!"

The voice brought Max forward. "Martin!"

The tousled brown head of Captain Martin Rotherbridge turned to greet his older brother. A winning grin spread across features essentially a more boyish version of Max's own. "Hello, Max. I'm back, as you see. Curst Frenchies put a hole in my shoulder."

Max's gaze fell to the bulk of bandaging distorting the set of his brother's coat. He clasped the hand held out to him warmly, his eyes raking the other's face. "Come into the library. Hillshaw?"

"Yes, Your Grace. I'll see to some food."

When they were comfortably ensconced by the fire, Martin with a tray of cold meat by his side and a large balloon of his brother's best brandy in his hand, Max asked his questions.

"No, you're right," Martin answered to one of these. "It wasn't just the wound, though that was bad enough. They tell me that with rest it'll come good in time." Max waited patiently. His brother fortified himself before continuing. "No. I sold out simply because, now the action's over, it's deuced boring over there. We sit about and play cards half the day. And the other half, we just sit and reminisce about all the females we've ever had." He grinned at his brother in a way Caroline, for one, would have recognised. "Seemed to me I was running out of anecdotes. So I decided to come home and lay in a fresh stock."

Max returned his brother's smile. Other than the shoulder wound, Martin was looking well. The difficult wound and slow convalescence had not succeeded in erasing the healthy glow from outdoor living which burnished his skin and, although there were lines present which had not been there before, these merely seemed to emphasize the fact that Martin Rotherbridge had seen more than twenty-five summers and was an old hand in many spheres. Max was delighted to hear he had returned to civilian life. Aside from

his genuine concern for a much loved sibling, Martin was
now the heir to the Dukedom of Twyford. While inheriting
the Delmere holdings, with which he was well-acquainted,
would have proved no difficulty to Martin, the Twyford estates were a different matter. Max eyed the long, lean frame
stretched out in the chair before him and wondered where
to begin. Before he had decided, Martin asked, "So how do
you like being 'Your Grace'?"

In a few pithy sentences, Max told him. He then embarked on the saga of horrors examination of his uncle's
estate had revealed, followed by a brief description of their
present circumstances. Seeing the shadow of tiredness pass
across Martin's face, he curtailed his report, saying instead, "Time for bed, stripling. You're tired."

Martin started, then grinned sleepily at Max's use of his
childhood tag. "What? Oh, yes. I'm afraid I'm not up to
full strength yet. And we've been travelling since first light."

Max's hand at his elbow assisted him to rise from the
depth of the armchair. On his feet, Martin stretched and
yawned. Seen side by side, the similarity between the brothers was marked. Max was still a few inches taller and his nine
years' seniority showed in the heavier musculature of his
chest and shoulders. Other than that, the differences were
few—Martin's hair was a shade lighter than Max's dark
mane and his features retained a softness Max's lacked, but
the intensely blue eyes of the Rotherbridges shone in both
dark faces.

Martin turned to smile at his brother. "It's good to be
home."

"GOOD MORNING. Hillshaw, isn't it? I'm Lizzie Twinning.
I've come to return a book to His Grace."

Although he had only set eyes on her once before, Hillshaw remembered his master's youngest ward perfectly. As
she stepped daintily over the threshold of Delmere House,
a picture in a confection of lilac muslin, he gathered his wits
to murmur, "His Grace is not presently at home, miss. Per-

haps his secretary, Mr. Cummings, could assist you.'' Hillshaw rolled one majestic eye toward a hovering footman
who immediately, if reluctantly, disappeared in the direction of the back office frequented by the Duke's secretary.

Lizzie, allowing Hillshaw to remove her half-cape, looked
doubtful. But all she said was, ''Wait here for me, Hen-
nessy. I shan't be long.'' Her maid, who had dutifully followed her in, sat primly on the edge of a chair by the wall
and, under the unnerving stare of Hillshaw, lowered her
round-eyed gaze to her hands.

Immediately, Mr. Joshua Cummings came hurrying forward from the dimness at the rear of the hall. ''Miss Lizzie?
I'm afraid His Grace has already left the house, but perhaps I may be of assistance?'' Mr. Cummings was not what
one might expect of a nobleman's secretary. He was of
middle age and small and round and pale, and, as Lizzie
later informed her sisters, looked as if he spent his days
locked away perusing dusty papers. In a sense, he did. He
was a single man and, until taking his present post, had lived
with his mother on the Rotherbridge estate in Surrey. His
family had long been associated with the Rotherbridges and
he was sincerely devoted to that family's interests. Catching sight of the book in Lizzie's small hand, he smiled. ''Ah,
I see you have brought back Lord Byron's verses. Perhaps
you'd like to read his next book? Or maybe one of Mrs.
Linfield's works would be more to your taste?''

Lizzie smiled back. On taking up residence at Twyford
House, the sisters had been disappointed to find that, although extensive, the library there did not hold any of the
more recent fictional works so much discussed among the
ton. Hearing of their complaint, Max had revealed that his
own library did not suffer from this deficiency and had
promised to lend them any books they desired. But, rather
than permit the sisters free rein in a library that also con-
tained a number of works less suitable for their eyes, he had
delegated the task of looking out the books they wanted to

his secretary. Consequently, Mr. Cummings felt quite competent to deal with the matter at hand.

"If you'd care to wait in the drawing room, miss?" Hillshaw moved past her to open the door. With another dazzling smile, Lizzie handed the volume she carried to Mr. Cummings, informing him in a low voice that one of Mrs. Linfield's novels would be quite acceptable, then turned to follow Hillshaw. As she did so, her gaze travelled past the stately butler to rest on the figure emerging from the shadow of the library door. She remained where she was, her grey-brown eyes growing rounder and rounder, as Martin Rotherbridge strolled elegantly forward.

After the best night's sleep he had had in months, Martin had felt ready to resume normal activities but, on descending to the breakfast parlour, had discovered his brother had already left the house to call in at Tattersall's. Suppressing the desire to pull on his coat and follow, Martin had resigned himself to awaiting Max's return, deeming it wise to inform his brother in person that he was setting out to pick up the reins of his civilian existence before he actually did so. Knowing his friends, and their likely reaction to his reappearance among them, he was reasonably certain he would not be returning to Delmere House until the following morning. And he knew Max would worry unless he saw for himself that his younger brother was up to it. So, with a grin for his older brother's affection, he had settled in the library to read the morning's news sheets. But, after months of semi-invalidism, his returning health naturally gave rise to returning spirits. Waiting patiently was not easy. He had been irritably pacing the library when his sharp ears had caught the sound of a distinctly feminine voice in the hall. Intrigued, he had gone to investigate.

Setting eyes on the vision gracing his brother's hall, Martin's immediate thought was that Max had taken to allowing his ladybirds to call at his house. But the attitudes of Hillshaw and Cummings put paid to that idea. The sight of a maid sitting by the door confirmed his startled perception that the vision was indeed a young lady. His boredom vanishing like a cloud on a spring day, he advanced.

Martin allowed his eyes to travel, gently, so as not to startle her, over the delicious figure before him. Very nice. His smile grew. The silence around him penetrated his mind, entirely otherwise occupied. "Hillshaw, I think you'd better introduce us."

Hillshaw almost allowed a frown to mar his impassive countenance. But he knew better than to try to avoid the unavoidable. Exchanging a glance of fellow feeling with Mr. Cummings, he obliged in sternly disapproving tones. "Captain Martin Rotherbridge, Miss Lizzie Twinning. The young lady is His Grace's youngest ward, sir."

With a start, Martin's gaze, which had been locked with Lizzie's, flew to Hillshaw's face. "Ward?" He had not been listening too well last night when Max had been telling him of the estates, but he was sure his brother had not mentioned any wards.

With a thin smile, Hillshaw inclined his head in assent.

Lizzie, released from that mesmerising gaze, spoke up, her soft tones a dramatic contrast to the masculine voices. "Yes. My sisters and I are the Duke's wards, you know." She held out her hand. "How do you do? I didn't know the Duke had a brother. I've only dropped by to exchange some books His Grace lent us. Mr. Cummings was going to take care of it."

Martin took the small gloved hand held out to him and automatically bowed over it. Straightening, he moved to her side, placing her hand on his arm and holding it there. "In that case, Hillshaw's quite right. You should wait in the drawing-room." The relief on Hillshaw's and Mr. Cummings's faces evaporated at his next words. "And I'll keep you company."

As Martin ushered Lizzie into the drawing-room and pointedly shut the door in Hillshaw's face, the Duke's butler and secretary looked at each other helplessly. Then Mr. Cummings scurried away to find the required books, leaving Hillshaw to look with misgiving at the closed door of the drawing-room.

Inside, blissfully unaware of the concern she was engendering in her guardian's servants, Lizzie smiled trustingly up at the source of that concern.

"Have you been my brother's ward for long?" Martin asked.

"Oh, no!" said Lizzie. Then, "That is, I suppose, yes." She looked delightfully befuddled and Martin could not suppress a smile. He guided her to the chaise and, once she had settled, took the chair opposite her so that he could keep her bewitching face in full view.

"It depends, I suppose," said Lizzie, frowning in her effort to gather her wits, which had unaccountably scattered, "on what you'd call long. Our father died eighteen months ago, but then the other Duke—your uncle, was he not?— was our guardian. But when we came back from America, your brother had assumed the title. So then he was our guardian."

Out of this jumbled explanation, Martin gleaned enough to guess the truth. "Did you enjoy America? Were you there long?"

Little by little his questions succeeded in their aim and in short order, Lizzie had relaxed completely and was conversing in a normal fashion with her guardian's brother.

Listening to her description of her home, Martin shifted, trying to settle his shoulder more comfortably. Lizzie's sharp eyes caught the awkward movement and descried the wad of bandaging cunningly concealed beneath his coat.

"You're injured!" She leaned forward in concern. "Does it pain you dreadfully?"

"No, no. The enemy just got lucky, that's all. Soon be right as rain, I give you my word."

"You were in the army?" Lizzie's eyes had grown round. "Oh, please tell me all about it. It must have been so exciting!"

To Martin's considerable astonishment, he found himself recounting for Lizzie's benefit the horrors of the campaign and the occasional funny incident which had enlivened their days. She did not recoil but listened avidly. He had always thought he was a dab hand at interrogation but her persistent questioning left him reeling. She even succeeded in dragging from him the reason he had yet to leave the house. Her ready sympathy, which he had fully expected to send him running, enveloped him instead in a warm glow, a sort of prideful care which went rapidly to his head.

Then Mr. Cummings arrived with the desired books. Lizzie took them and laid them on a side-table beside her, patently ignoring the Duke's secretary who was clearly waiting to escort her to the front door. With an ill-concealed grin, Martin dismissed him. "It's all right, Cummings. Miss Twinning has taken pity on me and decided to keep me entertained until my brother returns."

Lizzie, entirely at home, turned a blissful smile on Mr. Cummings, leaving that gentleman with no option but to retire.

AN HOUR LATER, Max crossed the threshold to be met by Hillshaw, displaying, quite remarkably, an emotion very near agitation. This was instantly explained. "Miss Lizzie's here. In the drawing-room with Mr. Martin."

Max froze. Then nodded to his butler. "Very good, Hillshaw." His sharp eyes had already taken in the bored face of the maid sitting in the shadows. Presumably, Lizzie had been here for some time. His face was set in grim lines as his hand closed on the handle of the drawing-room door.

The sight which met his eyes was not at all what he had expected. As he shut the door behind him, Martin's eyes lifted to his, amused understanding in the blue depths. He was seated in an armchair and Lizzie occupied the nearest corner of the chaise. She was presently hunched forward, pondering what lay before her on a small table drawn up between them. As Max rounded the chaise, he saw to his stupefaction that they were playing checkers.

Lizzie looked up and saw him. "Oh! You're back. I was just entertaining your brother until you returned." Max blinked but Lizzie showed no consciousness of the implication of her words and he discarded the notion of enlightening her.

Then Lizzie's eyes fell on the clock on the mantelshelf. "Oh, dear! I didn't realize it was so late. I must go. Where are those books Mr. Cummings brought?"

Martin fetched them for her and, under the highly sceptical gaze of his brother, very correctly took leave of her. Max, seeing the expression in his brother's eyes as they rested on his youngest ward, almost groaned aloud. This was really too much.

Max saw Lizzie out, then returned to the library. But before he could launch into his inquisition, Martin got in first. "You didn't tell me you had inherited four wards."

"Well, I have," said Max, flinging himself into an armchair opposite the one his brother had resumed.

"Are they all like that?" asked Martin in awe.

Max needed no explanation of what "that" meant. He answered with a groan, "Worse!"

Eyes round, Martin did not make the mistake of imagining the other Twinning sisters were antidotes. His gaze rested on his brother for a moment, then his face creased into a wide smile. "Good lord!"

Max brought his blue gaze back from the ceiling and fixed it firmly on his brother. "Precisely. That being so, I suggest you revise the plans you've been making for Lizzie Twinning."

Martin's grin, if anything, became even broader. "Why so? It's you who's their guardian, not I. Besides, you don't seriously expect me to believe that, if our situations were reversed, you'd pay any attention to such restrictions?" When Max frowned, Martin continued. "Anyway, good heavens, you must have seen it for yourself. She's like a ripe plum, ready for the picking." He stopped at Max's raised hand.

"Permit me to fill you in," drawled his older brother. "For a start, I've nine years on you and there's nothing about the business you know that I don't. However, quite aside from that, I can assure you the Twinning sisters, ripe though they may be, are highly unlikely to fall into any-one's palms without a prior proposal of marriage."

A slight frown settled over Martin's eyes. Not for a mo-ment did he doubt the accuracy of Max's assessment. But he had been strongly attracted to Lizzie Twinning and was disinclined to give up the idea of converting her to his way of thinking. He looked up and blue eyes met blue. "Re-ally?"

Max gestured airily. "Consider the case of Lord Darcy Hamilton." Martin looked his question. Max obliged. "Being much taken with Sarah, the second of the four, Darcy's been engaged in storming her citadel for the past five weeks and more. No holds barred, I might add. And the outcome you ask? As of yesterday, he's retired to his es-tates, to lick his wounds and, unless I miss my guess, to consider whether he can stomach the idea of marriage."

"Good lord!" Although only peripherally acquainted with Darcy Hamilton, Martin knew he was one of Max's particular friends and that his reputation in matters involv-ing the fairer sex was second only to Max's own.

"Exactly," nodded Max. "Brought low by a chit of a girl. So, brother dear, if it's your wish to tangle with any Twin-nings, I suggest you first decide how much you're willing to stake on the throw."

As he pondered his brother's words, Martin noticed that Max's gaze had become abstracted. He only just caught the last words his brother said, musing, almost to himself. "For, brother mine, it's my belief the Twinnings eat rakes for breakfast."

THE COACH SWAYED as it turned a corner and Arabella clutched the strap swinging by her head. As equilibrium returned, she settled her skirts once more and glanced at the other two occupants of the carriage. The glow from a street lamp momentarily lit the interior of the coach, then faded as the four horses hurried on. Arabella grinned into the darkness.

Caroline had insisted that she and not Lizzie share their guardian's coach. One had to wonder why. Too often these days, her eldest sister had the look of the cat caught just after it had tasted the cream. Tonight, that look of guilty pleasure, or, more specifically, the anticipation of guilty pleasure, was marked.

She had gone up to Caroline's room to hurry her sister along. Caroline had been sitting, staring at her reflection in the mirror, idly twisting one copper curl to sit more attractively about her left ear.

"Caro? Are you ready? Max is here."

"Oh!" Caroline had stood abruptly, then paused to cast one last critical glance over her pale sea-green dress, severely styled as most suited her ample charms, the neckline daringly *décolleté*. She had frowned, her fingers straying to the ivory swell of her breasts. "What do you think, Bella? Is it too revealing? Perhaps a piece of lace might make it a little less . . . ?"

"Attractive?" Arabella had brazenly supplied. "To be perfectly frank, I doubt our guardian would approve a fichu."

The delicate blush that had appeared on Caroline's cheeks had been most informative. But, "Too true," was all her sister had replied.

Arabella looked across the carriage once more and caught the gleam of warm approval that shone in their guardian's eyes as they rested on Caroline. It was highly unlikely that the conservative Mr. Willoughby was the cause of her sister's blushes. That being so, what game was the Duke of

Twyford playing? And, even more to the point, was Caro thinking of joining in?

Heaven knew, they had had a close enough call with Sarah and Lord Darcy. Nothing had been said of Sarah's strange affliction, yet they were all close enough for even the innocent Lizzie to have some inkling of the root cause. And while Max had been the soul of discretion in speaking privately to Caroline and Sarah in the hall before they had left, it was as plain as a pikestaff the information he had imparted had not included news of a proposal. Sarah's pale face had paled further. But the Twinnings were made of stern stuff and Sarah had shaken her head at Caro's look of concern.

The deep murmur of their guardian's voice came to her ears, followed by her sister's soft tones. Arabella's big eyes danced. She could not make out their words but those tones were oh, so revealing. But if Sarah was in deep waters and Caro was hovering on the brink, she, to her chagrin, had not even got her toes wet yet.

Arabella frowned at the moon, showing fleetingly between the branches of a tall tree. Hugo, Lord Denbigh. The most exasperating man she had ever met. She would give anything to be able to say she didn't care a button for him. Unfortunately, he was the only man who could make her tingle just by looking at her.

Unaware that she was falling far short of Caroline's expectations, Arabella continued to gaze out of the window, absorbed in contemplation of the means available for bringing one large gentleman to heel.

THE HEAVY TWYFORD coach lumbered along in the wake of the sleek Delmere carriage. Lady Benborough put up a hand to right her wig, swaying perilously as they rounded a particularly sharp corner. For the first time since embarking on her nephew's crusade to find the Twinning girls suitable husbands, she felt a twinge of nervousness. She was playing with fire and she knew it. Still, she could not regret it.

The sight of Max and Caroline together in the hall at Twyford House had sent a definite thrill through her old bones. As for Sarah, she doubted not that Darcy Hamilton was too far gone to desist, resist and retire. True, he might not know it yet, but time would certainly bring home to him the penalty he would have to pay to walk away from the snare. Her shrewd blue eyes studied the pale face opposite her. Even in the dim light, the strain of the past few days was evident. Thankfully, no one outside their party had been aware of that contretemps. So, regardless of what Sarah herself believed, Augusta had no qualms. Sarah was home safe; she could turn her attention elsewhere.

Arabella, the minx, had picked a particularly difficult nut to crack. Still, she could hardly fault the girl's taste. Hugo Denbigh was a positive Adonis, well-born, well-heeled and easy enough in his ways. Unfortunately, he was so easy to please that he seemed to find just as much pleasure in the presence of drab little girls as he derived from Arabella's rather more scintillating company. Gammon, of course, but how to alert Arabella to that fact? Or would it be more to the point to keep quiet and allow Hugo a small degree of success? As her mind drifted down that particular path, Augusta suddenly caught herself up and had the grace to look sheepish. What appalling thoughts for a chaperon!

Her gaze fell on Lizzie, sweet but far from demure in a gown of delicate silver gauze touched with colour in the form of embroidered lilacs. A soft, introspective smile hovered over her classically moulded lips. Almost a smile of anticipation. Augusta frowned. Had she missed something?

Mentally reviewing Lizzie's conquests, Lady Benborough was at a loss to account for the suppressed excitement evident, now she came to look more closely, in the way the younger girl's fingers beat an impatient if silent tattoo on the beads of her reticule. Clearly, whoever he was would be at the ball. She would have to watch her youngest charge like a hawk. Lizzie was too young, in all conscience, to be allowed the licence her more worldly sisters took for granted.

Relaxing back against the velvet squabs, Augusta smiled. Doubtless she was worrying over nothing. Lizzie might have the Twinning looks but surely she was too serious an innocent to attract the attentions of a rake? Three rakes she might land, the Twinnings being the perfect bait, but a fourth was bound to be wishful thinking.

CHAPTER SEVEN

MARTIN PUZZLED OVER Max's last words on the Twinnings but it was not until he met the sisters that evening, at Lady Montacute's drum, that he divined what had prompted his brother to utter them. He had spent the afternoon dropping in on certain old friends, only to be, almost immediately, bombarded with requests for introductions to the Twinnings. He had come away with the definite impression that the best place to be that evening would be wherever the Misses Twinning were destined. His batman and valet, Jiggins, had turned up the staggering information that Max himself usually escorted his wards to their evening engagements. Martin had found this hard to credit, but when, keeping an unobtrusive eye on the stream of arrivals from a vantage-point beside a potted palm in Lady Montacute's ballroom, he had seen Max arrive surrounded by Twinning sisters, he had been forced to accept the crazy notion as truth. When the observation that the fabulous creature on his brother's arm was, in fact, his eldest ward finally penetrated his brain all became clear.

Moving rapidly to secure a dance with Lizzie, who smiled up at him with flattering welcome, Martin was close enough to see the expression in his brother's eyes as he bent to whisper something in Miss Twinning's ear, prior to relinquishing her to the attention of the circle forming about her. His brows flew and he pursed his lips in surprise. As his brother's words of that morning returned to him, he grinned. How much was Max prepared to stake?

For the rest of the evening, Martin watched and plotted and planned. He used his wound as an excuse not to dance, which enabled him to spend his entire time studying Lizzie Twinning. It was an agreeable pastime. Her silvery dress floated about her as she danced and the candlelight glowed on her sheening brown curls. With her natural grace, she reminded him of a fairy sprite, except that he rather thought such mythical creatures lacked the fulsome charms with which the Twinning sisters were so well-endowed. Due to his experienced foresight, Lizzie accommodatingly returned to his side after every dance, convinced by his chatter of the morning that he was in dire need of cheering up. Lady Benborough, to whom he had dutifully made his bow, had snorted in disbelief at his die-away airs but had apparently been unable to dissuade Lizzie's soft heart from bringing him continual succour. By subtle degrees, he sounded her out on each of her hopeful suitors and was surprised at his own relief in finding she had no special leaning towards any.

He started his campaign in earnest when the musicians struck up for the dance for which he *had* engaged her. By careful manoeuvring, they were seated in a sheltered alcove, free for the moment of her swains. Schooling his features to grave disappointment, he said, "Dear Lizzie. I'm so sorry to disappoint you, but . . ." He let his voice fade away weakly.

Lizzie's sweet face showed her concern. "Oh! Do you not feel the thing? Perhaps I can get Mrs. Alford's smelling salts for you?"

Martin quelled the instinctive response to react to her suggestion in too forceful a manner. Instead, he waved aside her words with one limp hand. "No! No! Don't worry about me. I'll come about shortly." He smiled forlornly at her, allowing his blue gaze to rest, with calculated effect, on her grey-brown eyes. "But maybe you'd like to get one of your other beaux to dance with you? I'm sure Mr. Mallard would be only too thrilled." He made a move as if to summon this gentleman, the most assiduous of her suitors.

"Heavens, no!" exclaimed Lizzie, catching his hand in hers to prevent the action. "I'll do no such thing. If you're feeling poorly then of course I'll stay with you." She continued to hold his hand and, for his part, Martin made no effort to remove it from her warm clasp.

Martin closed his eyes momentarily, as if fighting off a sudden faintness. Opening them again, he said, "Actually, I do believe it's all the heat and noise in here that's doing it. Perhaps if I went out on to the terrace for a while, it might clear my head."

"The very thing!" said Lizzie, jumping up.

Martin, rising more slowly, smiled down at her in a brotherly fashion. "Actually, I'd better go alone. Someone might get the wrong idea if we both left."

"Nonsense!" said Lizzie, slightly annoyed by his implication that such a conclusion could, of course, have no basis in fact. "Why should anyone worry? We'll only be a few minutes and anyway, I'm your brother's ward, after all."

Martin made some small show of dissuading her, which, as he intended, only increased her resolution to accompany him. Finally, he allowed himself to be bullied on to the terrace, Lizzie's small hand on his arm, guiding him.

As supper time was not far distant, there were only two other couples on the shallow terrace, and within minutes both had returned to the ballroom. Martin, food very far from his mind, strolled down the terrace, apparently content to go where Lizzie led. But his sharp soldier's eyes had very quickly adjusted to the moonlight. After a cursory inspection of the surroundings, he allowed himself to pause dramatically as they neared the end of the terrace. "I really think..." He waited a moment, as if gathering strength, then continued, "I really think I should sit down."

Lizzie looked around in consternation. There were no benches on the terrace, not even a balustrade.

"There's a seat under that willow, I think," said Martin, gesturing across the lawn.

A quick glance from Lizzie confirmed this observation. "Here, lean on me," she said. Martin obligingly draped one arm lightly about her shoulders. As he felt her small hands gripping him about his waist, a pang of guilt shook him. She really was so trusting. A pity to destroy it.

They reached the willow and brushed through the long strands which conveniently fell back to form a curtain around the white wooden seat. Inside the chamber so formed, the moonbeams danced, sprinkling sufficient light to lift the gloom and allow them to see. Martin sank on to the seat with a convincing show of weakness. Lizzie subsided in a susurration of silks beside him, retaining her clasp on his hand and half turning the better to look into his face.

The moon was behind the willow and one bright beam shone through over Martin's shoulder to fall gently on Lizzie's face. Martin's face was in shadow, so Lizzie, smiling confidingly up at him, could only see that he was smiling in return. She could not see the expression which lit his blue eyes as they devoured her delicate face, then dropped boldly to caress the round swell of her breasts where they rose and fell invitingly below the demurely scooped neckline of her gown. Carefully, Martin turned his hand so that now he was holding her hand, not she his. Then he was still.

After some moments, Lizzie put her head on one side and softly asked, "Are you all right?"

It was on the tip of Martin's tongue to answer truthfully. No, he was not all right. He had brought her out here to commence her seduction and now some magical power was holding him back. What was the matter with him? He cleared his throat and answered huskily, "Give me a minute."

A light breeze wafted the willow leaves and the light shifted. Lizzie saw the distracted frown which had settled over his eyes. Drawing her hand from his, she reached up and gently ran her fingers over his brow, as if to smooth the frown away. Then, to Martin's intense surprise, she leaned forward and, very gently, touched her lips to his.

As she drew away, Lizzie saw to her dismay that, if Martin had been frowning before, he was positively scowling now. "Why did you do that?" he asked, his tone sharp.

Even in the dim light he could see her confusion. "Oh, dear! I'm s...so sorry. Please excuse me! I shouldn't have done that."

"Damn right, you shouldn't have," Martin growled. His hand, which had fallen to the bench, was clenched hard with the effort to remain still and not pull the damn woman into his arms and devour her. He realized she had not answered his question. "But why did you?"

Lizzie hung her head in contrition. "It's just that you looked...well, so troubled. I just wanted to help." Her voice was a small whisper in the night.

Martin sighed in frustration. That sort of help he could do without.

"I suppose you'll think me very forward, but..." This time, her voice died away altogether.

What Martin did think was that she was adorable and he hurt with the effort to keep his hands off her. Now he came to think of it, while he had not had a headache when they came out to the garden, he certainly had one now. Repressing the desire to groan aloud, he straightened. "We'd better get back to the ballroom. We'll just forget the incident." As he drew her to her feet and placed her hand on his arm, an unwelcome thought struck him. "You don't go around kissing other men who look troubled, do you?"

The surprise in her face was quite genuine. "No! Of course not!"

"Well," said Martin, wondering why the information so thrilled him, "just subdue any of these sudden impulses of yours. Except around me, of course. I dare say it's perfectly all right with me, in the circumstances. You are my brother's ward, after all."

Lizzie, still stunned by her forward behaviour, and the sudden impulse that had driven her to it, smiled trustingly up at him.

CAROLINE SMILED her practised smile and wished, for at
least the hundredth time, that Max Rotherbridge were not
their guardian. At least, she amended, not *her* guardian. He
was proving a tower of strength in all other respects and she
could only be grateful, both for his continuing support and
protection, as well as his experienced counsel over the affair of Sarah and Lord Darcy. But there was no doubt in her
mind that her own confusion would be immeasurably eased
by dissolution of the guardianship clause which tied her so
irrevocably to His Grace of Twyford.

While she circled the floor in the respectful arms of Mr.
Willoughby who, she knew, was daily moving closer to a
declaration despite her attempts to dampen his confidence,
she was conscious of a wish that it was her guardian's far
less gentle clasp she was in. Mr. Willoughby, she had discovered, was worthy. Which was almost as bad as righteous. She sighed and covered the lapse with a brilliant smile
into his mild eyes, slightly below her own. It was not that she
despised short men, just that they lacked the ability to make
her feel delicate and vulnerable, womanly, as Max Rotherbridge certainly could. In fact, the feeling of utter helpless-
ness that seemed to overcome her every time she found
herself in his powerful arms was an increasing concern.

As she and her partner turned with the music, she sighted
Sarah, dancing with one of her numerous court, trying, not
entirely successfully, to look as if she was enjoying it. Her
heart went out to her sister. They had stayed at home the
previous night and, in unusual privacy, thrashed out the
happenings of the night before. While Sarah skated somewhat thinly over certain aspects, it had been clear that she,
at least, knew her heart. But Max had taken the opportunity of a few minutes' wait in the hall at Twyford House to
let both herself and Sarah know, in the most subtle way, that
Lord Darcy had left town for his estates. She swallowed another sigh and smiled absently at Mr. Willoughby.

As the eldest, she had, in recent years, adopted the role of
surrogate mother to her sisters. One unfortunate aspect of

that situation was that she had no one to turn to herself. If
the gentleman involved had been anyone other than her
guardian, she would have sought advice from Lady Benborough. In the circumstances, that avenue, too, was closed
to her. But, after that interlude in the Overtons's summer-
house, she was abysmally aware that she needed advice. All
he had to do was to take her into his arms and her well-
ordered defences fell flat. And his kiss! The effect of that
seemed totally to disorder her mind, let alone her senses. She
had not yet fathomed what, exactly, he was about, yet it
seemed inconceivable that he would seduce his own ward.
Which fact, she ruefully admitted, but only to herself when
at her most candid, was at the seat of her desire to no longer
be his ward.

It was not that she had any wish to join the *demimonde*.
But face facts she must. She was nearly twenty-six and she
knew what she wanted. She wanted Max Rotherbridge. She
knew he was a rake and, if she had not instantly divined him
standing as soon as she had laid eyes on him, Lady Benborough's forthright remarks on the subject left no room for
doubt. But every tiny particle of her screamed that he was
the one. Which was why she was calmly dancing with each
of her most ardent suitors, careful not to give any one of
them the slightest encouragement, while waiting for her
guardian to claim her for the dance before supper. On their
arrival in the overheated ballroom, he had, in a sensual
murmur that had wafted the curls over her ear and sent
shivery tingles all the way down her spine, asked her to hold
that waltz for him. She looked into Mr. Willoughby's pale
eyes. And sighed.

"SIR MALCOLM, I do declare you're flirting with me!"
Desperation lent Arabella's bell-like voice a definite edge.
Using her delicate feather fan to great purpose, she flashed
her large eyes at the horrendously rich but essentially dim-
witted Scottish baronet, managing meanwhile to keep Hugo,
Lord Denbigh, in view. Her true prey was standing only feet

away, conversing amiably with a plain matron with an even plainer daughter. What was the matter with him? She had tried every trick she knew to bring the great oaf to her tiny feet, yet he persistently drifted away. He would be politely attentive but seemed incapable of settling long enough even to be considered one of her court. She had kept the supper waltz free, declaring it to be taken to all her suitors, convinced he would ask her for that most favoured dance. But now, with supper time fast approaching, she suddenly found herself facing the prospect of having no partner at all. Her eyes flashing, she turned in welcome to Mr. Pritchard and Viscount Molesworth.

She readily captivated both gentlemen, skilfully steering clear of any lapse of her own rigidly imposed standards. She was an outrageous flirt, she knew, but a discerning flirt, and she had long made it her policy never to hurt anyone with her artless chatter. She enjoyed the occupation but it had never involved her heart. Normally, her suitors happily fell at her feet without the slightest assistance from her. But, now that she had at last found someone she wished to attract, she had, to her horror, found she had less idea of how to draw a man to her side than plainer girls who had had to learn the art.

To her chagrin, she saw the musicians take their places on the rostrum. There was only one thing to do. She smiled sweetly at the three gentlemen around her. "My dear sirs," she murmured, her voice mysteriously low, "I'm afraid I must leave you. No! Truly. Don't argue." Another playful smile went around. "Until later, Sir Malcolm, Mr. Pritchard, my lord." With a nod and a mysterious smile she moved away, leaving the three gentlemen wondering who the lucky man was.

Slipping through the crowd, Arabella headed for the exit to the ballroom. Doubtless there would be an antechamber somewhere where she could hide. She was not hungry anyway. She timed her exit to coincide with the movement of a group of people across the door, making it unlikely that anyone would see her retreat. Once in the passage, she glanced about. The main stairs lay directly in front of her. She glanced to her left in time to see two ladies enter one of the rooms. The last thing she needed was the endless chatter of a withdrawing-room. She turned purposefully to her right. At the end of the dimly lit corridor, a door stood open, light from the flames of a hidden fire flickering on its panels. She hurried down the corridor and, looking in, saw a small study. It was empty. A carafe and glasses set in readiness on a small table suggested it was yet another room set aside for the use of guests who found the heat of the ballroom too trying. With a sigh of relief, Arabella entered. After some consideration, she left the door open.

She went to the table and poured herself a glass of water. As she was replacing the glass, she heard voices approaching. Her eyes scanned the room and lit on the deep window alcove; the curtain across it, if fully drawn, would make it a small room. On the thought, she was through, drawing the heavy curtain tightly shut.

In silence, her heart beating in her ears, she listened as the voices came nearer and entered the room, going towards the fire. She waited a moment, breathless, but no one came to the curtain. Relaxing, she turned. And almost fell over the large pair of feet belonging to the gentleman stretched at his ease in the armchair behind the curtain.

"Oh!" Her hand flew to her lips in her effort to smother the sound. "What are you doing here?" she whispered furiously.

Slowly, the man turned his head towards her. He smiled. "Waiting for you, my dear."

Arabella closed her eyes tightly, then opened them again but he was still there. As she watched, Lord Denbigh unfurled his long length and stood, magnificent and, suddenly, to Arabella at least, oddly intimidating, before her. In the light of the full moon spilling through the large windows, his tawny eyes roved appreciatively over her. He caught her small hand in his and raised it to his lips. "I didn't think you'd be long."

His lazy tones, pitched very low, washed languidly over Arabella. With a conscious effort, she tried to break free of their hypnotic hold. "How could you know I was coming here? *I* didn't."

"Well," he answered reasonably, "I couldn't think where else you would go, if you didn't have a partner for the supper waltz."

He *knew!* In the moonlight, Arabella's fiery blush faded into more delicate tints but the effect on her temper was the same. "You oaf!" she said in a fierce whisper, aiming a stinging slap at the grin on his large face. But the grin grew into a smile as he easily caught her hand and drew it down and then behind her, drawing her towards him. He captured her other hand as well and imprisoned that in the same large hand behind her back.

"Lord Denbigh! Let me go!" Arabella pleaded, keeping her voice low for fear the others beyond the curtain would hear. How hideously embarrassing to be found in such a situation. And now she had another problem. What was Hugo up to? As her anger drained, all sorts of other emotions came to the fore. She looked up, her eyes huge and shining in the moonlight, her lips slightly parted in surprise.

Hugo lifted his free hand and one long finger traced the curve of her full lower lip.

Even with only the moon to light his face, Arabella saw the glimmer of desire in his eyes. "Hugo, let me go. Please?"

He smiled lazily down at her. "In a moment, sweetheart. After I've rendered you incapable of scratching my eyes out."

His fingers had taken hold of her chin and he waited to see the fury in her eyes before he chuckled and bent his head until his lips met hers.

Arabella had every intention of remaining aloof from his kisses. Damn him—he'd tricked her! She tried to whip up her anger, but all she could think of was how wonderfully warm his lips felt against hers. And what delicious sensations were running along her nerves. Everywhere. Her body, entirely of its own volition, melted into his arms.

She felt, rather than heard, his deep chuckle as his arms shifted and tightened about her. Finding her hands free and resting on his shoulders, she did not quite know what to do with them. Box his ears? In the end, she twined them about his neck, holding him close.

When Hugo finally lifted his head, it was to see the stars reflected in her eyes. He smiled lazily down at her. "Now you have to admit that's more fun than waltzing."

Arabella could think of nothing to say.

"No quips?" he prompted.

She blushed slightly. "We should be getting back." She tried to ease herself from his embrace but his arms moved not at all.

Still smiling in that sleepy way, he shook his head. "Not yet. That was just the waltz. We've supper to go yet." His lips lightly brushed hers. "And I'm ravenously hungry."

Despite the situation, Arabella nearly giggled at the boyish tone. But she became much more serious when his lips returned fully to hers, driving her into far deeper waters than she had ever sailed before.

But he was experienced enough correctly to gauge her limits, to stop just short and retreat, until they were sane again. Later, both more serious than was their wont, they returned separately to the ballroom.

DESPITE HER STRATEGIES, Arabella was seen as she slipped from the ballroom. Max, returning from the card-room where he had been idly passing his time until he could, with reasonable excuse, gravitate to the side of his eldest ward, saw the bright chestnut curls dip through the doorway and for an instant had thought that Caroline was deserting him.

But his sharp ears had almost immediately caught the husky tone of her laughter from a knot of gentlemen near by and he realised it must have been Arabella, most like Caroline in colouring, whom he had seen.

But he had more serious problems on his mind than whether Arabella had torn her flounce. His pursuit of the luscious Miss Twinning, or, rather, the difficulties which now lay in his path to her, were a matter for concern. The odd fact that he actually bothered to dance with his eldest ward had already been noted. As there were more than a few ladies among the *ton* who could give a fairly accurate description of his preferences in women, the fact that Miss Twinning's endowments brought her very close to his ideal had doubtless not been missed. However, he cared very little for the opinions of others and foresaw no real problem in placating the *ton* after the deed was done. What was troubling him was the unexpected behaviour of the two principals in the affair, Miss Twinning and himself.

With respect to his prey, he had miscalculated on two counts. Firstly, he had imagined it would take a concerted effort to seduce a twenty-five-year-old woman who had lived until recently a very retired life. Instead, from the first, she had responded so freely that he had almost lost his head. He was too experienced not to know that it would take very little of his persuasion to convince her to overthrow the tenets of her class and come to him. It irritated him beyond measure that the knowledge, far from spurring him on to take immediate advantage of her vulnerability, had made him pause and consider, in a most disturbing way, just what he was about. His other mistake had been in thinking that, with his intensive knowledge of the ways of the *ton*, he would have no difficulty in using his position as her guardian to create opportunities to be alone with Caroline. Despite—or was it because of?—her susceptibility towards him, she seemed able to avoid his planned tête-à-têtes with ease and, with the exception of a few occasions associated with some concern over one or other of her sisters, had singularly failed to give him the opportunities he sought. And seducing a woman whose mind was filled with worry over one of her sisters was a task he had discovered to be beyond him.

He had, of course, revised his original concept of what role Caroline was to play in his life. However, he was fast coming to the conclusion that he would have to in some way settle her sisters' affairs before either he or Caroline would have time to pursue their own destinies. But life, he was fast learning, was not all that simple. In the circumstances, the *ton* would expect Miss Twinning's betrothal to be announced before that of her sisters. And he was well aware he had no intention of giving his permission for any gentleman to pay his addresses to Miss Twinning. As he had made no move to clarify for her the impression of his intentions he had originally given her, he did not delude himself that she might not accept some man like Willoughby, simply to remove herself from the temptation of her guardian. Yet if he told her she was not his ward, she would undoubtedly be even more vigilant with respect to himself and, in all probability, even more successful in eluding him.

There was, of course, a simple solution. But he had a perverse dislike of behaving as society dictated. Consequently, he had formed no immediate intention of informing Caroline of his change of plans. There was a challenge, he felt, in attempting to handle their relationship his way. Darcy had pushed too hard and too fast and, consequently, had fallen at the last fence. He, on the other hand, had no intention of rushing things. Timing was everything in such a delicate matter as seduction.

The congestion of male forms about his eldest ward brought a slight frown to his face. But the musicians obligingly placed bow to string, allowing him to extricate her from their midst and sweep her on to the floor.

He glanced down into her grey-green eyes and saw his own pleasure in dancing with her reflected there. His arm tightened slightly and her attention focused. "I do hope your sisters are behaving themselves?"

Caroline returned his weary question with a smile. "Assuming your friends are doing likewise, I doubt there'll be a problem."

Max raised his brows. So she knew at least a little of what had happened. After negotiating a difficult turn to avoid old Major Brumidge and his similarly ancient partner, he jettisoned the idea of trying to learn more of Sarah's thoughts in favour of spiking a more specific gun. "Incidently, apropos of your sisters' and your own fell intent, what do you wish me to say to the numerous beaux who seem poised to troop up the steps of Delmere House?"

He watched her consternation grow as she grappled with the sticky question. He saw no reason to tell her that, on his wards' behalf, he had already turned down a number of offers, none of which could be considered remotely suitable. He doubted they were even aware of the interest of the gentlemen involved.

Caroline, meanwhile, was considering her options. If she was unwise enough to tell him to permit any acceptable gentlemen to address them, they could shortly be bored to distraction with the task of convincing said gentlemen that their feelings were not reciprocated. On the other hand, giving Max Rotherbridge a free hand to choose their husbands seemed equally unwise. She temporized. "Perhaps it would be best if we were to let you know if we anticipated receiving an offer from any particular gentleman that we would wish to seriously consider."

Max would have applauded if his hands had not been so agreeably occupied. "A most sensible suggestion, my ward. Tell me, how long does it take to pin up a flounce?"

Caroline blinked at this startling question.

"The reason I ask," said Max as they glided to a halt, "is that Arabella deserted the room some minutes before the music started and, as far as I can see, has yet to return."

A frown appeared in Caroline's fine eyes but, in deference to the eyes of others, she kept her face free of care and her voice light. "Can you see if Lord Denbigh is in the room?"

Max did not need to look. "Not since I entered it." After a pause, he asked, "Is she seriously pursuing that line? If so, I fear she'll all too soon reach point non plus."

Caroline followed his lead as he offered her his arm and calmly strolled towards the supper-room. A slight smile curled her lips as, in the increasing crowd, she leaned closer to him to answer. "With Arabella, it's hard to tell. She seems so obvious, with her flirting. But that's really all superficial. In reality, she's rather reticent about such things."

Max smiled in reply. Her words merely confirmed his own reading of Arabella. But his knowledge of the relationship between Caroline and her sisters prompted him to add, "Nevertheless, you'd be well-advised to sound her out on that score. Hugo Denbigh, when all is said and done, is every bit as dangerous as..." He paused to capture her eyes with his own before, smiling in a devilish way, he continued, "I am."

Conscious of the eyes upon them, Caroline strove to maintain her composure. "How very... reassuring, to be sure," she managed.

The smile on Max's face broadened. They had reached the entrance of the supper-room and he paused in the doorway to scan the emptying ballroom. "If she hasn't returned in ten minutes, we'll have to go looking. But come, sweet ward, the lobster patties await."

With a flourish, Max led her to a small table where they were joined, much to his delight, by Mr. Willoughby and a plain young lady, a Miss Spence. Mr. Willoughby's transparent intention of engaging the delightful Miss Twinning in close converse, ignoring the undemanding Miss Spence and Miss Twinning's guardian, proved to be rather more complicated than Mr. Willoughby, for one, had imagined. Under the subtle hand of His Grace of Twyford, Mr. Willoughby found himself the centre of a general discussion on philosophy. Caroline listened in ill-concealed delight as Max blocked every move poor Mr. Willoughby made to polarise the conversation. It became apparent that her guardian understood only too well Mr. Willoughby's state and she found herself caught somewhere between embarrassment and relief. In the end, relief won the day.

Eventually, routed, Mr. Willoughby rose, ostensibly to return Miss Spence to her parent. Watching his retreat with laughing eyes, Caroline returned her gaze to her guardian, only to see him look pointedly at the door from the ball-room. She glanced across and saw Arabella enter, slightly flushed and with a too-bright smile on her lips. She made straight for the table where Sarah was sitting with a number of others and, with her usual facility, merged with the group, laughing up at the young man who leapt to his feet to offer her his chair.

Caroline turned to Max, a slight frown in her eyes, to find his attention had returned to the door. She followed his gaze and saw Lord Denbigh enter.

To any casual observer, Hugo was merely coming late to the supper-room, his languid gaze and sleepy smile giving no hint of any more pressing emotion than to discover whether there were any lobster patties left. Max Rotherbridge, however, was a far from casual observer. As he saw the expression in his lordship's heavy-lidded eyes as they flicked across the room to where Arabella sat, teasing her company unmercifully, His Grace of Twyford's black brows rose in genuine astonishment. Oh, God! Another one?

RESIGNED TO YET another evening spent with no progress in the matter of his eldest ward, Max calmly escorted her back to the ballroom and, releasing her to the attentions of her admirers, not without a particularly penetrating stare at two gentlemen of dubious standing who had had the temerity to attempt to join her circle, he prepared to quit the ballroom. He had hoped to have persuaded Miss Twinning to view the moonlight from the terrace. There was a useful bench he knew of, under a concealing willow, which would have come in handy. However, he had no illusions concerning his ability to make love to a woman who was on tenterhooks over the happiness of not one but two sisters. So he headed for the card-room.

On his way, he passed Arabella, holding court once again in something close to her usual style. His blue gaze searched her face. As if sensing his regard, she turned and saw him. For a moment, she looked lost. He smiled encouragingly. After a fractional pause, she flashed her brilliant smile back and, putting up her chin, turned back to her companions, laughing at some comment.

Max moved on. Clearly, Caroline did have another problem on her hands. He paused at the entrance to the card-room and, automatically, scanned the packed ballroom. Turning, he was about to cross the threshold when a disturbing thought struck him. He turned back to the ballroom.

"Make up your mind! Make up your mind! Oh, it's you, Twyford. What are you doing at such an occasion? Hardly your style these days, what?"

Excusing himself to Colonel Weatherspoon, Max moved out of the doorway and checked the room again. Where was Lizzie? He had not seen her at supper, but then again he had not looked. He had mentally dubbed her the baby of the family but his rational mind informed him that she was far from too young. He was about to cross the room to where his aunt Augusta sat, resplendent in bronze bombazine, when a movement by the windows drew his eyes.

Lizzie entered from the terrace, a shy and entirely guileless smile on her lips. Her small hand rested with easy assurance on his brother's arm. As he watched, she turned and smiled up at Martin, a look so full of trust that a newborn lamb could not have bettered it. And Martin, wolf that he was, returned the smile readily.

Abruptly, Max turned on his heel and strode into the card-room. He needed a drink.

CHAPTER EIGHT

ARABELLA SWATTED at the bumble-bee blundering noisily by her head. She was lying on her stomach on the stone surround of the pond in the courtyard of Twyford House, idly trailing her fingers in the cool green water. Her delicate mull muslin, petal-pink in hue, clung revealingly to her curvaceous form while a straw hat protected her delicate complexion from the afternoon sun. Most other young ladies in a similar pose would have looked childish. Arabella, with her strangely wistful air, contrived to look mysteriously enchanting.

Her sisters were similarly at their ease. Sarah was propped by the base of the sundial, her *bergère* hat shading her face as she threaded daisies into a chain. The dark green cambric gown she wore emphasized her arrestingly pale face, dominated by huge brown eyes, darkened now by the hint of misery. Lizzie sat beside the rockery, poking at a piece of embroidery with a noticeable lack of enthusiasm. Her sprigged mauve muslin proclaimed her youth yet its effect was ameliorated by her far from youthful figure.

Caroline watched her sisters from her perch in a cushioned hammock strung between two cherry trees. If her guardian could have seen her, he would undoubtedly have approved of the simple round gown of particularly fine amber muslin she had donned for the warm day. The fabric clung tantalizingly to her mature figure while the neckline revealed an expanse of soft ivory breasts.

The sisters had gradually drifted here, one by one, drawn by the warm spring afternoon and the heady scents rising

from the rioting flowers which crammed the beds and over-
flowed on to the stone flags. The period between luncheon
and the obligatory appearance in the Park was a quiet time
they were coming increasingly to appreciate as the Season
wore on. Whenever possible, they tended to spend it together, a last vestige, Caroline thought, of the days when
they had only had each other for company.

Sarah sighed. She laid aside her hat and looped the completed daisy chain around her neck. Cramming her head-
gear back over her dark curls, she said, "Well, what are we
going to do?"

Three pairs of eyes turned her way. When no answer was
forthcoming, she continued, explaining her case with all
reasonableness, "Well, we can't go on as we are, can we?
None of us is getting anywhere."

Arabella turned on her side better to view her sisters. "But
what can we do? In your case, Lord Darcy's not even in
London."

"True," returned the practical Sarah. "But it's just occurred to me that he must have friends still in London. Ones
who would write to him, I mean. Other than our guardian."

Caroline grinned. "Whatever you do, my love, kindly
explain all to me before you set the *ton* ablaze. I don't think
I could stomach our guardian demanding an explanation
and not having one to give him."

Sarah chuckled. "Has he been difficult?"

But Caroline would only smile, a secret smile of which
both Sarah and Arabella took due note.

"He hasn't said anything about me, has he?" came Lizzie's slightly breathless voice. Under her sisters' gaze, she
blushed. "About me and Martin," she mumbled, suddenly
becoming engrossed in her *petit point*.

Arabella laughed. "Artful puss. As things stand, you're
the only one with all sails hoisted and a clear wind blowing.
The rest of us are becalmed, for one reason or another."

Caroline's brow had furrowed. "Why do you ask? Has Max given you any reason to suppose he disapproves?"

"Well," temporized Lizzie, "he doesn't seem entirely... happy, about us seeing so much of each other."

Her attachment to Martin Rotherbridge had progressed in leaps and bounds. Despite Max's warning and his own innate sense of danger, Martin had not been able to resist the temptation posed by Lizzie Twinning. From that first undeniably innocent kiss he had, by subtle degrees, led her to the point where, finding herself in his arms in the gazebo in Lady Malling's garden, she had permitted him to kiss her again. Only this time, it had been Martin leading the way. Lizzie, all innocence, had been thoroughly enthralled by the experience and stunned by her own response to the delightful sensations it had engendered. Unbeknownst to her, Martin Rotherbridge had been stunned, too.

Belatedly, he had tried to dampen his own increasing desires, only to find, as his brother could have told him, that that was easier imagined than accomplished. Abstinence had only led to intemperance. In the end, he had capitulated and returned to spend every moment possible at Lizzie's side, if not her feet.

Lizzie was right in her assessment that Max disapproved of their association but wrong in her idea of the cause. Only too well-acquainted with his brother's character, their guardian entertained a grave concern that the frustrations involved in behaving with decorum in the face of Lizzie Twinning's bounteous temptations would prove overwhelming long before Martin was brought to admit he was in love with the chit. His worst fears had seemed well on the way to being realized when he had, entirely unintentionally, surprised them on their way back to the ballroom. His sharp blue eyes had not missed the glow in Lizzie's face. Consequently, the look he had directed at his brother, which Lizzie had intercepted, had not been particularly encouraging. She had missed Martin's carefree response.

Caroline, reasonably certain of Max's thoughts on the matter, realized these might not be entirely clear to Lizzie. But how to explain Max's doubts of his own brother to the still innocent Lizzie? Despite the fact that only a year separated her from Arabella, the disparity in their understandings, particularly with respect to the male of the species, was enormous. All three elder Twinnings had inherited both looks and dispositions from their father's family, which in part explained his aversion to women. Thomas Twinning had witnessed firsthand the dance his sisters had led all the men of their acquaintance before finally settling in happily wedded bliss. The strain on his father and himself had been considerable. Consequently, the discovery that his daughters were entirely from the same mould had prompted him to immure them in rural seclusion. Lizzie, however, had only inherited the Twinning looks, her gentle and often quite stubborn innocence deriving from the placid Eleanor. Viewing the troubled face of her youngest half-sister, Caroline decided the time had come to at least try to suggest to Lizzie's mind that there was often more to life than the strictly obvious. Aside from anything else, this time, she had both Sarah and Arabella beside her to help explain.

"I rather think, my love," commenced Caroline, "that it's not that Max would disapprove of the connection. His concern is more for your good name."

Lizzie's puzzled frown gave no indication of lightening. "But why should my being with his brother endanger my good name?"

Sarah gave an unladylike snort of laughter. "Oh, Lizzie, love! You're going to have to grow up, my dear. Our guardian's concerned because he knows what his brother's like and that, generally speaking, young ladies are not safe with him."

The effect of this forthright speech on Lizzie was galvanizing. Her eyes blazed in defence of her absent love. "Martin's not like that at all!"

"Oh, sweetheart, you're going to have to open your eyes!" Arabella bought into the discussion, sitting up the better to do so. "He's not only 'like that,' Martin Rotherbridge has made a career specializing in being 'like that.' He's a rake. The same as Hugo and Darcy Hamilton, too. And, of course, the greatest rake of them all is our dear guardian, who has his eye firmly set on Caro here. Rakes and Twinnings go together, I'm afraid. We attract them and they—" she put her head on one side, considering her words "—well, they attract us. It's no earthly good disputing the evidence."

Seeing the perturbation in Lizzie's face, Caroline sought to reassure her. "That doesn't mean that the end result is not just the same as if they were more conservative. It's just that, well, it very likely takes longer for such men to accept the...the desirability of marriage." Her eyes flicked to Sarah who, head bent and eyes intent on her fingers, was plaiting more daisies. "Time will, I suspect, eventually bring them around. The danger is in the waiting."

Lizzie was following her sister's discourse with difficulty. "But Martin's never...well, you know, tried to make love to me."

"Do you mean to say he's never kissed you?" asked Arabella in clear disbelief.

Lizzie blushed. "Yes. But I kissed him first."

"Lizzie!" The startled exclamation was drawn from all three sisters who promptly thereafter fell about laughing. Arabella was the last to recover. "Oh, my dear, you're more a Twinning than we'd thought!"

"Well, it was nice, I thought," said Lizzie, fast losing her reticence in the face of her sisters' teasing. "Anyway, what am I supposed to do? Avoid him? That wouldn't be much fun. And I don't think I could stop him kissing me, somehow. I rather like being kissed."

"It's not the kissing itself that's the problem," stated Sarah. "It's what comes next. And that's even more difficult to stop."

"Very true," confirmed Arabella, studying her slippered toes. "But if you want lessons in how to hold a rake at arm's length you shouldn't look to me. Nor to Sarah either. It's only Caro who's managed to hold her own so far." Arabella's eyes started to dance as they rested on her eldest sister's calm face. "But, I suspect, that's only because our dear guardian is playing a deep game."

Caroline blushed slightly, then reluctantly smiled. "Unfortunately, I'm forced to agree with you."

A silence fell as all four sisters pondered their rakes. Eventually, Caroline spoke. "Sarah, what are you planning?"

Sarah wriggled her shoulders against the sundial's pedestal. "Well, it occurred to me that perhaps I should make some effort to bring things to a head. But if I did the obvious, and started wildly flirting with a whole bevy of gentlemen, then most likely I'd only land myself in the suds. For a start, Darcy would very likely not believe it and I'd probably end with a very odd reputation. I'm not good at it, like Bella."

Arabella put her head on one side, the better to observe her sister. "I could give you lessons," she offered.

"No," said Caroline. "Sarah's right. It wouldn't wash." She turned to Lizzie to say, "Another problem, my love, is that rakes know all the tricks, so bamming them is very much harder."

"Too true," echoed Arabella. She turned again to Sarah. "But if not that, what, then?"

A wry smile touched Sarah's lips. "I rather thought the pose of the maiden forlorn might better suit me. Nothing too obvious, just a subtle withdrawing. I'd still go to all the parties and balls, but I'd just become quieter and ever so gradually, let my...what's the word, Caro? My despair? My broken heart? Well, whatever it is, show through."

Her sisters considered her plan and found nothing to criticise. Caroline summed up their verdict. "In truth, my dear, there's precious little else you could do."

Sarah's eyes turned to Arabella. "But what are you going to do about Lord Denbigh?"

Arabella's attention had returned to her toes. She wrinkled her pert nose. "I really don't know. I can't make him jealous; as Caro said, he knows all those tricks. And the forlorn act would not do for me."

Arabella had tried every means possible to tie down the elusive Hugo but that large gentleman seemed to view her attempts with sleepy humour, only bestirring himself to take advantage of any tactical error she made. At such times, as Arabella had found to her confusion and consternation, he could move with ruthless efficiency. She was now very careful not to leave any opening he could exploit to be private with her.

"Why not try...?" Caroline broke off, suddenly assailed by a twinge of guilt at encouraging her sisters in their scheming. But, under the enquiring gaze of Sarah and Arabella, not to mention Lizzie, drinking it all in, she mentally shrugged and continued. "As you cannot convince him of your real interest in any other gentleman, you'd be best not to try, I agree. But you could let him understand that, as he refused to offer marriage, and you, as a virtuous young lady, are prevented from accepting any other sort of offer, then, with the utmost reluctance and the deepest regret, you have been forced to turn aside and consider accepting the attentions of some other gentleman."

Arabella stared at her sister. Then, her eyes started to dance. "Oh, Caro!" she breathed. "What a perfectly marvellous plan!"

"Shouldn't be too hard for you to manage," said Sarah. "Who are the best of your court for the purpose? You don't want to raise any overly high expectations on their parts but you've loads of experience in playing that game."

Arabella was already deep in thought. "Sir Humphrey Bullard, I think. And Mr. Stone. They're both sober enough and in no danger of falling in love with me. They're quite coldly calculating in their approach to matrimony; I doubt they have hearts to lose. They both want an attractive wife, preferably with money, who would not expect too much attention from them. To their minds, I'm close to perfect but to scramble for my favours would be beneath them. They should be perfect for my charade."

Caroline nodded. "They sound just the thing."

"Good! I'll start tonight," said Arabella, decision burning in her huge eyes.

"But what about you, Caro?" asked Sarah with a grin. "We've discussed how the rest of us should go on, but you've yet to tell us how you plan to bring our dear guardian to his knees."

Caroline smiled, the same gently wistful smile that frequently played upon her lips these days. "If I knew that, my dears, I'd certainly tell you." The last weeks had seen a continuation of the unsatisfactory relationship between His Grace of Twyford and his eldest ward. Wary of his ability to take possession of her senses should she give him the opportunity, Caroline had consistently avoided his invitations to dally alone with him. Indeed, too often in recent times her mind had been engaged in keeping a watchful eye over her sisters, something their perceptive guardian seemed to understand. She could not fault him for his support and was truly grateful for the understated manner in which he frequently set aside his own inclinations to assist her in her concern for her siblings. In fact, it had occurred to her that, far from being a lazy guardian, His Grace of Twyford was very much *au fait* with the activities of each of his wards. Lately, it had seemed to her that her sisters' problems were deflecting a considerable amount of his energies from his pursuit of herself. So, with a twinkle in her eyes, she said, "If truth be told, the best plan I can think of to further my own ends is to assist you all in achieving your goals as soon as may be. Once free of you three, perhaps our dear guardian will be able to concentrate on me."

IT WAS LIZZIE who initiated the Twinning sisters' friendship with the two Crowbridge girls, also being presented that
year. The Misses Crowbridge, Alice and Amanda, were very
pretty young ladies in the manner which had been all the
rage until the Twinnings came to town. They were pale and
fair, as ethereal as the Twinnings were earthy, as fragile as
the Twinnings were robust, and, unfortunately for them, as
penniless as the Twinnings were rich. Consequently, the
push to find well-heeled husbands for the Misses Crowbridge had not prospered.

Strolling down yet another ballroom, Lady Mott's as it
happened, on the arm of Martin, of course, Lizzie had
caught the sharp words uttered by a large woman of horsey
mien to a young lady, presumably her daughter, sitting pas-
sively at her side. "Why can't you two be like that? Those
girls simply walk off with any man they fancy. All it needs
is a bit of push. But you and Alice..." The rest of the tirade had been swallowed up by the hubbub around them.
But the words returned to Lizzie later, when, retiring to the
withdrawing-room to mend her hem which Martin very
carelessly had stood upon, she found the room empty except for the same young lady, huddled in a pathetic bundle,
trying to stifle her sobs.

As a kind heart went hand in hand with Lizzie's innocence, it was not long before she had befriended Amanda
Crowbridge and learned of the difficulty facing both
Amanda and Alice. Lacking the Twinning sisters' confidence and abilities, the two girls, thrown without any prep-
aration into the heady world of the *ton*, found it impossible
to converse with the elegant gentlemen, becoming tongue-
tied and shy, quite unable to attach the desired suitors. To
Lizzie, the solution was obvious.

Both Arabella and Sarah, despite having other fish to fry,
were perfectly willing to act as tutors to the Crowbridge
girls. Initially, they agreed to this more as a favour to Lizzie
than from any more magnanimous motive, but as the week
progressed they became quite absorbed with their proté-

gées. For the Crowbridge girls, being taken under the collective wing of the three younger Twinnings brought a cataclysmic change to their social standing. Instead of being left to decorate the wall, they now spent their time firmly embedded amid groups of chattering young people. Drawn ruthlessly into conversations by the artful Arabella or Sarah at her most prosaic, they discovered that talking to the swells of the *ton* was not, after all, so very different from conversing with the far less daunting lads at home. Under the steady encouragement provided by the Twinnings, the Crowbridge sisters slowly unfurled their petals.

Caroline and His Grace of Twyford watched the growing friendship from a distance and were pleased to approve, though for very different reasons. Having ascertained that the Crowbridges were perfectly acceptable acquaintances, although their mother, for all her breeding, was, as Lady Benborough succinctly put it, rather too pushy, Caroline was merely pleased that her sisters had found some less than scandalous distraction from their romantic difficulties. Max, on the other hand, was quick to realize that with the three younger girls busily engaged in this latest exploit, which kept them safely in the ballrooms and salons, he stood a much better chance of successfully spending some time, in less populated surroundings, with his eldest ward.

In fact, as the days flew past, his success in his chosen endeavour became so marked that Caroline was forced openly to refuse any attempt to detach her from her circle. She had learned that their relationship had become the subject of rampant speculation and was now seriously concerned at the possible repercussions, for herself, for her sisters and for him. Max, reading her mind with consummate ease, paid her protestations not the slightest heed. Finding herself once more in His Grace's arms and, as usual, utterly helpless, Caroline was moved to remonstrate. "What on earth do you expect to accomplish by all this? I'm your *ward,* for heaven's sake!"

A deep chuckle answered her. Engaged in tracing her left brow, first with one long finger, then with his lips, Max had replied, "Consider your time spent with me as an educational experience, sweet Caro. As Aunt Augusta was so eager to point out," he continued, transferring his attention to her other brow, "who better than your guardian to demonstrate the manifold dangers to be met with among the *ton?*"

She was prevented from telling him what she thought of his reasoning, in fact, was prevented from thinking at all, when his lips moved to claim hers and she was swept away on a tide of sensation she was coming to appreciate all too well. Emerging, much later, pleasantly witless, she found herself the object of His Grace's heavy-lidded blue gaze. "Tell me, my dear, if you were not my ward, would you consent to be private with me?"

Mentally adrift, Caroline blinked in an effort to focus her mind. For the life of her she could not understand his question, although the answer seemed clear enough. "Of course not!" she lied, trying unsuccessfully to ease herself from his shockingly close embrace.

A slow smile spread across Max's face. As the steel bands around her tightened, Caroline was sure he was laughing at her.

Another deep chuckle, sending shivers up and down her spine, confirmed her suspicion. Max bent his head until his lips brushed hers. Then, he drew back slightly and blue eyes locked with grey. "In that case, sweet ward, you have some lessons yet to learn."

Bewildered, Caroline would have asked for enlightenment but, reading her intent in her eyes, Max avoided her question by the simple expedient of kissing her again. Irritated by his cat-and-mouse tactics, Caroline tried to withdraw from participation in this strange game whose rules were incomprehensible to her. But she quickly learned that His Grace of Twyford had no intention of letting her backslide. Driven, in the end, to surrender to the greater force,

Caroline relaxed, melting into his arms, yielding body, mind and soul to his experienced conquest.

IT WAS AT Lady Richardson's ball that Sir Ralph Keighly first appeared as a cloud on the Twinnings's horizon. Or, more correctly, on the Misses Crowbridge's horizon, although by that stage, it was much the same thing. Sir Ralph, with a tidy estate in Gloucestershire, was in London to look for a wife. His taste, it appeared, ran to sweet young things of the type personified by the Crowbridge sisters, Amanda Crowbridge in particular. Unfortunately for him, Sir Ralph was possessed of an overwhelming self-conceit combined with an unprepossessing appearance. He was thus vetoed on sight as beneath consideration by the Misses Crowbridge and their mentors.

However, Sir Ralph was rather more wily than he appeared. Finding his attentions to Amanda Crowbridge compromised by the competing attractions of the large number of more personable young men who formed the combined Twinning-Crowbridge court, he retired from the lists and devoted his energies to cultivating Mr. and Mrs. Crowbridge. In this, he achieved such notable success that he was invited to attend Lady Richardson's ball with the Crowbridges. Despite the tearful protestations of both Amanda and Alice at his inclusion in their party, when they crossed the threshold of Lady Richardson's ballroom, Amanda, looking distinctly seedy, had her hand on Sir Ralph's arm.

At her parents' stern instruction, she was forced to endure two waltzes with Sir Ralph. As Arabella acidly observed, if it had been at all permissible, doubtless Amanda would have been forced to remain at his side for the entire ball. As it was, she dared not join her friends for supper but, drooping with dejection, joined Sir Ralph and her parents.

To the three Twinnings, the success of Sir Ralph was like waving a red rag to a bull. Without exception, they took it as interference in their, up until then, successful development of their protégées. Even Lizzie was, metaphorically speaking, hopping mad. But the amenities offered by a ball were hardy conducive to a council of war, so, with admirable restraint, the three younger Twinnings devoted themselves assiduously to their own pursuits and left the problem of Sir Ralph until they had leisure to deal with it appropriately.

Sarah was now well down the road to being acknowledged as having suffered an unrequited love. She bore up nobly under the strain but it was somehow common knowledge that she held little hope of recovery. Her brave face, it was understood, was on account of her sisters, as she did not wish to ruin their Season by retiring into seclusion, despite this being her most ardent wish. Her large brown eyes, always fathomless, and her naturally pale and serious face were welcome aids in the projection of her new persona. She danced and chatted, yet the vitality that had burned with her earlier in the Season had been dampened. That, at least, was no more than the truth.

Arabella, all were agreed, was settling down to the sensible prospect of choosing a suitable connection. As Hugo Denbigh had contrived to be considerably more careful in his attentions to Arabella than Darcy Hamilton had been with Sarah, the gossips had never connected the two. Consequently, the fact that Lord Denbigh's name was clearly absent from Arabella's list did not in itself cause comment. But, as the Twinning sisters had been such a hit, the question of who precisely Arabella would choose was a popular topic for discussion. Speculation was rife and, as was often the case in such matters, a number of wagers had already been entered into the betting books held by the gentlemen's clubs. According to rumour, both Mr. Stone and Sir Humphrey Bullard featured as possible candidates. Yet not the most avid watcher could discern which of these gentlemen Miss Arabella favoured.

Amid all this drama, Lizzie Twinning continued as she always had, accepting the respectful attentions of the sober young men who sought her out while reserving her most brilliant smiles for Martin Rotherbridge. As she was so young and as Martin wisely refrained from any overtly amorous or possessive act in public, most observers assumed he was merely helping his brother with what must, all were agreed, constitute a definite handful. Martin, finding her increasingly difficult to lead astray, was forced to live with his growing frustrations and their steadily diminishing prospects for release.

The change in Amanda Crowbridge's fortunes brought a frown to Caroline's face. She would not have liked the connection for any of her sisters. Still, Amanda Crowbridge was not her concern. As her sisters appeared to have taken the event philosophically enough, she felt justified in giving it no further thought, reserving her energies, mental and otherwise, for her increasingly frequent interludes with her guardian.

Despite her efforts to minimize his opportunities, she found herself sharing his carriage on their return journey to Mount Street. Miriam Alford sat beside her and Max, suavely elegant and exuding a subtle aura of powerful sensuality, had taken the seat opposite her. Lady Benborough and her three sisters were following in the Twyford coach. As Caroline had suspected, their chaperon fell into a sound sleep before the carriage had cleared the Richardson House drive.

Gazing calmly at the moonlit fields, she calculated they had at least a forty-minute drive ahead of them. She waited patiently for the move she was sure would come and tried to marshal her resolve to deflect it. As the minutes ticked by, the damning knowledge slowly seeped into her consciousness that, if her guardian was to suddenly become afflicted with propriety and the journey was accomplished without incident, far from being relieved, she would feel let down, cheated of an eagerly anticipated treat. She frowned, recognizing her already racing pulse and the tense knot in her stomach that restricted her breathing for the symptoms they

were. On the thought, she raised her eyes to the dark face
before her.

He was watching the countryside slip by, the silvery light
etching the planes of his face. As if feeling her gaze, he
turned and his eyes met hers. For a moment, he read her
thoughts and Caroline was visited by the dreadful certainty
that he knew the truth she was struggling to hide. Then, a
slow, infinitely wicked smile spread across his face. Caroline stopped breathing. He leaned forward. She expected
him to take her hand and draw her to sit beside him. Instead, his strong hands slipped about her waist and, to her
utter astonishment, he lifted her across and deposited her in
a swirl of silks on his lap.

"Max!" she gasped.

"Sssh. You don't want to wake Mrs. Alford. She'd have
palpitations."

Horrified, Caroline tried to get her feet to the ground,
wriggling against the firm clasp about her waist. Almost
immediately, Max's voice sounded in her ear, in a tone quite
different from any she had previously heard. "Sweetheart,
unless you cease wriggling your delightful *derrière* in such
an enticing fashion, this lesson is likely to go rather further
than I had intended."

Caroline froze. She held her breath, not daring to so
much as twitch. Then Max's voice, the raw tones of an instant before no longer in evidence, washed over her in warm
approval. "Much better."

She turned to face him, carefully keeping her hips still.
She placed her hands on his chest in an effort, futile, she
knew, to fend him off. "Max, this is madness. You must
stop doing this!"

"Why? Don't you like it?" His hands were moving gently on her back, his touch scorching through the thin silk of
her gown.

Caroline ignored the sardonic lift of his black brows and
the clear evidence in his eyes that he was laughing at her. She
found it much harder to ignore the sensations his hands were

drawing forth. Forcing her face into strongly disapproving
lines, she answered his first question, deeming it prudent to
conveniently forget the second. "I'm your *ward*, remember? You know I am. You told me so yourself."

"A fact you should strive to bear in mind, my dear."

Caroline wondered what he meant by that. But Max's
mind, and hands, had shifted their focus of attention. As his
hands closed over her breasts, Caroline nearly leapt to her
feet. *"Max!"*

But, "Sssh," was all her guardian said as his lips settled
on hers.

CHAPTER NINE

THE TWYFORD COACH was also the scene of considerable activity, though of a different sort. Augusta, in sympathy with Mrs. Alford, quickly settled into a comfortable doze which the whisperings of the other occupants of the carriage did nothing to disturb. Lizzie, Sarah and Arabella, incensed by Amanda's misfortune, spent some minutes giving vent to their feelings.

"It's not as if Sir Ralph's such a good catch, even," Sarah commented.

"Certainly not," agreed Lizzie with uncharacteristic sharpness. "It's really too bad! Why, Mr. Minchbury is almost at the point of offering for her and he has a much bigger estate, besides being much more attractive. And Amanda *likes* him, what's more."

"Ah," said Arabella, wagging her head sagely, "but he's not been making up to Mrs. Crowbridge, has he? That woman must be all about in her head, to think of giving little Amanda to Keighly."

"Well," said Sarah decisively, "what are we going to do about it?"

Silence reigned for more than a mile as the sisters considered the possibilities. Arabella eventually spoke into the darkness. "I doubt we'd get far discussing matters with the Crowbridges."

"Very true," nodded Sarah. "And working on Amanda's equally pointless. She's too timid."

"Which leaves Sir Ralph," concluded Lizzie. After a pause, she went on: "I know we're not precisely to his taste, but do you think you could do it, Bella?"

Arabella's eyes narrowed as she considered Sir Ralph. Thanks to Hugo, she now had a fairly extensive understanding of the basic attraction between men and women. Sir Ralph was, after all, still a man. She shrugged. "Well, it's worth a try. I really can't see what else we can do."

For the remainder of the journey, the sisters' heads were together, hatching a plan.

ARABELLA STARTED her campaign to steal Sir Ralph from Amanda the next evening, much to the delight of Amanda. When she was informed in a whispered aside of the Twinnings' plan for her relief, Amanda's eyes had grown round. Swearing to abide most faithfully by any instructions they might give her, she had managed to survive her obligatory two waltzes with Sir Ralph in high spirits, which Sarah later informed her was not at all helpful. Chastised, she begged pardon and remained by Sarah's side as Arabella took to the floor with her intended.

As Sir Ralph had no real affection for Amanda, it took very little of Arabella's practised flattery to make him increasingly turn his eyes her way. But, to the Twinnings' consternation, their plan almost immediately developed a hitch.

Their guardian was not at all pleased to see Sir Ralph squiring Arabella. A message from him, relayed by both Caroline and Lady Benborough, to the effect that Arabella should watch her step, pulled Arabella up short. A hasty conference, convened in the withdrawing-room, agreed there was no possibility of gaining His Grace's approval for their plan. Likewise, none of the three sisters had breathed a word of their scheme to Caroline, knowing that, despite her affection for them, there were limits to her forbearance.

"But we can't just give up!" declared Lizzie in trenchant tones.

Arabella was nibbling the end of one finger. "No. We won't give up. But we'll have to reorganize. You two," she said, looking at Sarah and Lizzie, quite ignoring Amanda and Alice who were also present, "are going to have to cover for me. That way, I won't be obviously spending so much time with Sir Ralph, but he'll still be thinking about me. You must tell Sir Ralph that our guardian disapproves but that, as I'm head over heels in love with him, I'm willing to go against the Duke's wishes and continue to see him." She frowned, pondering her scenario. "We'll have to be careful not to paint our dear guardian in too strict colours. The story is that we're sure he'll eventually come around, when he sees how attached I am to Sir Ralph. Max knows I'm a flighty, flirtatious creature and so doubts of the strength of my affections. That should be believable enough."

"All right," Sarah nodded. "We'll do the groundwork and you administer the *coup de grâce*."

And so the plan progressed.

For Arabella, the distraction of Sir Ralph came at an opportune time in her juggling of Sir Humphrey and Mr. Stone. It formed no part of her plans for either of these gentlemen to become too particular. And while her sober and earnest consideration of their suits had, she knew, stunned and puzzled Lord Denbigh, who watched with a still sceptical eye, her flirtation with Sir Ralph had brought a strange glint to his hazel orbs.

In truth, Hugo had been expecting Arabella to flirt outrageously with her court in an attempt to make him jealous and force a declaration. He had been fully prepared to sit idly by, watching her antics from the sidelines with his usual sleepily amused air, waiting for the right moment to further her seduction. But her apparent intention to settle for a loveless marriage had thrown him. It was not a reaction he had expected. Knowing what he did of Arabella, he could not stop himself from thinking what a waste it would be.

True, as the wife of a much older man, she was likely to be even more receptive to his own suggestions of a discreet if illicit relationship. But the idea of her well-endowed charms being brutishly enjoyed by either of her ageing suitors set his teeth on edge. Her sudden pursuit of Sir Ralph Keighly, in what he was perceptive enough to know was not her normal style, seriously troubled him, suggesting as it did some deeper intent. He wondered whether she knew what she was about. The fact that she continued to encourage Keighly despite Twyford's clear disapproval further increased his unease.

Arabella, sensing his perturbation, continued to tread the difficult path she had charted, one eye on him, the other on her guardian, encouraging Sir Ralph with one hand while using the other to hold back Sir Humphrey and Mr. Stone. As she confessed to her sisters one morning, it was exhausting work.

Little by little, she gained ground with Sir Ralph, their association camouflaged by her sisters' ploys. On the way back to the knot of their friends, having satisfactorily twirled around Lady Summerhill's ballroom, Arabella and Sir Ralph were approached by a little lady, all in brown.

Sir Ralph stiffened.

The unknown lady blushed. "How do you do?" she said, taking in both Arabella and Sir Ralph in her glance. "I'm Harriet Jenkins," she explained helpfully to Arabella, then, turning to Sir Ralph, said, "Hello, Ralph," in quite the most wistful tone Arabella had ever heard.

Under Arabella's interested gaze, Sir Ralph became tongue-tied. He perforce bowed over the small hand held out to him and managed to say, "Mr. Jenkins's estates border mine."

Arabella's eyes switched to Harriet Jenkins. "My father," she supplied.

Sir Ralph suddenly discovered someone he had to exchange a few words with and precipitately left them. Arabella looked down into Miss Jenkins's large eyes, brown, of course, and wondered. "Have you lately come to town, Miss Jenkins?"

Harriet Jenkins drew her eyes from Sir Ralph's departing figure and dispassionately viewed the beauty before her. What she saw in the frank hazel eyes prompted her to reply, "Yes. I was...bored at home. So my father suggested I come to London for a few weeks. I'm staying with my aunt, Lady Cottesloe."

Arabella was only partly satisfied with this explanation. Candid to a fault, she put the question in her mind. "Pardon me, Miss Jenkins, but are you and Sir Ralph...?"

Miss Jenkins's wistfulness returned. "No. Oh, you're right in thinking I want him. But Ralph has other ideas. I've known him from the cradle, you see. And I suppose familiarity breeds contempt." Suddenly realizing to whom she was speaking, she blushed and continued, "Not that I could hope to hold a candle to the London beauties, of course."

Her suspicions confirmed, Arabella merely laughed and slipped an arm through Miss Jenkins's. "Oh, I shouldn't let that bother you, my dear." As she said the words, it occurred to her that, if anything, Sir Ralph was uncomfortable and awkward when faced with beautiful women, as evidenced by his behaviour with either herself or Amanda. It was perfectly possible that some of his apparent conceit would drop away when he felt less threatened; for instance, in the presence of Miss Jenkins.

Miss Jenkins had stiffened at Arabella's touch and her words. Then, realizing the kindly intent behind them, she relaxed. "Well, there's no sense in deceiving myself. I suppose I shouldn't say so, but Ralph and I were in a fair way to being settled before he took this latest notion of looking about before he made up his mind irrevocably. I sometimes think it was simply fear of tying the knot that did it."

"Very likely," Arabella laughingly agreed as she steered Miss Jenkins in the direction of her sisters.

"My papa was furious and said I should give him up. But I convinced him to let me come to London, to see how things stood. Now, I suppose, I may as well go home."

"Oh, on no account should you go home yet awhile, Miss Jenkins!" said Arabella, a decided twinkle in her eye. "May I call you Harriet? Harriet, I'd like you to meet my sisters."

THE ADVENT OF Harriet Jenkins caused a certain amount of reworking of the Twinnings' plan for Sir Ralph. After due consideration, she was taken into their confidence and willingly joined the small circle of conspirators. In truth, her appearance relieved Arabella's mind of a nagging worry over how she was to let Sir Ralph down after Amanda accepted Mr. Minchbury, who, under the specific guidance of Lizzie, was close to popping the question. Now, all she had to do was to play the hardened flirt and turn Sir Ralph's bruised ego into Harriet's tender care. All in all, things were shaping up nicely.

However, to their dismay, the Twinnings found that Mrs. Crowbridge was not yet vanquished. The news of her latest ploy was communicated to them two days later, at Beckenham, where they had gone to watch a balloon ascent. The intrepid aviators had yet to arrive at the field, so the three Twinnings had descended from their carriage and, together with the Misses Crowbridge and Miss Jenkins, were strolling elegantly about the field, enjoying the afternoon sunshine and a not inconsiderable amount of male attention. It transpired that Mrs. Crowbridge had invited Sir Ralph to pay a morning call and then, on the slightest of pretexts, had left him alone with Amanda for quite twenty minutes. Such brazen tactics left them speechless. Sir Ralph, to do him justice, had not taken undue advantage.

"He probably didn't have time to work out the odds against getting Arabella versus the benefits of Amanda," said Sarah with a grin. "Poor man! I can almost pity him, what with Mrs. Crowbridge after him as well."

All the girls grinned but their thoughts quickly returned to their primary preoccupation. "Yes, but," said Lizzie, voicing a fear already in both Sarah's and Arabella's minds, "if Mrs. Crowbridge keeps behaving like this, she might force Sir Ralph to offer for Amanda by tricking him into compromising her."

"I'm afraid that's only too possible," agreed Harriet. "Ralph's very gullible." She shook her head in such a deploring way that Arabella and Sarah were hard put to it to smother their giggles.

"Yes, but it won't do," said Amanda, suddenly. "I know my mother. She'll keep on and on until she succeeds. You've got to think of some way of...of removing Sir Ralph quickly."

"For his sake as well as your own," agreed Harriet. "The only question is, how?"

Silence descended while this conundrum revolved in their minds. Further conversation on the topic was necessarily suspended when they were joined by a number of gentlemen disinclined to let the opportunity of paying court to such a gaggle of very lovely young ladies pass by. As His Grace of Twyford's curricle was conspicuously placed among the carriages drawn up to the edge of the field, the behaviour of said gentlemen remained every bit as deferential as within the confines of Almack's, despite the sylvan setting.

Mr. Mallard was the first to reach Lizzie's side, closely followed by Mr. Swanston and Lord Brookfell. Three other fashionable exquisites joined the band around Lizzie, Amanda, Alice and Harriet, and within minutes an unexceptionable though thoroughly merry party had formed. Hearing one young gentleman allude to the delicate and complementary tints of the dresses of the four younger girls as "pretty as a posy," Sarah could not resist a grimace, purely for Arabella's benefit. Arabella bit hard on her lip to stifle her answering giggle. Both fell back a step or two from the younger crowd, only to fall victim to their own admirers.

Sir Humphrey Bullard, a large man of distinctly florid countenance, attempted to capture Arabella's undivided attention but was frustrated by the simultaneous arrival of Mr. Stone, sleekly saturnine, on her other side. Both offered their arms, leaving Arabella, with a sunshade to juggle, in a quandary. She laughed and shook her head at them both. "Indeed, gentlemen, you put me to the blush. What can a lady do under such circumstances?"

"Why, make your choice, m'dear," drawled Mr. Stone, a strangely determined glint in his eye.

Arabella's eyes widened at this hint that Mr. Stone, at least, was not entirely happy with being played on a string. She was rescued by Mr. Humphrey, irritatingly aware that he did not cut such a fine figure as Mr. Stone. "I see the balloonists have arrived. Perhaps you'd care to stroll to the enclosure and watch the inflation, Miss Arabella?"

"We'll need to get closer if we're to see anything at all," said Sarah, coming up on the arm of Lord Tulloch.

By the time they reached the area cordoned off in the centre of the large field, a crowd had gathered. The balloon was already filling slowly. As they watched, it lifted from the ground and slowly rose to hover above the cradle slung beneath, anchored to the ground by thick ropes.

"It looks like such a flimsy contraption," said Arabella, eyeing the gaily striped silk balloon. "I wonder that anyone could trust themselves to it."

"They don't always come off unscathed, I'm sorry to say," answered Mr. Stone, his schoolmasterish tones evincing strong disapproval of such reckless behaviour.

"Humph!" said Sir Humphrey Bullard.

Arabella's eyes met Sarah's in mute supplication. Sarah grinned.

It was not until the balloon had taken off, successfully, to Arabella's relief, and the crowd had started to disperse that the Twinnings once more had leisure to contemplate the

problem of Sir Ralph Keighly. Predictably, it was Sarah and
Arabella who conceived the plot. In a few whispered sentences, they developed its outline sufficiently to see that it
would require great attention to detail to make it work. As
they would have no further chance that day to talk with the
others in private, they made plans to meet the next morning at Twyford House. Caroline had mentioned her intention of visiting her old nurse, who had left the Twinnings'
employ after her mother had died and hence was unknown
to the younger Twinnings. Thus, ensconced in the back
parlour of Twyford House, they would be able to give free
rein to their thoughts. Clearly, the removal of Sir Ralph was
becoming a matter of urgency.

Returning to their carriage, drawn up beside the elegant
equipage bearing the Delmere crest, the three youngest
Twinnings smiled serenely at their guardian, who watched
them from the box seat of his curricle, a far from complaisant look in his eyes.

Max was, in fact, convinced that something was in the
wind but had no idea what. His highly developed social an-
tennae had picked up the undercurrents of his wards' plotting and their innocent smiles merely confirmed his
suspicions. He was well aware that Caroline, seated beside
him in a fetching gown of figured muslin, was not privy to
their schemes. As he headed his team from the field, he
smiled. His eldest ward had had far too much on her mind
recently to have had any time free for scheming.

Beside him, Caroline remained in blissful ignorance of her
sisters' aims. She had spent a thoroughly enjoyable day in
the company of her guardian and was in charity with the
world. They had had an excellent view of the ascent itself
from the height of the box seat of the curricle. And when
she had evinced the desire to stroll among the crowds, Max
had readily escorted her, staying attentively by her side, his
acerbic comments forever entertaining and, for once, totally unexceptionable. She looked forward to the drive back
to Mount Street with unimpaired calm, knowing that in the

curricle, she ran no risk of being subjected to another of His Grace's "lessons." In fact, she was beginning to wonder how many more lessons there could possibly be before the graduation ceremony. The thought brought a sleepy smile to her face. She turned to study her guardian.

His attention was wholly on his horses, the bays, as sweet a pair as she had ever seen. Her eyes fell to his hands as they tooled the reins, strong and sure. Remembering the sensations those hands had drawn forth as they had knowledgeably explored her body, she caught her breath and rapidly looked away. Keeping her eyes fixed on the passing landscape, she forced her thoughts into safer fields.

The trouble with Max Rotherbridge was that he invaded her thoughts, too, and, as in other respects, was wellnigh impossible to deny. She was fast coming to the conclusion that she should simply forget all else and give herself up to the exquisite excitements she found in his arms. All the social and moral strictures ever intoned, all her inhibitions seemed to be consumed to ashes in the fire of her desire. She was beginning to feel it was purely a matter of time before she succumbed. The fact that the idea did not fill her with trepidation but rather with a pleasant sense of anticipation was in itself, she felt, telling.

As the wheels hit the cobbles and the noise that was London closed in around them, her thoughts flew ahead to Lady Benborough, who had stayed at home recruiting her energies for the ball that night. It was only this morning, when, with Max, she had bid her ladyship goodbye, that the oddity in Augusta's behaviour had struck her. While the old lady had been assiduous in steering the girls through the shoals of the acceptable gentlemen of the *ton,* she had said nothing about her eldest charge's association with her nephew. No matter how Caroline viewed it, invoke what reason she might, there was something definitely odd about that. As she herself had heard the rumours about His Grace of Twyford's very strange relationship with his eldest ward, it was inconceivable that Lady Benborough had not been ed-

ified with their tales. However, far from urging her to behave with greater discretion towards Max, impossible task
though that might be, Augusta continued to behave as if
there was nothing at all surprising in Max Rotherbridge escorting his wards to a balloon ascent. Caroline wondered
what it was that Augusta knew that she did not.

THE TWINNING SISTERS attended the opera later that week.
It was the first time they had been inside the ornate struc-
ture that was the Opera House; their progress to the box
organized for them by their guardian was perforce slow as
they gazed about them with interest. Once inside the box itself, in a perfect position in the first tier, their attention was
quickly claimed by their fellow opera-goers. The pit below
was a teeming sea of heads; the stylish crops of the fashionable young men who took perverse delight in rubbing
shoulders with the masses bobbed amid the unkempt locks
of the hoi polloi. But it was upon the occupants of the other
boxes that the Twinnings' principal interest focused. These
quickly filled as the time for the curtain to rise approached.
All four were absorbed in nodding and waving to friends
and acquaintances as the lights went out.

The first act consisted of a short piece by a little-known
Italian composer, as the prelude to the opera itself, which
would fill the second and third acts, before another short
piece ended the performance. Caroline sat, happily absorbed in the spectacle, beside and slightly in front of her
guardian. She was blissfully content. She had merely made
a comment to Max a week before that she would like to visit
the opera. Two days later, he had arranged it all. Now she
sat, superbly elegant in a silver satin slip overlaid with
bronzed lace, and revelled in the music, conscious, despite
her preoccupation, of the warmth of the Duke of Twyford's blue gaze on her bare shoulders.

Max watched her delight with satisfaction. He had long
ago ceased to try to analyze his reactions to Caroline Twinning; he was besotted and knew it. Her happiness had

somehow become his happiness; in his view, nothing else mattered. As he watched, she turned and smiled, a smile of genuine joy. It was, he felt, all the thanks he required for the effort organizing such a large box at short notice had entailed. He returned her smile, his own lazily sensual. For a moment, their eyes locked. Then, blushing, Caroline turned back to the stage.

Max had little real interest in the performance, his past experiences having had more to do with the singer than the song. He allowed his gaze to move past Caroline to dwell on her eldest half-sister. He had not yet fathomed exactly what Sarah's ambition was, yet felt sure it was not as simple as it appeared. The notion that any Twinning would meekly accept unwedded solitude as her lot was hard to swallow. As Sarah sat by Caroline's side, dramatic as ever in a gown of deepest green, the light from the stage lit her face. Her troubles had left no mark on the classical lines of brow and cheek but the peculiar light revealed more clearly than daylight the underlying determination in the set of the delicate mouth and chin. Max's lips curved in a wry grin. He doubted that Darcy had heard the last of Sarah Twinning, whatever the outcome of his self-imposed exile.

Behind Sarah sat Lord Tulloch and Mr. Swanston, invited by Max to act as squires for Sarah and Arabella respectively. Neither was particularly interested in the opera, yet both had accepted the invitations with alacrity. Now, they sat, yawning politely behind their hands, waiting for the moment when the curtain would fall and they could be seen by the other attending members of the *ton*, escorting their exquisite charges through the corridors.

Arabella, too, was fidgety, settling and resetting her pink silk skirts and dropping her fan. She appeared to be trying to scan the boxes on the tier above. Max smiled. He could have told her that Hugo Denbigh hated opera and had yet to be seen within the portals of Covent Garden.

Lady Benborough, dragon-like in puce velvet, sat determinedly following the aria. Distracted by Arabella's antics, she turned to speak in a sharp whisper, whereat Arabella grudgingly subsided, a dissatisfied frown marring her delightful visage.

At the opposite end of the box sat Martin, with Lizzie by the parapet beside him. She was enthralled by the performance, hanging on every note that escaped the throat of the soprano performing the lead. Martin, most improperly holding her hand, evinced not the slightest interest in the buxom singer but gazed solely at Lizzie, a peculiar smile hovering about his lips. Inwardly, Max sighed. He just hoped his brother knew what he was about.

The aria ended and the curtain came down. As the applause died, the large flambeaux which lit the pit were brought forth and re-installed in their brackets. Noise erupted around them as everyone talked at once.

Max leaned forward to speak by Caroline's ear. "Come. Let's stroll."

She turned to him in surprise and he smiled. "That's what going to the opera is about, my dear. To see and be seen. Despite appearances, the most important performances take place in the corridors of Covent Garden, not on the stage."

"Of course," she returned, standing and shaking out her skirts. "How very provincial of me not to realize." Her eyes twinkled. "How kind of you, dear guardian, to attend so assiduously to our education."

Max took her hand and tucked it into his arm. As they paused to allow the others to precede them, he bent to whisper in her ear, "On the contrary, sweet Caro. While I'm determined to see your education completed, my interest is entirely selfish."

The wicked look which danced in his dark blue eyes made Caroline blush. But she was becoming used to the highly improper conversations she seemed to have with her guardian. "Oh?" she replied, attempting to look innocent and not entirely succeeding. "Won't I derive any benefit from my new-found knowledge?"

They were alone in the box, hidden from view of the other boxes by shadows. For a long moment, they were both still, blue eyes locked with grey-green, the rest of the world far distant. Caroline could not breathe; the intensity of that blue gaze and the depth of the passion which smouldered within it held her mesmerized. Then, his eyes still on hers, Max lifted her hand and dropped a kiss on her fingers. "My dear, once you find the key, beyond that particular door lies paradise. Soon, sweet Caro, very soon, you'll see."

Once in the corridor, Caroline's cheeks cooled. They were quickly surrounded by her usual court and Max, behaving more circumspectly than he ever had before, relinquished her to the throng. Idly, he strolled along the corridors, taking the opportunity to stretch his long legs. He paused here and there to exchange a word with friends but did not stop for long. His preoccupation was not with extending his acquaintance of the *ton*. His ramblings brought him to the corridor serving the opposite arm of the horseshoe of boxes. The bell summoning the audience to their seats for the next act rang shrilly. Max was turning to make his way back to his box when a voice hailed him through the crush.

"Your Grace!"

Max closed his eyes in exasperation, then opened them and turned to face Lady Mortland. He nodded curtly. "Emma."

She was on the arm of a young man whom she introduced and immediately dismissed, before turning to Max. "I think perhaps we should have a serious talk, Your Grace."

The hard note in her voice and the equally rock-like glitter in her eyes were not lost on the Duke of Twyford. Max had played the part of the fashionable rake for fifteen years and knew well the occupational hazards. He lifted his eyes from an uncannily thorough contemplation of Lady Mortland and sighted a small alcove, temporarily deserted. "I think perhaps you're right, my dear. But I suggest we improve our surroundings."

His hand under her elbow steered Emma towards the alcove. The grip of his fingers through her silk sleeve and the steely quality in his voice were a surprise to her ladyship, but she was determined that Max Rotherbridge should pay, one way or another, for her lost dreams.

They reached the relative privacy of the alcove. "Well, Emma, what's this all about?"

Suddenly, Lady Mortland was rather less certain of her strategy. Faced with a pair of very cold blue eyes and an iron will she had never previously glimpsed, she vacillated. "Actually, Your Grace," she cooed, "I had rather hoped you would call on me and we could discuss the matter in...greater privacy."

"Cut line, Emma," drawled His Grace. "You knew perfectly well I have no wish whatever to be private with you."

The bald statement ignited Lady Mortland's temper. "Yes!" she hissed, fingers curling into claws. "Ever since you set eyes on that little harpy you call your ward, you've had no time for me!"

"I wouldn't, if I were you, make scandalous statements about a young lady to her guardian," said Max, unmoved by her spleen.

"Guardian, ha! Love, more like!"

One black brow rose haughtily.

"Do you deny it? No, of course not! Oh, there are whispers aplenty, let me tell you. But they're as nothing to the storm there'll be when I get through with you. I'll tell—Ow!"

Emma broke off and looked down at her wrist, imprisoned in Max's right hand. "L...let me go. Max, you're hurting me."

"Emma, you'll say nothing."

Lady Mortland looked up and was suddenly frightened. Max nodded, a gentle smile, which was quite terrifyingly cold, on his lips. "Listen carefully, Emma, for I'll say this once only. You'll not, verbally or otherwise, malign my ward—any of my wards—in any way whatever. Because, if you do, rest assured I'll hear about it. Should that happen I'll ensure your stepson learns of the honours you do his father's memory by your retired lifestyle. Your income derives from the family estates, does it not?"

Emma had paled. "You...you wouldn't."

Max released her. "No. You're quite right. I wouldn't," he said. "Not unless you do first. Then, you may be certain that I would." He viewed the woman before him, with understanding if not compassion. "Leave be, Emma. What Caroline has was never yours and you know it. I suggest you look to other fields."

With a nod, Max left Lady Mortland and returned through the empty corridors to his box.

Caroline turned as he resumed his seat. She studied his face for a moment, then leaned back to whisper, "Is anything wrong?"

Max's gaze rested on her sweet face, concern for his peace of mind the only emotion visible. He smiled reassuringly and shook his head. "A minor matter of no moment." In the darkness he reached for her hand and raised it to his lips. With a smile, Caroline returned her attention to the stage. When she made no move to withdraw her hand, Max continued to hold it, mimicking Martin, placating his conscience with the observation that, in the dark, no one could see the Duke of Twyford holding hands with his eldest ward.

CHAPTER TEN

EXECUTION OF THE first phase of the Twinnings' master plot to rescue Amanda and Sir Ralph from the machinations of Mrs. Crowbridge fell to Sarah. An evening concert was selected as the venue most conducive to success. As Sir Ralph was tone deaf, enticing him from the real pleasure of listening to the dramatic voice of *Señorita Muscariña*, the Spanish soprano engaged for the evening, proved easier than Sarah had feared.

Sir Ralph was quite content to escort Miss Sarah for a stroll on the balcony, ostensibly to relieve the stuffiness in Miss Twinning's head. In the company of the rest of the *ton*, he knew Sarah was pining away and thus, he reasoned, he was safe in her company. That she was one of the more outstandingly opulent beauties he had ever set eyes on simply made life more complete. It was rare that he felt at ease with such women and his time in London had made him, more than once, wish he was back in the less demanding backwoods of Gloucestershire. Even now, despite his successful courtship of the beautiful, the effervescent, the gorgeous Arabella Twinning, there were times Harriet Jenkins's face reminded him of how much more comfortable their almost finalized relationship had been. In fact, although he tried his best to ignore them, doubts kept appearing in his mind, of whether he would be able to live up to Arabella's expectations once they were wed. He was beginning to understand that girls like Arabella—well, she was a woman, really—were used to receiving the most specific advances from the more hardened of the male population. Sir Ralph

swallowed nervously, woefully aware that he lacked th
abilities to compete with such gentlemen. He glanced at th
pale face of the beauty beside him. A frown marred h
smooth brow. He relaxed. Clearly, Miss Sarah's mind wa
not bent on illicit dalliance.

In thinking this, Sir Ralph could not have been furthe
from the truth. Sarah's frown was engendered by her futi
attempts to repress the surge of longing that had swep
through her—a relic of that fateful evening in Lady Over
ton's shrubbery, she felt sure—when she had seen Darc
Hamilton's tall figure negligently propped by the door. Sh
had felt the weight of his gaze upon her and, turning to see
its source, had met his eyes across the room. Fool that sh
was! She had had to fight to keep herself in her seat and n
run across the room and throw herself into his arms. Then
an arch look from Arabella, unaware of Lord Darcy's re
turn, had reminded her of her duty. She had put her han
to her head and Lizzie had promptly asked if she was feel
ing the thing. It had been easy enough to claim Sir Ralph'
escort and leave the music-room. But the thunderous loo
in Darcy's eyes as she did so had tied her stomach in knot

Pushing her own concerns abruptly aside, she trans
ferred her attention to the man beside her. "Sir Ralph,
hope you won't mind if I speak to you on a matter of som
delicacy?"

Taken aback, Sir Ralph goggled.

Sarah ignored his startled expression. Harriet had warne
her how he would react. It was her job to lead him by th
nose. "I'm afraid things have reached a head with Ara
bella. I know it's not obvious; she's so reticent about suc
things. But I feel it's my duty to try to explain it to you
She's in such low spirits. Something must be done or sh
may even go into a decline."

It was on the tip of Sir Ralph's tongue to say that he ha
thought it was Sarah who was going into the decline. An
the suggestion that Arabella, last seen with an enchantin
sparkle in her big eyes, was in low spirits confused him u

erly. But Sarah's next comment succeeded in riveting his mind. "You're the only one who can save her."

The practical tone in which Sarah brought out her statement lent it far greater weight than a more dramatic declaration. In the event, Sir Ralph's attention was all hers. "You see, although she would flay me alive for telling you, you should know that she was very seriously taken with a gentleman earlier in the Season, before you arrived. He played on her sensibilities and she was so vulnerable. Unfortunately, he was not interested in marriage. I'm sure I can rely on your discretion. Luckily, she learned of his true intentions before he had time to achieve them. But her heart was sorely bruised, of course. Now that she's found such solace in your company, we had hoped, my sisters and I, that you would not let her down."

Sir Ralph was heard to mumble that he had no intention of letting Miss Arabella down.

"Ah, but you see," said Sarah, warming to her task, "what she needs is to be taken out of herself. Some excitement that would divert her from the present round of balls and parties and let her forget her past hurts in her enjoyment of a new love."

Sir Ralph, quite carried away by her eloquence, muttered that yes, he could quite see the point in that.

"So you see, Sir Ralph, it's imperative that she be swept off her feet. She's very romantically inclined, you know."

Sir Ralph, obediently responding to his cue, declared he was only too ready to do whatever was necessary to ensure Arabella's happiness.

Sarah smiled warmly, "In that case, I can tell you exactly what you must do."

IT TOOK SARAH nearly half an hour to conclude her instructions to Sir Ralph. Initially, he had been more than a little reluctant even to discuss such an enterprise. But, by dwelling on the depth of Arabella's need, appealing quite brazenly to poor Sir Ralph's chivalrous instincts, she had

finally wrung from him his sworn agreement to the enti
plan.

In a mood of definite self-congratulation, she led the wa
back to the music-room and, stepping over the door sill, a
but walked into Darcy Hamilton. His hand at her elbo
steadied her, but, stung by his touch, she abruptly pulle
away. Sir Ralph, who had not previously met Lord Darc
stopped in bewilderment, his eyes going from Sarah
burning face to his lordship's pale one. Then, Darcy Han
ilton became aware of his presence. "I'll return Miss Twi
ning to her seat."

Responding to the commanding tone, Sir Ralph bowe
and departed.

Sarah drew a deep breath. "How *dare* you?" she uttere
furiously as she made to follow Sir Ralph.

But Darcy's hand on her arm detained her. "What
that...country bumpkin to you?" The insulting drawl in h
voice drew a blaze of fire from Sarah's eyes.

But before she could wither him where she stood, sever;
heads turned their way. "Sssh!"

Without a word, Darcy turned her and propelled her bac
out of the door.

"Disgraceful!" said Lady Malling to Mrs. Benn, noo
ding by her side.

On the balcony, Sarah stood very still, quivering with rag
and a number of other more interesting emotions, directl
attributable to the fact that Darcy was standing immed
ately behind her.

"Perhaps you'd like to explain what you were doing wit
that gentleman on the balcony for half an hour and more?"

Sarah almost turned, then remembered how close he wa;
She lifted her chin and kept her temper with an effor
"That's hardly any affair of yours, my lord."

Darcy frowned. "As a friend of your guardian—"

At that Sarah did turn, uncaring of the consequences, he
eyes flashing, her voice taut. "As a friend of my guardia

you've been trying to seduce me ever since you first set eyes on me!''

"True," countered Darcy, his face like granite. "But not even Max has blamed me for that. Besides, it's what you Twinning girls expect, isn't it? Tell me, my dear, how many other lovesick puppies have you had at your feet since I left?"

It was on the tip of Sarah's tongue to retort that she had had no lack of suitors since his lordship had quit the scene. But, just in time, she saw the crevasse yawning at her feet. In desperation, she willed herself to calm, and coolly met his blue eyes, her own perfectly candid. "Actually, I find the entertainments of the *ton* have palled. Since you ask, I've formed the intention of entering a convent. There's a particularly suitable one, the Ursulines, not far from our old home.''

For undoubtedly the first time in his adult life, Darcy Hamilton was completely nonplussed. A whole range of totally unutterable responses sprang to his lips. He swallowed them all and said, "You wouldn't be such a fool.''

Sarah's brows rose coldly. For a moment she held his gaze, then turned haughtily to move past him.

"Sarah!" The word was wrung from him and then she was in his arms, her lips crushed under his, her head spinning as he gathered her more fully to him.

For Sarah, it was a repeat of their interlude in the shrubbery. As the kiss deepened, then deepened again, she allowed herself a few minutes' grace, to savour the paradise of being once more in his arms.

Then, she gathered her strength and tore herself from his hold. For an instant, they remained frozen, silently staring at each other, their breathing tumultuous, their eyes liquid fire. Abruptly, Sarah turned and walked quickly back into the music-room.

With a long-drawn-out sigh, Darcy Hamilton leaned upon the balustrade, gazing unseeingly at the well-manicured lawns.

HIS GRACE OF TWYFORD carefully scrutinized Sarah Twinning's face as she returned to the music-room and joined her younger sisters in time to applaud the singer's operatic feats. Caroline, seated beside him, had not noticed her sister's departure from the room, nor her short-lived return. As his gaze slid gently over Caroline's face and noted the real pleasure the music had brought her, he decided that he had no intention of informing her of her sister's strange behaviour. That there was something behind the younger Twinnings's interest in Sir Ralph Keighly he did not doubt. But whatever it was, he would much prefer that Caroline was not caught up in it. He was becoming accustomed to having her complete attention and found himself reluctant to share it with anyone.

He kept a watchful eye on the door to the balcony and, some minutes later, when the singer was once more in full flight, saw Darcy Hamilton enter and, unobtrusively, leave the room. His eyes turning once more to the bowed dark head of Sarah Twinning, Max sighed. Darcy Hamilton had been one of the coolest hands in the business. But in the case of Sarah Twinning his touch seemed to have deserted him entirely. His friend's disintegration was painful to watch. He had not yet had time to do more than nod a greeting to Darcy when he had seen him enter the room. Max wondered what conclusions he had derived from his sojourn in Ireland. Whatever they were, he wryly suspected that Darcy would be seeking him out soon enough.

Which, of course, was likely to put a time limit on his own affair. His gaze returned to Caroline and, as if in response, she turned to smile up at him, her eyes unconsciously warm, her lips curving invitingly. Regretfully dismissing the appealing notion of creating a riot by kissing her in the midst of the cream of the *ton*, Max merely returned the smile and watched as she once more directed her attention to the singer. No, he did not need to worry. She would be his long before her sisters' affairs became pressing.

THE MASKED BALL given by Lady Penbright was set to be one of the highlights of an already glittering Season. Her ladyship had spared no expense. Her ballroom was draped in white satin and the terraces and trellised walks with which Penbright House was lavishly endowed were lit by thousands of Greek lanterns. The music of a small orchestra drifted down from the minstrels' gallery, the notes falling like petals on the gloriously covered heads of the *ton*. By decree, all the guests wore long dominos, concealing their evening dress, hoods secured over the ladies' curls to remove even that hint of identity. Fixed masks concealing the upper face were the order, far harder to penetrate than the smaller and often more bizarre hand-held masks, still popular in certain circles for flirtation. By eleven, the Penbright ball had been accorded the ultimate accolade of being declared a sad crush and her ladyship retired from her position by the door to join in the revels with her guests.

Max, wary of the occasion and having yet to divine the younger Twinnings' secret aim, had taken special note of his wards' dresses when he arrived at Twyford House to escort them to the ball. Caroline he would have no difficulty in detecting; even if her domino in a subtle shade of aqua had not been virtually unique, the effect her presence had on him, he had long ago noticed, would be sufficient to enable him to unerringly find her in a crowded room blindfold. Sarah, looking slightly peaked but carrying herself with the grace he expected of a Twinning, had flicked a moss-green domino over her satin dress which was in a paler shade of the same colour. Arabella had been struggling to settle the hood of a delicate rose-pink domino over her bright curls while Lizzie's huge grey eyes had watched from the depths of her lavender hood. Satisfied he had fixed the particular tints in his mind, Max had ushered them forth.

On entering the Penbright ballroom, the three younger Twinnings melted into the crowd but Caroline remained beside Max, anchored by his hand under her elbow. To her confusion, she found that one of the major purposes of a masked ball seemed to be to allow those couples who wished to spend an entire evening together without creating a scandal to do so. Certainly, her guardian appeared to have no intention of quitting her side.

While the musicians were tuning up, she was approached in a purposeful manner by a grey domino, under which she had no difficulty in recognizing the slight frame of Mr. Willoughby. The poor man was not entirely sure of her identity and Caroline gave him no hint. He glared at the tall figure by her side, which resulted in a slow, infuriating grin spreading across that gentleman's face. Then, as Mr. Willoughby cleared his throat preparatory to asking the lady in the aqua domino for the pleasure of the first waltz, Max got in before him.

After her second waltz with her guardian, who was otherwise behaving impeccably, Caroline consented to a stroll about the rooms. The main ballroom was full and salons on either side took up the overflow. A series of interconnecting rooms made Caroline's head spin. Then, Max embarked on a long and involved anecdote which focused her attention on his masked face and his wickedly dancing eyes.

She should, of course, have been on her guard, but Caroline's defences against her dangerous guardian had long since fallen. Only when she had passed through the door he held open for her, and discovered it led into a bedroom, clearly set aside for the use of any guests overcome by the revels downstairs, did the penny drop. As she turned to him, she heard the click of the lock falling into its setting. And then Max stood before her, his eyes alight with an emotion she dared not define. That slow grin of his, which by itself turned her bones to jelly, showed in the shifting light from the open windows.

She put her hands on his shoulders, intending to hold him off, yet there was no strength behind the gesture and instead, as he drew her against him, her arms of their own accord slipped around his neck. She yielded in that first instant, as his lips touched hers, and Max knew it. But he saw no reason for undue haste. Savouring the feel of her, the taste of her, he spun out their time, giving her the opportunity to learn of each pleasure as it came, gently guiding her to the chaise by the windows, never letting her leave his arms or that state of helpless surrender she was in.

Caroline Twinning was heady stuff, but Max remembered he had a question for her. He drew back to gaze at her as she lay, reclining against the colourful cushions, her eyes unfocused as his long fingers caressed the satin smoothness of her breasts as they had once before in the carriage on the way back from the Richardsons' ball, with Miriam Alford snoring quietly in the corner. "Caro?"

Caroline struggled to make sense of his voice through the haze of sensation clouding her mind. "Mmm?"

"Sweet Caro," he murmured wickedly, watching her efforts. "If you recall, I once asked you if, were I not your guardian, you would permit me to be alone with you. Do you still think, if that was the case, you'd resist?"

To Caroline, the question was so ridiculous that it broke through to her consciousness, submerged beneath layers of pleasurable sensation. A slight frown came to her eyes as she wondered why on earth he kept asking such a hypothetical question. But his hands had stilled so it clearly behoved her to answer it. "I've always resisted you," she declared. "It's just that I've never succeeded in impressing that fact upon you. Even if you weren't my guardian, I'd still try to resist you." Her eyes closed and she gave up the attempt at conversation as his hands resumed where they had left off. But all too soon they stilled again.

"What do you mean, *even* if I weren't your guardian?"

Caroline groaned. "Max!" But his face clearly showed that he wanted her answer, so she explained with what patience she could muster. "This, you and me, together, would be scandalous enough if you weren't my guardian, but you are, so it's ten times worse." She closed her eyes again. "You must know that."

Max did, but it had never occurred to him that she would have readily accepted his advances even had he not had her guardianship to tie her to him. His slow smile appeared. He should have known. Twinnings and rakes, after all. Caroline, her eyes still closed, all senses focused on the movement of his hands upon her breasts, did not see the smile, nor the glint in her guardian's very blue eyes that went with it. But her eyes flew wide open when Max bent his head and took one rosy nipple into his mouth.

"Oh!" She tensed and Max lifted his head to grin wolfishly at her. He cocked one eyebrow at her but she was incapable of speech. Then, deliberately, his eyes holding hers, he lowered his head to her other breast, feeling her tense in his arms against the anticipated shock. Gradually, she relaxed, accepting that sensation too. Slowly, he pushed her further, knowing he would meet no resistance. She responded freely, so much so that he was constantly drawing back, trying to keep a firm hold on his much tried control. Experienced as he was, Caroline Twinning was something quite outside his previous knowledge.

Soon, they had reached that subtle point beyond which there would be no turning back. He knew it, though he doubted she did. And, to his amazement, he paused, then gently disengaged, drawing her around to lean against his chest so that he could place kisses in the warm hollow of her neck and fondle her breasts, ensuring she would stay blissfully unaware while he did some rapid thinking.

The pros were clear enough, but she would obviously come to him whenever he wished, now or at any time in the future. Such as tomorrow. The cons were rather more substantial. Chief among these was that tonight they would have to return to the ball afterwards, usually a blessing if one merely wanted to bed a woman, not spend the entire night with her. But, if given the choice, he would prefer to spend at least twenty-four hours in bed with Caroline, a reasonable compensation for his forbearance to date. Then, too, there was the very real problem of her sisters. Despite the preoccupation of his hands, he knew that a part of his mind was taken up with the question of what they were doing while he and his love were otherwise engaged. He would infinitely prefer to be able to devote his entire attention to the luscious person in his arms. He sighed. His body did not like what his mind was telling it. Before he could change his decision, he pulled Caroline closer and bent to whisper in her ear. "Caro?"

She murmured his name and put her hand up to his face. Max smiled. "Sweetheart, much as I'd like to complete your education here and now, I have a dreadful premonition of what hideous scandals your sisters might be concocting with both of us absent from the ballroom."

He knew it was the right excuse to offer, for her mind immediately reasserted itself. "Oh, dear," she sighed, disappointment ringing clearly in her tone, deepening Max's smile. "I suspect you're right."

"I know I'm right," he said, straightening and sitting her upright. "Come, let's get you respectable again."

As soon as she felt sufficiently camouflaged from her guardian's eye by the gorgeously coloured throng, Lizzie Twinning made her way to the ballroom window further from the door. It was the meeting place Sarah had stipulated where Sir Ralph was to await further instructions. He was there, in a dark green domino and a black mask.

Lizzie gave him her hand. "Good!" The hand holding hers trembled. She peered into the black mask. "You're not going to let Arabella down, are you?"

To her relief, Sir Ralph swallowed and shook his head. "No. Of course not. I've got my carriage waiting, as Miss Sarah suggested. I wouldn't dream of deserting Miss Arabella."

Despite the weakness in his voice, Lizzie was satisfied. "It's all right," she assured him. "Arabella is wearing a rose-pink domino. It's her favourite colour so you should recognise it. We'll bring her to you, as we said we would.

Don't worry," she said, giving his hand a squeeze, "it'll all work out for the best, you'll see." She patted his hand and, returning it to him, left him. As she moved down the ballroom, she scanned the crowd and picked out Caroline in her aqua domino waltzing with a black domino who could only be their guardian. She grinned to herself and the next instant, walked smack into a dark blue domino directly in her path.

"Oh!" She fell back and put up a hand to her mask, which had slipped.

"Lizzie," said the blue domino in perfectly recognizable accents, "what were you doing talking to Keighly?"

"Martin! What a start you gave me. My mask nearly fell. Wh...what do you mean?"

"I mean, Miss Innocence," said Martin sternly, taking her arm and compelling her to walk beside him on to the terrace, "that I saw you come into the ballroom and then, as soon as you were out of Max's sight, make a bee-line for Keighly. Now, out with it! What's going on?"

Lizzie was in shock. What was she to do? Not for a moment did she imagine that Martin would agree to turn a blind eye to their scheme. But she was not a very good liar. Still, she would have to try. Luckily, the mask hid most of her face and her shock had kept her immobile, gazing silently up at him in what could be taken for her usual innocent manner. "But I don't know what you mean, Martin. I know I talked to Sir Ralph, but that was because he was the only one I recognized."

The explanation was so reasonable that Martin felt his sudden suspicion was as ridiculous as it had seemed. He felt decidedly foolish. "Oh."

"But now you're here," said Lizzie, putting her hand on his arm. "So I can talk to you."

Martin's usual grin returned. "So you can." He raised his eyes to the secluded walks, still empty as the dancing had only just begun. "Why don't we explore while we chat?"

Lately, Lizzie had been in the habit of refusing such invitations but tonight she was thankful for any suggestion that would distract Martin from their enterprise. So she nodded and they stepped off the terrace on to the gravel. They followed a path into the shrubbery. It wended this way and that until the house was a glimmer of light and noise beyond the screening bushes. They found an ornamental stream and followed it to a lake. There was a small island in the middle with a tiny summer-house, reached by a rustic bridge. They crossed over and found the door of the summer-house open.

"Isn't this lovely?" said Lizzie, quite enchanted by the scene. Moonbeams danced in a tracery of light created by the carved wooden shutters. The soft swish of the water running past the reed-covered banks was the only sound to reach their ears.

"Mmm, yes, quite lovely," murmured Martin, enchanted by something quite different. Even Lizzie in her innocence heard the warning in his tone but she turned only in time to find herself in his arms. Martin tilted her face up and smiled gently down at her. "Lizzie, sweet Lizzie. Do you have any idea how beautiful you are?"

Lizzie's eyes grew round. Martin's arms closed around her, gentle yet quite firm. It seemed unbelievable that their tightness could be restricting her breathing, yet she found herself quite unable to draw breath. And the strange light in Martin's eyes was making her dizzy. She had meant to ask her sisters for guidance on how best to handle such situations but, due to her absorption with their schemes, it had slipped her mind. She suspected this was one of those points where using one's wits came into it. But, as her tongue seemed incapable of forming any words, she could only shake her head and hope that was acceptable.

"Ah," said Martin, his grin broadening. "Well, you're so very beautiful, sweetheart, that I'm afraid I can't resist. I'm going to kiss you again, Lizzie. And it's going to be thoroughly enjoyable for both of us." Without further

words, he dipped his head and, very gently, kissed her.
When she did not draw back, he continued the caress, pro-
longing the sensation until he felt her response. Gradually,
with the moonlight washing over them, he deepened the
kiss, then, as she continued to respond easily, gently drew
her further into his arms. She came willingly and Martin was
suddenly unsure of the ground rules. He had no wish to
frighten her, innocent as she was, yet he longed to take their
dalliance further, much further. He gently increased the
pressure of his lips on hers until they parted for him. Slowly,
continually reminding himself of her youth, he taught her
how pleasurable a kiss could be. Her responses drove him to
seek more.

Kisses were something Lizzie felt she could handle. Being held securely in Martin's arms was a delight. But when
his hand closed gently over her breast she gasped and pulled
away. The reality of her feelings hit her. She burst into tears.

"Lizzie?" Martin, cursing himself for a fool, for pushing her too hard, gathered her into his arms, ignoring her
half-hearted resistance. "I'm sorry, Lizzie. It was too soon,
I know. Lizzie? Sweetheart?"

Lizzie gulped and stifled her sobs. "It's true!" she said,
her voice a tear-choked whisper. "They said you were a rake
and you'd want to take me to bed and I didn't believe them
but it's *true*." She ended this astonishing speech on a hic-
cup.

Martin, finding much of her accusation difficult to deny,
fastened on the one aspect that was not clear. "They—
who?"

"Sarah and Bella and Caro. They said you're *all* rakes.
You and Max and Lord Darcy and Lord Denbigh. They said
there's something about us that means we attract rakes."

Finding nothing in all this that he wished to dispute,
Martin kept silent. He continued to hold Lizzie, his face half
buried in her hair. "What did they suggest you should do
about it?" he eventually asked, unsure if he would get an
answer.

The answer he got was unsettling. "Wait."

Wait. Martin did not need to ask what for. He knew.

Very much later in the evening, when Martin had escorted Lizzie back to the ballroom, Max caught sight of them from the other side of the room. He had been forced to reassess his original opinion of the youngest Twinning's sobriety. Quite how such a youthful innocent had managed to get Martin into her toils he could not comprehend, but one look at his brother's face, even with his mask in place, was enough to tell him she had succeeded to admiration. Well, he had warned him.

ARABELLA'S ROLE in the great plan was to flirt so outrageously that everyone in the entire room would be certain that it was indeed the vivacious Miss Twinning under the rose-pink domino. None of the conspirators had imagined this would prove at all difficult and, true to form, within half an hour Arabella had convinced the better part of the company of her identity. She left one group of revellers, laughing gaily, and was moving around the room, when she found she had walked into the arms of a large, black-domino-clad figure. The shock she received from the contact immediately informed her of the identity of the gentleman.

"Oh, sir! You quite overwhelm me!"

"In such a crowd as this, my dear? Surely you jest?"

"Would you contradict a lady, sir? Then you're no gentlemen, in truth."

"In truth, you're quite right, sweet lady. Gentlemen lead such boring lives."

The distinctly seductive tone brought Arabella up short. He could not know who she was, could he? As if in answer to her unspoken question, he asked, "And who might you be, my lovely?"

Arabella's chin went up and she playfully retorted, "Why, that's not for you to know, sir. My reputation might be at

stake, simply for talking to so unconventional a gentleman
as you.''

To her unease, Hugo responded with a deep and attractive chuckle. Their light banter continued, Arabella making all the customary responses, her quick ear for repartee saving her from floundering when his returns made her cheeks burn. She flirted with Hugo to the top of her bent. And hated every minute of it. He did not know who she was, yet was prepared to push an unknown lady to make an assignation with him for later in the evening. She was tempted to do so and then confront him with her identity. But her heart failed her. Instead, when she could bear it no longer, she made a weak excuse and escaped.

THEY HAD TIMED their plan carefully, to avoid any possible mishap. The unmasking was scheduled for one o'clock. At precisely half-past twelve, Sarah and Sir Ralph left the ballroom and strolled in a convincingly relaxed manner down a secluded walk which led to a little gazebo. The gazebo was placed across the path and, beyond it, the path continued to a gate giving access to the carriage drive.

Within sight of the gazebo, Sarah halted. "Arabella's inside. I'll wait here and ensure no one interrupts."

Sir Ralph swallowed, nodded once and left her. He climbed the few steps and entered the gazebo. In the dimness, he beheld the rose-pink domino, her mask still in place, waiting nervously for him to approach. Reverently, he went forward and then went down on one knee.

Sarah, watching from the shadows outside, grinned in delight. The dim figures exchanged a few words, then Sir Ralph rose and kissed the lady. Sarah held her breath, but all went well. Hand in hand, the pink domino and her escort descended by the opposite door of the gazebo and headed for the gate. To make absolutely sure of their success, Sarah entered the gazebo and stood watching the couple disappear through the gate. She waited, silently, then the click of horses' hooves came distantly on the breeze. With a quick smile, she turned to leave. And froze.

Just inside the door to the gazebo stood a tall, black-domino-clad figure, his shoulders propped negligently against the frame in an attitude so characteristic Sarah would have known him anywhere. "Are you perchance waiting for an assignation, my dear?"

Sarah made a grab for her fast-disappearing wits. She drew herself up but, before she could speak, his voice came again. "Don't run away. A chase through the bushes would be undignified at best and I would catch you all the same."

Sarah's brows rose haughtily. She had removed her mask which had been irritating her and it hung by its strings from her fingers. She swung it back and forth nervously. "Run? Why should I run?" Her voice, she was pleased to find, was calm.

Darcy did not answer. Instead, he pushed away from the door and crossed the floor to stand in front of her. He reached up and undid his mask. Then his eyes caught hers. "Are you still set on fleeing to a convent?"

Sarah held his gaze steadily. "I am."

A wry smile, self-mocking, she thought, twisted his mobile mouth. "That won't do, you know. You're not cut out to be a bride of Christ."

"Better a bride of Christ than the mistress of any man." She watched the muscles in his jaw tighten.

"You think so?"

Despite the fact that she had known it would happen, had steeled herself to withstand it, her defences crumbled at his touch and she was swept headlong into abandonment, freed from restraint, knowing where the road led and no longer caring.

But when Darcy stooped and lifted her, to carry her to the wide cushioned seats at the side of the room, she shook her head violently. "Darcy, no!" Her voice caught on a sob. "Please, Darcy, let me go."

Her tears sobered him as nothing else could have. Slowly, he let her down until her feet touched the floor. She was openly crying, as if her heart would break. "Sarah?" Darcy put out a hand to smooth her brown hair.

Sarah had found her handkerchief and was mopping her streaming eyes, her face averted. "Please go, Darcy."

Darcy stiffened. For the first time in his adult life, he wanted to take a woman into his arms purely to comfort her. All inclinations to make love to her had vanished at the first hint of her distress. But, sensing behind her whispered words a confusion she had yet to resolve, he sighed and, with a curt bow, did as she asked.

Sarah listened to his footsteps die away. She remained in the gazebo until she had cried herself out. Then, thankful for the at least temporary protection of her mask, she returned to the ballroom to tell her sisters and their protégées of their success.

HUGO SCANNED the room again, searching through the sea of people for Arabella. But the pink domino was nowhere in sight. He was as thoroughly disgruntled as only someone of a generally placid nature could become. Arabella had flirted outrageously with an unknown man. Admittedly him, but she had not known that. Here he had been worrying himself into a state over her getting herself stuck in a loveless marriage for no reason and underneath she was just a heartless flirt. A jade. Where the hell was she?

A small hand on his arm made him jump. But, contrary to the conviction of his senses, it was not Arabella but a lady in a brown domino with a brown mask fixed firmly in place. "'Ello, kind sir. You seem strangely lonely."

Hugo blinked. The lady's accent was heavily middle European, her tone seductively low.

"I'm all alone," sighed the lady in brown. "And as you seemed also alone, I thought that maybe we could cheer one another up, no?"

In spite of himself, Hugo's glance flickered over the lady. Her voice suggested a wealth of experience yet her skin, what he could see of it, was as delicate as a young girl's. The heavy mask she wore covered most of her face, even shading her lips, though he could see these were full and ripe. The domino, as dominos did, concealed her figure. Exasperated, Hugo sent another searching glance about the room in vain. Then, he looked down and smiled into the lady's hazel eyes. "What a very interesting idea, my dear. Shall we find somewhere to further develop our mutual acquaintance?"

He slipped an arm around the lady's waist and found that it was indeed very neat. She seemed for one instant to stiffen under his arm but immediately relaxed. Damn Arabella! She had driven him mad. He would forget her existence and let this lovely lady restore his sanity. "What did you say your name was, my dear?"

The lady smiled up at him, a wickedly inviting smile. "Maria Pavlovska," she said as she allowed him to lead her out of the ballroom.

They found a deserted ante-room without difficulty and, without waiting time in further, clearly unnecessary talk, Hugo drew Maria Pavlovska into his arms. She allowed him to kiss her and, to his surprise, raised no demur when he deepened the kiss. His senses were racing and her responses drove him wild. He let his hand wander and she merely chuckled softly, the sound suggesting that he had yet to reach her limit. He found a convenient armchair and pulled her on to his lap and let her drive him demented. She was the most satisfyingly responsive woman he had ever found. Bewildered by his good fortune, he smiled understandingly when she whispered she would leave him for a moment.

He sighed in anticipation and stretched his long legs in front of him as the door clicked shut.

As the minutes ticked by and Maria Pavlovska did not return, sanity slowly settled back into Hugo's fevered brain. Where the hell was she? She'd deserted him. Just like Arabella. The thought hit him with the force of a sledgehammer. *Just like Arabella?* No, he was imagining things. True, Maria Pavlovska had aroused him in a way he had begun to think only Arabella could. *Hell!* She had even *tasted* like Arabella. But Arabella's domino was pink. Maria Pavlovska's domino was brown. And, now he came to think of it, it had been a few inches too short; he had been able to see her pink slippers and the pink hem of her dress. Arabella's favourite colour was pink but pink was, after all, a very popular colour. Damn, where was she? Where were they? With a long-suffering sigh, Hugo rose and, forswearing all women, left to seek the comparative safety of White's for the rest of the night.

CHAPTER ELEVEN

AFTER RETURNING to the ballroom with Caroline, Max found his temper unconducive to remaining at the ball. In short, he had a headache. His wards seemed to be behaving themselves, despite his premonitions, so there was little reason to remain at Penbright House. But the night was young and his interlude with Caroline had made it unlikely that sleep would come easily, so he excused himself to his eldest ward and his aunt, and left to seek entertainment of a different sort.

He had never got around to replacing Carmelita. There hardly seemed much point now. He doubted he would have much use for such women in future. He grinned to himself, then winced. Just at that moment, he regretted not having a replacement available. He would try his clubs—perhaps a little hazard might distract him.

The carriage had almost reached Delmere House when, on the spur of the moment, he redirected his coachman to a discreet house on Bolsover Street. Sending the carriage back to Penbright House, he entered the newest gaming hell in London. Naturally, the door was opened to His Grace of Twyford with an alacrity that brought a sardonic grin to His Grace's face. But the play was entertaining enough and the beverages varied and of a quality he could not fault. The hell claimed to be at the forefront of fashion and consequently there were a number of women present, playing the green baize tables or, in some instances, merely accompanying their lovers. To his amusement, Max found a number of pairs of feminine eyes turned his way, but was too wise to evince an interest he did not, in truth, feel. Among the patrons he found more than a few refugees from the Penbright ball, among them Darcy Hamilton.

Darcy was leaning against the wall, watching the play at the hazard table. He glowered as Max approached. "I noticed both you and your eldest ward were absent from the festivities for an inordinately long time this evening. Examining etchings upstairs, I suppose?"

Max grinned. "We were upstairs, as it happens. But it wasn't etchings I was examining."

Darcy nearly choked on his laughter. "Damn you, Max," he said when he could speak. "So you've won through, have you?"

A shrug answered him. "Virtually. But I decided the ball was not the right venue." The comment stunned Darcy but before he could phrase his next question Max continued. "Her sisters seem to be hatching some plot, though I'm dashed if I can see what it is. But when I left all seemed peaceful enough." Max's blue eyes went to his friend's face. "What are you doing here?"

"Trying to avoid thinking," said Darcy succinctly.

Max grinned. "Oh. In that case, come and play a hand of piquet."

The two were old adversaries who only occasionally found the time to play against each other. Their skills were well-matched and before long their game had resolved into an exciting tussle which drew an increasing crowd of spectators. The owners of the hell, finding their patrons leaving the tables to view the contest, from their point an unprofitable exercise, held an urgent conference. They concluded that the cachet associated with having hosted a contest between two such well-known players was worth the expense. Consequently, the two combatants found their glasses continually refilled with the finest brandy and new decks of cards made readily available.

Both Max and Darcy enjoyed the battle, and as both were able to stand the nonsense, whatever the outcome, they were perfectly willing to continue the play for however long their interest lasted. In truth, both found the exercise a welcome outlet for their frustrations of the past weeks.

The brandy they both consumed made absolutely no impression on their play or their demeanour. Egged on by a throng of spectators, all considerably more drunk than the principals, the game was still underway at the small table in the first parlour when Lord McCubbin, an ageing but rich Scottish peer, entered with Emma Mortland on his arm.

Drawn to investigate the cause of the excitement, Emma's bright eyes fell on the elegant figure of the Duke of Twyford. An unpleasant smile crossed her sharp features. She hung on Lord McCubbin's arm, pressing close to whisper to him.

"Eh? What? Oh, yes," said his lordship, somewhat incoherently. He turned to address the occupants of the table in the middle of the crowd. "Twyford! There you are! Think you've lost rather more than money tonight, what?"

Max, his hand poised to select his discard, let his eyes rise to Lord McCubbin's face. He frowned, an unwelcome premonition filling him as his lordship's words sank in. "What, exactly, do you mean by that, my lord?" The words were even and precise and distinctly deadly.

But Lord McCubbin seemed not to notice. "Why, dear boy, you've lost one of your wards. Saw her, clear as daylight. The flighty one in the damned pink domino. Getting into a carriage with that chap Keighly outside the Penbright place. Well, if you don't know, it's probably too late anyway, don't you know?"

Max's eyes had gone to Emma Mortland's face and seen the malicious triumph there. But he had no time to waste on her. He turned back to Lord McCubbin. "Which way did they go?"

The silence in the room had finally penetrated his lordship's foggy brain. "Er—didn't see. I went back to the ballroom."

MARTIN ROTHERBRIDGE paused, his hand on the handle of his bedroom door. It was past seven in the morning. He had sat up all night since returning from the ball, with his brother's brandy decanter to keep him company, going over his relationship with Lizzie Twinning. And still he could find only one solution. He shook his head and opened the door. The sounds of a commotion in the hall drifted up the stairwell. He heard his brother's voice, uplifted in a series of orders to Hillshaw, and then to Wilson. The tone of voice was one he had rarely heard from Max. It brought him instantly alert. Sleep forgotten, he strode back to the stairs.

In the library, Max was pacing back and forth before the hearth, a savage look on his face. Darcy Hamilton stood silently by the window, his face showing the effects of the past weeks, overlaid by the stress of the moment. Max paused to glance at the clock on the mantelshelf. "Seven-thirty," he muttered. "If my people haven't traced Keighly's carriage by eight-thirty, I'll have to send around to Twyford House." He stopped as a thought struck him. Why hadn't they sent for him anyway? It could only mean that, somehow or other, Arabella had managed to conceal her disappearance. He resumed his pacing. The idea of his aunt in hysterics, not to mention Miriam Alford, was a sobering thought. His own scandalous career would be nothing when compared to the repercussions from this little episode. He would wring Arabella's neck when he caught her.

The door opened. Max looked up to see Martin enter. "What's up?" asked Martin.

"Arabella!" said his brother, venom in his voice. "The stupid chit's done a bunk with Keighly."

"Eloped?" said Martin, his disbelief patent.

Max stopped pacing. "Well, I presume he means to marry her. Considering how they all insist on the proposal first, I can't believe she'd change her spots quite so dramatically. But if I have anything to say about it, she won't be marrying Keighly. I've a good mind to shove her into a convent until she comes to her senses!"

Darcy started, then smiled wryly. "I'm told there's a particularly good one near their old home."

Max turned to stare at him as if he had gone mad.

"But think of the waste," said Martin, grinning.

"Precisely my thoughts," nodded Darcy, sinking into an armchair. "Max, unless you plan to ruin your carpet, for God's sake sit down."

With something very like a growl, Max threw himself into the other armchair. Martin drew up a straight-backed chair from the side of the room and sat astride it, his arms folded over its back. "So what now?" he asked. "I've never been party to an elopement before."

His brother's intense blue gaze, filled with silent warning, only made him grin more broadly. "Well, how the hell should I know?" Max eventually exploded.

Both brothers turned to Darcy. He shook his head, his voice unsteady as he replied. "Don't look at me. Not in my line. Come to think of it, none of us has had much experience in trying to get women to marry us."

"Too true," murmured Martin. A short silence fell, filled with uncomfortable thoughts. Martin broke it. "So, what's your next move?"

"Wilson's sent runners out to all the posting houses. I can't do a thing until I know which road they've taken."

At that moment, the door silently opened and shut again, revealing the efficient Wilson, a small and self-effacing man, Max's most trusted servitor. "I thought you'd wish to know, Your Grace. There's been no sightings of such a vehicle on any of the roads leading north, north-east or south. The man covering the Dover road has yet to report back, as has the man investigating the road to the south-west."

Max nodded. "Thank you, Wilson. Keep me informed as the reports come in."

Wilson bowed and left as silently as he had entered.

The frown on Max's face deepened. "Where would they go? Gretna Green? Dover? I know Keighly's got estates somewhere, but I never asked where." After a moment, he glanced at Martin. "Did Lizzie ever mention it?"

Martin shook his head. Then, he frowned. "Not but what I found her talking to Keighly as soon as ever they got to the ball this evening. I asked her what it was about but she denied there was anything in it." His face had become grim. "She must have known."

"I think Sarah knew too," said Darcy, his voice unemotional. "I saw her go out with Keighly, then found her alone in a gazebo not far from the carriage gate."

"Hell and the devil!" said Max. "They can't all simultaneously have got a screw loose. What I can't understand is what's so attractive about *Keighly*?"

A knock on the door answered this imponderable question. At Max's command, Hillshaw entered. "Lord Denbigh desires a word with you, Your Grace."

For a moment, Max's face was blank. Then, he sighed. "Show him in, Hillshaw. He's going to have to know sooner or later."

As it transpired, Hugo already knew. As he strode into the library, he was scowling furiously. He barely waited to shake Max's hand and exchange nods with the other two men before asking, "Have you discovered which road they've taken?"

Max blinked and waved him to the armchair he had vacated, moving to take the chair behind the desk. "How did you know?"

"It's all over town," said Hugo, easing his large frame into the chair. "I was at White's when I heard it. And if it's reached that far, by later this morning your ward is going to be featuring in the very latest *on-dit* all over London. I'm going to wring her neck!"

This last statement brought a tired smile to Max's face. But, "You'll have to wait in line for that privilege," was all he said.

The brandy decanter, replenished after Martin's inroads, had twice made the rounds before Wilson again slipped noiselessly into the room. He cleared his throat to attract Max's attention. "A coach carrying a gentleman and a young lady wearing a rose-pink domino put in at the Crown at Acton at two this morning, Your Grace."

The air of despondency which had settled over the room abruptly lifted. "Two," said Max, his eyes going to the clock. "And it's well after eight now. So they must be past Uxbridge. Unless they made a long stop?"

Wilson shook his head. "No, Your Grace. They only stopped long enough to change horses." If anything, the little man's impassive face became even more devoid of emotion. "It seems the young lady was most anxious to put as much distance as possible behind them."

"As well she might," said Max, his eyes glittering. "Have my curricle put to. And good work, Wilson."

"Thank you, Your Grace." Wilson bowed and left. Max tossed off the brandy in his glass and rose.

"I'll come with you," said Hugo, putting his own glass down. For a moment, his eyes met Max's, then Max nodded.

"Very well." His gaze turned to his brother and Darcy Hamilton. "Perhaps you two could break the news to the ladies at Twyford House?"

Martin nodded.

Darcy grimaced at Max over the rim of his glass. "I thought you'd say that." After a moment, he continued, "As I said before, I'm not much of a hand at elopements and I don't know Keighly at all. But it occurs to me, Max, dear boy, that it's perfectly possible he might not see reason all that easily. He might even do something rash. So, aside from Hugo here, don't you think you'd better take those along with you?"

Darcy pointed at a slim wooden case that rested on top of the dresser standing against the wall at the side of the room. Inside, as he knew, reposed a pair of Mr. Joseph Manton's duelling pistols, with which Max was considered a master.

Max hesitated, then shrugged. "I suppose you're right." He lifted the case to his desk-top and, opening it, quickly checked the pistols. They looked quite lethal, the long black barrels gleaming, the silver mountings glinting wickedly. He had just picked up the second, when the knocker on the front door was plied with a ruthlessness which brought a definite wince to all four faces in the library. The night had been a long one. A moment later, they heard Hillshaw's sonorous tones, remonstrating with the caller. Then, an unmistakably feminine voice reached their ears. With an oath, Max strode to the door.

Caroline fixed Hillshaw with a look which brooked no argument. "I wish to see His Grace *immediately*, Hillshaw."

Accepting defeat, Hillshaw turned to usher her to the drawing-room, only to be halted by his master's voice.

"Caro! What are you doing here?"

From the library door, Max strolled forward to take the hand Caroline held out to him. Her eyes widened as she took in the pistol he still held in his other hand. "Thank God I'm in time!" she said, in such heartfelt accents that Max frowned.

"It's all right. We've found out which road they took. Denbigh and I were about to set out after them. Don't worry, we'll bring her back."

Far from reassuring her as he had intended, his matter-of-fact tone seemed to set her more on edge. Caroline clasped both her small hands on his arm. "No! You don't understand."

Max's frown deepened. He decided she was right. He could not fathom why she wished him to let Arabella ruin herself. "Come into the library."

Caroline allowed him to usher her into the apartment where they had first met. As her eyes took in the other occupants, she coloured slightly. "Oh, I didn't realize," she said.

Max waved her hesitation aside. "It's all right. They already know." He settled her in the armchair Hugo had vacated. "Caro, do you know where Keighly's estates are?"

Caroline was struggling with his last revelation. They already knew? How? "Gloucestershire, I think," she replied automatically. Then, her mind registered the fact that Max had laid the wicked-looking pistol he had been carrying on his desk, with its mate, no less, and was putting the box which she thought ought to contain them back, empty, on the dresser. A cold fear clutched at her stomach. Her voice seemed thin and reedy. "Max, what are you going to do with those?"

Max, still standing behind the desk, glanced down at the pistols. But it was Hugo's deep voice which answered her. "Have to make sure Keighly sees reason, ma'am," he explained gently. "Need to impress on him the wisdom of keeping his mouth shut over this."

Her mind spinning, Caroline looked at him blankly. "But why? I mean, what can he say? Well, it's all so ridiculous."

"Ridiculous?" echoed Max, a grim set to his mouth.

"I'm afraid you don't quite understand, Miss Twinning," broke in Darcy. "The story's already all over town. But if Max can get her back and Keighly keeps his mouth shut, then it's just possible it'll all blow over, you see."

"But... but why should Max interfere?" Caroline put a hand to her head, as if to still her whirling thoughts.

This question was greeted by stunned silence. It was Martin who broke it. "But, dash it all! He's her *guardian!*"

For an instant, Caroline looked perfectly blank. "Is he?" she whispered weakly.

This was too much for Max. "You know perfectly well I am." It appeared to him that his Caro had all but lost her wits with shock. He reined in his temper, sorely tried by the events of the entire night, and said, "Hugo and I are about to leave to get Arabella back—"

"No!" The syllable was uttered with considerable force by Caroline as she leapt to her feet. It had the desired effect of stopping her guardian in his tracks. One black brow rose threateningly, but before he could voice his anger she was speaking again. "You *don't* understand! I didn't *think* you did, but you kept telling me you *knew.*"

Caroline's eyes grew round as she watched Max move around the desk and advance upon her. She waved one hand as if to keep him back and enunciated clearly, "Arabella did not go with Sir Ralph."

Max stopped. Then his eyes narrowed. "She was seen getting into a carriage with him in the Penbrights' drive."

Caroline shook her head as she tried to work this out. Then she saw the light. "A rose-pink domino was seen getting into Sir Ralph's carriage?"

At her questioning look, Max thought back to Lord McCubbin's words. Slowly, he nodded his head. "And you're sure it wasn't Arabella?"

"When I left Twyford House, Arabella was at the breakfast table."

"So who...?"

"Sarah?" came the strangled voice of Darcy Hamilton. Caroline looked puzzled. "No. She's at home, too."

"*Lizzie?*"

Martin's horrified exclamation startled Caroline. She regarded him in increasing bewilderment. "Of course not. She's at Twyford House."

By now, Max could see the glimmer of reason for what seemed like the first time in hours. "So who went with Sir Ralph?"

"Miss Harriet Jenkins," said Caroline.

"*Who?*" The sound of four male voices in puzzled unison was very nearly too much for Caroline. She sank back into her chair and waved them back to their seats. "Sit down and I'll explain."

With wary frowns, they did as she bid them.

After a pause to marshal her thoughts, Caroline began. "It's really all Mrs. Crowbridge's fault. She decided she wanted Sir Ralph for a son-in-law. Sir Ralph had come to town because he took fright at the thought of the marriage he had almost contracted with Miss Jenkins in Gloucestershire." She glanced up, but none of her audience seemed to have difficulty understanding events thus far. "Mrs. Crowbridge kept throwing Amanda in Sir Ralph's way. Amanda did not like Sir Ralph and so, to help out, and especially because Mr. Minchbury had almost come to the point with Amanda and she favoured his suit, Arabella started flirting with Sir Ralph, to draw him away from Amanda." She paused, but no questions came. "Well, you, Max, made that a bit difficult when you told Arabella to behave herself with respect to Sir Ralph. But they got around that by sharing the work, as it were. It was still Arabella drawing Sir Ralph off, but the other two helped to cover her absences. Then, Miss Jenkins came to town, following Sir Ralph. She joined in the...the plot. I gather Arabella was to hold Sir Ralph off until Mr. Minchbury proposed and then turn him over to Miss Jenkins."

Max groaned and Caroline watched as he put his head in his hand. "Sir Ralph has my heart-felt sympathy," he said. He gestured to her. "Go on."

"Well, then Mrs. Crowbridge tried to trap Sir Ralph by trying to put him in a compromising situation with Amanda. After that, they all decided something drastic needed to be done, to save both Sir Ralph and Amanda. At the afternoon concert, Sarah wheedled a declaration of sorts from Sir Ralph over Arabella and got him to promise to go along with their plan. He thought Arabella was about to go into a decline and had to be swept off her feet by an elopement."

"My sympathy for Sir Ralph has just died," said Max. "What a slow-top if he believed that twaddle!"

"So that's what she was doing on the balcony with him," said Darcy. "She was there for at least half an hour."

Caroline nodded. "She said she had had to work on him. But Harriet Jenkins has known Sir Ralph from the cradle and had told her how best to go about it."

When no further comment came, Caroline resumed her story. "At the Penbrights's ball last night, Lizzie had the job of making sure Sir Ralph had brought his carriage and would be waiting for Sarah when she came to take him to the rendezvous later."

"And that's why she went to talk to Keighly as soon as you got in the ballroom," said Martin, putting his piece of the puzzle into place.

"All Arabella had to do was flirt outrageously as usual, so that everyone, but particularly Sir Ralph, would be convinced it was her in the rose-pink domino. At twelve-twenty, Arabella swapped dominos with Harriet Jenkins and Harriet went down to a gazebo by the carriage gate."

"Oh, God!" groaned Hugo Denbigh. The horror in his voice brought all eyes to him. He had paled. "What was the colour? Of the second domino?"

Caroline stared at him. "Brown."

"Oh, no! I should have guessed. But her *accent*." Hugo dropped his head into his large hands.

For a moment, his companions looked on in total bewilderment. Then Caroline chuckled, her eyes dancing. "Oh. Did you meet Maria Pavlovska?"

"Yes, I did!" said Hugo, emerging from his depression. "Allow me to inform you, Miss Twinning, that your sister is a minx!"

"I know that," said Caroline. "Though I must say, it's rather trying of her." In answer to Max's look of patent enquiry, she explained. "Maria Pavlovska was a character Arabella acted in a play on board ship. A Polish countess of—er—" Caroline broke off, blushing.

"Dubious virtue," supplied Hugo, hard pressed.

"Well, she was really very good at it," said Caroline.

Looking at Hugo's flushed countenance, none of the others doubted it.

"Where was I?" asked Caroline, trying to appear unconscious. "Oh, yes. Well, all that was left to do was to get Sir Ralph to the gazebo. Sarah apparently did that."

Darcy nodded. "Yes. I saw her."

Max waited for more. His friend's silence brought a considering look to his eyes.

"So, you see, it's all perfectly all right. It's Harriet Jenkins who has gone with Sir Ralph. I gather he proposed before they left and Miss Jenkins's family approved the match, and as they are headed straight back to Gloucestershire, I don't think there's anything to worry about. Oh, and Mr. Minchbury proposed last night and the Crowbridges accepted him, so all's ended well after all and everyone's happy."

"Except for the four of us, who've all aged years in one evening," retorted Max acerbically.

She had the grace to blush. "I came as soon as I found out."

Hugo interrupted. "But they've forgotten one thing. It's all over town that Arabella eloped with Keighly."

"Oh, no. I don't think that can be right," said Caroline, shaking her head. "Anyone who was at the unmasking at the Penbrights' ball would know Arabella was there until the end." Seeing the questioning looks, she explained. "The unmasking was held at one o'clock. And someone suggested there should be a...a competition to see who was the best disguised. People weren't allowed to unmask until someone correctly guessed who they were. Well, no one guessed who Maria Pavlovska was, so Arabella was the toast of the ball."

Max sat back in his chair and grinned tiredly. "So anyone putting about the tale of my ward's elopement will only have the story rebound on them. I'm almost inclined to forgive your sisters their transgression for that one fact."

Caroline looked hopeful, but he did not elaborate. Max stood and the others followed suit. Hugo, still shaking his head in disbelief, took himself off, and Darcy left immediately after. Martin retired for a much needed rest and Caroline found herself alone with her guardian.

Max crossed to where she sat and drew her to her feet and into his arms. His lips found hers in a reassuring kiss. Then, he held her, her head on his shoulder, and laughed wearily. "Sweetheart, if I thought your sisters would be on my hands for much longer, I'd have Whitney around here this morning to instruct him to break that guardianship clause."

"I'm sorry," mumbled Caroline, her hands engrossed in smoothing the folds of his cravat. "I did come as soon as I found out."

"I know you did," acknowledged Max. "And I'm very thankful you did, what's more! Can you imagine how Hugo and I would have looked if we *had* succeeded in overtaking Keighly's carriage and demanded he return the lady to us? God!" He shuddered. "It doesn't bear thinking about." He hugged her, then released her. "Now you should go home and rest. And I'm going to get some sleep."

"One moment," she said, staying within his slackened hold, her eyes still on his cravat. "Remember I said I'd tell you whether there were any gentlemen who we'd like to consider seriously, should they apply to you for permission to address us?"

Max nodded. "Yes. I remember." Surely she was not going to mention Willoughby? What had gone on last night, after he had left? He suddenly felt cold.

But she was speaking again. "Well, if Lord Darcy should happen to ask, then you know about that, don't you?"

Max nodded. "Yes. Darcy would make Sarah a fine husband. One who would keep her sufficiently occupied so she wouldn't have time for scheming." He grinned at Caroline's blush. "And you're right. I'm expecting him to ask at any time. So that's Sarah dealt with."

"And I'd rather thought Lord Denbigh for Arabella, though I didn't know then about Maria Pavlovska."

"Oh, I wouldn't deal Hugo short. Maria Pavlovska might be a bit hard to bear but I'm sure he'll come about. And, as

'm sure Aunt Augusta has told you, he's perfectly accept-
ble as long as he can be brought to pop the question.''

"And," said Caroline, keeping her eyes down, "I'm not
erfectly sure, but..."

"You think Martin might ask for Lizzie," supplied Max,
onscious of his own tiredness. It was sapping his will. All
orts of fantasies were surfacing in his brain and the devil of
t was they were all perfectly achievable. But he had already
nade other plans, better plans. "I foresee no problems
here. Martin's got more money than is good for him. I'm
ure Lizzie will keep him on his toes, hauling her out of the
crapes her innocence will doubtless land her in. And I'd
nuch rather it was him than me." He tried to look into
Caroline's face but she kept her eyes—were they greyish-
reen or greenish-grey? He had never decided—firmly fixed
n his cravat.

"I'm thrilled that you approve of my cravat, sweetheart,
ut is there anything more? I'm dead on my feet," he ac-
nowledged with a rueful grin, praying that she did not have
nything more to tell him.

Caroline's eyes flew to his, an expression he could not
ead in their depths. "Oh, of course you are! No. There's
othing more."

Max caught the odd wistfulness in her tone and correctly
livined its cause. His grin widened. As he walked her to the
loor, he said, "Once I'm myself again, and have recovered
rom your sisters' exploits, I'll call on you—say at three this
fternoon? I'll take you for a drive. There are some matters
wish to discuss with you." He guided her through the li-
rary door and into the hall. In answer to her questioning
ook, he added. "About your ball."

"Oh. I'd virtually forgotten about it," Caroline said as
Max took her cloak from Hillshaw and placed it about her
houlders. They had organized to hold a ball in the Twin-
ings' honour at Twyford House the following week.

"We'll discuss it at three this afternoon," said Max as he
issed her hand and led her down the steps to her carriage.

CHAPTER TWELVE

SARAH WRINKLED her nose at the piece of cold toast lying on her plate. Pushing it away, she leaned back in her chair and surveyed her elder sister. With her copper curls framing her expressive face, Caroline sat at the other end of the small table in the breakfast-room, a vision of palest cerulean blue. A clearly distracted vision. A slight frown had settled in the greeny eyes, banishing the lively twinkle normally lurking there. She sighed, apparently unconsciously, as she stared at her piece of toast, as cold and untouched as Sarah's, as if concealed in its surface were the answers to all unfathomable questions. Sarah was aware of a guilty twinge. Had Max cut up stiff and Caroline not told them?

They had all risen early, being robust creatures and never having got into the habit of lying abed, and had gathered in the breakfast parlour to examine their success of the night before. That it had been a complete and unqualified success could not have been divined from their faces; all of them had looked drawn and peaked. While Sarah knew the cause of her own unhappiness, and had subsequently learned of her younger sisters' reasons for despondency, she had been and still was at a loss to explain Caroline's similar mood. She had been in high feather at the ball. Then Max had left early, an unusual occurrence which had made Sarah wonder if they had had a falling-out. But her last sight of them together, when he had taken leave of Caroline in the ballroom, had not supported such a fancy. They had looked . . . well, intimate. Happily so. Thoroughly immersed in each other. Which, thought the knowledgeable

Sarah, was not especially like either of them. She sent a sharp glance to the other end of the table.

Caroline's bloom had gradually faded and she had been as silent as the rest of them during the drive home. This morning, on the stairs, she had shared their quiet mood. And then, unfortunately, they had had to make things much worse. They had always agreed that Caroline would have to be told immediately after the event. That had always been their way, ever since they were small children. No matter the outcome, Caroline could be relied on to predict unerringly the potential ramifications and to protect her sisters from any unexpected repercussions. This morning, as they had recounted to her their plan and its execution, she had paled. When they had come to a faltering halt, she had, uncharacteristically, told them in a quiet voice to wait as they were while she communicated their deeds to their guardian forthwith. She had explained nothing. Rising from the table without so much as a sip of her coffee, she had immediately called for the carriage and departed for Delmere House.

She had returned an hour and a half later. They had not left the room; Caroline's orders, spoken in that particular tone, were not to be dismissed lightly. In truth, each sunk in gloomy contemplation of her state, they had not noticed the passage of time. Caroline had re-entered the room, calmly resumed her seat and accepted the cup of coffee Arabella had hastily poured for her. She had fortified herself from this before explaining to them, in quite unequivocal terms, just how close they had come to creating a hellish tangle. It had never occurred to them that someone might see Harriet departing and, drawing the obvious conclusion, inform Max of the fact, especially in such a public manner. They had been aghast at the realization of how close to the edge of scandal they had come and were only too ready to behave as contritely as Caroline wished. However, all she had said was, "I don't really think there's much we should do. Thankfully, Arabella, your gadding about as Maria Pav-

lovska ensured that everyone knows you did not elope from
the ball. I suppose we could go riding.'' She had paused,
then added, ''But I really don't feel like it this morning.''

They had not disputed this, merely shaken their heads to
convey their agreement. After a moment of silence, Caroline had added, ''I think Max would expect us to behave as
if nothing had happened, other than there being some ridiculous tale about that Bella had eloped. You'll have to
admit, I suppose, that you swapped dominos with Harriet
Jenkins, but that could have been done in all innocence.
And remember to show due interest in the surprising tale
that Harriet left the ball with Sir Ralph.'' An unwelcome
thought reared its head. ''Will the Crowbridge girls have the
sense to keep their mouths shut?''

They had hastened to assure her on this point. ''Why, it
was all for Amanda's sake, after all,'' Lizzie had pointed
out.

Caroline had not been entirely convinced but had been
distracted by Arabella. Surmising from Caroline's use of her
shortened name that the worst was over, she had asked, ''Is
Max very annoyed with us?''

Caroline had considered the question while they had all
hung, unexpectedly nervous, on her answer. ''I think he's
resigned, now that it's all over and no real harm done, to
turn a blind eye to your misdemeanours. However, if I were
you, I would not be going out of my way to bring myself to
his notice just at present.''

Their relief had been quite real. Despite his reputation,
their acquaintance with the Duke of Twyford had left his
younger wards with the definite impression that he would
not condone any breach of conduct and was perfectly capable of implementing sufficiently draconian measures in
response to any transgression. In years past, they would
have ignored the potential threat and relied on Caroline to
make all right in the event of any trouble. But, given that the
man in question was Max Rotherbridge, none was sure how
successful Caroline would be in turning him up sweet. Re-

assured that their guardian was not intending to descend, in
ire, upon them, Lizzie and Arabella, after hugging Caroline and avowing their deepest thanks for her endeavours on
their behalf, had left the room. Sarah suspected they would
both be found in some particular nook, puzzling out the
uncomfortable feeling in their hearts.

Strangely enough, she no longer felt the need to emulate
them. In the long watches of a sleepless night, she had finally faced the fact that she could not live without Darcy
Hamilton. In the gazebo the previous evening, it had been
on the tip of her tongue to beg him to take her from the ball,
to some isolated spot where they could pursue their lovemaking in greater privacy. She had had to fight her own
nearly overwhelming desire to keep from speaking the
words. If she had uttered them, he would have arranged it
all in an instant, she knew; his desire for her was every bit
as strong as her desire for him. Only her involvement in their
scheme and the consternation her sudden disappearance
would have caused had tipped the scales. Her desire for
marriage, for a home and family, was still as strong as ever.
But, if he refused to consider such an arrangement, she was
now prepared to listen to whatever alternative suggestions
he had to offer. There was Max's opposition to be overcome, but presumably Darcy was aware of that. She felt sure
he would seek her company soon enough and then she
would make her acquiescence plain. That, at least, she
thought with a small, introspective smile, would be very easy
to do.

Caroline finally pushed the unhelpful piece of toast aside.
She rose and shook her skirts in an unconsciously flustered
gesture. In a flash of unaccustomed insight, Sarah wondered if her elder sister was in a similar state to the rest of
them. After all, they were all Twinnings. Although their
problems were superficially quite different, in reality, they
were simply variations on the same theme. They were all in
love with rakes, all of whom seemed highly resistant to
matrimony. In her case, the rake had won. But surely Max

wouldn't win, too? For a moment, Sarah's mind boggled at the thought of the two elder Twinnings falling by the wayside. Then, she gave herself a mental shake. No, of course not. He was their guardian, after all. Which, Sarah thought, presumably meant Caroline would even the score. Caroline was undoubtedly the most capable of them all. So why, then, did she look so troubled?

Caroline was indeed racked by the most uncomfortable thoughts. Leaving Sarah to her contemplation of the breakfast table, she drifted without purpose into the drawing-room and thence to the small courtyard beyond. Ambling about, her delicate fingers examining some of the bountiful blooms, she eventually came to the hammock, slung under the cherry trees, protected from the morning sun by their leafy foliage. Climbing into it, she rested her aching head against the cushions with relief and prepared to allow the conflicting emotions inside her to do battle.

Lately, it seemed to her that there were two Caroline Twinnings. One knew the ropes, was thoroughly acquainted with society's expectations and had no hesitation in laughing at the idea of a gentlewoman such as herself sharing a man's bed outside the bounds of marriage. She had been acquainted with this Caroline Twinning for as long as she could remember. The other woman, for some mysterious reason, had only surfaced in recent times, since her exposure to the temptations of Max Rotherbridge. There was no denying the increasing control this second persona exerted over her. In truth, it had come to the point where she was seriously considering which Caroline Twinning she preferred.

She was no green girl and could hardly pretend she had not been perfectly aware of Max's intentions when she had heard the lock fall on that bedroom door. Nor could she comfort herself that the situation had been beyond her control—at least, not then. If she had made any real effort to bring the illicit encounter to a halt, as she most certainly should have done, Max would have instantly acquiesced.

She could hardly claim he had forced her to remain. But it had been that other Caroline Twinning who had welcomed him into her arms and had proceeded to enjoy, all too wantonly, the delights to be found in his.

She had never succeeded in introducing marriage as an aspect of their relationship. She had always been aware that what Max intended was an illicit affair. What she had underestimated was her own interest in such a scandalous proceeding. But there was no denying the pleasure she had found in his arms, nor the disappointment she had felt when he had cut short their interlude. She knew she could rely on him to ensure that next time there would be no possible impediment to the completion of her education. And she would go to his arms with neither resistance nor regrets. Which, to the original Caroline Twinning, was a very lowering thought.

Swinging gently in the hammock, the itinerant breeze wafting her curls, she tried to drum up all the old arguments against allowing herself to become involved in such an improper relationship. She had been over them all before; they held no power to sway her. Instead, the unbidden memory of Max's mouth on her breast sent a thrill of warm desire through her veins. "Fool!" she said, without heat, to the cherry tree overhead.

MARTIN ROTHERBRIDGE kicked a stone out of his path. He had been walking for nearly twenty minutes in an effort to rid himself of a lingering nervousness over the act he was about to perform. He would rather have raced a charge of Chasseurs than do what he must that day. But there was nothing else for it—the events of the morning had convinced him of that. That dreadful instant when he had thought, for one incredulous and heart-stopping moment, that Lizzie had gone away with Keighly was never to be repeated. And the only way of ensuring that was to marry the chit.

It had certainly not been his intention, and doubtless Max would laugh himself into hysterics, but there it was. Facts had to be faced. Despite his being at her side for much of the time, Lizzie had managed to embroil herself very thoroughly in a madcap plan which, even now, if it ever became known, would see her ostracized by those who mattered in the *ton*. She was a damned sight too innocent to see the outcome of her actions; either that, or too naïve in her belief in her abilities to come about. She needed a husband to keep a firm hand on her reins, to steer her clear of the perils her beauty and innocence would unquestionably lead her into. And, as he desperately wanted the foolish woman, and had every intention of fulfilling the role anyway, he might as well officially be it.

He squared his shoulders. No sense in putting off the evil moment any longer. He might as well speak to Max.

He turned his steps toward Delmere House. Rounding a corner, some blocks from his destination, he saw the impressive form of Lord Denbigh striding along on the opposite side of the street, headed in the same direction. On impulse, Martin crossed the street.

"Hugo!"

Lord Denbigh halted in his purposeful stride and turned to see who had hailed him. Although a few years separated them, he and Martin Rotherbridge had many interests in common and had been acquainted even before the advent of the Twinnings. His lordship's usual sleepy grin surfaced. "Hello, Martin. On your way home?"

Martin nodded and fell into step beside him. At sight of Hugo, his curiosity over Maria Pavlovska had returned. He experimented in his head with a number of suitable openings before settling for, "Dashed nuisances, the Twinning girls!"

"Very!" The curt tone in Hugo's deep voice was not very encouraging.

Nothing loath, Martin plunged on. "Waltz around, tying us all in knots. What exactly happened when Arabella masqueraded as that Polish countess?"

To his amazement, Hugo coloured. "Never you mind," he said, then, at the hopeful look in Martin's eyes, relented. "If you must know, she behaved in a manner which...well, in short, it was difficult to tell who was seducing whom."

Martin gave a burst of laughter, which he quickly controlled at Hugo's scowl. By way of returning the confidence, he said, "Well, I suppose I may as well tell you, as it's bound to be all over town all too soon. I'm on my way to beg Max's permission to pay my addresses to Lizzie Twinning."

Hugo's mild eyes went to Martin's face in surprise. He murmured all the usual condolences, adding, "Didn't really think you'd be wanting to get leg-shackled just yet."

Martin shrugged. "Nothing else for it. Aside from making all else blessedly easy, it's only as her husband I'd have the authority to make certain she didn't get herself involved in any more hare-brained schemes."

"There is that," agreed Hugo ruminatively. They continued for a space in silence before Martin realized they were nearing Delmere House.

"Where are you headed?" he enquired of the giant by his side.

For the second time, Hugo coloured. Looking distinctly annoyed by this fact, he stopped. Martin, puzzled, stopped by his side, but before he could frame any question, Hugo spoke. "I may as well confess, I suppose. I'm on my way to see Max, too."

Martin howled with laughter and this time made no effort to subdue it. When he could speak again, he clapped Hugo on the back. "Welcome to the family!" As they turned and fell into step once more, Martin's eyes lifted. "And lord, what a family it's going to be! Unless I miss my guess, that's Darcy Hamilton's curricle."

Hugo looked up and saw, ahead of them, Lord Darcy's curricle drawn up outside Delmere House. Hamilton himself, elegantly attired, descended and turned to give instructions to his groom, before strolling towards the steps leading up to the door. He was joined by Martin and Hugo.

Martin grinned. "Do you want to see Max, too?"

Darcy Hamilton's face remained inscrutable. "As it happens, I do," he answered equably. As his glance flickered over the unusually precise picture both Martin and Hugo presented, he added, "Am I to take it there's a queue?"

"Afraid so," confirmed Hugo, grinning in spite of himself. "Maybe we should draw lots?"

"Just a moment," said Martin, studying the carriage waiting by the pavement in front of Darcy's curricle. "That's Max's travelling chaise. Is he going somewhere?

This question was addressed to Darcy Hamilton, who shook his head. "He's said nothing to me."

"Maybe the Twinnings have proved too much for him and he's going on a repairing lease?" suggested Hugo.

"Entirely understandable, but I don't somehow think that's it," mused Darcy. Uncertain, they stood on the pavement, and gazed at the carriage. Behind them the door of Delmere House opened. Masterton hurried down the steps and climbed into the chaise. As soon as the door had shut, the coachman flicked his whip and the carriage pulled away. Almost immediately, the vacated position was filled with Max's curricle, the bays stamping and tossing their heads.

Martin's brows had risen. "Masterton and baggage," he said. "Now why?"

"Whatever the reason," said Darcy succinctly, "I suspect we'd better catch your brother now or he'll merrily leave us to our frustrations for a week or more."

The looks of horror which passed over the two faces before him brought a gleam of amusement to his eyes.

"Lord, yes!" said Hugo.

Without further discussion, they turned *en masse* and started up the steps. At that moment, the door at the top opened and their prey emerged. They stopped.

Max, eyeing them as he paused to draw on his driving gloves, grinned. The breeze lifted the capes of his greatcoat as he descended the steps.

"Max, we need to talk to you."

"Where are you going?"

"You can't leave yet."

With a laugh, Max held up his hand to stem the tide. When silence had fallen, he said, "I'm so glad to see you all." His hand once more quelled the surge of explanation his drawling comment drew forth. "No! I find I have neither the time nor the inclination to discuss the matters. My answers to your questions are yes, yes and yes. All right?"

Darcy Hamilton laughed. "Fine by me."

Hugo nodded bemusedly.

"Are you going away?" asked Martin.

Max nodded. "I need a rest. Somewhere tranquil."

His exhausted tone brought a grin to his brother's face. "With or without company?"

Max's wide grin showed fleetingly. "Never you mind, brother dear. Just channel your energies into keeping Lizzie from engaging in any further crusades to help the needy and I'll be satisfied." His gaze took in the two curricles beside the pavement, the horses fretting impatiently. "In fact, I'll make life easy for you. For all of you. I suggest we repair to Twyford House. I'll engage to remove Miss Twinning. Aunt Augusta and Mrs. Alford rest all afternoon. And the house is a large one. If you can't manage to wrest agreement to your proposals from the Misses Twinning under such circumstances, I wash my hands of you."

They all agreed very readily. Together, they set off immediately, Max and his brother in his curricle, Lord Darcy and Hugo Denbigh following in Darcy's carriage.

THE SOUND OF male voices in the front hall drifted to Caroline's ears as she sat with her sisters in the back parlour. With a sigh, she picked up her bonnet and bade the three despondent figures scattered through the room goodbye. They all looked distracted. She felt much the same. Worn out by her difficult morning and from tossing and turning half the night, tormented by a longing she had tried valiantly to ignore, she had fallen asleep in the hammock under the cherry trees. Her sisters had found her but had left her to recover, only waking her for a late lunch before her scheduled drive with their guardian.

As she walked down the corridor to the front hall, she was aware of the leaping excitement the prospect of seeing Max Rotherbridge always brought her. At the mere thought of being alone with him, albeit on the box seat of a curricle in broad daylight in the middle of fashionable London, she could feel that other Caroline Twinning taking over.

Her sisters had taken her words of the morning to heart and had wisely refrained from joining her in greeting their guardian. Alone, she emerged into the hallway. In astonishment, she beheld, not one elegantly turned out gentleman, but four.

Max, his eyes immediately drawn as if by some magic to her, smiled and came forward to take her hand. His comprehensive glance swept her face, then dropped to her bonnet, dangling loosely by its ribbons from one hand. His smile broadened, bringing a delicate colour to her cheeks. "I'm glad you're ready, my dear. But where are your sisters?"

Caroline blinked. "They're in the back parlour," she answered, turning to greet Darcy Hamilton.

Max turned. "Millwade, escort these gentlemen to the back parlour."

Millwade, not in Hillshaw's class, looked slightly scandalized. But an order from his employer was not to be disobeyed. Caroline, engaged in exchanging courtesies with the gentlemen involved, was staggered. But before she could remonstrate, her cloak appeared about her shoulders and she was firmly propelled out the door. She was constrained to hold her fire until Max had dismissed the urchin holding the bays and climbed up beside her.

"You're supposed to be our guardian! Don't you think it's a little unconventional to leave three gentlemen with your wards unchaperoned?"

Giving his horses the office, Max chuckled. "I don't think any of them need chaperoning at present. They'd hardly welcome company when trying to propose."

"Oh! You mean they've asked?"

Max nodded, then glanced down. "I take it you're still happy with their suits?"

"Oh, yes! It's just that...well, the others didn't seem to hold out much hope." After a pause, she asked, "Weren't you surprised?"

He shook his head. "Darcy I've been expecting for weeks. After this morning, Hugo was a certainty. And Martin's been more sternly silent than I've ever seen him before. So, no, I can't say I was surprised." He turned to grin at her. "Still, I hope your sisters have suffered as much as their swains—it's only fair."

She was unable to repress her answering grin, the dimple by her mouth coming delightfully into being. A subtle comment of Max's had the effect of turning the conversation into general fields. They laughed and discussed, occasionally with mock seriousness, a number of tonnish topics, then settled to determined consideration of the Twyford House ball.

This event had been fixed for the following Tuesday, five days distant. More than four hundred guests were expected. Thankfully, the ballroom was huge and the house would easily cater for this number. Under Lady Benborough's guidance, the Twinning sisters had coped with all the arrangements, a fact known to Max. He had a bewildering array of questions for Caroline. Absorbed with answering these, she paid little attention to her surroundings.

"You don't think," she said, airing a point she and her sisters had spent much time pondering, "that, as it's not really a proper come-out, in that we've been about for the entire Season and none of us is truly a débutante, the whole thing might fall a little flat?"

Max grinned. "I think I can assure you that it will very definitely not be flat. In fact," he continued, as if pondering a new thought, "I should think it'll be one of the highlights of the Season."

Caroline looked her question but he declined to explain.

As usual when with her guardian, time flew and it was only when a chill in the breeze penetrated her thin cloak that Caroline glanced up and found the afternoon gone. The curricle was travelling smoothly down a well surfaced road, lined with low hedges set back a little from the carriageway. Beyond these, neat fields stretched sleepily under the waning sun, a few scattered sheep and cattle attesting to the fact that they were deep in the country. From the direction of the sun, they were travelling south, away from the capital. With a puzzled frown, she turned to the man beside her. "Shouldn't we be heading back?"

Max glanced down at her, his devilish grin in evidence. "We aren't going back."

Caroline's brain flatly refused to accept the implications of that statement. Instead, after a pause, she asked conversationally, "Where are we?"

"A little past Twickenham."

"Oh." If they were that far out of town, then it was difficult to see how they could return that evening even if he was only joking about not going back. But he had to be joking, surely?

The curricle slowed and Max checked his team for the turn into a beech-lined drive. As they whisked through the gateway, Caroline caught a glimpse of a coat of arms worked into the impressive iron gates. The Delmere arms, Max's own. She looked about her with interest, refusing to give credence to the suspicion growing in her mind. The

drive led deep into the beechwood, then opened out to run
along a ridge bordered by cleared land, close-clipped grass
dropping away on one side to run down to a distant river.
On the other side, the beechwood fell back as the curricle
continued towards a rise. Cresting this, the road descended
in a broad sweep to end in a gravel courtyard before an old
stone house. It nestled into an unexpected curve of a small
stream, presumably a tributary of the larger river which
Caroline rather thought must be the Thames. The roof
sported many gables. Almost as many chimneys, intricate
pots capping them, soared high above the tiles. In the setting sun, the house glowed mellow and warm. Along one
wall, a rambling white rose nodded its blooms and released
its perfume to the freshening breeze. Caroline thought she
had seen few more appealing houses.

They were expected, that much was clear. A groom came
running at the sound of the wheels on the gravel. Max lifted
her down and led her to the door. It opened at his touch. He
escorted her in and closed the door behind them.

Caroline found herself in a small hall, neatly panelled in
oak, a small round table standing in the middle of the tiled
floor. Max's hand at her elbow steered her to a corridor
giving off the back of the hall. It terminated in a beauti-
fully carved oak door. As Max reached around her to open
it, Caroline asked, "Where are the servants?"

"Oh, they're about. But they're too well trained to show
themselves."

Her suspicions developing in leaps and bounds, Caroline
entered a large room, furnished in a fashion she had never
before encountered.

The floor was covered in thick, silky rugs, executed in the
most glorious hues. Low tables were scattered amid piles of
cushions in silks and satins of every conceivable shade.
There was a bureau against one wall, but the room was
dominated by a dais covered with silks and piled with cushions, more silks draping down from above to swirl about it
in semi-concealing mystery. Large glass doors gave on to a

paved courtyard. The doors stood slightly ajar, admitting the comforting gurgle of the stream as it passed by on the other side of the courtyard wall. As she crossed to peer out, she noticed the ornate brass lamps which hung from the ceiling. The courtyard was empty and, surprisingly, entirely enclosed. A wooden gate was set in one side-wall and another in the wall opposite the house presumably gave on to the stream. As she turned back into the room, Caroline thought it had a strangely relaxing effect on the senses—the silks, the glowing but not overbright colours, the soothing murmur of the stream. Then, her eyes lit on the silk-covered dais. And grew round. Seen from this angle, it was clearly a bed, heavily disguised beneath the jumble of cushions and silks, but a bed nevertheless. Her suspicions confirmed, her gaze flew to her guardian's face.

What she saw there tied her stomach in knots. "Max..." she began uncertainly, the conservative Miss Twinning hanging on grimly.

But then he was standing before her, his eyes glinting devilishly and that slow smile wreaking havoc with her good intentions. "Mmm?" he asked.

"What are we doing here?" she managed, her pulse racing, her breath coming more and more shallowly, her nerves stretching in anticipation.

"Finishing your education," the deep voice drawled.

Well, what had she expected? asked that other Miss Twinning, ousting her competitor and taking total possession as Max bent his head to kiss her. Her mouth opened welcomingly under his and he took what she offered, gradually drawing her into his embrace until she was crushed against his chest. Caroline did not mind; breathing seemed unimportant just at that moment.

When Max finally raised his head, his eyes were bright under their hooded lids and, she noticed with smug satisfaction, his breathing was almost as ragged as hers. His eyes searched her face, then his slow smile appeared. "I notice you've ceased reminding me I'm your guardian."

Caroline, finding her arms twined around his neck, ran her fingers through his dark hair. "I've given up," she said in resignation. "You never paid the slightest attention, anyway."

Max chuckled and bent to kiss her again, then pulled back and turned her about. "Even if I were your guardian, I'd still have seduced you, sweetheart."

Caroline obligingly stood still while his long fingers unlaced her gown. She dropped her head forward to move her curls, which he had loosed, out of his way. Then, the oddity of his words struck her. Her head came up abruptly. *"Even?* Max . . ." She tried to turn around but his hand pushed her back.

"Stand still," he commanded. "I have no intention of making love to you with your clothes on."

Having no wish to argue that particular point, Caroline, seething with impatience, stood still until she felt the last ribbon freed. Then, she turned. "What do you mean, *even* if you were my guardian? You *are* my guardian. You told me so yourself." Her voice tapered away as one part of her mind tried to concentrate on her questions while the rest was more interested in the fact that Max had slipped her dress from her shoulders and it had slid, in a softly sensuous way, down to her feet. In seconds, her petticoats followed.

"Yes, I know I did," Max agreed helpfully, his fingers busy with the laces of the light stays which restrained her ample charms. "I lied. Most unwisely, as it turned out."

"Wh . . . what?" Caroline was having a terrible time trying to focus her mind. It kept wandering. She supposed she really ought to feel shy about Max undressing her. The thought that there were not so many pieces of her clothing left for him to remove, spurred her to ask, "What do you mean, you lied? And why unwisely?"

Max dispensed with her stays and turned his attention to the tiny buttons of her chemise. "You were never my ward. You ceased to be a ward of the Duke of Twyford when you turned twenty-five. But I arranged to let you believe I was still your guardian, thinking that if you knew I wasn't you would never let me near you." He grinned wolfishly at her as his hands slipped over her shoulders and her chemise joined the rest of her clothes at her feet. "I didn't then know that the Twinnings are . . . susceptible to rakes."

His smug grin drove Caroline to shake her head. "We're not . . . susceptible."

"Oh?" One dark brow rose.

Caroline closed her eyes and her head fell back as his hands closed over her breasts. She heard his deep chuckle and smiled to herself. Then, as his hands drifted, and his lips turned to hers, her mind went obligingly blank, allowing her senses free rein. As her bones turned to jelly and her knees buckled, Max's arm helpfully supported her. Then, her lips were free and she was swung up into his arms. A moment later, she was deposited in the midst of the cushions and silks on the dais.

Feeling excitement tingling along every nerve, Caroline stretched sensuously, smiling at the light that glowed in Max's eyes as they watched her while he dispensed with his clothes. But when he stretched out beside her, and her hands drifted across the hard muscles of his chest, she felt him hold back. In unconscious entreaty, she turned towards him, her body arching against his. His response was immediate and the next instant his lips had returned to hers, his arms gathering her to him. With a satisfied sigh, Caroline gave her full concentration to her last lesson.

CHAPTER THIRTEEN

'SARAH?'' Darcy tried to squint down at the face under the dark hair covering his chest.

"Mmm," Sarah replied sleepily, snuggling comfortably against him.

Darcy grinned and gave up trying to rouse her. His eyes drifted to the ceiling as he gently stroked her back. Serve her right if she was exhausted.

Together with Martin and Hugo, he had followed the strongly disapproving Millwade to the back parlour. He had announced them, to the obvious consternation of the three occupants. Darcy's grin broadened as he recalled the scene. Arabella had looked positively stricken with guilt, Lizzie had not known what to think and Sarah had simply stood, her back to the windows, and watched him. At his sign, she had come to his side and they had left the crowded room together.

At his murmured request to see her privately, she had led the way to the morning-room. He had intended to speak to her then, but she had stood so silently in the middle of the room, her face quite unreadable, that before he had known it he was kissing her. Accomplished rake that he was, her response had been staggering. He had always known her for a sensual woman but previously her reactions had been dragged unwillingly from her. Now that they came freely, their potency was enhanced a thousand-fold. After five minutes, he had forcibly disengaged to return to the door and lock it. After that, neither of them had spared a thought for anything save the quenching of their raging desires.

Much later, when they had recovered somewhat, he had managed to find the time, in between other occupations, to ask her to marry him. She had clearly been stunned and it was only then that he realized she had not expected his proposal. He had been oddly touched. Her answer, given without the benefit of speech, had been nevertheless comprehensive and had left him in no doubt of her desire to fill the position he was offering. His wife. The idea made him laugh. Would he survive?

The rumble in his chest disturbed Sarah but she merely burrowed her head into his shoulder and returned to her bliss-filled dreams. Darcy moved slightly, settling her more comfortably.

Her eagerness rang all sorts of warning bells in his mind. Used to taking advantage of the boredom of sensual married women, he made a resolution to ensure that his Sarah never came within arm's reach of any rakes. It would doubtless be wise to establish her as his wife as soon as possible, now he had whetted her appetite for hitherto unknown pleasures. Getting her settled in Hamilton House and introducing her to his country residences, and perhaps giving her a child or two, would no doubt keep her occupied. At least, he amended, sufficiently occupied to have no desire left over for any other than himself.

The light was fading. He glanced at the window to find the afternoon far advanced. With a sigh, he shook Sarah's white shoulder gently.

"Mmm," she murmured protestingly, sleepily trying to shake off his hand.

Darcy chuckled. "I'm afraid, my love, that you'll have to awaken. The day is spent and doubtless someone will come looking for us. I rather think we should be dressed when they do."

With a long-drawn-out sigh, Sarah struggled to lift her head, propping her elbows on his chest to look into his face. Then, her gaze wandered to take in the scene about them. They were lying on the accommodatingly large sofa before he empty fireplace, their clothes strewn about the room. She dropped her head into her hands. "Oh, God. I suppose you're right."

"Undoubtedly," confirmed Darcy, smiling. "And allow me to add, sweetheart, that, as your future husband, I'll always be right."

"Oh?" Sarah enquired innocently. She sat up slightly, her hair in chaos around her face, straggling down her back to cover his hands where they lay, still gently stroking her satin skin.

Darcy viewed her serene face with misgiving. Thinking to distract her, he asked, "Incidentally, when should we marry? I'm sure Max won't care what we decide."

Sarah's attention was drawn from tracing her finger along the curve of his collarbone. She frowned in concentration. "I rather think," she eventually said, "that it had better be soon."

Having no wish to disagree with this eminently sensible conclusion, Darcy said, "A wise decision. Do you want a big wedding? Or shall we leave that to Max and Caroline?"

Sarah grinned. "A very good idea. I think our guardian should be forced to undergo that pleasure, don't you?"

As this sentiment exactly tallied with his own, Darcy merely grinned in reply. But Sarah's next question made him think a great deal harder.

"How soon is it possible to marry?"

It took a few minutes to check all the possible pros and cons. Then he said, uncertain of her response, "Well, theoretically speaking, it would be possible to get married tomorrow."

"Truly? Well, let's do that," replied his prospective bride, a decidedly wicked expression on her face.

Seeing it, Darcy grinned. And postponed their emergence from the morning-room for a further half-hour.

THE FIRST THOUGHT that sprang to Arabella's mind on seeing Hugo Denbigh enter the back parlour was how annoyed he must have been to learn of her deception. Caroline had told her of the circumstances; they would have improved his temper. Oblivious to all else save the object of her thoughts, she did not see Sarah leave the room, nor Martin take Lizzie through the long windows into the garden. Consequently, she was a little perturbed to suddenly find herself alone with Hugo Denbigh.

"Maria Pavlovska, I presume?" His tone was perfectly equable but Arabella did not place any reliance on that. He came to stand before her, dwarfing her by his height and the breadth of his magnificent chest.

Arabella was conscious of a devastating desire to throw herself on that broad expanse and beg forgiveness for her sins. Then she remembered how he had responded to Maria Pavlovska. Her chin went up enough to look his lordship in the eye. "I'm so glad you found my little ... charade entertaining."

Despite having started the conversation, Hugo abruptly found himself at a loss for words. He had not intended to bring up the subject of Maria Pavlovska, at least not until Arabella had agreed to marry him. But seeing her standing there, obviously knowing he knew and how he found out, memory of the desire Arabella-Maria so readily provoked had stirred disquietingly and he had temporarily lost his head. But now was not the time to indulge in a verbal brawl with a woman who, he had learned to his cost, could match his quick tongue in repartee. So, he smiled lazily down at her, totally confusing her instead, and rapidly sought to bring the discussion to a field where he knew he possessed few defences. "Mouthy baggage," he drawled, taking her in his arms and preventing any riposte by the simple expedient of placing his mouth over hers.

Arabella was initially too stunned by this unexpected manoeuvre to protest. And by the time she realized what had happened, she did not want to protest. Instead, she twined her arms about Hugo's neck and kissed him back with all the fervour she possessed. Unbeknownst to her, this was a

onsiderable amount, and Hugo suddenly found himself
desperately searching for a control he had somehow mis-
placed.

Not being as hardened a rake as Max or Darcy, he struggled with himself until he won some small measure of rec-
titude; enough, at least, to draw back and sit in a large
armchair, drawing Arabella onto his lap. She snuggled
against his chest, drawing comfort from his warmth and
solidity.

"Well, baggage, will you marry me?"

Arabella sat bolt upright, her hands braced against his
chest, and stared at him. "Marry you? Me?"

Hugo chuckled, delighted to have reduced her to dither-
ing idiocy.

But Arabella was frowning. "Why do you want to marry
me?"

The frown transferred itself to Hugo's countenance. "I
should have thought the answer to that was a mite obvious,
m'dear."

Arabella brushed that answer aside. "I mean, besides the
obvious."

Hugo sighed and, closing his eyes, let his head fall back
against the chair. He had asked himself the same question
and knew the answer perfectly well. But he had not shaped
his arguments into any coherent form, not contemplating
being called on to recite them. He opened his eyes and fixed
his disobliging love with a grim look. "I'm marrying you
because the idea of you flirting with every Tom, Dick and
Harry drives me insane. I'll tear anyone you flirt with
limb from limb. So, unless you wish to be responsible for
murder, you'd better stop flirting." A giggle, quickly
suppressed, greeted this threat. "Incidentally," Hugo continued, "you don't go around kissing men like that all the
time, do you?"

Arabella had no idea of what he meant by "like that" but
as she had never kissed any other man, except in a perfectly

chaste manner, she could reply with perfect truthfulness, "No, of course not! That was only you."

"Thank God for that!" said a relieved Lord Denbigh. "Kindly confine all such activities to your betrothed in future. Me," he added, in case this was not yet plain.

Arabella lifted one fine brow but said nothing. She was conscious of his hands gently stroking her hips and wondered if it would be acceptable to simply blurt out "yes". Then, she felt Hugo's hand tighten about her waist.

"And one thing more," he said, his eyes kindling. "No more Maria Pavlovska. Ever."

Arabella grinned. "No?" she asked wistfully, her voice dropping into the huskily seductive Polish accent.

Hugo stopped and considered this plea. "Well," he temporized, inclined to be lenient, "Only with me. I dare say I could handle closer acquaintance with Madame Pavlovska."

Arabella giggled and Hugo took the opportunity to kiss her again. This time, he let the kiss develop as he had on other occasions, keeping one eye on the door, the other on the windows and his mind solely on her responses. Eventually, he drew back and, retrieving his hands from where they had wandered, bringing a blush to his love's cheeks, he gripped her about her waist and gently shook her. "You haven't given me your answer yet."

"Yes, please," said Arabella, her eyes alight. "I couldn't bear not to be able to be Maria Pavlovska every now and again."

Laughing, Hugo drew her back into his arms. "When shall we wed?"

Tracing the strong line of his jaw with one small finger, Arabella thought for a minute, then replied, "Need we wait very long?"

The undisguised longing in her tone brought her a swift response. "Only as long as you wish."

Arabella chuckled. "Well, I doubt we could be married tomorrow."

"Why not?" asked Hugo, his eyes dancing.

His love looked puzzled. "Is it possible? I thought all those sorts of things took forever to arrange."

"Only if you want a big wedding. If you do, I warn you it'll take months. My family's big and distributed all about. Just getting in touch with half of them will be bad enough."

But the idea of waiting for months did not appeal to Arabella. "If it can be done, can we really be married tomorrow? It would be a lovely surprise—stealing a march on the others."

Hugo grinned. "For a baggage, you do have some good ideas sometimes."

"Really?" asked Maria Pavlovska.

FOR MARTIN ROTHERBRIDGE, the look on Lizzie's face as he walked into the back parlour was easy to read. Total confusion. On Lizzie, it was a particularly attractive attitude and one with which he was thoroughly conversant. With a grin, he went to her and took her hand, kissed it and tucked it into his arm. "Let's go into the garden. I want to talk to you."

As talking to Martin in gardens had become something of a habit, Lizzie went with him, curious to know what it was he wished to say and wondering why her heart was leaping about so uncomfortably.

Martin led her down the path that bordered the large main lawn until they reached an archway formed by a rambling rose. This gave access to the rose gardens. Here, they came to a stone bench bathed in softly dappled sunshine. At Martin's nod, Lizzie seated herself with a swish of her muslin skirts. After a moment's consideration, Martin sat beside her. Their view was filled with ancient rosebushes, the spaces beneath crammed with early summer flowers. Bees buzzed sleepily and the occasional dragonfly darted by, on its way from the shrubbery to the pond at the bottom of the main lawn. The sun shone warmly and all was peace and tranquillity.

All through the morning, Lizzie had been fighting the fear that in helping Amanda Crowbridge she had unwittingly earned Martin's disapproval. She had no idea why his approval mattered so much to her, but with the single-mindedness of youth, was only aware that it did. "Wh... what did you wish to tell me?"

Martin schooled his face into stern lines, much as he would when bawling out a young lieutenant for some silly but understandable folly. He took Lizzie's hand in his, his strong fingers moving comfortingly over her slight ones. "Lizzie, this scheme of yours, m'dear. It really was most unwise." Martin kept his eyes on her slim fingers. "I suppose Caroline told you how close-run the thing was. If she hadn't arrived in the nick of time, Max and Hugo would have been off and there would have been no way to catch them. And the devil to pay when they came up with Keighly."

A stifled sob brought his eyes to her, but she had averted her face. "Lizzie?" No lieutenant he had ever had to speak to had sobbed. Martin abruptly dropped his stance of stern mentor and gathered Lizzie into his arms. "Oh, sweetheart. Don't cry. I didn't mean to upset you. Well, yes, I did. Just a bit. You upset me the devil of a lot when I thought you had run off with Keighly."

Lizzie had muffled her face in his coat but she looked up at that. "You thought... But whyever did you think such a silly thing?"

Martin flushed slightly. "Well, yes. I know it was silly. But it was just the way it all came out. At one stage, we weren't sure who had gone in that blasted coach." He paused for a moment, then continued in more serious vein. "But, really, sweetheart, you mustn't start up these schemes to help people. Not when they involve sailing so close to the wind. You'll set all sorts of people's backs up, if ever they knew."

Rather better acquainted with Lizzie than his brother was, Martin had no doubt at all whose impulse had started the

vhole affair. It might have been Arabella who had carried
ut most of the actions and Sarah who had worked out the
letails, but it was his own sweet Lizzie who had set the ball
olling.

Lizzie was hanging her head in contrition, her fingers idly
playing with his coat buttons. Martin tightened his arms
about her until she looked up. "Lizzie, I want you to
promise me that if you ever get any more of these helpful
deas you'll immediately come and tell me about them, before you do anything at all. Promise?"

Lizzie's downcast face cleared and a smile like the sun lit
her eyes. "Oh, yes. That will be safer." Then, a thought
truck her and her face clouded again. "But you might
not be about. You'll... well, now your wound is healed,
you'll be getting about more. Meeting lots of l-ladies
and ... things."

"Things?" said Martin, struggling to keep a straight face.
"What things?"

"Well, you know. The sort of things you do. With l-
ladies." At Martin's hoot of laughter, she set her lips firmly
and doggedly went on. "Besides, you might marry and your
wife wouldn't like it if I was hanging on your sleeve." There,
she had said it. Her worst fear had been brought into the
light.

But, instead of reassuring her that all would, somehow,
be well, Martin was in stitches. She glared at him. When that
had no effect, she thumped him hard on his chest.

Gasping for breath, Martin caught her small fists and
then a slow grin, very like his brother's, broke across his face
as he looked into her delightfully enraged countenance. He
waited to see the confusion show in her fine eyes before
drawing her hands up, pulling her hard against him and
kissing her.

Lizzie had thought he had taught her all about kissing,
but this was something quite different. She felt his arms lock
like a vice about her waist, not that she had any intention of
struggling. And the kiss went on and on. When she finally

emerged, flushed, her eyes sparkling, all she could do was gasp and stare at him.

Martin uttered a laugh that was halfway to a groan. "Oh, Lizzie! Sweet Lizzie. For God's sake, say you'll marry me and put me out of my misery."

Her eyes grew round. "Marry you?" The words came out as a squeak.

Martin's grin grew broader. "Mmm. I thought it might be a good idea." His eyes dropped from her face to the lace edging that lay over her breasts. "Aside from ensuring I'll always be there for you to discuss your hare-brained schemes with," he continued conversationally, "I could also teach you about all the things I do with l-ladies."

Lizzie's eyes widened as far as they possibly could.

Martin grinned devilishly. "Would you like that Lizzie?"

Mutely, Lizzie nodded. Then, quite suddenly, she found her voice. "Oh, yes!" She flung her arms about Martin's neck and kissed him ferociously. Emerging from her wild embrace, Martin threw back his head and laughed. Lizzie did not, however, confuse this with rejection. She waited patiently for him to recover.

But, "Lizzie, oh Lizzie. What a delight you are!" was all Martin Rotherbridge said, before gathering her more firmly into his arms to explore her delights more thoroughly.

A considerable time later, when Martin had called a halt to their mutual exploration on the grounds that there were probably gardeners about, Lizzie sat comfortably in the circle of his arms, blissfully happy, and turned her thought to the future. "When shall we marry?" she asked.

Martin, adrift in another world, came back to earth and gave the matter due consideration. If he had been asked the same question two hours ago, he would have considered a few months sufficiently soon. Now, having spent those two hours with Lizzie in unfortunately restrictive surroundings, he rather thought a few days would be too long to wait. But presumably she would want a big wedding, with all the trimmings.

However, when questioned, Lizzie disclaimed all interest in wedding breakfasts and the like. Hesitantly, not sure how he would take the suggestion, she toyed with the pin in his cravat and said, "Actually, I wonder if it would be possible to be married quite soon. Tomorrow, even?"

Martin stared at her.

"I mean," Lizzie went on, "that there's bound to be quite a few weddings in the family—what with Arabella and Sarah."

"And Caroline," said Martin.

Lizzie looked her question.

"Max has taken Caroline off somewhere. I don't know where, but I'm quite sure why."

"Oh." Their recent occupation in mind, Lizzie could certainly see how he had come to that conclusion. It was on the tip of her tongue to ask for further clarification of the possibilities Caroline might encounter, but her tenacious disposition suggested she settle the question of her own wedding first. "Yes, well, there you are. With all the fuss and bother, I suspect we'll be at the end of the list."

Martin looked much struck by her argument.

"But," Lizzie continued, sitting up as she warmed to her theme, "if we get married tomorrow, without any of the others knowing, then it'll be done and we shan't have to wait." In triumph, she turned to Martin.

Finding her eyes fixed on him enquiringly, Martin grinned. "Sweetheart, you put together a very convincing argument. So let's agree to be married tomorrow. Now that's settled, it seems to me you're in far too composed a state. From what I've learned, it would be safest for everyone if you were kept in a perpetual state of confusion. So come here, my sweet, and let me confuse you a little."

Lizzie giggled and, quite happily, gave herself up to delighted confusion.

THE CLINK OF CROCKERY woke Caroline. She stretched languorously amid the soft cushions, the sensuous drift of the silken covers over her still tingling skin bringing back clear memories of the past hours. She was alone in the bed. Peering through the concealing silk canopy, she spied Max, tastefully clad in a long silk robe, watching a small dapper servant laying out dishes on the low tables on the other side of the room. The light from the brass lamps suffused the scene with a soft glow. She wondered what the time was.

Lying back in the luxurious cushions, she pondered her state. Her final lesson had been in two parts. The first was concluded fairly soon after Max had joined her in the huge bed; the second, a much more lingering affair, had spun out the hours of the evening. In between, Max had, to her lasting shock, asked her to marry him. She had asked him to repeat his request three times, after which he had refused to do it again, saying she had no choice in the matter anyway as she was hopelessly compromised. He had then turned his attention to compromising her even further. As she had no wish to argue the point, she had meekly gone along with his evident desire to examine her responses to him in even greater depth than he had hitherto, a proceeding which had greatly contributed to their mutual content. She was, she feared, fast becoming addicted to Max's particular expertise; there were, she had discovered, certain benefits attached to going to bed with rakes.

She heard the door shut and Max's tread cross the floor. The silk curtains were drawn back and he stood by the bed. His eyes found her pale body, covered only by the diaphanous silks, and travelled slowly from her legs all the way up until, finally, they reached her face, and he saw she was awake and distinctly amused. He grinned and held out a hand. "Come and eat. I'm ravenous."

It was on the tip of Caroline's tongue to ask what his appetite craved, but the look in his eyes suggested that might not be wise if she wished for any dinner. She struggled to sit up and looked wildly around for her clothes. They had disappeared. She looked enquiringly at Max. He merely raised one black brow.

"I draw the line at sitting down to dinner with you clad only in silk gauze," Caroline stated.

With a laugh, Max reached behind him and lifted a pale blue silk wrap from a chair and handed it to her. She struggled into it and accepted his hand to help her from the depths of the cushioned dais.

The meal was well cooked and delicious. Max contrived to turn eating into a sensual experience of a different sort and Caroline eagerly followed his lead. At the end of the repast, she was lying, relaxed and content, against his chest, surrounded by the inevitable cushions and sipping a glass of very fine chilled wine.

Max, equally content, settled one arm around her comfortably, then turned to a subject they had yet to broach. "When shall we be married?"

Caroline raised her brows. "I hadn't really thought that far ahead."

"Well, I suggest you do, for there are certain cavils to be met."

"Oh?"

"Yes," said Max. "Given that I left my brother, Darcy Hamilton and Hugo Denbigh about to pay their addresses to my three wards, I suspect we had better return to London tomorrow afternoon. Then, if you want a big wedding, I should warn you that the Rotherbridge family is huge and, as I am its head, will all expect to be invited."

Caroline was shaking her head. "Oh, I don't think a big wedding would be at all wise. I mean, it looks as though the Twinning family will have a surfeit of weddings. But," she paused, "maybe your family will expect it?"

"I dare say they will, but they're quite used to me doing outrageous things. I should think they'll be happy enough that I'm marrying at all, let alone to someone as suitable as yourself, my love."

Suddenly, Caroline sat bolt upright. "Max! I just remembered. What's the time? They'll all be in a flurry because I haven't returned...."

But Max drew her back against his chest. "Hush. It's all taken care of. I left a note for Aunt Augusta. She knows you're with me and will not be returning until tomorrow."

"But... won't she be upset?"

"I should think she'll be dancing a jig." He grinned as she turned a puzzled face to him. "Haven't you worked out Aunt Augusta's grand plan yet?" Bemused, Caroline shook her head. "I suspect she had it in mind that I should marry you from the moment she first met you. That was why she was so insistent that I keep my wards. Initially, I rather think she hoped that by her throwing us forever together I would notice you." He chuckled. "Mind you, a man would have to be blind not to notice your charms at first sight, m'dear. By that first night at Almack's, I think she realized she didn't need to do anything further, just give me plenty of opportunity. She knows me rather well, you see, and knew that, despite my reputation, you were in no danger of being offered a *carte blanche* by me."

"I did wonder why she never warned me about you," admitted Caroline.

"But to return to the question of our marriage. If you wish to fight shy of a full society occasion, then it still remains to fix the date."

Caroline bent her mind to the task. Once they returned to London, she would doubtless be caught up in all the plans for her sisters' weddings, and, she supposed, her own would have to come first. But it would all take time. And meanwhile, she would be living in Twyford House, not Delmere House. The idea of returning to sleeping alone in her own bed did not appeal. The end of one slim finger tapping her lower lip, she asked, "How soon could we be married?"

"Tomorrow, if you wish." As she turned to stare at him again, Max continued. "Somewhere about here," he waved his arm to indicate the room, "lies a special licence. And our neighbour happens to be a retired bishop, a long-time friend of my late father's, who will be only too thrilled to officiate at my wedding. If you truly wish it, I'll ride over tomorrow

norning and we can be married before luncheon, after
which we had better get back to London. Does that pro-
gramme meet with your approval?''

Caroline leaned forward and placed her glass on the table. Then she turned to Max, letting her hands slide under
the edge of his robe. "Oh, yes," she purred. "Most definitely."

Max looked down at her, a glint in his eyes. "You, ma-
dam, are proving to be every bit as much a houri as I suspected."

Caroline smiled slowly. "And do you approve, my lord?"

"Most definitely," drawled Max as his lips found hers.

THE DUKE OF TWYFORD returned to London the next afternoon, accompanied by his Duchess. They went directly
to Twyford House, to find the entire household at sixes and
sevens. They found Lady Benborough in the back parlour,
reclining on the chaise, her wig askew, an expression of
smug satisfaction on her face. At sight of them, she abruptly
sat up, struggling to control the wig. "There you are! And
about time, too!" Her shrewd blue eyes scanned their faces,
noting the inner glow that lit Caroline's features and the
contented satisfaction in her nephew's dark face. "What
have you been up to?"

Max grinned wickedly and bent to kiss her cheek. "Securing my Duchess, as you correctly imagined."

"You've tied the knot already?" she asked in disbelief.

Caroline nodded. "It seemed most appropriate. That
way, our wedding won't get in the way of the others."

"Humph!" snorted Augusta, disgruntled at missing the
sight of her reprehensible nephew getting leg-shackled. She
glared at Max.

His smile broadened. "Strange, I had thought you would
be pleased to see us wed. Particularly considering your odd
behaviour. Why, even Caro had begun to wonder why you
never warned her about me, despite the lengths to which I
went to distract her mind from such concerns."

Augusta blushed. "Yes, well," she began, slightly flustered, then saw the twinkle in Max's eye. "You know very
well I'm *aux anges* to see you married at last, but I would
have given my best wig to have seen it!"

Caroline laughed. "I do assure you we are truly married.
But where are the others?"

"And that's another thing!" said Augusta, turning to
Max. "The next time you set about creating a bordello in a
household I'm managing, at least have the goodness to warn
me beforehand! I come down after my nap to find Arabella
in Hugo Denbigh's lap. That was bad enough, but the door
to the morning-room was locked. Sarah and Darcy Hamilton *eventually* emerged, but only much later." She glared at
Max but was obviously having difficulty keeping her face
straight. "Worst of all," she continued in a voice of long
suffering, "Miriam went to look at the roses just before
sunset. Martin had apparently chosen the rose garden to
further his affair with Lizzie, don't ask me why. It was an
hour before Miriam's palpitations had died down enough
for her to go to bed. I've packed her off to her sister's to re-
cuperate. Really, Max, you've had enough experience to
have foreseen what would happen."

Both Max and Caroline were convulsed with laughter.

"Oh, dear," said Caroline when she could speak, "I
wonder what would have happened if she had woken up on
the way back from the Richardsons' ball?"

Augusta looked interested but, before she could request
further information, the door opened and Sarah entered,
followed by Darcy Hamilton. From their faces it was clear
that all their troubles were behind them—Sarah looked radiant, Darcy simply looked besotted. The sisters greeted
each other affectionately, then Sarah drew back and surveyed the heavy gold ring on Caroline's left hand. "Married already?"

"We thought to do you the favour of getting our marriage out of the way forthwith," drawled Max, releasing

Darcy's hand. "So there's no impediment to your own nuptials."

Darcy and Sarah exchanged an odd look, then burst out laughing. "I'm afraid, dear boy," said Darcy, "that we've jumped the gun, too."

Sarah held out her left hand, on which glowed a slim gold band.

While the Duke and Duchess of Twyford and Lord and Lady Darcy exchanged congratulations all around, Lady Benborough looked on in disgust. "What I want to know," she said, when she could make herself heard once more, "is if I'm to be entirely done out of weddings, even after all my efforts to see you all in parson's mouse-trap?"

"Oh, there are still two Twinnings to go, so I wouldn't give up hope," returned her nephew, smiling down at her with transparent goodwill. "Apropos of which, has anyone seen the other two lately?"

No one had. When applied to, Millwade imparted the information that Lord Denbigh had called for Miss Arabella just before two. They had departed in Lord Denbigh's carriage. Mr. Martin had dropped by for Miss Lizzie at closer to three. They had left in a hack.

"A hack?" queried Max.

Millwade merely nodded. Dismissed, he withdrew.

Max was puzzled. "Where on earth could they have gone?"

As if in answer, voices were heard in the hall. But it was Arabella and Hugo who had returned. Arabella danced in, her curls bouncing, her big eyes alight with happiness. Hugo ambled in her wake, his grin suggesting that he suspected his good fortune was merely a dream and he would doubtless wake soon enough. Meanwhile, he was perfectly content with the way this particular dream was developing. Arabella flew to embrace Caroline and Sarah, then turned to the company at large and announced, "Guess what!"

A pregnant silence greeted her words, the Duke and his Duchess, the Lord and his Lady, all struck dumb by a

sneaking suspicion. Almost unwillingly, Max voiced it.
"You're married already?"

Arabella's face fell a little. "How did you guess?" she
demanded.

"No!" moaned Augusta. "Max, see what happens when
you leave town? I won't have it!"

But her words fell on deaf ears. Too blissfully happy
themselves to deny their friends the same pleasures, the
Duke and his Duchess were fully engaged in wishing the new
Lady Denbigh and her Lord all manner of felicitations. And
then, of course, there was their own news to hear, and that
of the Hamiltons. The next ten minutes were filled with
congratulations and good wishes.

Left much to herself, Lady Benborough sat in a corner of
the chaise and watched the group with an indulgent eye.
Truth to tell, she was not overly concerned with the absence of weddings. At her age, they constituted a definite
trial. She smiled at the thought of the stories she would tell
of the rapidity with which the three rakes before her had
rushed their brides to the altar. Between them, they had
nearly forty years of experience in evading parson's mouse-
trap, yet, when the right lady had loomed on their horizon,
they had found it expedient to wed her with all speed. She
wondered whether that fact owed more to their frustrations
or their experience.

Having been assured by Arabella that Martin had indeed
proposed and been accepted, the Duke and Duchess allowed themselves to be distracted by the question of the immediate housing arrangements. Eventually, it was decided
that, in the circumstances, it was perfectly appropriate that
Sarah should move into Hamilton House immediately, and
Arabella likewise to Denbigh House. Caroline, of course,
would henceforth be found at Delmere House. Relieved to
find their ex-guardian so accommodating, Sarah and Arabella were about to leave to attend to their necessary packing, when the door to the drawing-room opened.

Martin and Lizzie entered.

It was Max, his sharp eyes taking in the glow in Lizzie's
ace and the ridiculously proud look stamped across Mar-
in's features, who correctly guessed their secret.

"Don't tell me!" he said, in a voice of long suffering.
"You've got married, too?"

NEEDLESS TO SAY, the Twyford House ball four days later
vas hardly flat. In fact, with four blushing brides, sternly
vatched over by their four handsome husbands, it was, as
Max had prophesied, one of the highlights of the Season.

Take 4 bestselling love stories FREE

Plus get a FREE surprise gift!

Special Limited-time Offer

Mail to Harlequin Reader Service®

3010 Walden Avenue
P.O. Box 1867
Buffalo, N.Y. 14269-1867

YES! Please send me 4 free Harlequin Historical™ novels and my free surprise gift. Then send me 4 brand-new novels every month, which I will receive before they appear in bookstores. Bill me at the low price of $3.19 each plus 25¢ delivery and applicable sales tax, if any.* That's the complete price and—compared to the cover prices of $3.99 each—quite a bargain! I understand that accepting the books and gift places me under no obligation ever to buy any books. I can always return a shipment and cancel at any time. Even if I never buy another book from Harlequin, the 4 free books and the surprise gift are mine to keep forever.

247 BPA ANRM

Name _____ (PLEASE PRINT)

Address _____ Apt. No. _____

City _____ State _____ Zip _____

This offer is limited to one order per household and not valid to present Harlequin Historical™ subscribers. *Terms and prices are subject to change without notice. Sales tax applicable in N.Y.

UHIS-94R   ©1990 Harlequin Enterprises Limited

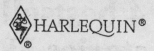

Where do you find hot Texas nights, smooth Texas charm and dangerously sexy cowboys?

Crystal Creek reverberates with the exciting rhythm of Texas.
Each story features the rugged individuals who live and love in the Lone Star State.

"...Crystal Creek wonderfully evokes the hot days and steamy nights of a small Texas community...impossible to put down until the last page is turned."
—*Romantic Times*

"...a series that should hook any romance reader. Outstanding."
—*Rendezvous*

Praise for Margot Dalton's *Even the Nights Are Better*

"...every bit as engrossing as the others. Ms. Dalton wraps you in sentiment...this is a book you don't just read, you feel."
—*Rendezvous*

Don't miss the next book in this exciting series. Look for
SOUTHERN NIGHTS by Margot Dalton

Available in June wherever Harlequin books are sold.

HARLEQUIN®

Diamonds of the first water, these exceptional heroines reflect the rare beauty and exquisite nature of priceless gems.

Fall in love with the past as Harlequin presents its latest Regency Romance collection, *Regency Diamonds.*

The collection features two stories by your favorite Regency authors. Brenda Hiatt brings us the passionate story of a heroine who must rekindle both the memory and the love of her husband in "Azalea," and Paula Marshall brings us a case of mistaken identity in "The Cyprian's Sister."

Capture the spirit and the passion of the Regency era with our latest collection, *Regency Diamonds.*

REG1